Storm Dragon's Desire

ROYAL DRAGON SHIFTERS OF MOROCCO #4

AVA WARD

A RED LETTER HOTEL PARANORMAL ROMANCE

COPYRIGHT

First Print Edition, 2019
ISBN 978-1-943199-34-1

Edited By: Jean Lowe Carlson.
Proofread By: Jean Lowe Carlson and Matt Carlson.
Cover Design: Copyright 2019 by Damonza. All Rights Reserved.
Chapter Graphics: FreeTiles http://www.dafont.com/ Free Commercial Use.

ACKNOWLEDGEMENTS

Many thanks to everyone who enjoys this series, especially Lela and Josh, Sam and Ben, Amber and Kyle, Marc and Claire, Dave S., and my sister Stephany.

Special shout-out to my amazing Beta Readers and Launch Team – Joy, Linda, April, Tanya, Jules, Georganne, Carrie, Fiona, Nikhil, Michelle, Kimmy, Penelope, Queen, Eileen, Marco, Jessica, Erin, Rosemarie, Christiane, Alfreda, Sierra, Joel, Jean, Brittany, Claire, Susanne, Kona, Ruth, Stephanie, Katie, Lynda, Melissa, Terry, Jeanette, Dottie, Raquel, Mike, Bill, Susan, Wendy, Melissa, Kim, Amy, Cori, Bobby, Alison, Angie, Kam, Cyndi, Daniel, Elizabeth, Terri, Robin, Felicia, Christine, Kahlia, Victoria, Julie, Susan, Juan, Hannelore, Jen, Bobbi, Tina, Jody, Shannon, Marlys, Sandra, Tara, Kathy, Heather, Jewell, Deborah, Sue, Catherine, Liz.

And last of all, a big thanks to my husband Matt – a constant inspiration in my life! I couldn't do any of this without you. :)

OTHER WORKS BY AVA WARD

RED LETTER HOTEL PARANORMAL ROMANCE

Royal Dragon Shifters of Morocco
Royal Dragon Bind
Crystal Dragon's Kiss
Sea Dragon's Command
Storm Dragon's Desire
Crystal Dragon King *(Forthcoming)*

Discover the entire series at
www.avawardromance.com

ABOUT STORM DRAGON'S DESIRE

When everything she loves is stolen, can she reclaim it?

Layla Price's life has never been more complex. With three sexy, passionate Royal Dragon billionaires bound to her, she's got all the hotness she can handle.

Add to that her debut as a Courtesan for the Red Letter Hotel – a deadly gamble to draw out her mate Adrian Rhakvir's enemies – and tensions couldn't be higher.

But when her human friends and her hot ex come to visit the Hotel, then are abducted, Layla must wrangle her Dragon lovers.

Can she unite her Royal Dragons and save her friends?

Or will they break – taking her down to darkness?

AUTHOR'S NOTE

Welcome to the passionate world of the Royal Dragon Shifters of Morocco!

This series is a *billionaire reverse harem dragon-shifter romance,* involving a strong, intelligent heroine who attracts multiple sexy bad-boy billionaire dragon lovers over the course of the series.

The world is racy, opulent, and sensual, with intense action sequences, political intrigue, and dangerous enemies. The themes are uplifting with HFN endings and for the best experience, the books should be read in sequence.

Thanks for joining the Royal Dragons at the Red Letter Hotel! *Are you ready for the heat?*

CHAPTER 1 – FRIENDS

Waiting on the promenade of the Red Letter Hotel Paris for her human friends to arrive in the Twilight Realm, Layla Price shifted from foot to foot as snow fell all around. Watching a car pass through the gilded wrought-iron gates of the Palace of Versailles' inner courtyard, Layla noted a silver Jaguar arrive rather than a black Hotel Mercedes. Juniper boughs with fae-lights like fireflies adorned the gilded French Baroque Hotel gates for Yule. Gold and white ribbon, sprigs of holly, and crimson berries had been woven through the wrought-iron, creating a filigreed tapestry of elegance in the winter day.

Opulence decorated the entire Palace of Versailles for the midwinter celebration of Yule. Evergreen and holly, gold and white twined up every column and through every rail. Though snow swirled down to the grand black and white marble courtyard, the afternoon was strangely bright from the natural magic of the Twilight Realm, every edge seeming diamond-touched and every color brighter than anything possible in the human world. Massive gilded braziers twisted with white-gold flames around the courtyard, highlighting enormous cream Hotel banners embroidered with their crimson 'R' and gilded crown, that sparkled through the falling snow.

The effect was gloriously elite – a winter wonderland for Yule.

Off-work for the week's celebrations, Layla stood in contrast to all that gold and fuss; wearing skinny jeans with russet leather boots rather than her professional Hotel finery today. Bundled in a navy peacoat with a cream scarf, her long sable curls pulled loosely over one shoulder, she was usually warm from her Desert Dragon's heat, but her nerves at her human friends' arrival were currently giving her a cold sweat. Layla knew her friends were going to love the Hotel; the interior had been decorated as thoroughly as the exterior for the holidays, though with the addition of mistletoe to kiss under. All the same, something moved restlessly inside Layla as a white Tesla Roadster drove through the gates, and she shifted again.

Waiting with her on the promenade, her boss in Concierge Services and bound Royal Crystal Dragon lover Dusk Arlohaim grinned as he glanced at her, a wave of light rippling through his artfully-styled dark hair. His sapphire eyes were luminous in the snowy day, serrated ridges of midnight Dragon-scales at his temples outlining his exquisite handsomeness. Wearing a slim charcoal Italian suit with a midnight-blue pocket square and matching tie, Dusk was comfortable in the cold. Grinning at her like a handsome devil as he tucked his hands nonchalantly in his pockets, he waited until Layla finally glanced over.

"What?" Layla spoke, her breath puffing in the late-December air.

"Layla Price, I do believe you're nervous to see your friends from Seattle." Dusk chuckled in his rolling baritone, though it was absent of his earth-shaking Crystal Dragon magics today.

"I'm not nervous." Layla spoke stubbornly, shoving her hands into the pockets of her peacoat to stop her fidgeting. "I just want to make sure my friends get a good impression of the Hotel while they're here, that's all. I've been working here almost six months and I've gotten used to the Twilight Realm, but this is their first time here, and I want everything to go well."

"You're more nervous than just making a good impression at the Hotel," Dusk watched her with humor glinting in his sapphire eyes, interrupting her anxiety with his bright banter and astuteness – which

7

came in handy for his position as Head Concierge of the Paris Hotel. "I can feel tension vibrating all through you. Not to mention it smells like a Yule-log soaked in bourbon out here. If I had to hedge a guess, I'd say you're concerned about Luke and I meeting. Your current hottie versus your ex."

"Thanks, but I'm actually thinking about a lot of things right now, not just your ego." Layla sassed with a lift of one dark eyebrow, though she was smiling now. It was hard to not smile at Dusk's handsomely cheeky nature. But she couldn't deny the intensity boiling off her, her Dragon-magics rioting as she waited for her friends to arrive. She and Dusk had only been standing in the snow a few minutes, but as Layla shifted her stance again, it felt like an hour.

"You're worried Luke's going to be jealous." Dusk spoke up cheekily beside her. "Even though he and I have talked on the phone about this trip, getting your friends ready for everything they'll encounter in the Twilight Realm, he's still your ex and I'm your current beau. One of three. That's got to be on your mind."

"So what if it is?" Layla glanced at him, though she knew he was one hundred percent right. Her nerves roiled, not knowing how to explain to her friends that she had not one, not two, but *three* bound lovers since Thanksgiving. All of them handsome-as-hell Royal Dragons and billionaires to boot – who could slay even the hottest human man Layla had ever met in the looks and sex appeal department.

"Well, I know how protective Luke is of you." Dusk held her gaze with gravitas now as snow settled into his sculpted hair and onto the shoulders of his slim Italian suit. "He's already taken my measure, and fortunately we get along. But he's going to size up Adrian and especially Reginald, once they get a chance to meet. Luke has already judged Adrian badly. And Reginald... well. We'll see how that goes."

Layla gave a short sigh; Dusk was right. Her human ex-boyfriend

Luke Murphy was a tempest in a teakettle, and Layla was already dreading him meeting Reginald Durant, Royal Siren and Head Courtier of the Hotel – and perpetual dick to anyone he judged as beneath him. As Dragons, Dusk and her bound Royal Desert Dragon Adrian Rhakvir were sexily arrogant, but Reginald was ten times that. "Small favors that Reginald is still away visiting his clan in the North Sea. Any word when he'll be back, by the way?"

"Not yet." Dusk sobered as he stared off into the settling snow. "The North Sea Sirens are a scary bunch, Layla. Reginald has a score to settle with his clan now that his brother Bastien is dead. Though Reginald won their Dragon-battle a month ago, it was with intervention. His brothers and father are debating if that raises Reginald into the Clan Second position or not. If it doesn't, he'll likely continue on here at the Paris Hotel as Head Courtier once his mandatory leave is finished. But if it does…"

"Reginald's going to be more embroiled in his clan's politics than ever." Layla spoke, her breath puffing in the chill air. Deep inside, her Dragon coiled through her veins with a tight, bitter worry, producing a scorched scent in the air like orange peels burned with a blowtorch. "What about Adrian? Any word from him yet?"

"Adrian's settled, finally." Dusk smiled gently as he slung an arm around Layla, hugging her close. "He's at one of his safe houses. Everything's going to be ok, Layla. Adrian's safe from the Hotel Board and Reginald's in no immediate danger from his clan. The Intercessoria are monitoring the Hotel closely for Hunter with all the new magical security they've installed, thanks to the information you provided Heathren Merkami with a month ago. Your friends are going to have a fantastic time this week at the Hotel, I've set up all kinds of fun activities for them. Everything is taken care of, I promise."

"I know. You've thought of everything, like always." Glancing up,

Layla cuddled close to Dusk, kissing his lips sweetly. "You're like this incredible grounding force in my life. Every time I start to worry, you're always there, cool and calm, planning six steps ahead of anyone else. Believe me, I'm grateful."

"Your welfare matters to me," he spoke, his bright sapphire gaze smiling at her like a high summer sky despite the cold day. "And as a Crystal Dragon, I have a lot more grounding than most. If I can use that to better your situation, I will. Besides, I enjoy taking advantage of your gratefulness when we get to see each other at night."

"But how are you not infernally jealous of the other bound men in my life?" Layla asked as she pulled back slightly, gazing up at him as she read beneath his cheeky innuendo about their currently blazing-hot sex life. "It's like you're always just smoothing tempers and helping us all get along in this crazy new world that you, Reginald, Adrian, and I have entered with our Bound power."

"I am jealous." Dusk's smile was wry though his blue eyes were honest. "But I get time with you while we're working at the Concierge desk. I get time when we sleep together at night. Adrian isn't around now that the Hotel Owners want his head on a platter, and Reginald is off at his clan home, working to get a handle on his Dragon and dealing with his clan's shit. Your Dragon attacked Luke as an inferior mate in the fall, so he's out of the running to be your beau. Plus, I understand complex relationships; you forget how many lovers I've juggled over the years. A Dragon's sex life is a crazy world, Layla, and you're just getting started. I'm jealous, but I know how to be practical. The last thing you need in your life is a pissy Crystal Dragon trying to encase the rest of your men in quartz cocoons and hide them outside in the snow."

Layla laughed; she couldn't help it. Dusk had an ego as big as the moon, but she couldn't deny his endless practicality. Lifting up, she gripped his lapels and kissed him again. It was deep and sensual, and he wound his strong arms around her with a deviant rumble to pull her close to his fit soccer-player's muscles as they kissed right out in the open. Their affair was no secret, and Layla didn't mind the hot kissing in public. It thrilled her, making her Dragon turn over deliciously inside her as she became breathless, her heart hammering. Dusk chuckled as he pulled away, his sapphire eyes luminous and impossibly cheeky as his breath came hot and fast also.

"Besides. You like me best. I can feel it."

"You wish!" Layla laughed as she slapped his chest lightly, though she was still buzzing from that kiss, her Dragon growling appreciatively inside her veins with a scalding surge of power. "Besides, you're one to talk about juggling multiple partners. How many lovers do you still have, Casanova, now that you and I are together? I mean, you've been with me almost every night this past month."

"Well, you might be pleased to know I've cut my impossibly long roster of lovers to only three these days." Dusk grinned as he nuzzled her nose, still not letting her wriggle out of his strong arms. "You, Amalia DuFane strictly because she makes me the best outfits after a good orgasm, and Rake André. I've discovered Royal Dragon Binds are a lot to handle in bed; sometimes three or four times a night. Not that I'm complaining."

"Wait, Rake is one of your lovers? Not Rikyava anymore?" Layla blinked, ignoring Dusk's innuendo about her ridiculously high libido, courtesy of her new Dragon-magics. He wasn't kidding that there were occasionally nights where Layla woke up numerous times needing to be satisfied – and Dusk was always happy to supply.

Layla had known her best friend and Head of the Hotel Guard Rikyava Andersen occasionally slept with Dusk, though it was a surprise to hear Dusk had cut that association off. She hadn't known Head Bartender Rake André, who was also interim Head Courtier now that Reginald was on hiatus, was one of Dusk's lovers. But Layla had known Dusk occasionally took men to bed and the thought suddenly made her body grip hard. A wash of sweet bourbon and orange peel scent wafted up around her as she imagined the fit-as-shit Dusk and the slender, gorgeous Rake André in bed together.

It was a hot image and she knew her cheeks burned as Dusk laughed.

"Rikyava's still pining for someone, though she won't tell anyone who. But you didn't know Rake was one of my regular partners, did you?" Dusk chuckled as he leaned in. Speaking by Layla's ear, he gave a delicious earth-shaking rumble of his magics that shuddered right to Layla's most intimate places. "Maybe I'll let you participate with Rake and I sometime. Rake's not a Dragon but he slays them in bed, believe me."

"Shut up." Layla rolled her eyes, solidly facing the promenade once more though she couldn't help it; she was smiling now. Dusk had a point with his lurid innuendo – all Dragons had disastrously high appetites for fighting and fucking, and Dragon-relationships were far more complicated than anything Layla could typify in human terms. She was still getting used to it, and managing the urges of her magic was an hourly task despite her control since she'd bound Reginald.

Especially with the temptingly sexy Dusk around night and day now.

But as Layla faced the promenade, her heat flooded away to tension once more. She saw more Black Bentleys and Jaguars had arrived as she and Dusk talked, guests being escorted into the Hotel with baggage hefted over the shoulders of crimson liveried Hotel Guards. But none of the cars held her friends yet, and watching the guests already dressed in their finery for the Yule celebrations tonight, Layla's impending position as a Hotel Courtesan hit her. Panic flooded her, thinking about her debut at the Yule Ball this evening – not knowing who would win her at her Courtesan's Debut auction, or what she would have to do for them in the sack tonight.

It was something Layla didn't want to think about just yet, but she had her final approval appointment with the Hotel's new Associate Head later this afternoon to discuss it. Since Reginald Durant, Partner to her Courtesan-in-Training, was currently away, she would face Master Vampire Quindici DaPonti solo today for her final Courtesan's interview. Reginald had more than prepared her for it, but that combined with her actual debut tonight and the fact that none of her human friends knew about any of it yet, was making Layla's tension ratchet up to the boiling point.

But even as a flood of scorched bourbon-orange scent cascaded off her skin in the bright winter day, Dusk stepped in behind her. Winding his strong arms around her, he set his chin on Layla's shoulder, kissing her neck with his soft lips and making a twist of passion surge through her rather than tension.

"I'm sorry you're having a hard time," he spoke knowingly, low and kind. "Stepping into a world where monogamy isn't the currency of the realm is tough. Not just with your three Bound men, but also your impending position as a Hotel Courtesan. I can't imagine what you're going through, trying to come to terms with it all."

"It's driving me insane trying to reconcile the values I was raised with, with my new Dragon-appetites." Layla agreed with a sigh, knowing she still had a lot of internal judgments to face about her own sexuality.

"I like how insane it's driving you." Dusk kissed her neck, grinning. "It's nice."

Layla smiled, feeling all the intimate time she and Dusk had shared these past weeks thrill through her as her Dragon turned over inside her veins with a delicious slither. Sex with Dusk was mind-blowing, and Layla heated as she thought about everything they'd been doing since Thanksgiving. Reginald had permitted them to be together while he was away, though Layla still needed to train with Rikyava in the fight-halls beneath the Hotel daily to blow off extra magical steam.

"Anyway," Layla spoke, trying to push down her libido since her human friends were soon to arrive, "monogamy is different for you and Reginald. He's lived his entire life as a Courtier, and you've had numerous lovers all of yours as a pressure-release for your crazy high energy. For Adrian and I... it's different."

"Is it different?" Dusk spoke, his voice strangely flat suddenly. "Or are you just less bothered by Reginald and me having sex with other people, rather than Adrian or yourself?"

That stopped her. Layla went utterly still, her Dragon frozen inside her. She suddenly felt like a rabbit pinned by a snowy owl's talons from Dusk's astute statement. He'd said it with glib panache, but Layla could feel him waiting for her answer with a tense stillness. He wanted a response, and Layla smelled his cool river-water scent blossom up around him like a whitewater flood. Dusk was casual about sex, but he wasn't casual about love. Layla could feel how much he'd given his heart to her these past months.

And the fierce alertness in him – as he waited to hear if he was less important to her than Adrian Rhakvir.

But Layla was saved from answering as a cadre of Hotel Guards in 1800's crimson uniforms suddenly marched out the main doors of the Hotel and formed a chevron before the Hotel's primary entrance. Glancing around, Layla smiled, recognizing Dusk's handwork: he'd arranged a formal Hotel welcome for her friends, just as Layla had received when she'd started in Concierge Services. It was something the Hotel only did for the highest dignitaries, and Layla smiled wider as her Blood Dragon friend and Head of the Hotel Guard Rikyava Andersen strode forward, clasping arms with Dusk, then snapping her black boots together and bowing smartly before Layla. Rikyava rose with a reckless grin on her full Swedish lips and high cheekbones, her lavender eyes sparkling as she set a hand to the rapier at her hip and swept her long blonde French braid back over her shoulder.

"Hey girl." Rikyava grinned at Layla with a wink. "The Guard heard there were some important folks coming in today. So we came to show our respects."

"Is this your doing?" Layla laughed, gesturing at the Guardsmen and women lined up in their chevron, standing at stiff attention in their uniforms with long pikes and baldrics of frightfully impressive weapons. Some of them looked human, but most didn't – including four enormous Red Giants at the rear whom Layla knew were intensely loyal to Adrian.

"Oh, a little birdie might have whispered in my ear." Rikyava winked at Dusk, who was smiling now with a devious wit.

"A little birdie with crystal Dragon-scales?" Layla turned to Dusk, grinning also now.

"A royal welcome is sometimes approved for human guests," he chuckled. "Though I can't say I ran this one by the new Associate Hotel Head, or the Hotel Head herself. Quindici DaPonti's a dick, and don't even get me started on Lulu Duvall and all the shit she's—"

Dusk was about to say more, when a black Bentley suddenly pulled up before them at the edge of the checkered marble courtyard. Layla's friends from Seattle were suddenly spilling out of the car with squeals of delight and her joy surged, watching her friends gape at all the opulence of the Red Letter Hotel.

15

Moving forward, Layla was already in their arms. Laughter was in her heart as she did a happy dance with geek-chic Celia Carron, wearing a quilted orange parka that squished fluffily as they hugged. Big buff Charlie Avondale was next, swaddling Layla in his massive arms, clad in a UW sweatshirt and jeans. Layla laughed into his Adonis-blond curls, longer and more stoner-like than ever. Her best friend Arron Jacobs pushed in third, wearing a lean navy pinstriped suit with a hot pink pocket square and sweeping Layla up into his tall frame. Lifting her off her feet, Arron made Layla laugh breathlessly as his goodness poured through her.

But Arron set Layla down with a twinkle in his grey eyes as Layla's last housemate from Seattle rounded the car. Wearing a blue blazer with nice jeans that fit his lean, mean body to a T, Luke Murphy was gorgeous as ever. Moving close, he ran a hand through his Irish-thick dark hair as he watched Layla with a careful gaze. She suddenly forgot all her troubles as she stared into his impossibly green eyes. Like emeralds shining through spring grass, those eyes spoke of tempestuous heat and renegade fury – and Luke's incredibly deep love. Their history held Layla as she drowned in his eyes for a moment.

And then Luke swept forward, gathering her into his arms.

The feeling was like coming home as Layla let out a deep sigh, cradled close to his strong, lean CrossFitter's body. Luke's hand slid up her neck, holding her, and she felt him relax as her hands lifted to clutch his blazer. His cheek turned to hers and Layla felt her passion leap to him just as it always had. He didn't kiss her, just breathed her in as they held each other. Tears pricked Layla's eyes, though the drakaina that lived inside her veins was coolly silent.

Her Dragon didn't want Luke as a mate, human as he was, but Layla would always love him.

"Hey." Luke murmured at last, nuzzling his nose into her jaw.

"Hey," Layla breathed back, smiling.

"I missed you." He spoke, pulling her closer.

"I missed you, too."

Layla felt a deep tenderness pass between them, the best of what they'd once had as a couple. But it held sadness now, something poignant that hadn't been there before as Luke set his lips to her temple in a soft kiss, then pulled back. His eyes were luminous with pain as he hesitated to let her go, and Layla felt emotion stretch between them. All their history bound her close – something that could never be replaced for all the magic in the world.

But as they watched each other, movement suddenly caught Layla's attention. At Luke's open shirt collar, she saw a silver chain with a dark pendant resting in the cleft of his sculpted chest. Layla perked as her gaze moved to it. Jewelry was something Luke had been adamant against all the years she'd known him. But his new teardrop pendant was a forest-green bloodstone flecked with rust-red, twined into an ornate silver filigree like Celtic knot work. As Layla watched, the dark stone writhed with veins of gold twisting through it, like currents of smelted blood.

It was so stunning that Layla blinked.

And so obviously magical that she glanced up at Luke in alarm.

CHAPTER 2 – DISH

The forest green bloodstone around Luke's neck was either being affected by magic, or it was magic in and of itself. Layla didn't know which, but as she stared at it as she and Luke stood on the snowy promenade with a thrill of shock passing through her, she felt her Dragon suddenly coil up and snarl inside her veins. As if the drakaina that lived inside Layla's flesh recognized something dire about that stone, Layla suddenly felt everything inside her go on high alert. If she'd had scales and a mantle full of Dragon-spines, she'd have bristled like a cat. As it was, every hair on her body stood up straight as a wave of adrenaline passed through her.

"Luke! This pendant—!" Layla spoke as she blinked.

"It's just something Dusk found for me." Luke dismissed with a wry smile, though Layla felt him clam up, tense. "Something to protect me from magic while I'm here at the Hotel."

"Why do you need protection from magic? Didn't Dusk tell you the Hotel has plenty of security systems to protect humans from extraneous magic while they stay here?" Layla frowned, knowing Luke wasn't giving her a full answer but not knowing why. Deep inside, her drakaina still bristled like she wanted to rake talons at that pendant, or perhaps at Luke, to shred it and cast it someplace far away.

"The pendant has to do with how your Dragon affected me back in September." Luke spoke more tersely, his Irish temper flashing in his eyes now. "It's nothing, Layla. Really. Just leave it."

Luke was rebuffing her, and Layla pulled back, concern rushing through her that her magic had done something to him in Seattle when it had attacked him in the fall – something that made him extremely susceptible to magic now. But rather than get all feisty and prickly like usual, Luke suddenly mastered himself, his temper sliding away even as it had risen. With a shock, Layla realized Luke was more in control of his emotions than she had ever seen him. She blinked, astounded, as she watched the pendant on Luke's chest writhe with currents as his storm was washed away.

"I'll tell you all about it later, Layla, I promise." Gazing down at her, Luke suddenly smiled, his green eyes lovely and bright. "So this is the Hotel? I heard there was more to it. Are we just going to see snow all morning or what?"

Layla's lips fell open, amazed that Luke's scalding temper had suddenly cleared. Luke was a tempestuous ass sometimes, but he could also be the best. And right now he was being the charming hottie Layla had fallen in love with years ago. Pleasure flowed from him in the snowy winter day and Layla shook her head. Threading her arm through his, she gave him a tug.

"Fine, we can talk about it later. Come on, you. Come meet Dusk."

"I've already met your odious Concierge Services boss, Layla. Whom you're also sleeping with." But Luke teased now as his gaze strayed to Dusk waiting with Rikyava. His words were said with no jealousy, and as Layla laughed, still astounded, their baggage was hefted from the Bentley's trunk to the brawny shoulders of the Hotel Guard, moving towards the main doors. As Layla and her friends moved to Rikyava and Dusk, Dusk beamed his most welcoming Head Concierge smile as he greeted everyone with a kiss to both cheeks.

"Welcome to the Red Letter Hotel Paris – Celia, Charlie, Arron. Luke." Dusk spoke in his lovely clear baritone.

"Dusk. Great to finally see you in person. When I'm well." Luke was in amazingly good spirits as he shook Dusk's hand, his green eyes bright as if he and Dusk were on excellent terms. It made Layla wonder what the two of them had been talking about during their phone calls these past months – and how many calls there had been. As if they had an extended acquaintance, Dusk was just as affable, clapping Luke's shoulder with a smile.

"Great to see you so hale, Luke. Glad that pendant is working for you."

"Absolutely. Thanks, Dusk." Luke meant it, his demeanor no-bullshit today.

"Anytime." Dusk smiled back, calm and generous.

Layla glanced between both men, impressed. She'd been almost certain Luke was going to be a bulldog this week with her Bound men, but watching him now, Layla saw something else. A deep understanding passed between Luke and Dusk, and as Rikyava stepped forward, seizing Luke's hand and giving it a solid pump, Layla blinked to realize her Blood Dragon friend had been in on those calls also. In a moment of instinct, Layla realized Luke's calls with Dusk and Rikyava had something to do with the bloodstone – and why Luke needed protection from magic.

"Luke! Shit, you're handsome! Even more than on the video cam." Rikyava grinned, a vicious flirtation taking her as she beamed at him.

"Thanks?" But though Luke laughed, Layla could feel a sudden tension between him and the Blood Dragon Head Guardswoman as Luke raked a hand through his thick Irish hair, blushing. Layla was about to ask what was going on when Dusk cleared his throat, continuing his welcome speech as Rikyava and Luke stepped awkwardly back from each other.

"Friends. Everything has been arranged for your stay over the next week, and please let me know if there is anything I can do for you while you're here. The Red Letter Hotel lives to serve, and so do I. You four are my utmost priority this week, and Rikyava will have her Guards on-hand at all times to make sure you're safe."

"I know what *I'll* need during my stay." Arron Jacobs sidled forward with a sexy smile on his ash-blond good looks as he eyeballed Dusk's sculpted frame. Arron was unabashedly gay and Dusk was the epitome of his type – soccer-player fit and tall. Layla watched as Dusk responded to the attention, turning his sex appeal up to an eleven as he gave Arron a deviantly hot laugh. Dusk's laugh contained a roll of his Crystal Dragon-power in it and Layla saw Arron rock, receiving the full blast of that carnal wave. Arron's hand shot out, steadying himself on Charlie's brawny shoulder as his eyes rolled up and his eyelashes fluttered.

"Holy hell…!" Arron gasped. "That was nice."

"If you think my powers are nice, Arron," Dusk chuckled, sly, "just wait until I introduce you to a few of our more prominent Courtiers. They make my magic feel like parlor tricks. Come on. Let's get you four settled in. This way."

Turning, Dusk threw Layla a sexy smile before he stepped into his brisk Head Concierge mode and began escorting the housemates inside the Hotel. Rikyava flicked her fingers for her Guardsmen in the chevron to come to attention, and they snapped their pikes out to form a vaulted arch. Leading everyone beneath the arch, Dusk proceeded through the Hotel's main doors. Stepping to Layla's side, Arron linked her by the arm and gave her an amazed shake of his head, his grey eyes sparkling as he spoke.

"Um. We are *so* going to discuss your man-situation in the coming days, chica. I am going to need *all* the scoop. Especially if your main beau can do that rumble thing in the bedroom."

"Oh, you are going to get all the sordid details, believe me." Layla grinned back. "And then you're going to head right down to the Concierge desk to schedule Assignations and have your mind blown with the things Courtiers can do here."

"Oh, honey." Arron grinned back like a tall blond devil. "I am going to get a lot more than my mind blown here, I assure you."

Laughing like two kids in a candy store, they moved inside. As Dusk held the door, Arron blew Dusk a cheeky kiss. Dusk grinned and winked, playing the cad. But as they entered the Red Letter Hotel Paris' grand main lobby, all of Layla's housemates stopped, ogling around in wide-eyed surprise – even Luke unable to stop his lips dropping open at the opulence.

Decorated to the nines for Yule, the massive French Baroque palace positively glittered with twenty-foot magical icicles, holly boughs, and greenery of cedar and juniper, with faerie lights winding around every grand column and gilded arch. Layla gazed around as her friends did, seeing it as if for the first time. This was the original Palace of Versailles, and rather than cherubs gazing down from the painted frescoes, the grandly-lit ceilings sported dragons, chimera, and fanciful beasts. Crystal chandeliers lit every soaring dome; gilded floor-candelabra illuminated every cavernous niche. Every marble column writhed with satyrs, sphinxes, and griffons rutting in scintillating decadence. So ornate it was disorienting, the Hotel's glory was augmented by crimson accents that bound everything together, letting no one forget what this place really was.

A domain of unforgettable red-letter experiences.

The Hotel was packed for Yule, and Twilight folk of every sort, along with human tycoons and royalty, moved through the grand foyer. Layla appreciated the excitement as they moved through the enormous, airy hall burbling with the echo of fountains. Dusk was gregarious as he pointed out the sights, Layla's Seattle friends speechless at the racy, fae opulence.

Even Arron blushed as they passed the *bacchanalios* orgy on its crimson dais, led by the Hotel's resident Smoke Faunus Imogene Cereste. Arrestingly haunting with her skin mottled like silver tree-bark, corkscrewing ram's horns, shaggy silver-white hair on her legs, and slender branch-like fingers, Imogene fucked three men simultaneously in the center of the forty-person orgy, exhaling white-blue smoke from her luscious lips to push the fevered revelry higher. Charlie became rooted in place, his blue eyes enormous as Celia stared with her mouth open. With a clearing of his throat, Dusk steered the group past the spectacle and up the grand double-staircase.

Leading them up to the third level, Dusk brought them at last to their rooms. Hotel Guards stood at attention by each set of double-doors, throwing them wide as Dusk indicated each room, Arron's suite next to Layla's own apartment. Layla smiled as her housemates moved into their suites. She heard a squeal from Celia, and a laugh from Arron, and an astounded exclamation from Charlie. Stepping over to Dusk, who was grinning to beat the band, Layla lifted her eyebrows.

"What did you leave in their rooms?"

"Oh, just a little welcome present, as per their tastes." Dusk winked.

Arron soon stepped back out his open doorway, shaking his head as he grinned at Dusk. "You are just *impossible*, aren't you?"

"Some have said so." Dusk grinned, then addressed all of Layla's friends as Luke, Charlie, and Celia gathered also. "I've arranged an early dinner for you all at four p.m. in Arron's suite, though after that, you'll need to get ready for the Yule Ball. Feel free to explore the Hotel until dinner, though I warn you, you're going to have your mind blown.

Don't worry about getting lost; ask any Guard in crimson and they can get you back here. I will be escorting you all to the Ball after dinner. I do need to attend a few details now for tonight's gala, however. If you will excuse me. Layla, a moment?"

As Layla stepped over to a marble column with Dusk, she laughed. "You didn't tell me you arranged dinner for everyone!"

"It's casual. Nothing special. Just slightly ostentatious and definitely delicious." Dusk chuckled, delight flashing in his summer-blue eyes as he stepped close. Clasping his arms around Layla's waist, he pressed his body close to hers. "I want this night to be special, Layla. I want this week to be full of pleasure while your friends are here. You're debuting as a Hotel Courtesan tonight; that's a tremendous event. With Adrian on the lam and Reginald away—"

But Dusk had no more time to talk as Luke stepped hesitantly towards them, clearing his throat. Layla flushed to be caught in an embrace with Dusk. But Dusk released her like a gentleman, flashing a kind smile as he kissed her hands and turned to face Luke. "Luke. Is there something you need?"

"Dusk, do you have a moment to speak about... that thing we've been discussing?" Luke spoke, his emerald gaze uncertain.

"Of course." Dusk was all Head Concierge professionalism as he nodded. "Let's move into your rooms where we'll have fewer prying ears."

"Sure." Luke was strangely tense as he ran a hand through his thick black hair, his gaze darting to Layla.

"Layla, I need to attend this," Dusk spoke to her as he gave a squeeze to Layla's hands, kind but firm. "Have fun visiting with your friends and don't forget your interview with the Associate Hotel Head at three p.m. I'll be back at four to have dinner with you all. Enjoy."

With a sweep of his arm, Dusk beckoned to Luke, moving into his rooms and leaving Layla out in the hall wondering what the hell was going on. Clearly, Luke felt he could entrust the details about his magical susceptibility to Dusk but not Layla, which was a first. Her brows knit as she stripped off her scarf and peacoat, bundling them over her arm. But before she could mull the situation over further, Arron stepped close, seizing her hands and hauling her towards his suite.

"Honey, your beau is so next-level!" Arron gushed as he tugged Layla into his rooms.

"What do you mean?" She asked, confused as she shut Arron's doors behind her and tossed her coat and scarf to a table.

"Observe." Striding to the walk-in closet of his sprite-themed apartment, Arron threw the gilded doors wide. Inside, the closet had been populated by twenty of the hottest suits Layla had ever seen, each one of them cut to perfection for Arron's tall, lanky frame. They were Head Clothier Amalia DuFane's work, in shimmering fabrics and ornate weaves humans just didn't make. Each and every one was fancier than Prada or Armani, and Arron immediately strode into all that opulence and began rolling himself through the suits with a laugh, stroking everything.

"Wow!" Layla grinned as she touched a cream and baby-blue paisley smoking jacket with shiny cobalt lapels that was going to look amazing on Arron's ash-blond coloring. "Well, Dusk does love a good suit."

"And clearly he appreciates a good man wearing them." Arron grinned back, lecherous. "My gaydar gets hits with him. Are you sure he's hetero?"

"Dusk is bi." Layla grinned, loving that her best friend was here at last. "A lot of Dragons enjoy both sexes. Though some are same-sex, and others are strictly hetero."

"Ok. Dish. I'm here now, so you can't avoid telling me all the sordid details. Are you and Dusk exclusive?" Arron gave an inquisitive lift of his blond eyebrows.

"Not exactly." And here they were, coming into Arron's favorite topic – Layla's love life. As they moved to the massive four-post bed with a spring green silk duvet and flopped down, Arron snatched up a box of chocolates Dusk had left on his pillows. They were Layla's favorite; alcoholic cordials from a Dionysian-fae chocolatier in Paris, *Tout Chocolat*. She and Arron tucked in, sampling this and that on his ample bed as Arron cocked his head, his grey eyes missing nothing.

"Last I heard, you were hot for Adrian." Arron spoke as he ate a lavender bonbon with purple striping.

"I still am." Glad she had a cherry cordial in her fingers, Layla licked it in lieu of fidgeting. None of her housemates knew the details about her Bind-magic, and they didn't know about her becoming a Courtesan tonight. It was going to be a big surprise, if she couldn't find a way to break the news before the Yule Ball – especially to Luke.

"So you've got *both* Adrian and Dusk on the line?" Arron blinked with a rascally grin. "Naughty madonna!"

"Actually…" Layla cleared her throat, licking her cherry cordial. "There are three of them."

"*Three?!*" Arron's grin was scandalized as he put his bonbon down. "What – I mean, *how*?"

"It's my Dragon-magic. It's sort of… pushed me into relationships with all of them." Gazing at her best friend, Layla suddenly knew it was time to spill all the details she'd been holding back since August. "Actually, it's all pretty difficult."

"Tell Arron." He smiled kindly, reaching out to take her hand. "What's wrong, hun-bun? You have three men on the line, yet I sense that's a problem."

"It is." Layla nodded, opening her heart to her best friend. "I was raised to value monogamy, but my Dragon can't get enough of anyone with power. She reaches out, tasting people and seeing if she can Bind them. I've got more control over it, because I bound someone at Thanksgiving who can control my Dragon's appetites. But I still feel it trying to reel in new mates. And now, I'm becoming a Hotel Courtesan tonight, and—"

"Um, *excuse* me?!" Arron's eyes went enormous as he blinked, staring at her like she'd grown six heads. "Back up, chica. What do you mean, *bind?* And becoming a Courtesan? Isn't that the whole reason you were skeptical of the Hotel in the first place?"

"Yes and yes." Taking a deep breath, Layla gathered herself. "You know I'm a Dragon. But the kind of Dragon I am is called a Royal Dragon Bind. My magic has the ability to create a connection with someone else powerful, a *bind*. It's like this cord that unites their magic with mine and lets me feel their emotions and memories. But it's more than that. It's like—"

"Love." Arron's gaze was deep as he watched her. "When you bind these men, you love them, don't you? All of them."

"I do." Layla breathed, twisting deep inside. "And not only that… my magic wants me to take more lovers, or it gets pissed, explosive. It's part of why—"

"Why you've decided to become a Courtesan." Arron's gaze was intense.

"I debut tonight at the Yule Ball." She nodded, feeling sick. "Tonight someone will win my debut auction and I have to sleep with them. Other Assignations will be my choice. But this first one… I haven't told any of this to Celia or Charlie. Or Luke."

"Fucksticks. Luke is going to birth a porcupine when he hears about it." Arron spoke as he smoothed his hand over hers. His grey eyes were deep, holding all the emotion Layla was too afraid to face. On the verge of tears, she gave a sick laugh that made her heart hammer. Blinking, she reached up, wiping a tear away. Arron wiped the next one as it came sliding down, then wrapped his long arms around her. "Hey, hey now…"

"What am I doing, Arron?" Layla hitched a breath, not ready to break down just yet.

"You're doing what you're supposed to, Layla." Arron spoke gently as he held her, warm and good. "Wherever you walk, men's eyes follow. Luke used to complain about it, that you were so magnetic he had to beat other men away with a stick. So what if you earn *millions* for sleeping with hot guys who don't care if you keep them? That's what a Hotel Courtesan earns, right?"

"Yeah. And the position carries tremendous status in the Twilight Realm." Layla sighed, her heart still heavy even though Arron's words made sense. "But I don't care about the money, Arron. I care about the fact that my Dragon is intrigued thinking about sleeping with random men. My Dragon is roaring for the mystery, the challenge – the whole messy business of having multiple partners, and strangers."

"It's not wrong, hun-bun." Reaching out, Arron tucked one of Layla's curls behind her ear, his gaze kind as he impressed his point. "None of it is wrong, as long as you're up-front about it. You've changed from who you were as a human, and you have to let your ideas about a happy life change with it. Nobody's saying you have to be some 1950's housewife, Layla. Lord knows I gave up on that ages ago when I found out I was gay. And that I like dick so much it's hard to settle on just one partner. Are other Dragons monogamous?"

"Not generally." Layla sighed, realizing the crux of the problem as Arron pointed it out. Having sex for money bothered her, but what was really tough was that she would always be a slave to her Dragon's urges, never human again. "But Dragons also tend to settle with a primary mate later in life. The problem is, even though I feel like Adrian's my primary, he's never around. Dusk is always here for me, and Reginald... well, Reginald is Head Courtier of the Paris Hotel, and a Royal Siren. Everything you've heard about Sirens is true."

"So what you're saying is," Arron gave a sly grin, "*Oops, I tripped and fucked three of the hottest men ever. And now I get to fuck more of them and make some ridiculous cash.*"

"Arron!" Layla laughed, slapping his chest. "I haven't actually had sex with Adrian yet, and Dragon males are intensely competitive. They're trying to not fight over me, but Dusk and Adrian are adopted family. And Reginald and Adrian have some feud I don't know about, constantly giving each other the deep cold shoulder."

"Juggling three powerful men with big egos is going to be tough." Arron became thoughtful as he settled to his stomach on the duvet, propping his head on his hands. "But Dusk is at least willing to play ball."

"Yeah, but he's jealous." Layla heaved another sigh, settling back on the duvet also. "Just today, he wanted to know if he was lower on the totem pole than the other two."

"Wanting to know if the *helpful provider* routine is going to get him benched from your bed when the other two are at full hotness."

"Something like that." Suddenly, Layla realized it was exactly like that – Dusk was afraid whenever Adrian or Reginald returned, he would get sidelined. She frowned, and was about to ask Arron what he'd observed about Dusk when Celia and Charlie suddenly pushed in through Arron's apartment doors with twin breathless laughs.

"Guys!" Charlie exclaimed, his baby-blue eyes alight. "Holy shit! I just walked downstairs and saw people getting erotic massages by these giant bird-women with like, sixteen breasts!"

"And I saw a naked mud-fight with over a hundred people!" Celia laughed as she pushed her horn-rimmed glasses up her button nose. "I *have* to get in on that! What are you two doing in here, being slouches when we should be out exploring?"

"We're talking over Layla's immensely complicated love life." Arron grinned as he pushed up from the bed. "Chica here takes priority. And we all need to start getting ready for this dinner."

"Dusk is probably planning something spectacular, even though he said it was casual." Layla commented, pushing up from the bed. "As for the Yule Ball tonight, you'll want to wear whatever Dusk put in your closets. Opulence doesn't even begin to describe the Hotel's masquerades, and you'll want to fit in."

"You mean wear those *gorgeous* ballgowns? And that jewelry? I mean, are those real diamonds?" Celia spoke with big eyes, adjusting one of her artsy enameled pink earrings.

"Oh, yeah." Charlie chimed in as he pulled a key fob from his jeans pocket. "What's this? It was left on my breakfast table with a note that said, *Have fun. – Dusk.*"

"It's probably a sports car or a motorcycle." Layla grinned, enjoying that her friends were getting a taste of Hotel life. "Something you can play with here and Dusk will ship back with you at the end of your stay."

"Holy crap!" Charlie looked at the keys in his hand with a shit-eating grin. "Goddamn, Layla! Your boyfriend is the best!"

Suddenly, Layla realized Charlie was right – Dusk was the best. He was there for her in a way her other two Bound men just weren't, and it made her heart swell for him. All at once, she realized he didn't have second-place status in her life. In certain ways he was coming in first and always would – simply because of who he was, day in and day out. As she and Arron exchanged a glance, he gave her an eyebrow lift that spoke volumes.

"Dusk is the best." Layla smiled.

Just then, another knock came at the door. Layla rose to admit a duo of Hotel employees from Wardrobe come to style Arron for dinner. Arron laughed as he rose, seeing they had brought mani-pedi supplies on a gilded cart, plus a full hairstyling setup. Settling into a chair before one tall mirror, Arron let the Wardrobe folks attend him like a king as Charlie and Celia moved back to their own rooms. Layla went to the doors also, exiting to get ready for her Courtesan's interview with Quindici DaPonti.

But as she moved to her apartment, at the last moment Layla changed course, stepping to Luke's doors. With a knock, she waited. But no one answered and when at last Layla knew no one was coming, she turned away with a sinking feeling in her heart.

CHAPTER 3 – INTERVIEW

At her Courtesan's interview, it took everything Layla had to not fidget as she sat across a broad mahogany desk from the Paris Hotel's new Associate Head, the Barone Quindici DaPonti. Quindici's office of floor-to-ceiling bookshelves and high-gabled windows breathed with the hiss of radiators in the midwinter afternoon, snow swirling down beyond the massive windows with their forest-green velvet drapes. But though he sat in the bright winter light without concern, the Master Vampire seeped with the cold breath of the grave as he sat back in his tall mahogany chair and steepled his long white fingers, watching Layla.

Ancientness rested in Quindici's gaze, his irises so dark they were nearly black, though Layla had no clue how old he really was. Wearing a dark maroon suit, his shirt a flat black, the new Associate Hotel Head let no one deny what he was – a creature of darkness, despite his Master's ability to walk in the day. A vivid crimson pocket square complemented his ensemble, his dark auburn hair styled expertly back from his beautifully masculine features, gold and ruby rings glinting on his long fingers. Cufflinks of gold and copper filigree held large onyx stones the same color as his eyes, piercing the French cuffs of his shirt.

"Ms. Price, thank you for meeting with me today." Quindici spoke, a pleasant smile curling his full lips. It flashed the points of his fangs – on purpose, Layla was certain. "I know this is a busy day for you with your friends arriving at the Hotel, and I appreciate your dedication to your impending position as a Hotel Courtesan."

"Associate Hotel Head. Thank you for the opportunity." Layla lifted her chin as she settled her hands on the lap of her cream cocktail dress with its burgundy lace shoulders. She'd changed into a far more elegant outfit for this meeting, to show her understanding of a Courtesan's niceties. Her blush patent leather heels were platform stilettos and Layla sat tall, crossing her ankles and tucking them to the side. It was an elegant position, one Reginald had grilled into her mercilessly these past months.

"I'd like to discuss your upcoming duties as a dual-position at this Hotel." Quindici continued in a gracious baritone. Glancing at a leather folio on his desk with gilded edges, embossed with the crimson 'R' of the Hotel, he flicked the cover open, his dark eyes scanning Layla's employee file. "Head Courtier-in-absentia Reginald Durant has been thorough in his reports on your training. He is confident you are ready for your Courtesan's Debut tonight at the Yule Ball. It is a prestigious event, Ms. Price, both the Ball and the debut of a new Courtesan. This meeting is informal; you have all the qualifications to satisfy your impending position and your application has already been approved by the Owners' Board. I simply wish to see how you are feeling about your auction tonight for your first Assignation."

"Reginald has prepared me for everything I will experience tonight." Layla spoke, keeping her head high though something deep inside her clenched. But she kept her posture; she'd be damned if she'd display discomfort before the new Associate Hotel Head, even though she was intensely nervous about being auctioned off like a piece of meat tonight. Technically, Quindici was Adrian's ally, watching over the Paris Hotel while Adrian was on the lam. But the Master Vampire had once been Head Courtier of the Florence Hotel, and an aura of decadent sexuality breathed from him still – scandalously intimate even for this informal meeting.

And as Layla watched Quindici, she wasn't entirely certain he was a friend.

"Reginald is a force of nature in the bedchamber. He understands all the regular sexual arts as well as those far more obscure." Quindici continued amiably. "You are lucky he has been your Partner. As his protégé, you stand to earn this branch a considerable sum in the coming years, and yourself as well. Our representatives have already been spreading word that Reginald has a Royal Dragon Bind as his *ingénue*, and it has provoked much interest. So. Tell me how you are really feeling about your impending position as a Hotel Courtesan."

Layla took a deep breath, re-crossing her ankles. Their new Associate Hotel Head wasn't going to let her off the hook. Quindici's dark gaze was deep as he watched her, and in it, Layla saw Reginald's uncanny awareness. The Vampire noted everything about Layla; her posture, her rigidity, her scorched bourbon scent that flooded the air. Layla knew she couldn't hide her true feelings from Quindici and it made her feel intensely vulnerable as they stared each other down.

"I think I'm ready." She spoke at last, stubborn.

"Thinking you're ready to have sex with a stranger and knowing you're ready are entirely different things." Quindici countered with a deeply knowing gaze. "Every Courtier and Courtesan is nervous for their first Assignation. No one knows how it will go, who it will be, what will be demanded of them. Though you will pre-approve subsequent partners, your first Assignation is determined by the auction – and the price will drive high for you. Not just because you come from a rare Lineage, but also because debuts at Grand Masquerades go for extraordinary sums. Which is important for our Hotel right now, making up for running in the red for much of the autumn as we are. Reginald knows this; so does the Board. And so do I."

Layla heard condescension in Quindici's tone against Adrian's management of the Paris Hotel. Indeed, Quindici's influence on the Hotel had been nothing short of astonishing these past weeks, establishing a BDSM technoclub in the basement, semi-secret 1920's speakeasies behind the walls, and an Escape Room with magical puzzles so extreme that it was attracting the best minds in the human and Twilight Realms to solve it. Though he was countless centuries old, the business-savvy Vampire Barone had his pulse on modernity, implementing upgrades that attracted a younger audience of new money. And as a former Head Courtier and a current Clan First of his Dark Haven in Florence, he had a long-standing association with the Florence Hotel that gave him exquisite knowledge of people's darker desires – something the Paris Hotel lacked.

Settling his elbows on his chair, Quindici's onyx gaze was penetrating as he sat back, an amused smile curling his full lips. "Did Reginald tell you he trained under me at the Florence Hotel?"

"I've heard it mentioned," Layla spoke, wondering where this was going. "Though he's not said much about it."

"Indeed." Quindici smiled amiably. "Our association occurred a little over two hundred years ago. I was his Partner for a time, and he my protégé, just as you are to him now. The Florence Red Letter Hotel has always been known for the darker arts of pleasure, and Reginald became a master of them during our time together. He is a considerable asset to this Hotel, and his patrons bring in nearly a fifth of our annual revenue."

"If he's so valuable," Layla countered, lifting an eyebrow, "then why don't you officially re-instate him as Head Courtier?" Though Reginald hadn't been dismissed after his Siren-fight with his older brother Bastien at Thanksgiving, his current position-in-absentia was still technically a demotion. Heads had rolled in the wake of that event, invoking a re-organization of the Paris Hotel – Adrian fleeing under pain of death as the scapegoat for it all.

"By Hotel law," Quindici spoke, his dark eyes piercing Layla, "anyone who has endured a significantly *destabilizing* event must abide a three-months suspension until they are deemed fit to return to work. Reginald slaughtered his brother Bastien in cold blood, destroying a Hotel ballroom and taking many lives. He and I have spoken, and he is not fighting his current suspension, especially now that he is embroiled in his clan's politics after Bastien's death. Please do not push the matter, Layla, if you would like to stay on the right side of the new Hotel Head."

"Lulu Duvall wanted to dismiss Reginald and you prevented it?" Layla's eyebrows raised. As Adrian's strongest ally on the Owners' Board, Quindici had been appointed to lead the Paris Hotel in Adrian's place, but only as Associate Hotel Head. As Layla stared at Quindici now, she realized he held a tenuous position, bridging the gap between Adrian's allies on the staff and the mouthpiece for the Owners' Board – their new Hotel Head, the frighteningly elegant French Faunus Ms. Lulu Duvall.

Just then, the door to the grand office behind Layla opened. A statuesque woman entered without knocking, a stack of leather folios carried in her graceful, slender arms. Naked but for the soft tawny velvet that covered her, growing into thicker, sleek hair down over her gazelle-legs, she looked like a supermodel, all lovely elegance and striking bones. Gold torques wound up her corkscrewing antlers, the same decorating her slim arms, wrists, and curling around her small breasts. She glanced at Layla with big dark doe-eyes as she rounded Quindici's desk and set the folios upon it. Her hands were long, her nails done in perfect French manicure as she lifted the top folio and extended it.

"Quindici, please set appointments to review these staff members in the next week." Ms. Duvall spoke, her voice low and melodious with its purring French accent. "We need to make assessments to see if they would be a better fit at other Hotels. Begin with this one here."

"Yes, Ms. Duvall." Quindici received the folio from his boss with a pleasant smile, flashing fang as he slipped it beneath Layla's.

"I'd also like a report on the Grand Ballroom re-build," Lulu Duvall continued. "I would like to create a placard for guests to read tonight, if they are curious why the Ballroom is under construction during Yule."

"Yes, Hotel Head." Quindici nodded graciously. But though he was elegantly poised, Layla could see his clever mind noting every word Lulu Duvall had spoken, and everything she hadn't said. Ms. Duvall was the kingpin of the Hotel Board's re-organization of the Paris branch in the last month. Their mouthpiece and their hands, Ms. Duvall received orders from higher-ups and relayed them through Quindici to help ease the Paris Hotel's transition into a compliant establishment with the Board's desires. A far cry from Adrian's stern but compassionate running of the Hotel, Lulu Duvall didn't care about feelings, only results. She was getting them by invoking a deep *Risorgimento* of the branch, but it was pissing off the Department Heads – most notably Dusk.

With a gracious nod, Ms. Duvall departed, giving Layla a smile as she left and closing the office's gilded double-doors behind her.

"So." Quindici continued with Layla as if they had never been interrupted, something astute easing through his eyes. "Tell me: what fears do you have about your debut tonight that I may assuage?"

"You think you can help calm my fears?" Layla lifted an eyebrow at the Vampire.

"Perhaps." He spoke quietly, intensely sensual. "I can smell fear all over you, though you're trying to reason through it. You're worrying about sleeping with a stranger who has paid to have your first Assignation. You're afraid of the implication that you will be owned for the night; it runs against every moral you have. Yet this is how you and Adrian Rhakvir have decided to flush out his enemies on the Owners' Board. This is the course of action agreed on with the Intercessoria Judiciary, to create a Venusian fly-trap for the Crimson Circle, that Heathren Merkami wants to bring to justice. This is how you have all planned to get close enough to the Twilight Realm's über-elite to dig for information on your own personal enemy – Hunter. That's a lot riding on your shoulders. Or between your legs, as it were."

Layla stilled, her fingers clenching in her lap, even though she tried to breathe through it. The Vampire was right on all counts, though gods knew how he had gotten all that information. Layla supposed Adrian had filled him in sometime in the past month, though it bothered her that Quindici knew all those reasons for her becoming a Courtesan.

"You're right," Layla spoke at last, holding Quindici's dark gaze. "I am afraid. Afraid of what I might have to do tonight; afraid of the outcome, whether it goes well or badly. Everything in me screams that fucking for money is wrong, and I think auctioning a person off is disgusting."

"Yet the Dragon in you is eager to take a new partner, and another, and another. All a mystery to be discovered." Quindici spoke, his gaze drilling right to Layla's core.

Layla drew a deep breath, trying to slow her suddenly pounding heart and the way her Dragon roiled inside her veins with a spiced blaze, wanting to devour Quindici's dark gaze and everything it promised. Not to mention the countless unknown partners she might have as a Courtesan. "My Dragon doesn't discriminate in the bedchamber. Only in matters of true mates."

"Only in matters of true love, you mean." Quindici corrected softly, his dark eyes searching hers. "I have known Binds in my time, Ms. Price. They never do anything without love. Just as I can taste your fear, I also feel your heart. Your blood rushes through your veins at the mention of Adrian Rhakvir. He is a true love, is he not? And would you not do anything to protect him?"

"Yes." Layla's answer was immediate. It was all true, and if Quindici really was an ally, he'd understand. If he was an enemy, then Layla wasn't going to mince words.

"Lay your plans carefully, then." Quindici's dark eyes glittered as if he could read her fierce thoughts. "Infiltrating the Crimson Circle is a severe danger. You will be in the center of that danger if you are alone in a bedchamber tonight with any of them."

"Is that a threat?" Layla prickled, narrowing her eyes.

"I am not your enemy, Layla," Quindici spoke softly, his dark eyes ancient, his tall frame utterly still in a way that alive creatures just didn't have. "I only warn that you pit yourself against a deadly conglomerate. I fear that by attempting to infiltrate the Circle, you are attracting attention which *will* harm you behind closed doors. Many with far stronger magics than you could ever dream of. I have assured Adrian I would protect those he loves while he is away, but blood will flow if you follow this course. Maybe yours; maybe people you care about. I know a thousand ways to devastate people, but the Crimson Circle know a million. Your heart will break before they are done with you. And that is not a threat I make – that is one which has been well-known in the Twilight Realm for ten thousand years since the Hotel was established."

"No one asks for the head of my lover and gets it," Layla growled, bristling as a wave of furious heat washed through her veins from her Dragon.

"No one asked for your heart or your sanity," Quindici countered smoothly, "but that is what you will give them if you step into this matter."

Quindici sat back in his throne-like chair, watching as Layla fell silent. His dark eyes perused her face and he inhaled, flaring his nostrils. Layla knew he was smelling her scorched-bourbon scent, like orange trees set fire with burning liquor. As he went utterly still, Layla saw a tyrant of the ages. This was a man who had killed his Maker, who had learned every manipulation and seduction in the book to rise high and dominate the Vampire clans of Italy. He wasn't King of his Lineage, but Layla knew Quindici was damn close to it. Like a viper in the dark who knew how to strike at the most opportune moment, Quindici held deep secrets in his stillness, though Layla didn't know his motivations.

And it was that detail which made her shiver as Quindici watched her.

"The Red Letter Hotel and its Crimson Circle were formed for a reason," Quindici spoke at last, "though its shadowy purpose is deeper than even I have been able to discover over the years. From its birth, the Hotel has built itself into the most powerful empire in the Twilight Realm – prostitution is an ancient profession, and those who profit from it at the point of a knife are nearly as old. Become a stronger player in the game and feel the cut of that knife, Layla."

"Fear doesn't control me." Layla spoke stubbornly, crossing her arms in a raging defiance.

Falling silent, Quindici watched her, then at last gave a sigh. Rising to his lean six-foot-plus height, the Vampire rounded his desk in a wave of slow, sexual grace. He offered his hand to Layla and she took it like a Courtesan should, rising. Reaching out, Quindici brushed his long fingertips over her cheek and Layla shivered, his touch so very cold yet somehow flooded with heat. Though the Master Vampire could stand in the winter sunlight without effect, his skin didn't warm, and his power flowed out in a chill nimbus around him, dimming the light. His onyx eyes held hers as he ran his thumb slowly over her lower lip – an exquisitely erotic sensation that made Layla shiver, though not from cold.

"You are the brightest Bind I have ever seen…" Quindici murmured with a dark poetry. "I would not see such a lovely creature become a beast of rage, claimed by darkness rather than light. But oh, how brightness can darken under the right circumstances."

"What do you mean?" Layla blinked, pulling back from his touch as alarm shot through her.

"Tell me you have not felt the darkness of the void inside you," Quindici spoke quietly, some ancient knowledge in his eyes. "I too have met the creature that hunts you, Layla, for once he also hunted me. He never hunts anyone who does not have his same blackness inside their hearts."

"You know Hunter?" Layla stepped back in severe alarm now, a wave of cold shivers taking her at the topic Quindici had switched to.

"The Hunter and I have met." The dire quirk of the Vampire's lips was not lost on Layla, nor was the haunting in his eyes. "He does not suffer those he deems powerful to rest. He pushes the powerful into their inner blackness by his actions, but what if he didn't have to? What if by pursuing the Crimson Circle, you do the job for him – and the sacrifice is your unholy soul?"

Quindici's gaze spoke of terrible things as he watched her. Not of things the Crimson Circle would do to her if she pursued this path – but of things Layla would do if she ever went dark like Hunter. His warning shuddered through Layla's bones, a blow deeper than any other he could have struck as she stared at him.

His gaze softening, an ancient sadness moved through Quindici's eyes. Stepping in close to Layla, he set a hand to her shoulder, then leaned down and set his lips to hers, exhaling a gentle wave of heat down her throat. It was like a reversal of his seeking, dark Vampire-energy, and strangely not unlike something Adrian could do.

Layla was at first startled that he'd kissed her, but something about that smooth, calm power was compelling. Called to draw a breath from Quindici's lips, Layla felt that warmth curl deep into her body, and soon found herself steadier and less bleak. As if he had given her something a Vampire would normally take, it was a tender gift – and as Layla pulled away, she found herself staring up at him, captured by his presence in a way she couldn't describe.

As Quindici stared down at her with his dark onyx eyes, they suddenly seemed sympathetic rather than calculating. Touching his full lips to hers one last time, Layla felt a gentle press of his fangs as he murmured softly, "Do as you will, Layla Price, for I cannot stop you. But take my warning to heart as advice from a friend. The Crimson Circle are dangerous, but what lives inside you as a Royal Dragon Bind may be more dangerous still. I will fill you in on the things I know about Hunter at a later time, just as I have for Adrian. But right now, you need to prepare for your debut. Go with my blessing on behalf of the Hotel, and go with your head high to protect those you love from the Crimson Circle. I will see you at the Ball."

Stepping back, Layla shuddered hard as she stared at Quindici. A million questions thundered through her, but he was right – now was not the time. Gathering herself, Layla became steady on her stiletto heels.

And with a nod, departed the Associate Hotel Head's office with poise and grace.

CHAPTER 4 – YULE

Layla was pacing before the Yule Ball. Back and forth across the Persian rug in her apartment between her door and breakfast table, she wrung her hands as she moved. Her magic was as restless as she was tonight; a simmering aura of scorched orange groves as her Dragon coiled over inside her. Turning by her breakfast table, she took up the bourbon she'd poured with a splash of water, her nerves as high-strung as she'd ever felt. It was the same feeling she'd had before her PhD dissertation's review.

But there was so much more on the line tonight.

Layla paced again, trying to breathe through her nerves and magic. Setting her bourbon down, she massaged her hands, cramping from tension. Glancing at the mantle-clock above the fireplace, she noted Dusk was twenty minutes late now to escort her to the ball. It wasn't like him and Layla took up her bourbon again, glancing out the windows and seeing the sun had set. Cerulean blanketed the snowy horizon, stars popping out like diamonds in the stark winter sky. But though everything tonight would be gold, silver, and white for Yule, Layla had taken the traditional Hotel color for her Courtesan's Debut – crimson.

Her gown was a sleek affair of flowing crimson silk chiffon, so sheer it nearly revealed everything though in Head Clothier Amalia DuFane's clever ways, it actually hid everything. Tight-wrapped at the waist with long fitted sleeves, the gown had a scandalous slit to Layla's hip and a plunging bodice that dove almost to her waist. Gold ribbon edged the v-neck, wrists, and hem, making the silk chiffon flow around her feet like a bloody seashore. A gold wrist-cuff and curling gold torque around her neck complemented the gown, her platform heels a sheer gold silk that made her feet seem bare. Coaxed into waves, Layla's sable curls were pinned back on one side, her makeup in golds and smoky hues that brought out the color of her eyes since her Dragon had become stronger at Samhain – a dark hunter-green, jade, and gold.

Glancing in the mirror, Layla saw a goddess staring back at her, and the sudden image shocked her into stillness as she watched her reflection. In the platform stilettos, she was statuesque, over six feet tall. The simplicity of her attire would stand out in a night famed for Twilight Realm ostentatiousness. But Layla's wealth was fury, she realized as she stared at herself in the mirror, and the passion and power that came with it. The entire ensemble screamed *back the fuck off* – sexy and vicious. With a sigh, she began pacing again, hoping she could live up to the whispers her attire would start tonight.

But as she reached the breakfast table, she heard a soft knock upon the door at last.

Turning quickly, she hauled one side of the massive double-doors open. As she stepped back, Dusk entered with his customary briskness. Relief filled Layla to see him. Wearing a dark maroon tux rather than his usual blues or greys, Dusk's lapels were black satin with a matching red paisley vest in an almost Victorian fashion. He wore a black tie, a gold pocket watch tucked into the vest. On his wrist, he wore a matching cuff to Layla's and she smiled, realizing Amalia DuFane's brilliance. Dusk was a darker, more simmering version of Layla's fierce grace, and with a modern cut but Victorian details, his entire ensemble screamed *dangerous.*

Layla didn't hesitate. She flowed to him, feeling their bodies pulled together by the golden cord that bound them. He caught her close, his eyes shining sapphire-diamond with pleasure at her greeting. A smile curled his lips, but as Layla lifted up to kiss him, he held a finger to her mouth, stopping her with a sexy glint in his eyes.

"We mustn't muss your lipstick before your debut. Are you ready?"

"Ready as I'll ever be, I guess." Layla gave a wry smile, but inside, she felt nauseous. Everything should have been perfect. Layla's human friends were at the Hotel, getting to experience it for the first time. Adrian was somewhere safe, no longer on the run. Layla's Dragon-magic was contained even without her talisman now, thanks to Reginald. Life was the best it had been in months.

And yet.

"Layla? Are you alright?" Dusk frowned at her, concern in his eyes as a subtle sheen of navy and cerulean rippled through his hair. "Your magic is coiling over and over like you're deeply worried about tonight." Dusk ran his warm hands over her shoulders with a comforting rumble and Layla sighed, aware of her tension as he helped her release it.

"I just feel like so much is up in the air," she spoke honestly as she gazed up at him. "Everything should be perfect with my friends here and my magic under control now from Reginald's influence on our Bind. But Adrian's in danger of being discovered by the Board, Reginald is in an unknown situation with his clan, and Luke is being secretive in a way that worries me. And at my interview... Quindici said some things that rattled me."

"What did he say?" Dusk frowned at her, something dark moving though his gaze at the mention of the Associate Hotel Head.

"Later." Layla spoke quietly, not quite ready to talk about everything Quindici had said to her, though she wanted to discuss it with Dusk soon. "But I'm worried about Luke. Out on the promenade, he said he's developed some kind of magical sensitivity since my Dragon attacked him in the fall. Did my magic… bind him?"

"He's ok." Dusk's sapphire gaze was honest as he rubbed her shoulders. "Your magic did have an affect on Luke, but not necessarily anything bad, and it didn't Bind him. It's just a change he needs perspective on, and I've been happy to provide it. And Rikyava also. He'll be fine, just trust me when I say it's not my matter to divulge."

Dusk had stonewalled Layla before, and she knew it was no use pushing. Even though concern moved through Layla, she could tell Dusk was in Head Concierge mode and not about to spill the details of someone else's private life. He was immutable when he wanted to be, and though Layla found it frustrating, she admired his ability to keep personal matters confidential. It was part of what made him an impeccable Head Concierge.

"What about Celia and Charlie, and Arron?" Layla fretted.

"I've already escorted your friends down to the Yule Ball twenty minutes ago." Dusk spoke, his gaze kind. "Rikyava will have her most trusted Guards close at all times this evening. Relax, Layla. Everything's under control."

"What about me?" Layla whispered, her words so soft even she could barely hear them. Fear twisted through her on the wake of Quindici's words this afternoon, and Layla couldn't forget them. All she saw was darkness inside herself for a moment, as her Dragon coiled over in her veins with a tight, deep panic.

But as always, Dusk knew just what to do. With a gentle, mysterious smile, Dusk lowered his lips, touching hers in the softest kiss. It was delicate to not muss her makeup, but as his smooth lips pressed hers, biting and lingering gently, he gave a deep growl, leaving her entire body breathless. A dark, hot look simmered in his eyes as he pulled away, cupping her neck in a distinctly possessive way as he caressed the angle of her jaw with his thumb.

"*You* are a goddess," Dusk spoke, holding her gaze with his fierce sapphire-bright eyes, "and *everyone* will see it tonight. Don't worry about your first Assignation. Adrian and I have it under control. You'll be safe, I promise. And you'll enjoy it."

"What?" Layla blinked in surprise.

But Dusk said no more, and taking a deep breath, he pulled back as if with a will. Offering his arm, he lifted one dark eyebrow, smoldering with a sexy, intense mystery. Still wondering what he'd just meant, Layla took his arm as they turned toward the door. But as they exited her apartment, Layla found her tension easing, knowing Dusk was a master of plans within plans. If he said he and Adrian had her first Assignation under control somehow, she believed it – her Dragon breathing a deep exhalation at last.

Layla's magic settled and so did her nerves as they exited her apartment, two Hotel Guards coming to attention as she and Dusk moved down the gilded hall. As they descended the grand staircase to the first floor, Layla beheld the massive crowd in the Hotel's main lobby, experiencing déjà vu. Her last Grand Masquerade had been at Samhain, Dusk keeping her safe with his magics as he'd maneuvered her through the crowd. But that night had gone disastrously when he and Adrian had decided to fight over her, resulting in Layla nearly dying from Reginald's Siren-power when he'd used it to calm Adrian.

And also resulting in Layla's abduction by Hunter.

She shivered as they descended the grand staircase, thinking about Hunter and darkness and the Crimson Circle again, and Dusk glanced over. But Layla shook her head, taking a deep breath and facing the night with her head high. As they gained the main floor, moving toward the Diamond Ballroom rather than the Grand Ballroom, Layla found herself managing the seething press of magic and people better than at Samhain. No one was masqued, and it helped her to see faces. Though the Yule Ball was technically one of the Grand Masquerades, the event was more of a black-tie formal. And though a wall of magic hit Layla like a sledgehammer just as before, she found she could breathe through it this time as she and Dusk moved through the crowd.

Far more developed than at Samhain, Layla's power formed a spontaneous shield around her as she moved, strong coils of heat pushing back other magic as she walked. People in gold and silver blinked as she moved through, pulling back with wide eyes as if the press of her magic was too much. Layla saw Dusk's lips quirk as they gained the Diamond Ballroom, practically glowing with pleasure as he felt Layla's magic push gawkers back in smooth waves – not having to use his own power to defend her at all.

As they entered the long hall, luminous with decorations, Layla saw the party was already in full swing. A fae orchestra played a waltz in haunting tones, couples dancing over the silver-diamond floor like snowflakes whirling over ice. Diamonds were everywhere, embedded in silver and white. Fanciful designs twisted up every marble column, cascading across the high vaults of the ceiling like a winter sky, rippling through the floor like a moonlit lake. Caught in the beauty, Layla stared as she realized sex was not the focus here tonight, elegance was.

Elegance and money.

The attendees sparkled in ornate tiaras and arresting cufflinks, and waterfall necklaces of real pearls and diamonds. Their costumes were glamorous, dripping with gems, silk, lace, and cascading feathers. Few people wore color, most of the party-goers dressed in the customary Yule tones of gold, white, black, and silver, and it made Layla and her date stand out. As she glanced around, she saw Arron and

Celia near a table with Charlie, all wearing blue to stand out also. Nearby, Luke nodded as he received a martini, dressed in a forest green and black tux that made his Irish colors stunning.

As their gazes connected, Luke's eyes widened, and Layla halted on Dusk's arm. Suddenly, she felt jealousy rip from Luke like a lance. It struck Layla's shield as if driving for her heart and she gasped, feeling a spasm in her chest. Dusk stiffened and Layla felt a flow of crystal-power spike from him, slamming up between her and Luke. Staggering as if Dusk had shoved him with power, Luke's entire body shuddered, his bloodstone pendant whirling. His breath was fast and Layla saw an intense energy spark in Luke's eyes like a flash of lightning before it was washed away, as his cheeks flamed with embarrassment and frustration.

But Layla knew what she'd felt. Her lips fell open as she realized what was happening to Luke. Magic. Somehow, her Dragon's attack in the fall had given Luke magic, and the bloodstone pendant was not protecting him – it was containing him. A talisman to prevent Luke from using his newly opened magic, like Layla's Moroccan cuff had once been.

Layla's head whirled, and Dusk glanced at her as if he knew what she was thinking. Somehow, Luke had magic now, and Dusk had known. Leading her through the throng, around couples waltzing across the silver-diamond floor, Dusk didn't say anything, merely escorted Layla to the gilded diamond stage where the orchestra played. Even though it was early, everyone was already inebriated, and Layla felt magic press her on all sides as people laughed raucously behind silver fans.

It only increased her stunned disorientation, and as the music concluded and people began crowding the stage at Layla's arrival, she saw the Associate Hotel Head standing on the left of the stage with the

Madame. Quindici was resplendent in a white tux with gold lapels, and blinked in surprise at Layla's crimson attire as Dusk led her over. The Vampire's grave-cool energy followed them as they approached, his onyx eyes pinning Layla. All of a sudden, Layla could feel the echo of his kiss from earlier in his office, as if those dark eyes watching her called up the memory. She felt a press of fang at her lips and all at once her breath was higher, faster. But as they watched each other, Quindici gave only a subtle nod, then beckoned Layla and Dusk into their group with a cordial gesture of his hand.

Standing with them, Ms. Lulu Duvall lifted an eyebrow at Layla's gown as she and Dusk arrived, but inclined her head graciously, her corkscrewing gazelle-antlers twined with golden torques set with diamonds tonight. The same graced her slim upper arms and wrists, her body with its lower gazelle-half sleek and elegantly naked as usual. But though Ms. Duvall was demure, Layla felt the penetrating notice of those fawn-brown eyes as Dusk escorted Layla up, their new Hotel Head giving Layla shivers. But her concerns were doused as Madame Etienne Voulouer – dressed in a fabulous gold zebra-striped gown with a starched lace collar and an old Hollywood tiara – beamed at Layla and opened her arms.

"Layla! You are radiant, darling!" Gathering Layla in and kissing both her cheeks, the Madame squeezed Layla's hands with a reassuring smile. Quiet enough to not be overheard, she whispered at Layla's ear next, "Have no fear. Your friends are here for you."

As Madame Voulouer stepped back, Layla blinked, wondering what in blazes was going to happen as she watched people push closer for the auction. White and gold auction paddles with crimson numbers were in numerous hands, but as Dusk smoothed his fingers over hers, giving a calming rumble, Layla understood he somehow had everything in hand – and the Madame was in on it.

As her gaze passed over people at the front, seeing familiar faces, Layla's tension eased further. Standing right before the stage was the teensy bee-fae Head Clothier Amalia DuFane, dressed in an ornate gown of black lace made of woven filaments. Beaming at Layla, she gave a buzzing wave with her paddle. Head Bartender and interim Head Courtier Rake André was with her, his yoga-lean body dressed in a sleek suit of Tibetan tan and gold silk tonight. Rake gave Layla a pleased smile from his beautiful green eyes, and even from a distance she felt his calming breath ease into her lips from his slow, meditative exhalation. Standing with Rake and Amalia, the stout old Fumerole Clan First Valdo Chermour sipped a martini, dressed in a classic black tux to complement his scaly brick-red skin. Built like a squat boulder, Valdo raised his martini, grinning and emitting a voluminous laugh as Layla's glance found him.

Relief filled Layla, and glancing around, she saw more welcome faces – like the startlingly sexy Rhennic Erdhelm standing with Rikyava and her uncle King Huttr Erdhelm. The enormous Viking King of the Blood Dragons with his dragon-shaven mane of a mohawk was dressed in his usual black tux with a massive white polar bear pelt chained around his shoulders. Standing beside him was Rikyava, dressed in a luminous silver gown that showed off the most of her buxom Swedish curves and long blonde hair.

But dressed in a white tux with a storm-blue sash slung over it, Rhennic had medals of valor clipped to his breast tonight. His bright blond hair was gladiator-cut, his short beard neat. Strong and towering like his father but elegantly trim, Rhennic looked far more stunning than when Layla had met him before. As he caught her looking, he gave a lift of one straight blond eyebrow, his vivid lavender eyes arresting her. A storm wind flavored with heather and lavender caressed her and Rhennic laughed in his musical baritone; a subtle, sexy sound that shivered Layla all the way across the hall.

Just the same as when he had once mate-tasted her.

But even as Layla's Dragon came to eager attention inside her to be touched by Rhennic's power again, Layla spied Luke and her housemates standing beside Rikyava. Holding paddles, they all cheered drunkenly, except Luke. Layla could feel the daggers of Luke's new magic seeking her as his emerald eyes burned with fury. She shivered and Dusk smoothed his hand over hers. Layla felt Dusk firm his barrier between her and her ex – Luke's sudden ability to wield magic a mystery to be dealt with some other night.

But there was no more time to scan the crowd as the Madame took center stage. Giving Layla's hand a squeeze with a tight smile, Dusk didn't kiss Layla as he took his leave, only held her with his suddenly pained eyes. Layla could only imagine what he was feeling, having his woman be auctioned off right in front of him tonight. Spotlights were cast down upon Layla and the Madame as a round of clapping began – which the Madame indulged like old Hollywood royalty, raising her hands until the clapping eased.

"Friends!" Madame Voulouer called out in her purring alto. "Welcome to the Red Letter Hotel Paris' annual Yule Ball! Tonight, we bear witness to a very special event – a new Courtesan to induct into our ranks! Though such a thing is rare, tonight's debut is far more rare than most. Tonight, we introduce a young woman who has not only been a Concierge here, but is the only Partner our dear Head Courtier Reginald Durant has taken in the past fifty years! In addition, she hails from a nearly extinct Lineage, the famed Royal Dragon Binds. Please allow me to introduce to you our very own, our dear and beloved, Ms. Layla Price!"

Thunderous applause surged through the crowd. As Layla sank into the proper curtsey in the scorching spotlights, she heard her human friends cheer like they were at a UW football game. It made her smile as she stood tall, as elegantly as Reginald had drilled into her these past months. As the applause quieted, the Madame commenced with a dossier of Layla's life – how she'd been raised human, how her magic had only opened recently. How she'd become a Concierge and how she was becoming a strong Bind, training not only in the bedroom arts but also the martial ones. All of Layla's positive qualities were lauded, and none of her tense escapades these past months were mentioned.

When the dossier was finished, the Madame concluded with, "Now, ladies and gentlemen of the Twilight Realm and Human world, we open the bidding for Ms. Price's debut Assignation. Because of her Lineage's rarity and her status as our Head Courtier's only protégé this past fifty years, we shall open the bidding at one million human Euros. Let the auction begin."

With another wave of applause, the auction suddenly opened. The Madame stepped aside for an auctioneer, a tall man in a classic black tux with russet feathers cresting from his head. Clutching an old-fashioned silver microphone in his taloned hand, he spoke into it rapidly with a chirruping speech – and paddles were suddenly flashing in the crowd.

Layla's heart raced as a spike of adrenaline surged through her that the auction was finally happening. As bids began, she saw old Valdo flag the auctioneer right away, a darkly competitive glint in the Fumarole's eyes. Others flashed paddles; Dusk at the front with Amalia and Rake, Rikyava's cousin Rhennic flashing his paddle with a sexy smile. Arron and Celia, then Luke. Quindici DaPonti flashed his paddle with dark calm, the savvy businessman driving up the price for the Hotel's benefit, Layla was almost certain.

And then Ms. Lulu Duvall.

Layla blinked at that one, and Dusk glowered at the French

Faunus as Layla heard the auctioneer say *ten million Euros.* More paddles flashed in the hands of strangers, and suddenly the auctioneer was saying *twenty million Euros.* Layla let out a breath, steadying herself. Reginald had prepared her for this, but all the same the bidding was shocking. Valdo Chermour flashed his paddle again and so did Rhennic, the two sharing a cordially competitive lift of drinks. Amalia, then Rake. Layla's human friends had dropped out of the race now, watching with eager eyes, though Luke glowered. Quindici raised his paddle again and Dusk was fast on his heels, his sapphire eyes murderous.

Thirty million Euros. Layla drew deep breaths, trying to not lock her knees and faint under the lights, or let her magic surge at the tension in the ballroom. For it was tense, many lesser players now dropped out of the race with shakes of their heads, the bidding down to a few key hotshots. Valdo flashed his paddle again, but with a wry laugh, Rhennic Erdhelm gave up, saluting Valdo with his drink and giving an apologetic smile to Layla. Quindici was not done, nor was Lulu Duvall. Dusk raised his paddle once more, but beside him, Amalia gave up with a buzzing laugh and so did Rake.

Suddenly, Layla realized it was down to four. The auctioneer returned to Valdo, who raised his paddle with a fierce nod. Quindici was next, though Lulu Duvall finally bowed out with a gracious shake of her antlers, and something inside Layla breathed in relief. Dusk grit his teeth, but waved his paddle again.

The bidding kept on until Layla heard *fifty million Euros.* As the auctioneer came around to Quindici again, he was suddenly out. With a tight smile that flashed fang, he bowed elegantly to Layla. Layla had thought the business-savvy Vampire had just been in to earn the Hotel more money, but as he put his paddle aside, she saw a subtly furious look in his onyx eyes. Quindici had actually wanted to win Layla tonight, but his business sensibilities outweighed his passions, and he wasn't about to bid more than he could afford.

But Dusk and Valdo would, and Layla watched them now. They were technically friends; it had been Dusk who'd introduced Layla to the old Fumarole when she had begun as a Concierge. But as the bidding drove up past seventy million, Dusk and Valdo scowling at each other with a dark fury, Layla felt rumbles issuing from both of them, shuddering the chandeliers in the hall. Crystal Dragons and Fumeroles were famous for causing earthquakes with their magic, and Layla was suddenly concerned their bidding war was going to cause an actual eruption between them.

But as the bidding hit one hundred million Euros, Dusk suddenly looked bleak. He glanced to Layla, a horrible loss in his sapphire eyes. As if the auction had reached in and ripped out his heart, he hitched a hard breath and set his paddle aside on a table. Holding Layla's gaze with a wretched agony, he shook his head.

Dusk was out.

The auctioneer glanced to Valdo. With a dark grin, the old Fumarole flashed his paddle.

One hundred million Euros.

CHAPTER 5 – RUMI

Part of Layla was relieved that a friend had won her Courtesan's Debut auction, and part of her was more tight-wound than ever. As she waited on the stage while stout old Valdo Chermour received applause and shook hands, making his way to the front, Layla trembled with nerves, her Dragon twisting inside her. Though she'd shared walks and banter with Valdo, and even meals, she realized suddenly that she didn't really know the old Fumerole. He came to the Hotel to relax, engaging Courtiers and Courtesans to make him laugh for stress relief, but Layla had no clue what his tastes were in the bedroom.

Or where his allegiances lay.

As Valdo stepped up the stairs of the gilded stage, a furiously pleased energy radiating from his five-foot-nothing yet heavily-muscled frame, Layla recalled what people said about him. That Valdo was a tyrant with his clan, a volcano that burst with little provocation. As his brick-red eyes pinned her, Valdo giving a snappy bow before taking her hand up in his roughly scaled one, Layla suddenly worried perhaps he was an enemy, a member of the Crimson Circle who had won her as a way to retaliate against Adrian, or to hurt Layla. Some dark part of her wondered that perhaps she didn't know Valdo well at all – if he'd bid so high against Dusk.

But watching him now, Layla recognized the old Fumerole Clan First's bombastic energy was just the same tonight as it had always been around her. Here was her friend, someone she'd impressed with her wits right away when she'd come to the Hotel. The same man who had asked her quite bluntly to have an Assignation at their very first meeting, even though she'd only been a Concierge at the time. And now old Valdo grinned at her, clasping her hand and patting it just like he always did, giving his booming laugh and making her smile.

"Busting my balls, girlie!" Valdo laughed in his room-devouring basso, grinning at her with his red eyes sparkling. "I could have bought a whole new palace for that sum! Fuck, six palaces!"

"Joke's on you," Layla sassed him immediately, falling into a familiar pattern. "You did purchase six palaces. The auction for my Debut Assignation was just a sham. Your palaces will be delivered by FedEx tomorrow, in an unmarked beige envelope."

"HA! Beige envelope. Good one, you little smartass!" Valdo roared a laugh, actually slapping his knee, before turning her by the hand towards the stage's stairs. "Come on. Let's get out of this crowd and go somewhere we can talk, eh?"

Layla nodded, then took Valdo's well-muscled arm. He was built like a boulder, and even though worries still flitted through her, she felt far more calm in his presence suddenly. Valdo and Layla received more applause as they moved through the ballroom, but the orchestra had taken up playing and people were once again enjoying their revelry now that the spectacle was over. Valdo walked Layla past Dusk, his sapphire eyes dark as they passed. But Dusk nodded stiffly, and though Layla tried to talk to him, it was Rikyava who came abreast of Dusk and pulled him back by the shoulder. Rikyava shook her head and Layla knew why.

After the auction, she was the winner's prize for the night – not supposed to interact with anyone unless the winner gave permission.

It seemed foreign to Layla, to walk past all her friends without speaking to them. She'd prepped Arron on the etiquette so her human friends didn't attempt to engage her, though Luke watched her with probably the darkest scowl she'd ever seen. Wrath surged from him, his bloodstone talisman writhing upon his chest as it worked to contain his livid energy.

Layla met Luke's gaze, but there wasn't time for more as Valdo led her past into the Hotel proper. Revelry consumed the main level of the Hotel, every copper bar along the halls filled with people drinking, laughing, and carousing. Fancy clothing was starting to be shed as couples, trios, and more started making out on the chaises and up against the tall marble columns, magic careening around them. But though the party was stirring up to deviant heights as the phoenix grandfather clock near the main Concierge desk chimed ten p.m., Layla realized the night was far from over.

And she still had no clue as to what would be required of her by the man who had won her.

"So what are we doing tonight?" Layla asked Valdo with her usual directness, knowing she didn't need to engage any Courtesan's niceties with him.

"Patience, girlie. This way." The old Fumerole glanced at her, a humorously deviant glint in his red eyes as they made it to the grand staircase and headed up away from the main party. Confused to the max now, Layla wondered what the hell was going on. Dusk had insinuated he had the night under control and so had the Madame, but then he'd bid fiercely against Valdo and Layla thought things hadn't gone to plan. But as they gained the third floor, suddenly arriving at Layla's own apartment door, she paused.

"Don't you have your own room? For… whatever it is we're doing?"

"Patience, dear heart." Valdo winked with a sly grin. "In we go. I believe there is a surprise waiting for you in your bathroom." As Valdo ushered Layla into her apartment and shut the doors behind them, Layla found herself frowning deeply, utterly confused. Her apartment looked just as she had left it earlier, and as she stepped to her gilded bathroom everything looked normal – except someone had written on her mirror with one of her lipsticks.

Moving over, Layla read the message.

When will you begin that long journey into yourself? Begin our night at the place my kiss first found your fury.

Blinking at her reflection in the mirror, astonishment opened Layla's lips as she recognized the Rumi quote that began the message. The rest of it was a riddle, but one Layla knew the answer to. A riddle *only* she would know the answer to. Shaking her head, she whispered, "Adrian, you bastard." Moving back out, Layla gave Valdo an incredulous look. "You're in league with Adrian and Dusk! You were bidding on me for Adrian tonight!"

"Wouldn't spend that much of my own cash on a bidding war, cute as you are." Reaching up, Valdo patted Layla's cheek in a grandfatherly way, his red eyes positively burning with humor as he gave a deep basso chuckle. "It's my task to escort you tonight. No one harms my sweet Layla. So. Shall we begin to unravel the riddle?"

Suddenly, Layla laughed. A black void she hadn't even known inside her was suddenly banished as her world brightened a hundredfold, luminous. In a wash of understanding, Dusk's entire plot for the evening suddenly became clear. He'd planted patsies in the audience to bid on her tonight for Adrian, most likely the larger portion of those who had been bidding hard at the end. Rake, Amalia, Valdo, maybe even Rikyava's cousin Rhennic. In a spontaneous joy, Layla bent and kissed the old Fumerole right on the lips. He blushed a dark puce, then gave a basso chuckle again. Extending his arm, he winked at Layla and she took it, feeling like she was floating on clouds.

"Though I'd love to participate in something this fun and

scandalous, this mystery-hunt is yours, dearie." Valdo chuckled kindly, eager to begin the night as much as Layla. "I'm afraid only you know where to go next. As per the riddle, you know."

"Outside." Layla spoke immediately, knowing where Adrian's enigmatic words led her. "Out back to the gardens."

"Right. Shall we get started?"

As the old Fumerole escorted her out through an enormous set of double-doors to the winter gardens behind the palace, Layla realized the brilliance of Adrian and Dusk's plot. Valdo was a respected member of the Twilight community and known to love strolling around the Hotel having a laugh with his Courtesans. That was precisely what it looked like they were doing now as he escorted Layla, both of them beaming with the excitement of Dusk and Adrian's arranged intrigue. Together, they pushed out the Hotel doors into the snowy gardens and glimmering fairy-lights, crunching along the gravel path through the deepening night. As diamond-bright stars shone high above, the snow long ceased, Layla glanced to Valdo.

"So this is all Dusk's doing?"

"Not all." Valdo winked. "A few others were involved to pull off this heist right under the noses of the Crimson Circle tonight. Other friends of yours, I believe, though I wasn't told who."

"You know about the Crimson Circle?" Layla blinked as they rounded the snowy topiaries, though her idea now about the rest of her friends' involvement in the plan had been confirmed.

"Everyone who's anyone knows about the Circle." Valdo rumbled casually, though his mood darkened as they lost themselves in the barren maze of hedges, out of earshot from the palace now in the extensive winter gardens. "Did I ever tell you I had a niece once? Cute as a button, like you. She wanted to live a life of excitement, so I bought her into Hotel Ownership. I was never much interested in

Owning, but she loved it, the galas and parties and such. But she had a temper like me, and was executed by the Circle for crimes against the Hotel that were never disclosed. I never had a chance to defend her for whatever happened. I regret it to this day, and it sparked my fury for many hundreds of years. Still does."

"My god." Layla didn't know what to say to that. All the jokes in the world couldn't heal such a horrible story.

"The Hotel has ancient laws no one can touch," Valdo glanced at her with a dark presence, "not even powerful Clan Firsts like me. They are a world unto themselves, and only unto themselves are they accountable. If you learn anything about the Twilight Realm, dear heart, learn this: no-one at the highest echelons of the Hotel are to be trusted. Use their services, but keep a wary eye on any Owner."

"Why are you doing this to help Adrian, then?"

"Well I'm not, am I?!" Valdo laughed loudly. "I'm doing it for you! Can't have you threatened by the Circle on your very first night as a Courtesan, can we? Dusk asked me for this favor and I was more than happy to play such a devious game. It amuses me. And anything I can do to stick it to the Circle... well. That amuses me more."

They'd arrived at the place Adrian had indicated in his message on Layla's mirror. But as she gazed around the secluded nook of topiaries where Adrian had once kissed her neck and they'd ended up having their first truly heinous fight, Layla frowned. Not seeing any message in the topiaries with their wisping fae-lights, she wondered if they'd come to the right spot. But then she saw the fish pond before her was partially frozen over – a message scrawled into the ice.

Life is a balance of holding on and letting go. I let you go once, and then I held you as the rain kept us warm. You came to find that solace again, and found the soft nose of a good friend before the real storm broke.

Layla took a deep breath of chill winter air. There were two locations this quote indicated, but she was almost certain it was the second location Adrian meant, since the first would be virtually impossible to find. Leading the way, Layla headed them deeper into the greenery. She'd not worn a coat and as she began to shiver in her gown, Valdo removed his tux jacket and draped it around her shoulders. They soon gained the horse barns at the edge of the forest and as Layla pushed inside, she saw a piece of paper tucked into the stall-gate of the horse she'd once ridden during the Dragon-hunt. The big bay gelding was happy to see her and snuffled her hair, lipping her curls as Layla retrieved the note from his stall door.

Dance until you shatter yourself. You shattered me here, when I found you in his arms first, though his was the heart made of crystal. Come, shatter me again.

This note hitched Layla's heart as she remembered Adrian's face the night he'd discovered her and Dusk in the crystal bath-house. Layla turned, heading east, the small crystal house not far from the stables. As she pushed inside, she found it quiet. With so much revelry happening inside the main Hotel tonight, it was empty, only mist from the pools and waterfalls swirling up to the high dome, enormous white trumpet-flowers open to the vivid winter stars. Glancing around, Layla saw a stack of white towels placed oddly on one wrought-iron rack. Lifting them up, she found another note beneath.

The source of now is here. Let your companion remain, and enter the pool alone.

"I think this is our last stop together." Layla glanced up from the note, feeling strangely sad to be leaving old Valdo's company.

"Well. It was a bit of excitement while it lasted, eh?" Reaching out, Valdo clasped Layla's hands in a firm, warm grip. Patting her hands, his gaze was hard-edged. "Go with fire in your blood, Layla

Price. I cannot say whether you are out of danger tonight, but know your friends have done what we can. I was wary when Owners were betting on you tonight, and I'll keep our secret from any prying ears. To anyone who asks, I will regale them with stories of your fiery wit. But be careful, wherever you're going next."

"I will be, thank you." Layla felt gratefulness well up in her for old Valdo, but there was a question she still wondered if he could answer. "Valdo, before you go… do you know why Dusk was betting so hard against you at the end of the auction? If he set all this up—"

"I think he realized how jealous he was." Valdo reached up, patting Layla's cheek with a rough hand. "Just because a man plans a deception doesn't mean his heart goes along with it. Be careful with our Crystal Dragon, young lady. He's more delicate than he seems."

With that, Valdo gave her a nod towards the pool. Standing at the edge, Layla had a flashback of her first tryst with Dusk. Her cheeks flamed as a simmering sensation heated her. As she stepped into the pool, she felt that simmering passion quadruple, then expand. The crystal of the pool lit up bright as day, flooding luminescence through the water. And suddenly, all that tremendous vibration caused a crystal cocoon to flare up around Layla – sealing her in.

Panic raced in Layla's chest as she beat on the thick crystal cocoon with her fists. Terrified, her Dragon roared in her veins, but even though her magic flared, it was as nothing inside the cocoon. She was trapped. And though Layla tried to be calm, telling herself this was Dusk's work, a darker part of her nature howled – wondering if it had all been a ploy by someone to capture her.

As crystal flared all around, flooding her with power and light, Layla cast up a hand to shield her eyes. With a wrenching sensation that made her ears pop, she felt herself released from all that power suddenly. Staggering as the crystal cocoon shattered around her, exploding and releasing water in a wave, Layla fell to her hands and knees.

Landing in red sand as water cascaded down a desert dune all around.

She'd been transported somewhere out of France entirely by the crystal cocoon, Layla realized as she came back to her feet, gazing around the deep midnight desert. As she stood atop the dune, seeing the shine of stars far above in the velvet night and undulations of midnight sand in every direction, she realized she knew this place. She knew the feel of the cold desert air as it blew past, teasing her curls. She knew the twilight nimbus that rode every horizon with an otherworldly light, a phenomenon that didn't happen in the human world. She knew the scents of jasmine, cinnamon, and oranges that swirled all around her in the dry winds.

Adrian's scent – and her own.

Brushing sand from her hands, Layla gazed down the dune's slope as her Dragon stirred deeply inside her, compelled by this beautiful, haunting place. A compound sprawled below, surrounded by red sandstone walls edged in cobalt tiles. Within its confines, palm trees swayed in the midnight breeze, the palatial compound devouring the land like a dragon. Set on bedrock, sand curled around the structure in the luminous night. But though the wall was red sandstone like the desert, everything inside the compound was made of a shining white alabaster, inset with colored tiles. Moroccan minarets rose to the starry sky, alabaster domes luminous with gold that reminded Layla of the Temple Mount in Jerusalem, vivid with accents of blue and purple.

Amazed, Layla stared as an ornate wrought-iron gate parted in the compound's wall. As she watched, a man walked out – stepping off the bedrock and walking up the dune. Tall and slim, he wore a fitted charcoal vest and trousers and a white shirt with the collar open, his sleeves rolled up to his elbows. His dark hair was ruffled by the wind, his hands thrust deep in his pockets. The wind whirled as if the man's presence had stirred it, and far up the slope, Layla caught a curl of cinnamon and desert jasmine scent. With it came a sensation of heat caressing her and slipping up her ankles – a dark heat that threw her head back in ecstasy.

She knew his scent in the air. She knew his touch rippling the silk chiffon of her gown, teasing up her bare thigh. Licking her belly, it curled around her breasts, stroking her throat and diving in at her lips – kissing her.

Adrian.

Layla swayed as Adrian Rhakvir kissed her in the cool desert night. Her eyelashes flickered and her lips parted, her heartbeat fast as her own magic rose. Spilling out of her, it rushed down the slope with an eager pleasure to find him. She felt her power reach Adrian, coiling up his body. Making him inhale with a shudder as it dove in at his lips also – kissing him back.

They kissed from a distance as he walked slowly up the dune. Layla swayed with pleasure, barely able to stand as he came for her, taking her deep as she took him back. Muscles of heat and power coiled around her, sliding, stroking her skin. Layla's power responded, coiling around Adrian, making him falter with a sigh as he gained the top of the slope.

Adrian's aqua-gold eyes were penetrating in the night, the same color as the midnight nimbus that rode the rim of the desert. His full lips parted as he neared, his achingly high cheekbones beautiful, a short stubble on his starkly-defined jaw. His cropped dark hair was ruffled by the midnight wind and by magic; as he stepped close, Layla could smell jasmine and a heady musk coiling out from him. Sliding in over her tongue, Adrian kissed her with his power as he held his distance. She kissed him back and saw his dark eyelashes flicker, his head falling back as he tasted her on the midnight wind.

When his eyes opened again, they cored her deep – every color all at once.

"You came." He breathed, letting his utterance coil around Layla, stroking her in the night.

"How could I not?" Layla spoke back, pleasured by his power. She felt a cord braiding between them as their magics touched, warm and strong, gold and bright. It pulled them closer, like magnets towards their mate. Adrian's eyes brightened with gold; breathing hard, Layla could almost feel his heart pounding in his chest to match hers. But he held himself back, watching her as if taking in everything about this moment, making it last.

With a sudden insight through their Bind, Layla knew why. She saw this scene through Adrian's eyes – everything he'd been dreaming about since they'd first met. His dreams had been haunted by her, over and over. In a thousand ways, he'd dreamt of her just like this; standing upon this dune at sunset, at midnight, or at dawn; dressed in silk, dressed in lace, dressed in nothing but desert winds and starlight. Layla had experienced those dreams in her dark midnights; of meeting Adrian upon a dune with a Moroccan palace sprawling below. As she reeled, Layla felt those dreams crash into reality – making and re-making this moment over and over like a thousand grains of sand upon the wind.

"Your heart knows the way. Run in that direction." Adrian's murmur curled upon the midnight zephyrs, stroking Layla as he experienced his memories being unearthed by their Bind. "A woman with sable curls haunted my dreams ever since I can remember. I dated women with dark hair over and over, looking for one whose eyes shone gold and green at the same time. When you and I met, I knew you were her. And after Hunter abducted you… there you were, with the right

color in your eyes at last. Suddenly, a drakaina of incredible power had come into my life – had followed where her visions had gone before. I don't know how any of this Bind-magic works, Layla. All I know is what I feel in my heart. You are my mate; you always will be. Whether you want to be is up to you. But know I will do right by you unto the ends of the earth. This Desert drake's heart is yours. I love you, Layla Price. I will never love another."

Tears filled Layla's eyes. She loved Adrian and hated him at the same time, feeling their Bind, their hearts coiled so deep together. Adrian was frustrating as shit. He was handsome as a god; tempestuous and beautiful. But in that moment, Layla felt his heart. He wasn't lying as he held her gaze, as he stroked her with his desert winds, still keeping himself carefully away.

Suddenly, she saw why he tucked his hands in his pockets when he was around her. It was because he was afraid he would coil around her and never let her go; that he would trap her. He didn't want to take away her choices. He didn't want to Bind her if she didn't want to be with him. He would stay away and suffer the consequences, rather than take away her decision to be in this relationship with him or not.

He wanted her to be free – even though he wanted her.

"Oh, Adrian," Layla's words spilled out in a sigh as she watched him. "I want to be Bound. To you, with you. As long as we can be. I love you, too. From the moment I first saw you walk in that art gallery door, you captured my heart, and have been capturing it every day since. I don't want to be free. I want to be *yours*."

An every-color fire flashed in Adrian's eyes as he heard her words. And just like that, his hesitation broke. Before Layla knew it, he'd closed the distance – removing his hands from his pockets and wrapping them fiercely around her. Kissing her, tasting her, pressing her – needing her. It was everything Layla wanted, everything they'd both dreamed of, kissing beneath the velvet sky as a cool desert wind and Dragon-power surged around them – Binding them as one.

As she tasted his lips and tongue, breathing together as he cradled her close, Layla felt completion lock deep inside her. As if she and Adrian had only been playing before, as if they'd only been testing this thing out, something suddenly clicked into place as they breathed each other in beneath the spreading midnight sky. He was hers, and she was his. Others would be hers, too, but he was the first. Though she might hate him over the years, though she might scream and rage against his asinine actions, his heart was hers and her heart was his.

And that was all there was to it.

Adrian's kiss paused at her lips, as if he could feel it too. Lingering together, they breathed softly, and Layla realized their breaths were in synch now. Pulling back, he stared down at her, something amazed shining in his golden aqua eyes. "Layla…what have we done?"

"What we were meant to." Layla reached up, stroking his soft stubble. "We've become life-mates. Just as we were supposed to all along."

Adrian swallowed hard. He blinked and for a moment, Layla had a flash of intense fear, like he might run. Like it might be too much, and he would take off around the world again trying to process his emotions and failing. But then he took a deep breath. The terror cleared from his eyes, replaced by determination. And with his determination came love, flooding through him as his eyes blazed – his magic coiling around Layla and stroking her tenderly from every side.

She surrendered to his love. She fell to it – hard. She didn't collapse in his arms, but she broke open deep inside; something that had been black suddenly filled with the brightest light. Gazing up at Adrian, Layla knew there was nothing she wouldn't do for him. She would kill for him; she would slay enemies. Adrian was her heart and she would do terrible things to protect it. She wouldn't hesitate if someone threatened this most precious piece of her. She would do everything dark and awful or bright and beautiful.

And she would do it all without hesitation or regret.

"I love you, Adrian Rhakvir," Layla spoke softly, stroking his jaw with her fingertips. "And I will do whatever it takes to keep you safe. Always."

He stared down at her in the luminous dark. Something in his gaze sharpened and softened at the same time, and Layla saw him understand the gravity of the oath she'd just made. She saw him understand perhaps even more thoroughly than she did, what she might do to protect him – or any of the people she loved. As he reached up, cradling her face with his hands, a sad smile curled his beautiful lips.

"I won't let it go that far, Layla," he breathed, watching her with his blazing aqua eyes. "I won't ever let things get so bad that you have to live up to that promise. I swear."

And then Adrian lifted his lips, smoothing them over hers.

Kissing her deep in the endless desert night.

CHAPTER 6 – HOME

Adrian scooped Layla up in his arms, not releasing her from his kiss as he walked them down the dune. She could feel his strong, lean muscles moving beneath his vest and shirt, his Dragon's passion making a hot, sweet jasmine scent rise around them as Adrian walked them to the massive wrought-iron gates in the palace's wall. They parted with a whisper, sighing open to reveal a sprawling courtyard of opal-white stone. The courtyard stretched into gardens inside the wall, lush with tropical plants and flowers. Layla broke from Adrian's kiss as she gazed around in astonishment, and Adrian let her slide down his strong body, setting her on her feet so she could take it all in.

Wrapped in Adrian's arms, Layla stared around his palatial home. For that's what it was – the immense grounds of Riad Rhakvir, the Rhakvir family home where Layla had been born. Fountains of blue tile burbled in the courtyard, feeding streams that wound out to water enormous palm trees, bird of paradise plants, and trailing jasmine vines. Waterfalls stepped down tiers of blue and white tile, into ponds filled with fish that looked like small water-dragons, flashing through the pools like miniature white and gold leviathans in the starry night. Like a dragon snaking through the desert, the palace and garden formed a perfect fit, like an endlessly writhing yin-yang. High domes sprawled through the enormous palace, joined by arched walkways of alabaster stone lattice and cobalt tile. Wrought-iron votives with blue and red Moroccan glass hung from every arch, flickering with lit candles.

Ushering her forward, a mystic smile lifted Adrian's lips as he watched her. All around, patios were set for outdoor living, chaises and tables gathered around enormous clay cook-stoves – even a nook up in the greenery sporting an outdoor bed surrounded by jasmine. Layla reeled from the heady air, realizing that every scent in Adrian's magic was present here. Cinnamon trees grew in enormous pots by the house; jasmine vines crawled through the compound, spilling out of windows. Vines of black peppercorn grew beside a grove of orange trees with emerald moss carpeting their roots, watered by a cobalt-tiled waterway.

Domes and minarets rose all around, made of the same smooth agate-stone that formed everything inside the walls. Tiled Moroccan arches, ornate columns, and high domes wound through the garden, the buildings far enough apart that one had to meander between them using outdoors walkways. Night-birds trilled in the trees, while white moths floated by the pools amidst winking golden fireflies. It was a city created by an incredible mixture of Moroccan and Persian architecture, and as Layla gazed around, she realized the palace was large enough to provide a home to a thousand people.

Yet as they moved through the desert paradise, Layla saw no one. Layla glanced at Adrian curiously as they wandered a mossy agate-stone path. He caught her watching and glanced over, giving a wry smile. As he motioned them through a grand arch and up a short ingress of red and blue-tiled stairs, Layla finally broke the silence.

"It's so quiet."

"No one lives here but me." Adrian glanced at her, a complex emotion in his eyes. "I need the quiet."

But Layla knew he was lying as he ushered her into a vaulted living-area nearly as enormous as one of the Hotel's ballrooms. Ornately tiled with Moroccan *zellij*, the room flowed with scenes of Desert Dragons writhing through dunes, swimming through the Mediterranean Sea, and carving out arroyos with fire. The furniture was classically Moroccan; rolled-back silk chaises in shining teals and turquoise, reds and purples. Wrought-iron votives of Moroccan glass hung from every arch, and were set into sconces in the walls. A massive wrought-iron chandelier of glass votives hung suspended from the highest vault, while indoor greenery with hand-carven teak and ebony screens created cozy niches.

The only thing missing from a classical Moroccan palace were fans; neither circular ceiling fans high above or long paddle-fans in rattan baskets. But the room held a comfortable breeze through its ornately carved vents above the doors, as if the space had been designed for optimal air flow. It invigorated and soothed Layla, as if the night-breeze was lulling her to sleep while also heightening her passions.

Yet as she gazed around, it was as if she could feel ghosts sighing through the space. It was a hall that should have been enjoyed by a hundred people chatting over bourbon and mint tea, watching children play in the floor-pools, or drinking coffee as they gamed on ornate chess-sets and backgammon boards. But like a fancy hotel of the 1920's that had been abandoned during the Great Depression, Riad Rhakvir had a sadness about it. Though every surface was clean, every alabaster arch pristine and clear water burbling through every fountain, it only enhanced the sensation of emptiness.

"Why do you need all this quiet, Adrian?" Layla asked suddenly, confused that such an incredible home would be left so empty. "This palace could hold a thousand people. Don't you at least have servants?"

"I don't keep servants, not anymore." Adrian's smile was wry as he caressed a lock of Layla's hair back from her face. "The palace and grounds are imbued with magic that keeps the environment healthy. Barring wars or damage, the palace will continue just like this, long after I am dead and dusted. And I live alone… because it's not that quiet when two powerful Royal Desert Dragons are smashing the courtyards apart with their fights. And the domes, and the fish-ponds. And anything else they barrel through in their rage."

"Your parents." Layla blinked, suddenly understanding. Dusk had said Adrian's parents had fought terribly when he was young, but Layla hadn't considered they'd done it in Dragon-form. She reached out, taking his hand. "I'm so sorry, Adrian."

"It's ancient history. My father died when I was a young man, and my mother was happier after that. With your mother Mimi." Lifting her hand in his, Adrian's aqua eyes were deep as he kissed her fingers. "Besides, I'm not alone all the time. Dusk comes here, and Rachida. Sometimes I invite the entire clan to stay for a season, to enjoy the palace while I'm away on business. But when my mother was killed, I just… didn't want anyone around for a while."

"Because you mistrusted people?" Layla frowned. "After Hunter murdered her?"

"Because I mistrusted myself." Adrian stroked his thumb over Layla's cheek as he cupped her face tenderly. "I went crazy after my mother was killed, Layla. I smashed through the palace in Dragon-form for a full week. Dusk talked me down, got me to change back, though I couldn't calm my rage for a while afterwards. I'm not the only one who has crashed through this place in a blind rage, though. It's been destroyed many times over the centuries by Dragon-wars or internal fights. Most of what you see now was restored between the fifteenth and nineteenth centuries after a major war with the Desert Dragons of Tunisia. There's only one spot that is original, just as it was built three thousand years ago."

"The blue courtyard." Layla had a sudden flash of it, just as she had seen it in her dreams. It was the one spot in the entire palace she remembered vividly from her brief time here as a child.

"Yes. Come see." Adrian's smile was genuine as he stepped away, tugging her hand. Layla suddenly felt like Indiana Jones being invited to see the Arc of the Covenant as she followed him through a series of halls, some extremely formal, some far more cozy and familial. They passed extensive kitchens, larders, and halls of palatial bedrooms, then turned into a back-area that Layla suddenly recalled. This area of the palace looked identical to Adrian's apartment at the Hotel. With a stunned blink, Layla realized he'd recreated the back-palace from his young life to be his living quarters in Paris.

The place where his family had lived was homey and bright, a smaller, cozier version of the first hall they'd entered. It was the part of the palace where Adrian's family had spent time together, where Mimi and Juliette had been happy. Layla saw flashes from Adrian as they gazed around; him as a child running through the back-palace, chasing Dusk and laughing. Mimi growling after both children in play, still young and looking almost exactly like Layla looked now. The family sharing meals on the stout ebony table, passing rustic dishes Mimi had cooked. Juliette vibrant with her flowing copper hair and sparkling emerald eyes, wearing a dark green evening caftan and telling stories on the veranda at night as a fire crackled in the pot-bellied fireplace. Adrian and Dusk releasing hundreds of crickets into the formal living room while Rachida and the rest of the clan were visiting – shrieking and running away in glee at the uproar.

But Adrian's father was in none of those memories. Frowning, Layla had a brief vision of Issam knocking politely at the ingress to the back-palace, asking Juliette if he could enter. He looked like Adrian, tall and handsome, striking in his later years with streaks of silver at his temples and in his short beard. She saw Adrian's parents sitting together stiffly to discuss political matters for the clan, after which Issam promptly departed. He'd not been permitted back here. This area of the palace had been a place of solace for Juliette, her children, and her lover Mimi – as Adrian's father and mother fought more and more over the years.

"No more." With a sad smile, Adrian stepped close to Layla, kissing her lips. "I don't want to see it, Layla. Please. My father was a good man, and he and my mother were life-mates, but when you've lived with someone for hundreds of years… sometimes it's not so easy anymore. He had his lovers, and she had hers. He kept his other families in another part of the palace, and she kept her family here."

"Your father had other wives? Other children?" Layla blinked, astounded to hear that Adrian's father had kept a harem, but not seeing any more of Adrian's memories through their Bind as he shut it down.

"He did. But they're all gone now."

"What happened to them?" Layla frowned.

"A plague swept through the palace when I was fifteen." Adrian sighed. "Normally, Dragons are impervious to disease, but this was something extremely deadly that went around at that time, something Twilight physicians couldn't figure out how to stop until years later. It wiped out over half the Desert Dragons in Africa. My clan was decimated. My father died in that plague; as did his five other wives and all my half-siblings. Only Dusk and I survived, and Adam. After that… it was just my mother, Mimi, Rachida, and us three younglings. Our clan is still suffering from that plague, at one-quarter the strength we should be – even though we encompass all the sub-clans of the Mediterranean now."

"I'm so sorry, Adrian." Layla reached up, cradling his face.

Taking one of her hands, he moved it to his lips, kissing her fingers. "Come see the Blue Courtyard. Come live a better memory."

As Layla nodded, Adrian led them through the back-palace into a rustic kitchen of enormous iron ovens and stoves hung with copper pots

75

and garlands of spices. And through a vaulted arch, she saw the Blue Courtyard. Square, it was surrounded by vaulted halls and accessed by tiled ingresses. Made of alabaster stone, every arch was tiled in cobalt glass, an ornate pattern of cobalt tiles forming the courtyard walk. The courtyard held ancient potted palms and jasmine, votives of blue glass flickering from every arch of the long quadrangle halls. In the center burbled a three-tiered fountain, shining under the starlight with vivid cobalt *zellij* like blue dragon-hide beneath the midnight sky. As Layla stepped to the fountain, she saw gold and white Dragon-fish flickering through the blue-tiled basin.

The effect was deeply mystical. As Layla gazed around, seeing glowing white and blue reflecting the light of the stars all around, she felt the courtyard's ancientness. A sensation of homecoming filled her – as if this was where she was supposed to be in life. Turning, she saw Adrian watching her, his aqua eyes penetrating as his lips quirked. "You look so at-home here."

"I feel that way." Layla spoke, feeling a tremendous belonging filling her. "I can't describe it, but it feels like I've always been here. Like I'm *supposed* to be here."

"Desert Dragons all feel that way when they come here." He spoke softly, moving toward her with a wistful grace. "This is the Well of Arcadia. The palace was built around the well, to house our entire clan long ago. Arcadia was the first Desert Dragon. A shape-shifter of immense ability tens of thousands of years ago, it's said she dreamed for thirty days and thirty nights while wandering the desert. When she finally transformed into a Dragon for the first time, a wellspring thrust up from the sands as she clawed her talons into the dunes. This is that spring."

"It is true?" Layla asked him, smiling at the fable.

"Who knows," he shrugged, gazing at the fountain. "But all

Desert Dragons feel a homecoming here. The waters feed the entire palace, and are said to have healing properties."

"Do they?" Layla asked.

"They helped soothe me when I got into scrapes with Dusk as a child." Adrian smiled sadly. "But they couldn't heal my father. Or his other families when the plague came."

"Do you miss him, your father?" Layla asked, watching him.

"Issam died over a hundred years ago, Layla." Adrian glanced at her. "I can barely remember his face now. Only that he was tall like I am. And I have his eyes."

"Does Dusk remember Issam?"

"Not really." Adrian spoke softly. "My father was simply the man who rescued him. Dusk was raised by my mother Juliette and your mother Mimi. Juliette was my father's first life-mate, so it was her responsibility to raise the adopted son."

"This palace is so full of memories."

"Too full." Adrian spoke sadly.

Stepping close, Layla took his hand and Adrian gazed down at their twined fingers, then up at her. "We should make some new memories here."

"I'd like that." A true smile curled Adrian's lips at last, his aqua eyes shining in the luminous dark. "As per the terms of your Debut Assignation, I do have you for the next twenty-four hours, you know. Plenty of time to make new memories. If you want."

Layla laughed at Adrian's devious quip, and suddenly the night didn't seem so dark. Tonight, it was just her and Adrian. For the first time, they would have no interruptions, no intrigue, and no games. Just two people able to truly be together for the first time. The thought suddenly made Layla heat as her Dragon turned over in her veins with a wash of spiced bourbon scent. Lifting a mantle of golden spikes inside

Layla, the drakaina shifted her coils eagerly. Layla's Dragon was done sifting through old memories like the wandering sands of time. She wanted what she had been denied these many months.

And so did Layla.

"I *do* want." Layla breathed as she stepped close, and Adrian wound her in his arms. "Did you really give old Valdo Chermour *carte blanche* to win my auction tonight?"

"It was Dusk who arranged it, but I told him no sum was too high to win you." Adrian gazed down at her soberly, cradling her close to his strong, lean body. "I told Dusk I would spend my entire worth to claim you tonight. Because you are worth more to me than any sum."

"My renegade Royal billionaire." Layla's lips quirked, teasing him lightly.

Adrian laughed at last. It was a soft laugh, nowhere near his sudden guffaws Layla loved so much, but it was a start. He was moving away from dire things as he wound her in his arms, corralling her close to his strong chest. Layla felt the coils of his magic rise once more in a scintillating wind, curling around her as he held her, slipping up her ankles and caressing her thighs. Lowering his head, Adrian nuzzled her nose as he let out a sensual breath, his magics stealing from his lips and kissing hers as he gave a slow grin.

"My tempestuous, ball-busting Bind."

It was Layla's turn to laugh. Lifting up, she closed the distance between them, giving him a deep, solid kiss before she pulled back. Tension heated between them now, simmering with power and passion as Layla felt their Dragons slide against each other with a sensual press of scales and etheric heat. It gripped things deep inside Layla, making her clench deliciously and shiver with anticipation. As Adrian's incredible aqua eyes burned into hers, her breath was stolen. He was amazing, he was powerful, he was beautiful.

And he was all hers tonight.

"Come on, you." Layla murmured, her heart hammering as her body surged with need. "It's high time I saw your bedroom. Because I *am* fucking you tonight and I will not take no for an answer."

"As my lady commands." Adrian was truly grinning now, his eyes bright with gold. With a masculine chuckle, he escorted her out of the Blue Courtyard and back into the kitchens, grinning like a sexy devil.

A sexy devil that was hers tonight – all night long.

CHAPTER 7 – DRAGON

Layla didn't know what she expected Adrian's bedroom to be like, but
as they stepped through a set of enormous ebony doors carven with
dragons, what she saw was not what she'd anticipated. They had
entered a circular hall with two sets of doors at the far end. All around,
smooth white agate-stone created the floor, the curved walls and stout
columns, arching in vaults to a dome far above. The alabaster walls
were entirely carved into ornate filigree, a delicate lattice that let in the
soothing midnight air. As Layla gazed through the walls, she saw a
dense garden ringing the hall. Choked with jasmine vines, fireflies
moved lazily through the greenery and in through the walls, swirling up
into the vaulted dome.

Niches had been carven into the walls, each decorated with ornate
lanterns of Moroccan silver and colorful glass. Candles burned in the
lanterns, casting vivid color through the space in the midnight hour.
High above where the ribs of the dome came together, an enormous
silver chandelier of votives was suspended from the ceiling by a stout
chain. Below that was the only furniture in the room – an enormous
canopied bed that could have slept ten. Carved of luscious ebony like
the room's doors, the bed had a soft white duvet with thin white netting
tied up at each towering bedpost. The entire room breathed with peace
and pleasure, and as Layla inhaled the cool air, she drowned in the
scent of night-blooming jasmine.

Opulent and elegant yet simple, the room held every aspect of
Adrian's personality. The blue-green color of his eyes was in the glass

votives and Moroccan lanterns. The depth of his intrigue showed in the ornately filigreed stone walls leading out to the dense chaos of foliage. The passion of his nature was in the enormity of the bold bed, solidly dominating the center of the room. As Layla gazed around, she had only one word to sum it all up.

"Wow."

"You like it?" Adrian glanced at her, hesitant – the same glance he'd given her when he'd first taken her to his apartment in the Hotel. It was his look of vulnerability, as if he'd suddenly showed too much of himself.

"It's amazing." Layla spoke, feeling strangely reverent in the airy, elegant space. "Is this hall supposed to be a bedroom?"

"Not originally." Adrian shook his head as he led her into the hall. "It was a meditation space, a place where any Desert Dragon who was having trouble with their shift could come and relax. There are three of them on the palace's grounds. They're all unique."

"Why did you take it for your bedroom?" Looking up, Layla did a slow turn, examining the opulent room from all angles.

"Because it's fireproof."

"Excuse me?" She stopped, glancing at him with a frown.

"The agate-stone is fireproof." Adrian nodded at the floor, the walls, and dome far above. "It won't catch fire, crack, or shatter under high heat. It's a specially smelted stone that Desert Dragons have built with for eons. It was sand, sculpted and carved, then blasted by Dragon-fire until it burnished into an indestructible glass, rather than a stone exactly. Some people call it desert-glass."

"Why do you need your bedroom to be fireproof?" Layla raised an eyebrow at him.

"There was a time when my dreams were not as pleasant as they are now." Adrian spoke quietly to her. "I've been able to spontaneously change into my Dragon since I was in my teens, Layla. But I've had a hard life, and with it came nightmares from a young age. Sometimes, if I had a particularly bad one…"

"You'd shift into your Dragon in the middle of sleep and blast your surroundings with fire." Layla gave a long, slow blink. "Does that still happen?"

"It hasn't happened for about two years." Adrian went still.

"Just two years?" Layla's eyes went wide.

"Rake André has been working with me on meditations, since my mother died." Adrian spoke quietly. "It went away after my twenties, but surfaced again after my fiancé was killed by Hunter, then again after Hunter killed my mother. I'm in control of my nighttime shifts now, but I just wanted you to know… before we spent our first evening together."

"Wow. Ok." Layla didn't have any words for a moment, trying to process. "So you could set fire to me in my sleep. That's a thing."

"It's been a long while." Adrian protested again, something careful in his eyes as he let Layla process.

"Still. Bedding with you might just make me a crispy critter."

A small smile quirked his lips, but it didn't touch his eyes. "We don't have to sleep in the same bed, Layla. There are other guest rooms —"

"No." Reaching up, Layla cradled his jaw with her hands. "I want this, Adrian. I want you, I want the whole meal deal. If that means I have to wear flame-retardant jammies to bed or whatever, I'm still in."

"I don't think it'll come to that." Adrian grinned now, and Layla felt something inside him ease. "In any case, you've stood in my flames before and not had them harm you. It's a phenomenon that happens sometimes with life-mates. That the fire of one won't burn the other, at least not casually. Not unless the flames are specifically aimed at that person."

"So you're saying there's a chance I'm all good." Layla cuddled closer, lifting up to kiss his lips. "Good. Because I want to be close to you. No matter what."

"So do I." Adrian curled her in his arms, and Layla felt their connection heat again. Passion sparked in Adrian's eyes now that he'd admitted his secret and not been turned away. "I want you more than anything, Layla."

"More than the hundred million Euros you spent to acquire me tonight?" She grinned.

"Jesus!" Adrian grimaced as he reached up to run a distraught hand through his short black hair. "Did the bidding really go that high?"

"Dusk pushed it way up at the end." Layla smoothed her hands down Adrian's lapels. "He got in a bidding war with Valdo after Quindici and Lulu dropped out."

"Lulu Duvall was bidding on you?" Adrian frowned, and the look was not a good one. "Who else?"

Layla recalled to him all the people who had bid on her during her Courtesan's Debut, including detailed descriptions of people she hadn't known, most of whom had dropped out mid-way. But Adrian's dark brows knit as he smoothed his hands over Layla's shoulders. "Most of those bidders are of no consequence. But Lulu Duvall is the mouthpiece for the Owners' Board. Neither Quindici nor I know if she's Crimson Circle, and even though she's Head of the Paris Hotel now, Quinn can't get a straight answer out of her. We know she has a high position on the Board, yet a subservient one at the same time. Was Dusk trying to out-bid her?"

"Valdo thinks Dusk got jealous of you, actually." Layla mused, recalling Valdo's words. "Dusk drove the bidding up thirty million Euros after Lulu and Quindici dropped out."

"Thirty million?" Adrian blinked, pulling back from their embrace as if she had slapped him. "Layla. Did something I don't know about happen with Dusk recently?"

"Well, I mean we have been sleeping together." Layla spoke, crossing her arms and feeling her Dragon rush up inside her veins with an irate heat as Adrian watched her like a hawk. "Pretty much every night for the past month, Adrian. I thought you were ok with me being with him?"

"Every night? Seriously? How many times a night?" Adrian spoke, blinking rapidly now. Layla watched him struggle with rage as he pulled away from her. As his hands slid from her waist, Adrian went from tender to tense in about two-point-five seconds. As he stood there suddenly fuming with his hands set on his hips, his beautiful eyes darkening to a vicious cobalt, Layla blinked. Here she was, his for the night, and he couldn't help but ask who she'd been fucking while he was unavailable – typical guy bullshit, even though he'd said he was okay with her and Dusk.

"Yes, Adrian, Dusk and I have been together. A lot." Layla tensed, her posture tightening as her hands gripped her arms now, a hot fury rushing through her as her drakaina gave a strangled roar of frustration inside her veins. "If I'm going to be a Courtesan and infiltrate the Crimson Circle for you, you need to pull yourself up out of your raging jealousy! Dusk and I are Bound just as much as you and I are. And he's only doing it with me so often because he can help me discharge my power. My Dragon needs to fuck – it's either that or fight – multiple times a day. I'm still training with Rikyava, but Dusk has graciously agreed to help me discharge the rest of my hcat. Which happens to be in the bedroom."

"You know that's not true." Adrian's gaze was withering, as a scalding wind of scorched jasmine flickered the candles. "Dusk fucks you because he wants to. Twisting a dagger in my heart that he can have you while I'm away and I can't."

"Adrian, you're acting like I'm not a willing participant." Layla crossed her arms tighter, feeling her Dragon roar in her veins now. Her own searing wind picked up, filled with the scent of burning orange peels. Layla felt she and Adrian's Dragons snarl at each other as the two winds heaved with barbed coils. "I want Dusk. He's important to me. And it's good, Adrian. It's exactly what I need."

"I bet." Adrian's gaze was scalding now, burning with molten gold. "Dusk knows all the right buttons to push in the bedroom to make a woman break to his *charms*."

"What is your problem?!" Layla shouted as she threw up her hands in an exasperation, her magic whipping out at him like a barbed tail. "You seemed fine with this last time! What about me being a Royal Dragon Bind don't you understand?! My magic binds people. Men. Powerful men. It's not just a bind of power and magic! It's a bind of emotions, connection, feelings—"

"Love." Adrian blinked at her, putting the pieces together just like Arron had earlier. "You love him."

"Yes!" Layla yelled, setting her hands feistily to her hips in a posture that mimicked Adrian's. "I love Dusk, and I love *you*, Adrian! I can't help it that I feel your moods and his, that I can see into his mind and memories as well as yours. Every horror of your life, they're mine now. Every love, every remembrance… I could feel it all if I dug deep enough. And I could do the same with Dusk and Reginald. But if I did, who would I become, feeling hundreds of years of lives I've never lived? What would happen to me if I dug into everything Reginald felt as he was drowning an entire village of Blood Dragons? What about when Dusk watched his clan and the Tunisians slaughter each other? What about you, standing over the body of your murdered fiancée?

How dark would I go, if I carried all that – if I gave in to the Bind?"

Layla was shuddering now, shaking with fury and heartache. Tears rolled down her cheeks even as she wrapped her arms tight, trying to stop from breaking. She hadn't even known how much she could see into her Bound men until the words tumbled out of her. But suddenly, all those memories of Reginald's and Dusk's and Adrian's were careening through her – horrible images she'd touched but had pushed away, terrified.

And with the stress of everything else recently, it was suddenly all too much.

As fury and heartbreak filled her that Adrian was being such an ass tonight, Layla was suddenly flooded by her men's nightmares. Seeing throats gurgle and eyes bulge as Reginald drowned the Blood Dragon village with seawater rising up their throats. Watching a battle of hundreds of Crystal Dragons slashing each other, biting out gullets, the sands of the Sahara flowing red with blood. Staring at her hands – Adrian's hands – as he turned over a beautiful lump of white satin and long, dark hair and saw enormous talon-marks ripping his fiancée's chest. His hands were covered in blood as he clutched the dead woman, screaming, sobbing.

Hysterical.

Without warning, the horror of memories Hunter had shared with Layla in the Phoenix King's bower suddenly opened inside Layla's mind. The combined darkness was disastrous, and Layla was down on her knees without knowing she had fallen, flooded with obliterating terror. Gasping for air, she felt like she was choking on seawater, being ripped apart by talons, and stabbed through the heart all at the same time.

As an enormous black void opened up inside her, cavernous and horrible.

Her chest was spasming as she hyperventilated, trying to escape that devouring blackness. Fire ripped along her spine in a burning wave of heat, fighting the darkness that wanted to consume her, and Layla screamed, shuddering. But the wave only spread as her Dragon thrashed against the grips of the cold terror, fighting it with everything she had. Washing through every limb, the ferocious power of Layla's beast devoured her all the way to the ends of her fingers and toes as pain roared through every nerve.

Layla screamed again, feeling like she was blazing with fire even as she was held suspended above that cavernous black hole inside her. Spines shot from her back, tearing the fabric of her gown and Layla screamed – her voice now roaring with impossible overtones. Talons shot from her fingertips in a wave of light and she roared again, the agony excruciating. Collapsed to the floor, she shuddered like she was going to shake apart, though she knew what was happening. She'd gone through a partial Dragon-shift twice before, but Dusk wasn't here to control her this time – and as she glanced up at Adrian with panic, she saw his fury evaporate.

Adrian went to her fast. Kneeling over her and wrapping her in his arms with her back to his front, he crushed her to his body even as she struggled and surged, fighting him, fighting the pain and darkness – fighting the change. She felt Adrian's energy expand around her, enormous, his Dragon coiling around her from head to heels, pulsing like a bellows. He was breathing in her power with his magic, breathing in her scalding waves of heat – taking them into himself and forestalling her change.

"Adrian!" Layla gasped, in a brief moment of clarity. "Help me!"

"Breathe, Layla." He spoke low by her ear, his voice a growl of sub-basso Dragon tones also now. "Let the shift wash through you; let it happen. I'll keep you safe, I promise."

"But I can't shift tonight!" She struggled, still fighting the ripping heat flooding through her, along with the crushing sensations of darkness. "You and I… we have to—!"

"Sex can wait; it'll have to." Adrian growled by her ear, still cradling her close, his body a scalding fire now to match hers as his power struggled to siphon her change away for a few moments. "Be the wind, Layla; be the fire. Let the pain of the memories you're feeling from Dusk and Reginald and I wash through you, but don't just be that. Be our joys also. Be our love for you, and your love for us – all of us. We're not just darkness, not like Hunter. And neither are you."

Some part of Layla registered that Adrian was using *we* to mean himself, Reginald, and Dusk. Somehow, he had seen what was happening to her through their Bind; seen the horror of Hunter's darkness opening up inside her as a reaction to her bound men's painful memories. But comprehension was pushed aside as Layla's Dragon rose again inside her, thundering back Adrian's winds at last. Hot like lava, furious like tornadoes, her inner Dragon raised its head high – and Layla's flesh was an obstacle.

She screamed as the beast inside her roared, spilling out her throat. She spasmed as it stretched muscled coils, pressing up against every last inch of her skin from the inside like a burning fire, swirling her up and devouring her. The fury of Layla's Dragon was suddenly pouring down every limb with a crash like asteroids hitting the earth.

And Layla's flesh gave in.

Layla's entire body was suddenly splitting. She screamed, feeling her skin shred and roil. She roared, feeling every limb surge outward, bones snapping and sinews remaking. Her chest scorched, and as she stretched her long neck up to the high vaults, she roared, a gout of furious red-gold flame heaving through the filigreed walls of the dome.

Coiling with pain, Layla surged and roiled, flailing. Her coils hit the walls and columns, not strong enough to crack them, but strong enough to scatter Moroccan lanterns across the room. She felt like fire-ants devoured her as pain burned in and in – scales blossoming out and out. Golden spines shot from her serpentine back, her head suddenly heavy with a corkscrewing mantle of horns. She flailed again, massive gold-red talons punching into the agate floor, her head whipping and her long, corkscrewing golden horns getting stuck in the upper frame of the canopied bed.

She screamed, her head now trapped. She heaved her body to get free and the entire bed frame lifted up from the floor – but it didn't shatter to her weak, newly-changed muscles. She heard another roar in the room. Big, male, that roar was all power and it made her panic even as she felt a blistering wind whirl around her. Suddenly, an enormous drake was coiled around her – crimson and aqua with a row of massive black spines protruding from his back. His burning aqua eyes pierced her as his head snaked high above hers, his snout full of enormous black fangs.

She panicked, flailing, straining the muscles of her neck as she shrieked in terror. She was caught. She was caught and he was going to eat her. As his jaws opened, baring those enormous, cruel fangs, she snarled at him, heaving a gout of fire from her lungs. With an agile side-winding movement, he dodged it, flowing around her flames. And then those enormous jaws were descending. She shrieked like a harpy, trying to split his ears with her power, but his jaws were were on her. Biting, crunching – cracking through the stout canopy of the bed.

Freeing her.

She heaved free with a scathing roar. It was so foolish of him to break her prison! But even as she roiled, she felt how uncoordinated her muscles were. Roaring in frustration, she tried to rake him with her talons; tried to whip her head and butt him with her stout skull. But her body was too weak, too new. She flailed and he was suddenly coiling around her, securing her with his massive strength. Fury coursed through her to be restrained. But even as her head whipped again and her talons tried to rip chunks from him, he pinned her talons beneath his, wrapping his serpentine body tight around hers.

She whipped her head to hammer him, but he was too fast. His enormous jaws seized her by the back of her neck, pinning her, letting her feel his strength. She felt him gather his formidable power with an enormous inhalation.

And then all that power was pouring into her through his bite – deep into her body.

CHAPTER 8 – MATE

The drakaina shuddered under the drake's wave of power, flowing into her armored neck through his bite. His fangs hadn't pierced deep, and at his basso growl, the sensation surging through her changed suddenly from terror to a vast pleasure. She roiled in his grip, feeling his ironbound strength and nearness. Feeling his powerful muscles holding her, adjusting to her every move. She felt their scales slide against each other, silken and scalding, as his wind of hot power poured through her body. Shuddering, she slid her body against his, purposefully this time.

And felt him shudder also.

His breath was suddenly hotter on her neck. His fangs ground delicately into his bite and he growled; a sensation that poured through her with a cascading scent of cinnamon and jasmine. She made a sound, but not one of fear as she writhed beneath him, a sweet smell of oranges and bourbon flowing out around her. As he began to move, sliding his enormous, strong coils over her, she understood he was letting her feel him. Letting her feel how strong he was, how dominant, how much he boiled with heat. The drakaina snarled, feeling him, wanting him – but in that moment, Layla's human mind suddenly snapped back.

Her breathing changed from the slow roil of the beast's to a fast pant of terror and amazement as she came partially back into her human mind. Layla's body felt enormous; coiling around half the room before the mangled bed, she realized she had arms but no legs anymore, her legs somehow all one long serpentine appendage now. A tail. She had a tail. As she realized it, it roiled, and she felt Adrian's enormous body pin her solidly yet again, holding her tight.

Adrian.

The thought of him rose and she was suddenly hot, pressed up against him. She was trapped beneath Adrian's armored, powerful body, his talons and bite sinking into her – deliciously. There was pain as he held her, as he bit his fangs into her neck, but it wasn't the kind of pain that made her shriek anymore. It was a soothing, delicious pain, and as Layla had that thought, she arched back against him – feeling him press his jaws deeper upon her, holding her still.

Suddenly, a long tongue licked up her neck between his fangs. Layla shuddered, feeling him lick her with sensual strokes, raspy like a cat's tongue. She surrendered to it, bending her neck so he licked her deeper, slower. Stronger. She heaved against his coils, but it wasn't to get away now. Adrian felt it, moving with her. They were suddenly coiling together, braiding around and through each other, sliding all those hot scales and strong muscles against each other. Slithering over the damaged bed; draping themselves around the frame as they coiled together.

With a powerful stroke, Adrian somehow rolled Layla over to her back, draping her over the damaged bed. Releasing her neck, he ran his smooth-scaled cheek over hers as they slid against each other belly to belly now. Layla heaved, pressing up against him as he pressed her down, draping his strong coils over her and pinning her again. But this pinning had motion to it; undulating waves that reminded Layla's human mind of sex. As if Adrian was heaving his coils against her to fuck her deep and slow, it was an inescapable sensation, and Layla shuddered all along the length of her new body.

As Adrian pulled back, gazing deep into her eyes from his beautiful aqua-gold ones in a Dragon's face, she suddenly heard his voice in her mind. *Layla? Are you in there?*

Yes. It was hard to form speech in the confused recesses of her mind. The part of her that was nothing but beast wanted to simply fight him until he fucked her. But the part that was Layla fought back, wrestling that animal mind down and forming language. *Adrian, I... need you...*

I need you, too. He thought back clearly, nuzzling his scaled lips over her face and fangs. *But I don't want our first time to be like this. It's too brutal, having sex as our Dragons. Can you let go, Layla? If you breathe with my power while holding on to your human mind, I can bring us both back to our regular forms.*

How...? She struggled with that thought, with the sensation of having a human body. Her beast wanted to stay in her powerful new body, even as uncoordinated as it was. Her weakness wouldn't last. The longer she stayed in this form, the greater control she would gain, until she could fight this Desert drake.

Fight him until he fucked her – brutally.

No. Adrian spoke as if he could read her Dragon's thoughts, as he nuzzled her lips again. *Breathe, Layla. Stay in your human mind and breathe in my power. Let me bring us both back...*

Layla saw a brief flicker through her mind, an image of placing her lips to Adrian's. Of opening her jaws and letting him breathe his power down her throat, holding her down with his talons and coils as he did it. But it was a terribly vulnerable position. He could breathe fire down her throat from that position, and she couldn't fight him. She couldn't scratch or flail to get away. Somehow, Layla's drakaina knew fire breathing from her own throat was safe, but if he breathed fire down her throat, it was deadly. No Dragon's fire burned the same as another's; no-one's power and magic breathed quite the same way. If she drank someone else's fire, it would burn her up from the inside out, devouring her body like high-molarity acid.

Layla blinked, the thought of chemical reactions pulling her back from her beast. Her beast didn't understand chemical compounds or acidic reactions, only danger and instinct. Closing her eyes, Layla rested her muzzle against Adrian's, forcing herself to stay conscious in her human mind by holding on to images of a long-ago college chemistry class. *I'm ready.*

Hold on. Breathe.

Adrian rested his lips against hers and Layla fought to remain calm even as her Dragon shrieked inside her. She fought to relax and not fight him, even though everything inside her roared at the danger. But this was Adrian; this was her true mate.

Her true mate wouldn't kill her.

That thought was the only thing that calmed her drakaina. As Layla felt the idea of *true mate* make sense to her Dragon, relaxing the last bit of fighting-tension in her coils and jaws, she felt Adrian press his lips deep to hers. As he slowly opened his jaws, he forced hers gently open. Layla felt their fangs scrape together; she felt their tongues meet in a deep, sensually terrifying kiss as he opened her jaws as wide as they would go, locking his fangs upon hers.

Layla's neck strained as Adrian curved his neck in a powerful movement, forcing her head back. Her panic rose to screaming as she was bent into a position of utter submission beneath him, and still she fought to breathe, to think of the periodic table and electron orbits as he bent her into the deepest kiss she had ever known. And then his tongue slid across hers, curling hers up in an erotic, delicious sensation – as the first wave of his cinnamon-jasmine winds breathed over her tongue and down her throat.

Breathe, Layla. Drink me in. Breathe and let go.

It was the last thing she heard before she was obliterated. As if wind and breath could carry thickness and weight, Adrian's power suddenly roared down her throat and Layla gasped it down, feeling it spread in a thick wave through her neck and chest. She roiled beneath him as that hot wave spread through her entire body, down to every last barb and scale. Adrian orchestrated that flow, pushing it into her with every breath, heaving it deep into her lungs – commanding that it fill every part of her.

Layla flailed; too full, too hot. Her skin was going to burst with all that power coursing through her; her muscles and bones were going to snap with it. But Adrian held her, giving not an inch as he held his jaws locked upon hers, his tongue holding her from the throat all the way down her long, muscled body.

In her mind, she saw a picture. Of him and her, wrapped around each other but naked in their human forms. Of having soft hair again and smooth contours and tender flesh. Of having fingernails rather than talons and soft lips rather than scales and rasping tongues. Of having sweet parts that could join gently, rather than the barbed, heaving fury of what would happen in Dragon-form. That thought more than any other shocked Layla back into her human mind.

No way. She was *so* not doing it with Adrian if his junk had barbs.

And then his power took her. Like a hot wind, it gathered her up, surging through her and tumbling her back solidly into her human form once more. Layla felt her skin split and writhe; she felt her bones crack and melt down, along with the snapping of diminishing muscles. She felt her fangs slide back into her skull and her talons do the same at her fingertips. She felt her long tail split back into legs once more and cascade down.

But none of it was as painful or terrifying as it had been the first time. In a wave of scalding heat and fullness, Layla was suddenly folded back down into her human body as her Dragon-scales raced back through her hair follicles like ants burrowing beneath desert sands. As she flowed back to human in a sweep of wind and light, Adrian did the same atop her. Twined together, they were naked on the broken bed as he pinned her to the mattress beneath his long, strong body – kissing her deep as she fell back beneath him, her entire body surrendering to his.

"Layla…" He breathed at her lips, moving his body against hers, sliding with her as deliciously as they'd done in Dragon-form.

"Adrian…" She sighed back, feeling him move, remembering all the power in his beast and feeling it still present in his human body.

"Make love to me." He sighed at her lips, kissing her softly now, sliding his hips lower, angling them close so she could feel how hot and thick he was, pressed against her.

"Yes." Layla breathed, sliding her hips up beneath him. "Please. I want you. I need you…"

"I need you, too. God, I want you so much…" He breathed back, nuzzling his lips over hers just like he'd done in Dragon-form. But he was already sliding down atop her, already pressing his hips in. Already forcing her legs gently apart, bracing his upper body on his elbows as he corralled her close with his hands like he'd done with his coils.

With a sigh, Layla opened to him, to his power and need. Sliding her thighs up, she trapped his hips as she eased her hands up his strong shoulders. She felt him press the tip of himself at her opening, and she was so wet already, it was only with a will that he held himself away. Setting his lips to hers, he kissed her with a sweetness Layla had never felt before. And then he pulled back, enough to watch her with his devastating aqua eyes as he tensed, firming his intent.

And sliding in deep.

Layla gasped, drinking him in, glorious as Adrian shuddered, gripping his hand behind her neck as he set his forehead to hers with a gasp. She writhed beneath him as Adrian moved his hips, riding her slowly. It wasn't just his body he'd slid inside her with that thrust, it was his power also. As he pulled back, watching her eyes while they moved so slow and so deep, Layla saw her same glory shining in his gaze. It was more than power as they fucked each other, Layla's magic flowing deep within her body now, coiling around his and pinning him inside her. It was more than love as he gazed into her eyes, seeing her, knowing her, understanding her. It was more than bliss radiating from their hearts and twining into a thick cord of gold that bound their passions more closely than ever before.

It was truth. True mates. Life-mates.

A sensation Layla knew to the depths of her soul.

She watched Adrian's eyes as they made love, deep and slow and complete. She watched them change from bliss and lust into knowledge. She saw their sharing affect him just as much as it affected her, and Layla's breath hitched as he thrust again, stronger now. His lips fell open and his eyes blazed as she cried out, unable to contain this enormous, living sensation inside of her.

It was more than just their Dragons and magic they were joining – it was everything.

She clutched his face as he thrust again, and this time it was he who cried out, closing his eyes and shuddering at the sensation of their togetherness. Layla wrapped her arms around his neck, gripping him tight, burying her lips and nose in his chest. Securing a strong arm around her back, Adrian suddenly lifted them up without losing their connection. Raising her with his hand on her spine and one beneath her ass, he rocked them back to a cross-legged seat on the bed with Layla's legs locked around his hips.

His hands held her firmly upon him as much as his coils had held her; she was pinned and there was no slipping as they changed position.

As Adrian leaned back in his cross-legged seat, he flexed his pelvis – driving deeper inside her. Layla arched as he cored her to her depths, Adrian leaning back on one hand, holding her with just one arm, pinning her to his chest and phallus as he made the angle deeper, more secure. Layla cried out at his deep thrust, feeling him come to the very end of her, struggling with pain and exquisite pleasure.

But he had her, his arm pinning her from the middle of her back where his elbow rested, up her spine to the base of her neck where his hand spread. His strong fingers gripped her neck like his fangs had done in Dragon-form, scintillating and decadent. Adrian thrust again, watching her with his burning aqua eyes, riveted as if he wanted to watch the beauty of her writhing upon him. And she did, arching against his body and gasping.

Trapped, pinned upon her mate.

A decadent knowing lifted Adrian's lips as he thrust again, so slow, so hard, so thick and deep that Layla cried out, throwing her head back in ecstasy. She writhed upon him, she bucked as her mate held her, as he rolled his pelvis so she could feel every last inch of him deep inside her. Moving his hips so he fucked her in a coiling wave, Layla roiled with him, undulating against his body, feeling a flow of barbed muscles in their fucking now.

Roiling through each other, writhing around each other, their Dragons reveled, coiling in a vicious, heated dance as they fucked. Adrian dug his fingertips into Layla's neck and she cried out, her Dragon roaring inside her with pleasure as the drake sank fangs into her neck yet again. Adrian tensed his body and thrust deeper, lifting his hips off the bed to take her as deeply as he could, and Layla felt his drake roar with glory as her drakaina did also.

As he thrust, coring her to her most intimate depths, Adrian's power suddenly surged in – down Layla's open lips. As he fucked her with his body, he took Layla with his power, kissing her hard, sliding inside her and making her gasp in a wave of passion as his power locked inside her both above and below.

Layla screamed his name as she felt his power take her, orgasming as a tremendous wave of golden flame burst from her skin. It flowed over the bed, burning nothing but touching everything, burnishing the duvet and the ebony wood and the floor as it rushed out into the night. She felt Adrian's power explode also, and he was suddenly spasming as he came upon the backlash of her magic, roaring as a wave of crimson and aqua flame burst from his skin also, coating everything the same way Layla's had and dancing through her power in a shimmering play of fire and light.

Racing out into the night, their power smelted into each other, exploding through the bower in a tirade of scalding wind and brilliance. Writhing together, Layla came again and Adrian did also as their twinned powers took each other, devouring and re-making each other. Layla's mind broke open as pleasure crashed over her again and again, and through Adrian also, bringing them over and over in an endless loop. Color coated the night; color expanded inside Layla's mind as pleasure devoured her for an unknown eternity.

And suddenly, she saw the sky far above. Sky. Night. Stars. As she stared up at a midnight desert sky bright with stars, she and Adrian clutched each other, heaving hard breaths and covered in sweat with their hearts pounding against each other's ribs. Vaguely, she was aware that something had crashed down beside the bed in a shattering of glass and metal, smashing the remnants of the broken canopy. Adrian laughed. Staring up at the stars also, he laughed, clutching her close to his chest and shuddering as he held her deep.

"It melted!" He gasped with that beautiful laugh Layla loved so much. "We melted an un-meltable dome!"

Layla blinked, finally realizing what she was seeing as her ecstasy shuddered with aftershocks. She was seeing the midnight sky. All around, the alabaster dome of desert-glass had been melted, and the Moroccan chandelier of votives had smashed down beside the bed in the ruins of the bed's canopy, shattering glass over the floor. The walls and columns and ceiling of the chamber were gone, replaced by a fluid ring of sublimated color swirling with aqua, crimson, and golden veins. Cast over the bed was a shimmering sand of gold, red, and blue, though neither the bed nor the greenery beyond the dome had melted.

As night winds rushed through the decimated space, swirling sand over the chamber with the scent of jasmine and oranges, Layla laughed. She laughed and laughed, breathless with glory.

And Adrian laughed with her, clutching her close as he eased them both down to the bed.

CHAPTER 9 – TAKEN

A puff of colorful dust heaved up from the duvet as Adrian and Layla fell down to it, laughing. All around the ruined dome, color coated everything, even the greenery thoroughly dusted with it. The strange product of their incredible lovemaking decorated Layla's skin, smudging Adrian also as he heaved hard breaths on his back, staring up at the night sky through the melted dome and still laughing breathlessly as Layla did the same beside him. Rumbling with chuckles, Adrian extended a hand to stroke Layla's thigh. Glancing over, Layla saw his cheek smudged with colorful dust like he'd been dancing out in a parade for India's festival of Holi.

Adrian glanced over, meeting her gaze and grinning like a brigand.

"Yowza, Batman!" Layla cough-laughed. "What the hell did we just do?"

"Something unprecedented, I'd wager. It looks like the apocalypse in here." Adrian chuckled, rolling to his side and sliding a hand over her ribs, palming her ribcage deliciously.

"I think it's safe to say we brought the house down with that last number." Layla quipped.

Adrian laughed. He threw his head back and laughed with that bright, winsome sound she loved so much. His eyes sparkled with every color like a Mediterranean dawn as he leaned down and kissed her, deep and delicious. His hand slid over her skin, and as he pulled away smiling, Layla felt him tracing patterns on her abdomen. She glanced down, seeing that he was playing in the streaks of colorful dust that coated her, painting her body with it.

"Trying to become Picasso?" She grinned, lifting an eyebrow at him.

"Trying to make you come again." He growled, leaning in and pressing her with his deliciously sculpted body.

"I don't think I can!" Layla laughed, mock-pushing him away. But it only made Adrian growl more, pinning her to the duvet with his hips, kissing her deep though she could feel he was truly spent now. Layla laughed as they kissed, struggling beneath him, which only made him grin at her lips and move his head – biting the side of her neck and making her melt with pleasure.

"Dammit!" She gasped, as Adrian bit her neck deeper. "Why does that feel so good?"

"Dragons like a little biting in the bedroom." Adrian chuckled, pulling away and kissing the spot he'd bit. He hadn't broken the skin, but Layla could tell it was going to leave a nice hickey she'd have to cover up tomorrow.

"What else do Dragons like?" She spoke as Adrian settled to her side again, propped up on one elbow and tracing patterns on her skin.

"Well, they certainly like whatever we just did in here." He lifted a straight dark eyebrow at the ruined bedroom.

"They certainly do." Layla lifted up, stealing a kiss from his lips, which lasted longer as he pressed into it, palming her ribcage so she couldn't get away. At last he let her go with a soft growl, and Layla settled back to the dusty duvet with a satisfied sigh.

Gazing down at her, Adrian kept smoothing his palm over her abdomen and breasts as if he couldn't stop himself from touching her. It was erotic and calming, and as Layla heaved another sigh, he beamed with a smile that went all the way through him, lighting up his eyes.

She reached up, stroking his jaw and soft stubble, then down his neck to his strong, lean chest, painting him with her fingertips as much as he did her. It was lovely, slow and tender, and as they touched each other in the afterglow, Layla felt the Bind between them brighten.

"You are a wonder of a woman, Layla Price." Adrian spoke, still tracing her skin with his fingers.

"Don't you mean Wonder Woman?" Layla grinned, her fingers skating up to touch his striking jaw again. "If you're Batman, then I should get to be a superhero, too."

Adrian turned his head, pressing his soft lips to her fingers. "Wonder Woman ain't got nothing on you."

Adrian's voice held a trace of southern accent in his lazy bliss, reminding Layla of his bayou alter-ego John LeVeque. Which suddenly reminded her of the massively dangerous game they were playing in the wider world, and how this was only a brief reprieve. Quindici's words before her debut suddenly came rushing back, and despite the afterglow, Layla sighed, her ecstasy slipping. Deep inside, a faint edge of that fearful darkness tried to open, though it was quickly rolled back by her Dragon's bliss after such a profound and incredible lovemaking. But Adrian felt it through their Bind and reached up, clasping Layla's hand and pressing a kiss to her fingers as his beautiful eyes sobered.

"What's wrong?" He asked quietly.

"I don't want to go back to the real world." Layla spoke, meeting his gaze.

"I don't either." He murmured, watching her. "I want to stay here with you, doing this over and over until we bring down every room in the house."

His statement made Layla smile, though it was hard to stay smiling now with everything suddenly flooding through her brain. "What are we doing, Adrian?"

"Enjoying the afterglow." He smiled against her hand as he kissed it again.

"No, I mean. What are we doing, going after the Crimson Circle?" Layla frowned, unable to stop thinking about it. Beyond the dome, crickets chirruped in the night, moths and fireflies swirling lazily now that the destruction was over and peace had settled in. "Are we just going to get ourselves killed?"

"Maybe." He kissed her fingers one last time, then lowered her hand to his color-smeared chest, pressing it to his heart. "But I would risk it all for you, Layla. You know that."

"I do." She spoke, feeling his sincerity, feeling the strength of his heart beating beneath her touch. "But what if the price this time is losing me? What if I die, or if you die? Or if I go bad, like Hunter? Now that I can change into my Dragon fully… it could be really bad." Inside Layla, that dark void tried to open up again – and yet again, her Dragon's slow heat rolled it back.

"I won't let you go bad." Adrian spoke with a sudden fierceness, pressing her hand deeper to his heart, a heat in his intense blue-green eyes. "Not now, not ever. Your Dragon is a powerful creature, but already you're able to hear your human voice of reason inside its mind. Not everyone can on their first shift, Layla. That shows you have more control over your inner darkness than many people. And the Circle already want me dead. If I run again, it's only a matter of time before they catch me. Their resources far outweigh mine."

"Which are now diminished by one hundred *million* Euros." Layla's lips quirked.

"I am going to insist Dusk pony up for that bidding war he started." Adrian lifted an eyebrow, a flash of anger moving through him. "He was only supposed to out-bid the third nearest person. Not crank the whole damn thing up into the stratosphere."

"He's jealous of how I feel about you." Layla spoke, smoothing her hand over Adrian's chest. "Give him a break, huh?"

"Dusk can be as jealous as he wants to be." Adrian snorted, settling on his elbow and cuddling his hips closer to Layla's. "But he'll damn well pay me back. He's got the funds. He's a sight wealthier than anyone we know, Layla – far wealthier than I am."

"How so?" Layla asked, intrigued. It was something Dusk never spoke about, just how much money he had stashed away. He was so meticulous about making nice things last that Layla had once thought he didn't have much money other than his Head Concierge income. But hints had been dropped around the Hotel that he was wealthier than any Hotel patron and many of the Owners, only it was a wealth he couldn't touch.

"You know Dusk is the last of his clan," Adrian eyed her as he smoothed his hand over her belly again. "What you don't know is that the Egyptian Crystal Dragons were the wealthiest Lineage in the Twilight Realm before they got massacred. They have secret hoards of gems and precious metals all over the world, hidden deep in the earth."

"Hoards?" Layla blinked with a slight grin. "Come on. Like the treasure of Smaug, hoards?"

"You joke, but this is real, Layla." Adrian spoke back soberly. "The Egyptian Crystal Dragon clan were once the most brutal conquerors in the Twilight Realm, and the Tunisian clan were second. Since they killed each other off, the Czech and Swiss clans have risen to prominence, thanks to King Markus Ambrose's brutality in killing off anyone who even hints at becoming his rival, but once that honor belonged to Dusk's people. Since Dusk is the last, he's inherited *all* their spoils. His clan left their vibrational imprint on their wealth so future generations could find it – the caches call to the ones who are supposed to have them. Dusk has discovered a few, and well, *ostentatious* is the mildest term one could use."

"Wow." Layla spoke, processing it. "So he's what, like Scrooge McDuck, diving into a swimming pool of money?"

"Like Scrooge McDuck times a million." Adrian spoke soberly. "My wealth is tied up in industry, Layla. I have money but in order to liberate it, I have to withdraw it from investments, which hurts my overall capital and resources. Many key players in the Twilight and Human Realms operate like I do, and I learned from them. My clan didn't always have exorbitant wealth. My father built his wealth over time, and I followed in his footsteps. But Dusk has no investments that will suffer if he makes a withdrawal. He simply liberates what he needs from the bowels of the earth, whenever he needs it."

"But won't the gems and such run out eventually?" Layla asked, frowning.

"Eventually." Adrian shook his head with a wry smile. "But what he's found so far makes my wealth look like a pile of coal. And he says he can feel *thousands* of caches out there, just like the ones he's already discovered."

"If someone ever… captured Dusk. Could they use him to get to his wealth?" Layla frowned.

"You're thinking about King Markus, aren't you?" Adrian eyed her shrewdly.

"Or Hunter." Layla nodded. "Or the Crimson Circle. Or anyone powerful enough, really."

"Technically, yes." Adrian nodded. "Why do you think Dusk pretends like he only has what he earns from the Hotel? Not to mention keeping a low profile with his magics."

"So your enemies will underestimate him." Layla reached up, smoothing her hand over Adrian's chest again. "Is it working?"

"So far." But again, Adrian frowned deeply. "Though I don't

know how much longer we'll be able to keep all that under wraps."

Layla was about to say something more, when she suddenly heard a buzzing sound in the room. It was like something vibrating against the stone floor, and as she frowned, Adrian perked, glancing around. In one lithe movement he was up off the bed, striding through the rubble and shuffling away glass with his feet. Lifting an enormous beam from the ruined canopy one-handed, demonstrating a strength in his human form that truly lifted Layla's eyebrows, he reached down – taking up the remnants of his shredded pants and fishing in one pocket.

It was his cellphone he pulled out, still buzzing. Wiping colored dust from it, he glanced at the number and frowned. "No one has this number but Dusk, Rikyava, Rachida, and Emir, but it's not a number I recognize. Do you mind if I take this?"

"Go ahead." Layla waved a hand, knowing it was probably important if either of those four people were calling Adrian right now, in the middle of the night, in the middle of their Assignation. Perhaps Adrian's aunt and Clan Second Rachida Rhakvir and his Battle-Lord Emir Tousk didn't know about tonight, but Layla was nearly certain Rikyava had been in on the plan. As Adrian unlocked the phone and tapped the screen, holding it up to his ear, she saw his face brighten.

"Dusk! You bastard." Adrian chuckled wryly. "You owe me a pile of money from that bidding war you—" But Adrian stopped suddenly, frowning. And then he scowled, a hard, furious energy radiating from him as he lifted his glance, staring at Layla. She felt his magics writhe around the room in a rush of burned jasmine, lifting colored dust and swirling it up into sand-funnels as it raced across the floor. Viciously intense now, Adrian nodded to what he was hearing on the phone.

"Shit." Adrian spoke darkly, wrath in his posture as he raked a hand through his hair, then set his hand to his hip, gazing up at the midnight sky. "Shit, shit, shit. Uh huh. And Quindici has someone in custody? And you're *sure* there's no vibrational trace of the assailants, or her friends? Fucking hells. Yeah, I hear you. Will Rake and Jenna Ostlheim recover?"

Something dropped inside Layla, and deep within, she felt that black pit yawn wide. Her ecstasy from lovemaking evaporated as her Dragon gave a terrified snarl deep inside her, fraught with pain. She stared at Adrian, feeling through their Bind that something was horribly wrong, knowing the news was bad. Sitting up with alarm racing through every part of her, she held Adrian's searing aqua gaze as it returned to her. Something terrible was in his eyes as he watched her, then finally turned away, nodding to whatever Dusk was saying on the other end of the phone.

"I got it." He murmured. "Hold tight, I'm sending her back, and I'm coming with her. Be ready for us in the crystal bath-house. Have some clothes handy. I know it's not a good idea for me to come. I know, Dusk. Tough, I'm coming. I know. Yes, I'll wear my talisman. Twenty minutes. Ciao."

With a hard sigh, Adrian touched the phone to hang up. Turning back to Layla, he let out a long, slow breath. Terror writhed through Layla as Adrian moved back to the bed, then set the phone carefully down. Layla shivered at the set of his jaw, knowing to her bones that something had gone horribly wrong tonight.

But before she could say anything, Adrian reached out, touching her ankle. "Layla, just listen before you say anything. There's been a development at the Hotel, and you need to go back right away. And I'm coming with you."

"Why? What's happened?" Fear drilled through her, every sense heightening in a rush as that black pit raced upward. "Isn't it dangerous for you to come back to the Hotel right now?"

"Yes, but your friends are missing." Adrian kept his eye contact, his voice low and calm. "They didn't make it back to their rooms tonight after the main party wound down in the Diamond Ballroom, so Rikyava sent a few extra Guards to find them. Luke was in his rooms, but not the rest."

Panic gripped Layla's chest as her heart dropped through her heels. Her chest tightened until she could barely breathe, and faster than thought, that enormous black pit of horror and darkness was suddenly rushing up, engulfing her. "I thought they were being guarded!"

"They were," Adrian spoke tensely. "Apparently, all their Guards got drugged. Rikyava found them in the Waterfall Grotto. Rake André, Jenna Ostlheim, Lars Kurs, and Amalia DuFane were there also, all drugged pretty bad but they'll live. Rake's woken in the infirmary and Dusk is with him now. Apparently, all your friends except Luke went to an after-party Dusk arranged in the Waterfall Grotto to show them a good time, and a group of unknown Faunus crashed it. They were Smoke Faunus, and they weren't associated with the Hotel. Quindici is interrogating our only Smoke Faunus on staff now, Imogene Cereste, but we don't know where your friends were taken; Dusk has been unable to trace their vibrations, and the Intercessoria can't either."

Terror froze Layla, gripping her in ice. Deep inside, her Dragon wailed, roaring and gnashing its fangs. Layla could practically feel that black pit sending tentacles out, wrapping its strangling fear and darkness around her Dragon and choking her passions. It sent a deep chill through her entire body, and suddenly everything felt numb, frozen – like everything inside her was somehow going to a dark, empty place.

"Are they…?" She breathed.

"We don't know." Adrian spoke quietly, holding her gaze with his strong commander's presence now. "I need to help Dusk get in touch with the Intercessoria, with Heathren Merkami and Insinio Brandfort.

We need to get back to the Hotel to provide any information that might aid Dusk and Rikyava's search efforts. I know you're terrified right now, but I need you to take a deep breath and get your head clear so we can handle this situation. Layla? Can you hear me?"

Layla had begun to get lost in her ice-cold darkness, but Adrian's words suddenly echoed what he'd said when her beast had been trying to take her over. Even though her black despair had roared up, swamping her, Layla suddenly realized her fear was the same as her passions. Her dark obliteration was the same as her bright fury – an animal trying to immobilize her saner mind. And if she was immobile, she was no good to her friends.

If she froze in that utter darkness now, chances were they wouldn't be found alive.

"Let's go. Now." Without thinking, Layla was up from the bed fast. She didn't even remember rising or moving, and was halfway to the egress of the ruined rotunda before Adrian snagged her arm. Her drakaina growled at him, swiping talons of magic through the air, and Adrian grunted, flinching as if she'd struck him like she'd once done before the Dragon-hunt. Layla turned back, confused at why he would try to stop her helping her friends – barely restraining her drakaina from lashing out at her mate again.

"You need something to wear." Adrian spoke gently, as if to a person in shock.

Layla blinked. Gazing down, she realized she was still naked and covered in colored dust, and it was then that she realized she was in shock, like a trauma patient after a car accident. The realization calmed her Dragon, though the beast of Layla's magic merely coiled up again, gnashing its fangs at the abduction of people she loved.

It all seemed like a lifetime ago, the passion Layla had shared with Adrian tonight. Glancing up to the sky, she saw it was lightening into dawn. She missed Adrian going to one of the other sets of double-doors in the ruined rotunda, but when he threw them open with a boom, she nearly jumped out of her skin. Her heartbeat was fast, her breath in her throat as he returned, extending a cobalt-blue silk robe to her and shrugging on a crimson quilted one for himself as he clasped something around his left wrist beneath the robe's cuff.

Layla hauled on her robe with jerky, shocky movements. Her hands were shaking so hard she couldn't get the sash tied and Adrian stepped in, doing it for her. Her eyes rose to him, and she knew they were enormous, her breath too fast. Tenderly, he cupped her face in his hands, giving her the full compassion of his deep aqua eyes. "This is all my fault. I'm so sorry, Layla. If I had never provoked the Crimson Circle—"

"It's not your fault. It's mine." Layla hitched a breath, still feeling that black void trying to swallow her. "I encouraged Dusk's plans to have my friends visit because I was selfish; I wanted to see them. Are you certain the Crimson Circle are behind this?"

"I'm almost certain of it." Adrian nodded, stroking her neck. "But we need to find out specifically who. When we find them, we'll find your friends."

Layla nodded. She still felt cold despite the robe, and reached up, clutching it closed at the collar. But the deep cold wasn't around her, it was inside her, as if that black pit of despair was empty as the vastness of outer space. Taking her hand, Adrian led them out of the ruined rotunda and back the way they had come, through the quiet palace and gardens. Layla hardly saw any of it. As they gained the front gates and proceeded up the dune, she knew she was still in shock, but couldn't push through it. All she could think about were her friends being tortured at the hands of faceless Crimson Circle members, laughing in the darkness.

She shuddered in the pre-dawn wind as they gained the top of the dune. Adrian turned to her, rubbing her shoulders through her silk robe, his face deadly serious. "We'll go back through the crystal bath-house where you came in. Dusk has set up a portal attuned to only you, him, and I. Layla? Are you listening?"

"Dusk can make portals?" She blinked, surfacing from dark thoughts.

"Through the earth," Adrian nodded. "But it's a rare Royal Crystal Dragon talent, and he can only do it with much time and energy spent, and thoroughly knowing the vibration of the person he wishes to transport. Are you ready?"

Was she ready? Layla's answer was *no*. She wasn't ready for this. She hadn't been ready to have her friends get abducted by the Crimson Circle. She hadn't been ready to face not knowing if they were alive or dead. She wasn't ready if it happened to Dusk, or Reginald, Rikyava, or Adrian. Rake André had been harmed in whatever had happened tonight. So had little Amalia DuFane and her friends Jenna and Lars from Concierge Services. Adrian and Dusk's plans to get her here tonight and keep her safe from the Crimson Circle had resulted in other people getting hurt.

The message was clear: if their enemies couldn't get to Adrian or Layla, they would get to anyone they could.

"What are we going to do?" Layla whispered, glancing up at Adrian, knowing her eyes were still too wide as that terrible blackness roared deep inside her.

"Whatever we can." Adrian spoke with a dire calm, as he smoothed his hands over her shoulders.

CHAPTER 10 – SHATTER

Adrian led Layla to a small patch of rose quartz on top of the dune that she'd missed in the suddenness of her arrival, a two-by-two foot flagstone partially covered by red sand. They stood upon it, and as he pulled her close in his arms, a similar vibration as when she'd arrived thundered through the air. The patch of crystal they stood upon shivered, the dune's sand sloughing away in waves until a clear crystal cocoon shuddered up around them, sealing her and Adrian in. The whole thing vibrated like a wailing banshee, but Layla wasn't panicked this time. In a flash, she felt like she was sucked into the earth and hurtled through it, her ears popping – before she and Adrian surged back up inside the pool of the crystal bath-house.

Plumes of water jetted up around them, sloshing back as the crystal cocoon shattered, the shards quickly reabsorbed into the pool's floor beneath the water. Dusk was waiting for them inside the bath-house, and as they made eye contact, Layla saw how disheveled he was. His tie from the night before was askew, his shirt half-unbuttoned, his immaculate dark hair mussed like he'd been raking his hands through it all night.

Blood stained one French cuff of his shirt.

As Layla and Adrian arrived, his eyes raked them quickly, and seeing they had robes, he put aside the one he was holding for Layla, taking up a pile of clothes instead. As Adrian helped Layla rinse colored dust from her body, doing the same himself, Dusk stepped in with their clothing.

"Dammit, Adrian!" Dusk cussed as he handed over a pile of clothes to Layla and then one to Adrian, his sapphire eyes flashing fury. "You shouldn't be here. I told you that you could help handle this from a distance, safe at Riad Rhakvir."

"Layla needs me here." Adrian growled back, tense but with a readiness about him. "It's not a move I make lightly, Dusk. But if the Crimson Circle's agents see me, it will let them know we're not afraid."

"It's not just your own life you're placing in danger. My god! Do I have to spell it out for you, Adrian?" Dusk had stepped up beside Adrian, growling so low he made the floor of the bath-house shudder beneath their feet. High above, the crystal dome rattled as Dusk ripped a hand through his hair, a hard wave of light refracting through his midnight-scaled ridges. "You always do this! Thinking only about yourself, not considering the whole network of people who will be affected by your actions! And now it falls to me to clean up your bullshit – again!"

Dusk was working himself into a fury, trembling with a vicious vibration like a porcupine on the defense. Waves of light refracted through his scales and hair now, and the cutting intensity of it made Layla's eyes widen. Her Dragon was fully alert, watching Dusk with a coiled wariness. Layla could feel her power trying to decide between snapping at him in his unbridled wrath or trying to reach out and soothe him.

"Dusk! Easy!" Adrian made a soothing gesture, reaching out to Dusk with his magic in a calming wind. But Dusk wasn't having it, throwing up one palm with a surge in his growling intensity that actually thrust ruby crystals into the air now. Layla had never seen him do that, and it shocked her into stepping back a pace – her hands coming up automatically in a protective gesture to form a shield-wall.

Dusk saw her step into her sudden defensive posture, still naked, and something in him broke. Stepping away from her and Adrian, he moved to the waterfall that poured down one crystal wall of the bathhouse. Turning away from them and setting both palms against the crystal so they were immersed in the waterfall's flow, he hung his head and Layla heard him breathe deeply, trying to get his shit under control. Gradually, the spearing nimbus of power around him disappeared, as the refractions flowing down the back of his neck slowed.

"Dusk? Are you alright?" Adrian's voice was low and careful as Dusk's shuddering quieted.

"No." Dusk didn't turn around, and Layla heard him let out a long, slow breath. "You just don't *think*, Adrian. You plot and plan, but you don't *think*. Layla's friends were *my responsibility* while they were here! Their safety is my responsibility. This whole damn Hotel's safety and everyone in it is my responsibility! Because of our plans to make Layla a Courtesan to infiltrate the Crimson Circle – which she and I are doing for *you*, Adrian – people got hurt. Rake and Amalia, Jenna and Lars! Because you can't ever keep a fucking low profile and not poke the bear, our friends are *in the fucking infirmary* and Layla's have been abducted! I'm trying, Adrian, God knows I am. I am *really* trying to keep all this shit together. For you. For Layla. For us."

"I know. I'm sorry." Adrian's words were soft, and as Layla glanced at him, she saw tenderness in his face. Adrian rarely apologized for anything and she saw Dusk respond to it, straightening with a hard sigh though he still didn't look around. Despite how much the two adopted brothers fought, despite how much they railed against each other, Layla suddenly saw the truth shining in Adrian's eyes as he moved to Dusk. Adrian's brother meant more to him than anything, and Layla heard it with the words Adrian spoke next. "I know how hard all this is for you, Dusk. I know what you're sacrificing to keep us all safe."

"Do you? Because it just might make us all significantly less safe. Sooner than later." Fury was hot in Dusk's eyes as he turned, setting his hands to his hips and staring Adrian down. His words were cryptic, and though Layla didn't understand them, when his tormented gaze flicked to her, there was so much hurt in his eyes that she stepped towards him. He watched her come, still naked, and she saw his gaze flick over her body as she neared, his eyes disastrously pained.

As Layla reached out, he held up a palm. "Don't."

"Tough." Completing her reach, she took his raised hand, winding her fingers through his. Dusk glanced down at their twined fingers and Layla heard him hitch a hard breath. It wasn't quite a sob but it wasn't far from it, and it made alarm race through her all over again. Stepping close, Layla reached her other hand up, stroking her fingers gently through his hair.

"Talk to me, Dusk." She spoke softly. "What's going on? I've never seen you like this…"

"I couldn't protect them." Dusk looked up from their twined hands, giving her the full force of his startlingly blue eyes – all the more vivid for the red that ringed them. As Layla stared up into his handsome, devastated face, a tear blinked from his dark lashes and rolled down his cheek. "I had one job for you… one thing I could do that *he* couldn't." Dusk nodded his chin at Adrian. "I could protect you, hold your heart. Keep you safe here at the Hotel and keep you happy by bringing your friends here to be with you. But I *failed*, Layla. I failed to keep them safe, and now your heart is broken because of *my plans*. And now there is nothing I can do for you. Do you know how it feels to always be in *his* shadow? My own fucking older brother?"

Cupping his cheek, Layla felt the impossible smoothness of Dusk's skin contrasting with the ridges of serrated scale that began at the end of his high cheekbone, and the soft dark stubble he wore now for winter. Gazing up into his eyes, Layla poured all of her love into her touch, making him feel what she felt for him. It caught Dusk's breath and his eyes burned white-hot like diamonds as he watched her, though they were still haunted.

"You are *not* in his shadow, Dusk," Layla spoke softly. "Everybody knows it, especially me."

"Don't lie to me, Layla." His snort was awful. "You and I know each other too well for that."

"Yes, we do. And because you know me, you know I would never lie to you."

Layla stared Dusk down, not relinquishing their touch, but digging in with the force of her heart and magic. She felt something luminous and golden spear out from her, flooding down her arm into her palm upon his cheek. It startled him, making him blink, his gaze becoming terrible with hope and hurt. Lifting up, Layla set her lips to his. She poured all that golden sensation into their kiss, feeling it flood up from her heart and in through his lips – down into his heart.

Dusk gasped against her lips – and then he was crushing her close in his arms, fierce and tender, kissing her hard as tears slid down his face. And from the combination of his severe exhaustion, his misery, and his fury, he suddenly broke. With a hard shudder, Dusk gasped as he clutched her tight, shivering and shaking.

"I was supposed to protect them! I'm supposed to protect you! I have to—!"

Suddenly, Dusk's vibrating rose to a fever pitch, so hard and fast that if it hadn't been for his strong grip on Layla, he would have shuddered himself right down through the floor. With a hard jerk, he screamed. The entire bath-house shuddered around them, water sloshing as the rose quartz floor heaved. Layla had to clutch Adrian to keep from falling over as the floor roiled beneath her, but even so, she felt vibrations shuddering from Dusk unlike anything she'd ever felt before. It was enormous, fundamental, and as it built and built inside him, a nimbus of ruby crystals manifested in the air around them.

Alarm raced through Layla as the entire bath-house began to roil like a category 8 earthquake.

"Dusk!" With terror flooding her that Dusk was going to bring the structure down on them, Layla seized his face, forcing him to look at her. But he was gone. His beautiful blue eyes were unfocused, lost somewhere terrible. As the bath-house heaved all around and beneath them, water splashing everywhere, blossoms of crimson began to lance in Dusk's eyes like a Blood Dragon. But these were terrible spikes of vicious ruby light rather than dark like blood. Fear flooded Layla as she felt a screaming uptick in Dusk's energy, like he was going to blow an entire fault-line straight to the Atlantic Ocean.

Layla didn't know what to do. She panicked, her world flashing black like a deep, dark nowhere. Her friends were gone; Dusk was losing it. She was going dark and there was nothing to stop it, Reginald far away in the North Sea with his clan. A devouring terror swamped Layla and she froze.

But in that moment, Adrian moved. Gripping Dusk's neck, he stepped in fast, holding Layla as he pulled their trio tight together. Hauling Dusk's lips to his, hard and deep, Adrian forced his lips upon his adopted brother, pouring his magic down Dusk's throat in a scalding rush of wind. It was like what Adrian had done to Layla when she'd been her Dragon, but rather than coaxing his brother back from the brink, Adrian forced the roar of his Dragon deep inside Dusk, forcing him to listen. In that moment, Layla felt Adrian's fear through their Bind. He was just as afraid as Dusk and Layla. He was just as annihilated by what had happened. But they had to fix this, and they would.

And Adrian would never give in until they did.

As Layla felt his determination and his strength, as she felt Adrian pour his power down Dusk's throat to stabilize the fracturing crystal, a golden light opened up inside Layla. And where she'd been afraid her own black fear would devour her, she was suddenly flooding light into Dusk through their Bind, inundating him with it. It was bright and pure, and it held all the love she felt for him and Adrian both.

Dusk broke from Adrian's kiss with a gasp, like a drowning man suddenly coming up for air as he was flooded with Layla's light and Adrian's fierce heat. His lips found hers, and she felt him cry out as she kissed him and he kissed her back, fiercely. Like a quake rippling away through the bowels of the earth, the shuddering in his body finally died, the bath-house around them ceasing to heave.

"Layla! Gods, I'm so sorry!" Dusk gasped as he broke from their kiss, reaching up to clasp her face gently between his hands. "I didn't mean to lose control!"

"It's ok. It's ok." She spoke, lifting up to kiss him again as Adrian blew a deep exhalation of relief, corralling Dusk's head and kissing his temple tenderly. Layla hadn't felt Adrian's tension until just now – now that Dusk was no longer going to blow the place sky-high.

"I lost your friends!" Dusk choked, clutching Layla close, his beautiful blue eyes so raw that Layla lifted up, kissing his lips.

"Shh, we'll find them. We'll find them." Layla kissed him as he shuddered against her. Tears sprung to her eyes as they clutched each other, and she felt Adrian wrap his arms around her and Dusk both, holding them safe. Dusk's face was buried in Layla's shoulder as he suddenly sobbed, and the sound broke Layla's heart. Running her fingers through his hair, she pressed her cheek to his as Adrian set his lips to Dusk's temple, heaving a hard sigh.

"We'll find Layla's friends, Dusk," Adrian spoke gently, corralling

Dusk's head with his hand and setting their foreheads together. "I promise."

It was a long moment before Dusk nodded with a hard sigh, moving his forehead back to Layla's. She could feel his incredible exhaustion running all through him now like a thousand fractures as Dusk breathed softly. Turning his head, he glanced to Adrian as he massaged a hand at his chest, gripping his heart. "I just – I feel so raw, like all my control has been stripped away by our Bind. But I can't break down, though god, I want to. Because it would place us all in too much danger."

"You're fighting your Dragon." Adrian spoke in a knowing voice. "My rage, Layla's passion, Reginald's situation with his clan, all this stress… you're feeling all our emotions resonating through the Bind and it's pushing you towards your first full Dragon-shift, isn't it?"

"More than ever." Dusk nodded, closing his eyes as if a great weight rested on his shoulders. "When I joined you and Layla's Bind, I think it started unleashing my buried rage. I used to be able to just stuff down everything I feel about my situation, my clan… my King. But with all of your emotions flooding me, plus Reginald in the Bind now working with a brand-new ability to shape-shift, it's pushing my Dragon to surface. Not to mention Layla's first shift tonight."

Layla stilled in Dusk and Adrian's arms at Dusk's revelation, that he had felt her shift tonight. She suddenly wondered what else he might have felt from her and Adrian's time together, and how much all of that might have caused his current state. But it was a question for another time, and as Layla reached up, smoothing her fingers through Dusk's hair again, he sighed heavily with his forehead still resting upon hers.

"Are you still able to fight your first shift, Dusk?" Adrian asked, his gaze intense.

"A little while longer." Dusk nodded, though it was tired, his voice quiet now. "But I don't know for how much more. My Dragon's just beneath the surface now… god, I can feel his breath on my neck…"

"Whose breath?" Layla frowned. "Your Dragon's?"

"No." Dusk shook his head quietly. "King Markus."

"Are you worried about receiving a summons from King Markus Ambrose if you shift?" Layla asked, finally realizing the depth of Dusk's worries from things he'd told her about his Lineage's Crystal King.

"Yes." Dusk spoke, opening his eyes and lifting his head so they could see each other, his gaze bleak. "King Markus already has ten good reasons to kill me to stop me becoming his rival – most of which he knows nothing about yet. If I shift, *really* shift… he's going to notice. I've lived a hundred and fifty years and never allowed myself to fully shift once. The longer a Dragon goes in life without shifting, the stronger their magic becomes when they finally do."

"By being able to prevent a full shift for so long, Dusk has practically ensured his magic is going to go ballistic once it finally happens, and be an intense challenge to King Markus." Adrian spoke softly to Layla. "It's like damming up a geyser. Watch out when it finally blows."

Layla blinked slowly, finally understanding as she looked back to Dusk. "Our emotions push your magic towards shifting. All of us, though the Bind… we're putting thousands of tons of pressure behind that trapped geyser, aren't we?"

"It's not your fault." Dusk kissed her lips, though his sigh was tired. "But it is proving tremendously difficult to fight, especially with all this stress right now." At last, Dusk heaved a sigh, and something in him seemed to clear. "Dammit. We need to get moving. Quindici's got Imogene down in the Guardhall and he's interrogating the shit out of her. We need to get Layla there so Imogene can speak to her before she passes out."

"We will." Adrian gripped Dusk's shoulder with a firm camaraderie. "But as soon as we have a moment, we are going to have a serious talk about all of this. It's long past time we started putting you first, Dusk. I'm sorry I didn't see it sooner."

"Is this how you feel, all the time?" Dusk spoke with a wry smile. "This rage like a goddamn volcano?"

"Mostly." Adrian gave a soft laugh, but there was something sad in his smile. The brothers shared a glance, deep with an understanding Layla didn't share. She didn't know the extent of their past hundred and fifty years together, everything they had helped each other with, all the ways they had fought. She suddenly felt like the one on the outside, looking in at something deeply precious.

"Come on." Adrian spoke gently as he cradled Dusk's head close to his, in a gesture so brotherly that it broke Layla's heart. "Tell us everything while we get dressed. Give Layla the run-down. Focus. We need you."

Dusk nodded briskly as he pulled back from Adrian at last. As he straightened with a deep breath, Layla saw him gather his brisk nature as Head Concierge back around himself like a well-known cloak, palming his wavy hair back into perfection once more. His sapphire eyes glanced upon Layla, but Dusk didn't apologize for anything he'd said or done. Honest to his bones, it included honesty with his emotions, and Dusk didn't gainsay anything he'd voiced.

But he was focused again, and that was how they needed him. Though for the first time, Layla wondered how long that focus might last, feeling like there was a lot more hidden beneath Dusk than he showed, more than perhaps he'd even let Adrian see over the years. For the first time, she wondered how long they had.

Before their Crystal Dragon finally shattered.

CHAPTER 11 – STORM

Dusk was finally calm and Layla turned, reaching for her clothes where they had fallen on the floor of the crystal bath-house. They were nothing special, just skinny jeans, a grey v-neck and a charcoal wrap sweater with her tall fawn boots. Though they were splashed with wet now, her casual clothes were comforting, and it was everything Layla hadn't known she needed. Dusk had brought clothing for Adrian also, trim grey slacks, a white shirt, and russet Oxfords, and he finally began speaking with his crisp no-bullshit Head Concierge attitude as Layla and Adrian pulled everything on.

"Your friends disappeared from the Waterfall Grotto around three hours ago, Layla, the place where I arranged their after-party." Dusk spoke as he watched them dress. "Their Guards were flooded with the equivalent of magical roofies – it's what Smoke Faunus magic does – but inundated with so much that we're still not certain a few of them will wake from the infirmary without a Purifier brought in, a special type of healer. Rake, Jenna, Lars, and Amalia fought back; they were far enough from the initial smoke-flood that they only got mildly dosed. The Furies fought hard and so did Rake, but Jenna and Lars got cut up pretty bad; they're still unconscious. Rake was cut up less; he was able to tell me what happened about an hour ago."

"Cut up?" Layla spoke as she sat on a wet chaise and zipped up her tall boots. "With talons, by a Dragon?"

"No. Branch-whips, like you'd get being drug through a forest canopy. Smoke Faunus are vicious slashers with those long branch-like hands of theirs." Dusk's dark gaze spoke volumes. "There were eight who busted into the Grotto – none of them Hotel employees. They escaped with Charlie, Celia, and Arron, we think they had access to a Nexus Realm. Quindici took our resident Smoke Faunus Imogene Cereste into custody, he's got her down in the Guardhall now and he and Rikyava have been interrogating her. But she asked for you, Layla. She won't talk until she can talk directly to you."

"Why me?" Layla frowned, trying to think through her fear. "Isn't it Adrian she'd want to talk to, if this is Crimson Circle related?"

"We're not entirely sure it is." Dusk's gaze was eloquent. "No one's mentioned the Circle, though Quindici's been adamant about asking on that point. Rake didn't hear it mentioned during the fight, either."

"Is it Hunter?" Layla's gut dropped as she stood, facing Dusk fully dressed now.

"From everything we've seen so far, Hunter works alone, so I doubt it." Dusk shook his head, a complex look on his face as he opened the crystal door to the bath-house and held it, gesturing Layla and Adrian out into the bright snowy morning. "It feels like Smoke Faunus retaliation for something. But gods if I can figure out what."

"I don't have any association with Smoke Faunus, and Imogene and I don't really even know each other." Layla glanced at Dusk as they stepped out onto the snowy path, their trio walking fast back towards the Hotel under a bright blue sky. "So why would Smoke Faunus take my friends?"

"I don't know." He glanced at her. "But maybe if she'll talk to you, we can find out."

They didn't say anything more as they moved at a brisk trot through the snowy gardens, making it to the Hotel and walking fast through the Yuletide crowds. The Hotel was still raging with a new kind

125

of party this morning, sensual breakfasts with decadent orgiastic events. But Layla had no time for any of it as she and Dusk headed quickly through it all.

Their entire walk, Adrian received astonished stares and provoked tirades of whispers and open mouths. Everyone knew the ex-Hotel Head, everyone knew he was a fugitive, and everyone was gaping as their trio gained the south wing and headed down the subterranean stairs to the Guardhall.

But they plowed through it all, down to Rikyava's domain, which was bustling like a kicked-up hornet's nest from the sudden emergency. Even though they startled to see Adrian, Guardsmen nodded to their trio as they passed, some saluting Adrian with a hand to the heart and a fierce clack of their bootheels. As Layla, Adrian, and Dusk marched through the Guard's catacombs and past the storehouses of weaponry, Layla saw arcane silver blades inscripted with runes being distributed to all hands.

"Silver?" She asked Dusk as they headed to the magical fight-halls. "Isn't that for werewolves?"

"It works against various types of deep-forest fae." Dusk answered, as he glanced at her with dark eyes. "Silver is caustic to Smoke Faunus. It won't kill them unless you stab the heart or decapitate them, but it gives them a nasty burn and makes them heal slow."

Reaching the end of the catacombs, Dusk gestured to a reinforced magical fight-hall to the right and Layla and Adrian pushed in through the rose quartz shielded door. What Layla saw inside made her stop with a sudden shock. On one wall of the quartz chamber, chains had been attached to a depression. From those chains dangled the Smoke Faunus Courtesan who normally ran their daily public *bacchanalios* orgy, Imogene Cereste.

Badly brutalized, scratches from knives ripped across Imogene's long, slender arms with their silver-bark mottling, weeping a silver sap-like blood. Her beautifully haunting face was bruised as if she'd been hit, her full red lips swollen. Silver sap-tears rolled down her high cheeks, her dark eyes mostly closed and her long eyelashes fluttering with exhaustion. Her cascades of silver hair were tangled around her corkscrewing ram's horns like she'd been yanked around, more silver sap streaking down her shaggy legs and hooves.

No fewer than thirty Guards in crimson lingered in the hall, leaning against the walls, straddling chairs and watching. All had an assortment of runic silver weapons bristling about their persons, some even holding long silver spears covered in runes. Wearing her Guard uniform, Rikyava stood ten feet from the chained Imogene, her arms crossed and a furious wrath on her lovely face. Her eyes had bled to a bloody crimson, drips of blood leaking down her cheeks as a nimbus of blood-droplets whirled around her.

Rikyava's Blood Dragon magic, raised to such catastrophic heights she couldn't contain it.

The entire scene flooded Layla with horror. She didn't know what Imogene had done to merit such abuse – she was a treasured Courtesan of the Hotel family. But even as she took in the scene, Layla saw none of the interrogation had been done by the Guard. Before the chained Smoke Faunus, Quindici DaPonti stood with a wrathful stillness, dressed in his vest and shirtsleeves from the ball. His sleeves were rolled to his elbows, his hands and forearms splattered in silver sap. In his left hand, he held a sickled knife covered in runes. The handle was leather but the blade was pure silver, and as he crossed his arms, setting the point of the knife against his chin, Layla saw his skin sizzle.

Quindici didn't move, staring at the bound Smoke Faunus and tapping the silver blade coldly against his burning skin.

"Jesus." Adrian swore softly as their trio moved into the hall, shutting the door. Rikyava glanced over as a number of Guards turned, the Head Guardswoman's gaze going from wrath to surprise at seeing Adrian. Rikyava said nothing as Layla, Adrian, and Dusk moved into the hall, though her bleak red eyes said it all. Her Guardsmen and women were similarly hard, parting for Layla, Dusk, and their former Hotel Head as they moved forward to access the spectacle.

"What's her crime?" Adrian spoke softly as he stepped abreast of the Vampire. "Please tell me it merits this kind of severity, Quinn."

"Poisoning." Quindici answered coolly. "Betrayal of Hotel Guests. Betrayal of Hotel Employees. Associate to Abduction. Associate to Murder."

"Murder?" Adrian growled softly. "Has someone died from the attack?"

"Chief Guardsman Benvolio Duetti died in the infirmary from smoke over-inhalation twenty minutes ago." Quindici responded levelly. "Imogene wasn't directly involved in the raid, but she was a lookout outside the Grotto, and kept the Guards there heavily dosed with smoke until Ms. Price's friends were captured. Hence, the Associate to Murder charge."

Quindici glanced to Adrian, but his austere face held no emotion; not anger, wrath, nor fury. He held only the same coolness with which Layla had seen him manage the Hotel this past month, the same calculation with which he did everything. Rikyava had no sap-blood on her; all the Guardsmen had clean hands. Only Quindici's were coated silver from what had clearly been his interrogation. As he glanced at Layla with his onyx eyes so perfectly calm and his russet hair still so perfectly coiffed, but his white hands so gruesomely filthy, Layla finally understood him.

The Barone Quindici DaPonti was not a creature of passion or emotion. He could brutalize one of their own Hotel family members and feel nothing. He was able to dissociate feelings from action, to calculate any situation no matter how heated passions got. Because deep down inside, his passions didn't touch him. Suddenly, it wasn't just Quindici's grave-cool magic flowing over Layla's skin that made her shudder, it was knowing they were aligned with someone far darker than she had ever suspected.

Knowing that Adrian was aligned with a bad guy – for reasons she still didn't understand.

"Ms. Price, at last." Quindici spoke as their gazes connected. Reaching over to a rose quartz table, he set the knife down among what Layla saw was a gruesome collection of torture implements – all silver and thoroughly etched with runes, most of them sap-coated. "Perhaps you will succeed where my efforts have failed. Something blocks her mind from me; I cannot access it. And she will not loose her tongue for all the pain in the Spanish Inquisition."

"You can read minds?" Layla blinked, her Dragon coiling up inside her with a nasty growl, fangs bared at that information. She suddenly recalled their kiss in his office – and now wondered if that had all been a manipulation for some strange reason, maybe even a result of him reading her mind.

"I can read minds of lesser magic, yes. Usually." Quindici's onyx gaze was eloquent as he waved a hand at Imogene, her lean beauty sagging painfully in her manacles, though her dark eyes were open now, watchful. "I am curious what she has to say to you, since she says she will speak only with *the Royal Dragon Bind*."

Though Layla's gut dropped further at everything she was learning about the Master Vampire who was supposedly their ally, she took a deep breath, turning and facing their resident Smoke Faunus. Imogene watched Layla with a dark intelligence, though neither said anything, the Faunus breathing hard from her interrogations.

"I'm here, Imogene. Talk." Layla crossed her arms at her chest, staring the woman down.

"As if it was that simple…" Imogene Cereste laughed in her beautiful alto, though her voice was grating as if she'd spent a lot of time screaming in the past hours. Sap-blood trickled from her mouth and she looked pale as if she'd suffered tremendous blood loss. She'd been chained up over a drain in the floor, sap trickling down her shaggy hooves down through the grate.

Layla tore her gaze from the blood-drain, making herself meet Imogene's dark eyes again. "It is simple. Tell me who took my friends, and maybe you'll get to live."

"I'm already dead." Imogene laughed, then coughed in pain. "You heard them. Associate to Murder. No one lives charged with something like that. The Hotel Owners will make certain of it."

"So why do it?" Layla pushed. "Why abduct my friends and risk yourself?"

"Because I had no choice." Imogene spoke sadly, a bleak wistfulness taking her dark eyes. "What my High Priest asks for, he receives. He took your friends because he wants to meet you, Dragon Bind, and the new *nullax* risen among you. Your friends are collateral to ensure you'll come to him. They will not be harmed… unless you don't come."

"So this guy you serve took my friends just to make sure I'd come talk to him?" Layla narrowed her eyes on Imogene, but the Smoke Faunus' eyes were closed now, her head resting back against the wall as if she were about to pass out.

"Not just you," Imogene breathed tiredly. "Him, also. The *nullax*."

"What is a *nullax*?" Layla glanced to Adrian. "Some kind of Vampire?"

"It's a Storm Dragon." Watching the barely-conscious Imogene, Adrian had set his hands to his hips, his straight brows furrowed. "But not unlike a Vampire. They're mystics of a religious sect called the White Chalice that used to be a problem in France, Britain, and Scandinavia. Their sect developed a method of draining magic from others by line-breeding Royal Storm Dragons with Vampire Revenants, creating a talent called *nullax*. The Chalice used their *nullax*-power to break strong Blood and Storm Dragons from prominent clans throughout Europe for many thousands of years."

"What does a Storm Dragon religious sect have to do with the Smoke Faunus?" Layla frowned, not understanding.

"The Faunus clans in Europe and Scandinavia used to have an alliance with the White Chalice." Rikyava stepped forward now, horror upon her lovely face as she stared at Imogene. "The Faunus believed the Chalice were the strongest group that could protect their forests. In exchange, the Chalice used Faunus clans to seduce enemies and capture them. But that's not been the case for hundreds of years since my uncle King Huttr Erdhelm and Queen Justine Toulet combined forces and routed the Chalice out."

"Apparently, they weren't routed thoroughly enough." Quindici spoke, something in his cold aura sharpening beside Layla. "One sect must have survived. Tell us, traitor, do you serve the White Chalice?"

"Yes." Imogene spoke softly, her beaten beauty tired now rather than defiant. "I must send the new *nullax* to my High Priest, and the Dragon Bind also."

"Who is this new *nullax* the White Chalice mystics wish to recruit?" Quindici was frigid now in his serene calm.

"He is strong." Imogene raised her head, barely able to look at Quindici in her flickering fatigue. "My High Priest feels his awakening power, like the High Priests of old."

"Who? Give us a name." Quindici spoke quietly, dark and vicious.

Just then, the door to the vaulted hall chunked open, and Layla turned to see Luke being escorted in by two of Rikyava's senior Guardsmen. He still wore his dark green suit from the evening, his bright emerald eyes red-rimmed as if he'd been crying. As his gaze met Layla's he moved forward, not even glancing at anyone else in the room. She was already moving to him. She was in his arms, and his arms were around her, holding her tight. She felt a furious tremor in him, and just before she closed her eyes, swathed in Luke's clean lemon-balm scent, she saw the bloodstone pendant upon his chest seethe with vicious twists of red in the green.

"Layla, thank god you're ok!" Luke breathed by her ear.

"Luke, what happened?" She choked, gripping him close with her hands clutched in his slender suit jacket.

"I don't know. I wasn't there." His breath hitched as he spoke, and she felt that tremor of fury in him again. "I was pissed after your Courtesan's auction and went back to my rooms, I didn't go to the after-party Dusk arranged for us. I wasn't there when Celia, Arron, and Charlie were taken. I should have been—"

"The *nullax* rages…" Imogene sighed from her chains, interrupting them.

"What?" Layla turned slowly, feeling like she'd just fallen into a horror movie.

"Him." Imogene's dark eyes were open now, watching Luke. "His fury drinks magic… just like his ancestors."

"What the fuck?" Luke growled, bristling as he tucked Layla into his arm and turned to face the chained-up Smoke Faunus. "If you know something about my magical bloodlines, you'd better spill it. Now."

"Blood and thunder," Imogene breathed softly. "Blood and storms. Blood of the High Priests come to its pinnacle… who would have thought to find a *nullax* hidden in the Human Realm?"

But before she could say anything more, Imogene's long eyelashes fluttered, her dark eyes rolling up in her head as she passed out cold.

Everyone turned, staring at Luke. Layla watched him bristle as he became the center of attention at this astounding new information. And then, she felt a searing shock of energy pass through Luke, so fast and hard that it zapped her where she stood touching him. With a gasp, Layla pulled away, feeling like she'd just been shocked by an ungrounded power cord. As she stared at Luke, watching him simmer with fury, she saw the bloodstone on his chest seethe with such hard currents she thought it might explode. Luke's emerald eyes flashed with power just like she'd seen the night before, magic lancing through his eyes like lightning as it rolled from his skin like thunder.

It was then that Layla realized Luke had Dragon-magic.

And more than that – he was a Storm Dragon.

CHAPTER 12 – RISK

Back in her apartment, Layla was getting dressed for dinner, Adrian with her. Pinning her curls over one shoulder, she caught Adrian's gaze in the mirrors and he gave a reassuring smile as he dressed also, though his eyes were tight. The past twenty-four hours felt surreal as Layla dressed in a gown of cream silk that cascaded down her body in sleek drifts, moving like feathers as she adjusted her mother Mimi's diamond and pink topaz jewelry set at her throat and ears. With a corset of cross-wrapped silk that dipped low in back, the gown was simple yet stunning, accentuating the wintertime paleness of Layla's skin and the darkness of her hair. But she was actually pale tonight, riven through with worry as her Dragon coiled tight inside her. Adrian was also, and Layla could almost feel what he was thinking through their Bind.

That tonight could break their lives if bad decisions were made.

After Imogene had passed out and Layla had been shocked by Luke, Adrian had quietly called an end to the interrogation. No one had gainsaid Adrian as he'd disbanded everyone and called for a formal dinner to discuss matters. The Guard had taken their unconscious prisoner to a secure room and Rikyava had summoned Infirmary crew. The Red Letter Hotel would have a trial for Imogene later, but Layla, Adrian, and the rest had decisions to make before that.

As Adrian moved by, adjusting one French cuff, Layla watched him, thinking about everything that had happened in the past day. Though so much had changed between them now that she had fully shifted into her Dragon and they'd also had sex for the first time, so many things were still the same. Her heart pounded faster suddenly as she watched him move around her apartment like it was home to him. Adrian's dinner-jacket was a sleek cream silk matching Layla's gown, beautifully paired with a dark navy shirt sans tie. Navy slacks and black oxfords completed his ensemble, with stunning diamond cufflinks. Layla could just see the edge of a gold talisman on his left wrist as he adjusted his French cuffs.

Adrian's eyes were a deep aqua as he watched her also, his straight black brows knit above his achingly high cheekbones. Moving to Layla's bar by her vaulted windows as the winter sun set over the snowy gardens, Adrian uncapped her crystal bottle of bourbon and poured two tumblers. As he extended one to her, his talisman showed, an ornate men's cuff of twisted gold, copper, and platinum writhing around his left wrist. He'd retrieved it from Riad Rhakvir before they left, and Layla had missed it in her shock. It was a Dragon, mimicking the coiling of his red, gold, and black tattoo up his forearm but done in a three-inch-wide piece. Set into the design were rubies, garnets, citrine, and topaz – the eyes of the Dragon a burning blue topaz the same color as Adrian's own eyes.

Moving forward, Layla accepted her bourbon. Reaching down, she touched his cuff, turning his wrist over so she could admire it fully. "That is one bombastic piece, Batman."

"It's my talisman, I've used it since my magics opened as a child." Adrian smiled wistfully, gazing at it also. "It's a Rhakvir family heirloom, only allowed to be worn by a strong Royal. It keeps my magic bound to a five-foot radius, mostly. If someone isn't close to me, they can't feel my fire and I can't be traced by magical means. It keeps me safe in times like these. It's what I wore the whole time I was on the lam, changing visages and hiding in safe houses to escape detection..."

"I was wondering how you were able to keep your magic on

lockdown while you were running, and how you were so confident the Crimson Circle couldn't trace you here." Layla's fingers strayed from the talisman, sliding up Adrian's forearm beneath his sleeve, admiring his Dragon-tattoo. Setting aside his bourbon and hers, Adrian obliged her, unbinding his French cuff and shrugging off his jacket so she could see the entire tattoo. Layla traced Adrian's snarling Desert Dragon with slow fingers, coiling like a serpent up his forearm. "You've never told me what this is for. Does it have magical properties like your cuff?"

"It's a symbol of my dominance. And yes, it is somewhat magical." Adrian watched her trace his ink, something darkly thoughtful in his gaze. "Desert Dragons have a tradition of inking our left forearm when we ascend to Clan First. My tattoo was done by a Marquist – a special kind of Twilight Lineage that can ink shape-shifters. No matter how much I shift visages, when I come back to my original human form, the tattoo comes back also. If I ever ascend to become King of the Desert Dragons, I'd take a matching one on my right forearm. Though there's not much chance of that."

"Why not?" Pausing, Layla glanced up at him.

"Because our King was turned to stone by a curse. And he's never been replaced."

"What do you mean?" Layla blinked, his answer unexpected. She'd thought Adrian would say the Desert Dragon King was a fierce beast like the Crystal Dragon King Markus Ambrose. "Like... turned to stone, stone?"

"Stone, stone." Adrian agreed with a wry smile, rolling his sleeve back down and affixing his cufflink, then donning his jacket. Turning, he claimed Layla's bourbon and handed it to her, then took up his own. "King Lethou Mathii is still alive inside the prison of his stone body. His power rushes out, wild, attacking anyone who gets near. No Desert Dragon has ever defeated him, and as he's *stone* now, he's indestructible to Desert magic these past two thousand years. We built a temple around him, out in the middle of the Sahara. But our Lineage is ruled by a Regent now. I might eventually rise to become Regent, but I doubt anyone will ever figure out a way to best King Lethou Mathii. So I'll probably never take a second tattoo."

"How are you so calm right now?" Layla murmured as she stared at Adrian's wrist, even though his tattoo and talisman were hidden now. "My friends abducted by these White Chalice zealots and Luke maybe having their magic? The Crimson Circle after you? Me binding Dusk and Reginald, and oh right, I'm also a Courtesan now. And Hunter, still out there somewhere...?"

"I don't know exactly," Adrian's lips quirked in a sober smile as he gazed at her. "Once I would have been wound tight as a tornado about all of it. But I feel myself changing, Layla. Our Bind is changing me, as much as it's changing Dusk. I still think and plan like me, and my magic still has my own flavor, but I have a greater perspective now. It's as if I get to see the world through your eyes, and Dusk's – even Reginald's. It's... starting to give me an understanding I lacked before."

"You were so tender with Dusk today, even though you were so irate with him for the bidding war, and his time with me this past month," Layla breathed, watching Adrian. "What changed?"

"I just... I saw him, Layla." Adrian's face was complex as he downed his bourbon. "I saw him through your eyes as well as my own this time. How ruined he was; how close he is to breaking. Though we're not blood-kin, Dusk is my family and I understand him; I love him. But in that moment," Adrian's brows knit, and Layla saw something new in his eyes, some deep inner knowledge, "I *loved* him. He's my best friend, he's my comrade-in-arms... I'm still processing what I felt. But I suddenly realized that despite my raging jealousies, there was nothing I wouldn't do for him. It's not just you that needs my strength right now. Dusk needs me to be strong. Because he's breaking."

"What happens when the crystal breaks?" Layla spoke quietly.

"I don't know." Adrian inhaled a deep breath, letting it out slow. "But for a lot of reasons, it's a very bad idea right now. Your shift I could help moderate. But Dusk's… I don't think anyone could help moderate his full shift when it finally comes. Not even his own King." Adrian set his empty bourbon glass aside on the bar. "Are you ready to go to dinner?"

"Yes." Layla nodded, downing her bourbon also. "But aren't you worried about being discovered tonight? About your whereabouts being passed to the Crimson Circle?"

"Deeply." Something moved through Adrian, some dark fear that Layla could feel, coiling through his Dragon. "But the risk is worth it. I need to be here, for you, for Dusk. For all of us."

At that, Adrian went silent. Watching her, something complex moved through his eyes. Moving to her, he wrapped his strong arms around her, setting his lips to her temple and stroking his long fingers over her back in smooth, languid patterns. Layla suddenly realized it was something Dusk might have done, and on the heels of that thought was that Adrian was acquiring Dusk's grounding. If that was happening, then Dusk was probably acquiring Adrian's tempestuousness, which would explain why he was breaking recently.

Relaxing her cheek onto Adrian's shoulder, Layla sighed. He didn't say anything, just held her, and it was everything Layla needed. It was strange, relaxing into Adrian in a way she would normally have done with Dusk, letting him smooth her worries with the simplicity of his touch. Yet as Layla breathed into it, feeling Adrian's magics moving in warm, gentle patterns around her, she realized it was perfect.

Drawing back, she gazed up at him. He watched her with

something tender yet strong in his eyes; determined. Reaching one hand up, he stroked her neck, and Layla lifted a hand to touch his fingers. His hand stilled beneath hers as his eyes lit with a golden fire.

"Is this risk worth it?" Layla asked, needing to know, needing his strength to bolster her. "You being here?"

"It is." Adrian spoke softly as he gazed deep into her eyes. "I want to be here for you, Layla. I want to be here *with* you, not on the run. Not tending a hundred empires against a shadowy enemy. When I was on the run these past weeks, I found the further I got from you, the more my heart screamed. I don't care if it's a risk. I don't care if Crimson Circle eyes and ears are all around. My place is here with you. And I didn't know that until I traveled halfway around the world… and found that no place was home to me anymore. Except when I'm by your side."

It was everything Layla had been wishing for these past months. Yet as she gazed up at him, she trembled, finding herself more afraid than ever as that black pit tried to open up inside her. "But if you're far away from me, you're safe from the Crimson Circle – and whatever other trouble I attract, like these White Chalice mystics."

"If I'm far away from you," Adrian countered softly, "I'm dead, Layla. Maybe not dead in the flesh, but dead inside. You are my mate. You are the woman I love. It's not just the Bind; it's my heart. I want to be your partner. I love you, Layla. It's my place to be here, protecting you."

"Adrian…" Layla gazed up at him, flooded with tenderness. Her heart swelled and the combined emotions of the day were suddenly too much. Tears pricked her eyes and Adrian saw it, or perhaps felt it. His gaze softened to an aching beauty, the same look he'd given her long ago when he'd stood outside her garden window in the deep summer midnight. As Layla gasped, feeling her heart break at the thought that something might happen to him, that tender beauty in Adrian's eyes deepened.

"I can't lose you, Layla." He spoke as he twined his fingers through hers. "But if I keep running, I will lose you. More deeply than if the Crimson Circle wrenched you from my cold, dead hands."

Layla knew it was true. If Adrian kept running, their Bind might live but their love would die. Lifting up, Layla set her lips to his, pouring out her heart. As she did, a tender wave of heat and light passed through her, spilling from her lips in through Adrian's. He inhaled as they kissed, feeling it, breathing in her emotions and magic. With a tender growl, Adrian wound her close in his arms and Layla touched his beloved face with her fingertips as he delved deeper into their kiss; hotter. Her eyelashes fluttered as she felt their magics whirl in a rush of heat and energy. Her breath was fast and her heart faster as Adrian finally broke their kiss, lingering. As he gazed down, she saw his eyes blaze with every color, burning hot and fierce.

"You are my mate, Layla Price." He growled, with basso tones in his voice as he nuzzled her nose. "I will not abandon you. Ever. I hate thinking about other men being with you. It rips me up to think I may never be your one and only. But I have to endure it, and I will. You are a woman unlike any I've ever met, and it demands for me to be a better man than I've ever been. I don't run from a challenge, or from danger, and I won't run from any of this. Our Bind is protection, for all of us. I won't screw that up, not like I did before."

"What about the Crimson Circle?" Layla asked, worry still moving in her despite everything. "And these arcane Storm Dragon mystics? Do you think they're connected?"

"I don't know." Adrian drew a deep breath, the blaze in his eyes simmering. "My hunch is that these things are connected, but I'll be damned if I can see it. But I've only been a Hotel Owner sixteen years,

Layla, I don't know anything about how the Crimson Circle work or who they may get to wash their dirty laundry – or even who they are. Some people Quindici suspects of being Circle have held ownership in the Hotel since its inception. They've seen empires rise and fall. I'm nothing compared to that."

"But you're on their radar as a threat now, Adrian," Layla breathed, "otherwise they wouldn't have resurrected some arcane Hotel law to try and get you murdered. How long until they start caring about me and Dusk, Reginald, the Madame, or Rikyava? From Imogene's words, people in scary places are caring about me already, like that White Chalice High Priest."

"That's because people are beginning to recognize how powerful you are," Adrian reached up, stroking her cheek as his eyes became fierce. "Progressing in battle-magics, learning to become a Courtesan in record time, trained by a Royal Siren. Magics that compel the strongest of any Lineage to do your bidding. It's a *La Femme Nikita* combination."

"I'm not a *femme fatale*, Adrian."

"Not yet." Adrian spoke as he kissed her gently. "But you might be."

That stopped her, and Layla blinked at Adrian. He watched her, his aqua eyes fierce, and she realized he believed his words. He believed she was going to become some sort of super-spy with bedroom talents and status that could get her in places no other spy could possibly access. It was too much for Layla suddenly. A cold spear chilled her, her Dragon coiling up into that tight fangs-out position deep within her gut as the black void threatened.

But Layla couldn't go there right now. Her friends were missing, and she couldn't allow herself to be mind-blind tonight. Kissing Adrian's lips one last time, she stepped back, taking a deep breath.

Adrian lifted her hand, kissing her fingers, watching her with his stunning aqua eyes. Layla watched him back, feeling even more nervous than before.

"Are you ready?" He asked – about far more than just dinner.

"No." Layla breathed, shaking her head. "I feel like I just want to run away."

"I'm right here with you." Adrian spoke gently as he lifted her hand to his arm, ready to escort her. "This situation isn't more dangerous than twenty different scrapes I've been in before."

"You're lying." Layla spoke, knowing the truth. "You have more to lose than you've ever had, Adrian. Maybe you can hide your fear from everyone else, but I feel it. You just don't want to break, so you won't even allow a glimmer of fear in your mind. But I feel your heart. You care. More now than you ever have before. And for the first time, your enemies have something they really will try to use against you. Your love."

That sobered him. Adrian paused, then turned to face her. His energy was fierce, the set of his tall, lean frame ferocious in a way she'd only seen a few times. As he simmered with power, Layla watched his eyes flash with a dark passion. Suddenly, he released her hand from his arm. Before she knew what he was doing, he had slipped his talisman from his wrist, setting it to a gilded table beside Layla's apartment doors.

Adrian's power flared through the room like a seething fire. Layla gasped, inhaling scorched jasmine on the wind of heat that swirled up all around her. A blast of crimson-aqua flame surged out around them, and though it burned nothing, the entire room suddenly flared hotter. Roiling with power as if all the sands of the Sahara could catch fire, Adrian's eyes blazed every color as a deep growl poured from his throat. Layla gasped, rocked by his passion so suddenly unleashed. As he lifted her hand, curling it around his arm again, she saw the ferociousness of Adrian's Dragon in his face and eyes; in the power of his sculpted shoulders and lean height. Turning his head, Adrian laid the full force of those terrible eyes upon her as he spoke.

"Let the Crimson Circle see my love and the power it gives me. I'm done hiding. Their spies can tell them I was here – and that *I'm the hunter now*. Anyone they try to use against us will be scorched by my winds. The hours of their sands have drawn short before the dawn of our Bind."

Layla blinked at Adrian's words, an echo of the language her nemesis Hunter had once used, the Royal Dragon Bind who had abducted her at Samhain. But this wasn't her enemy speaking, this was her mate. And suddenly, Layla saw the power inside Adrian. He wasn't the strongest Royal Dragon out there, he wasn't the most wealthy. He wasn't the largest in his Dragon-form, and he wasn't the most diabolical.

But a torrent of ferocious passion roared through Adrian's veins, and feeling it, Layla finally understood why everyone she'd met in the Twilight Realm considered Adrian a force to be reckoned with. He was a blaze, an inferno of passion and lance-sharp intent. Righteousness roared from his marrow, and in his moment of ferocious determination, Layla felt all his fears banished.

It bolstered her, flooding her as they stood together. Drawing a deep breath, Layla felt her energy lifted by his, rushing up into a tower of heat and light through their Bind. Suddenly, she was ready for whatever they might face in the coming days and weeks – good, bad, or terrible. She was ready for whomever might see them and for the consequences. She was ready to stand strong with him against their enemies, no matter where those enemies hid.

She was ready to be Adrian's mate – and to show the world how powerful they could be.

Adrian saw her become steady, and gave a regal nod. As a knock came at the door, Layla already knew who it was as Adrian reached out, opening one door. Dusk stood beyond, resplendent in a dark navy suit with cream lapels that made the color of his eyes bright like a noontime sky, a flash of iridescence flowing through his artfully-sculpted hair. As he stepped inside, Layla saw the same power and determination flowing through him from their Bind, brightening his fierce gaze and putting a briskness in his step.

Twenty Guards in crimson flanked Layla's doors along with six Red Giants – no one was taking any chances now with security – but as Dusk moved inside, shutting the door behind him, he was more ferocious than all of them. Layla felt a hard rush of crystal power surge from him like a wave of river-water as he glanced to her and Adrian.

"Are you both ready to go down?" He spoke with a sub-basso growl like he was ready for a fight. "I've already escorted Luke down to the Waterfall Grotto with Rikyava. Quindici's on his way. The Grotto is guarded for the night; Rikyava's most trustworthy, the ones that are still healthy at least. When the soirée is done, I'll take you back to the portal, Adrian."

"I'm not going back to Riad Rhakvir, Dusk." Adrian spoke firmly. "I'm not going back into hiding. This issue demands my full attention until it's resolved. I go where Layla goes."

Though Dusk eyeballed him, he didn't gainsay Adrian's words. "Then let's go."

With a brisk nod, Dusk turned, throwing open the gilded doors and leading the way out into the hall.

CHAPTER 13 – FALLING

The Waterfall Grotto was a natural formation on the Red Letter Hotel Paris grounds, augmented by magic. As Layla, Dusk, Adrian, and their retinue of Guards came to a break in the winter-barren trees, the snowy path suddenly ended at an ornately-fashioned door formed entirely of flowing water. Beyond the door was a dome created by water flowing down in a constant fall. None of it was frozen despite the chill evening. Fractal patterns flowed through the water as it cascaded down, creating pillars and arches like an ancient Roman rotunda.

The winter sky was clear, the twilight darkening to vivid blues and purples as the stars emerged above. With a nod to the Guards to remain, Dusk stepped to the wall of water, which parted at his approach. As Layla entered the Waterfall Grotto after Dusk, a calming sensation filled her. A smell of clear springs and ozone hit her with a refreshing spray as they stepped beneath the waterfall's curtain, only touched by a few drops as water cascaded all around them.

Stone stairs covered in flowering mosses led down into the grotto, and as Layla gazed up, she watched water flow from the center of the dome to every buttressed edge, pouring down in fanciful patterns and cascades. In the middle of the mossy grotto sat an enormous natural pool, at the center of which five massive pillars of twisting water cascaded up in glossy columns, the water converging far above to become the domed ceiling. The sound of rushing water filled the space as they descended the stone stairs. Winter held no court here, tiers of thick moss and blooming flowers devouring the lower levels, the grotto warm with mist.

As they arrived, Layla saw nearly everyone invited to this meeting was already sitting at an arrangement of velvet settees, a massive formal dining-table set up at the center of the space. Gilded floor-candelabra were lit all around, fireflies swirling in the dusk. A string quartet played music near a bank of ferns, but as Layla glanced over, she saw the musicians wore crimson uniforms of the Hotel Guard. As she stepped down the final set of stairs, Dusk escorting her on left and Adrian on her right, Layla saw the attendees turn.

Every person watched them come. Employees of the Hotel who were trusted friends stepped forward to clasp arms with Adrian and kiss his cheeks – Rake André with a pleased smile and looking amazingly recovered, dressed in a cream suit jacket that fit his lean height to perfection. Amalia DuFane, dressed in a somber blue gown, buzzing in a tender way as she seized Layla's cheeks and gave her a teensy shake. And though they looked pale, Layla's friends from Concierge Services, the statuesque blonde Furies Jenna Ostlheim and Lars Kurs came up to exchange Parisian kisses. Clad in a lavender gown with a sweetheart bodice that made the most of her strong Swedish curves, Rikyava Andersen kissed Dusk's cheeks, then embraced Layla.

"Finally! I was just about to send a second cadre of Guards up to your room!"

"How are things here, Rikyava?" Dusk spoke, gazing around and noting drinks in every hand and plates of small bites decorating the table.

"Fine." Rikyava nodded, glancing around also. "We're still missing a few people, though."

Layla saw they were missing Quindici DaPonti, along with the Madame. The new Hotel Head Lulu Duvall was not aware of this meeting, close as Quindici suspected she was to the Hotel Board and possibly the Crimson Circle. Everyone looked tense, though they were trying to appear casual. Energy from different magical Lineages hummed through the Grotto as everyone gazed upon Adrian, knowing what he was risking to come here.

But then Layla's gaze found Luke. Resplendent in a slim charcoal jacket and pants with an emerald shirt and paisley emerald pocket square, Luke stood alone by the central pool of the Grotto, his green eyes tight and his dark brows knit in a complex gaze. Layla saw him square his shoulders, drawing up tall as her glance found him. With a bitter quirk of his lips, he drew a breath and stepped towards her. As he neared, people around Layla parted. Walking up, he pinned her with his emerald gaze, and Layla felt Luke's tempestuous magic rush out in a wave of crackling intensity. But before that storm-energy could find Layla, a hot wind matched it – Adrian thrusting Luke's energy back.

"Touch her with your storms and feel my burn, young drake." Adrian growled hotly, bristling as he stepped bodily in front of Layla so Luke couldn't touch her.

"Who the fuck are you to give me ultimatums?" Luke snarled back, a vicious Irish heat flashing in his eyes with a burst of lightning.

"I'm her mate." Adrian spoke in a low tone, as his magic achieved a dangerous stillness. "And it's my duty to protect her."

Even though they'd seen each other down in the Guardhall, it was technically the first time Adrian and Luke were meeting for real. But as Adrian's magic went into a terrible stillness like the eye of a hurricane, everything inside Layla went on disastrously high alert. She suddenly recalled Luke's interactions with John LeVeque back in Seattle, and how much of a bad impression Adrian and Luke had made on each other right from the first. Power raged between the two men now, Luke's forest-green bloodstone writhing hard with red and gold as magic cascaded off him, Adrian's dark silence intensified as a biting wind began to curl around them like a tornado just starting to funnel.

As their magic faced off, Luke's green eyes brightened in a hot fury, flashing. "You're him, aren't you? Adrian fucking Rhakvir, billionaire Dragon asshole. In the flesh."

"Luke Murphy." Adrian spoke in a cold wrath as his eyes blistered with red now in the aqua. "Not a pleasure to meet you. Nor was it the first time."

"Adrian." Stepping in, Layla laid a hand on Adrian's arm. She felt him shudder almost as if he'd been in a trance, rising up to protect her in a red rage. But Layla couldn't imagine why he was on such high alert trying to protect her from Luke. At her intervention, Dusk slid forward, and Layla felt a hard wall of crystal build between the two drakes. But even Dusk formed his wall carefully, eyeballing Luke and Adrian as if the standoff between them was far more scary than even Layla knew.

But as Dusk's wall went up between them, it was like the searing connection between Adrian and Luke was suddenly cut. With a deep inhalation, the power in Luke seemed to settle and the air around him ceased to crackle, his bloodstone pendant slowing its mad currents. His gaze breaking from Adrian's, Luke glanced at Layla. Stepping forward, he reached out as if to take her hands – and was immediately blocked by Dusk's outstretched hand.

"Not until we discuss what you are." Dusk spoke quietly. "I'm sorry, Luke. Please understand that you might be a danger to Layla right now."

"Sure." Layla watched Luke contain himself with a deep breath, nodding tersely. But as Layla stared at him, amazed to now know what he and Dusk had been talking about all these weeks, Luke held her gaze – a sad quirk to his lips that twisted Layla's heart.

"So. You're a Dragon." Layla spoke, aware that everyone in the hall was watching. "Maybe a Storm Dragon."

"I'm sorry I didn't tell you earlier." Luke spoke as he held her gaze. "I didn't even know I had magical blood until your Dragon attacked me in Seattle. Turns out, I have a number of different Dragon bloodlines warring within me. All awake now."

"What about your parents—" Layla began.

"They don't know, and I'd appreciate if it stays that way." Luke held her gaze. "They're human, Layla. Just human."

"Luke's bloodlines were latent." Rikyava spoke as she moved to Luke's side, as if protecting him. "I traced his ancestry, and his most recent Twilight ancestor was four generations back in Ireland, a British Isles Blood Dragon. But there have been others. A Swedish Blood Dragon six generations ago. A French Royal Storm Dragon ten generations back. And, unfortunately… a White Chalice Storm Dragon High Priest, I discovered today after Imogene's interrogation. Sixteen generations back."

"Chalice blood runs strong, and infernally deep."

A smooth voice entered the conversation, and Layla looked up to see the Associate Hotel Head Quindici DaPonti descending the stone steps with Madame Etienne Voulouer on his arm. Madame Voulouer was resplendent in a gold and tan leopard taffeta ballgown, Quindici tall and sexily haunting in a dark blood-red suit with a black silk shirt framing all that pale Vampire skin. Onyx and gold rings glittered on his long fingers as he escorted the Madame down, matching his dark, clever eyes as he scanned the gathering. Sweeping forward, the Madame clasped Adrian's hands with tears shining in her feline tiger eyes as she kissed his cheeks. She was quiet as she greeted the rest of the company, while Quindici turned to face Adrian.

"Hotel Head." The Vampire spoke pleasantly, emotionless. "Shall we sit for dinner?"

"Indeed." Adrian nodded, some accord passing between the two men.

It was not lost on anyone that Quindici had ceded his authority in this gathering to Adrian. As the Vampire beckoned to the table and everyone moved over, selecting seats, Quindici took a place at the side of the table, leaving Adrian the table's head with Layla seated to his right. Dusk settled on Layla's other side, while Luke took a seat next to the Madame and Rikyava on the opposite side of the table.

Dinner was served by the Guards from the string quartet, who went promptly back to playing after everyone settled. The meal was opulent, with everything from lobster fettuccine to Kobe beef, to an edible dragon-sculpture made from tropical fruits only found in the Twilight Realm. Rake mixed drinks, and they were enjoyed, though a simmering tension still lay unaddressed in the assembly. Even the Vampire filled a small plate, having Kobe beef and a helping of fruit. He relished a cocktail Rake made with a blood-red color – though when Layla smelled it, she realized it was only grenadine, not blood. As everyone was finally set, a quiet tension took the table, only the sound of clinking cutlery and falling water heard for a time.

Someone needed to start this insane conversation they were all about to have, and Layla figured she might as well. Glancing at Luke, she took a deep drink of her cocktail, then set it down. But before she could say anything, it was as if Adrian read her mind, speaking up from the head of the table in a resonant baritone that smote all ears.

"So you're the descendant of a White Chalice High Priest, and they abducted your friends to get you to come join them." Adrian's gaze was hard as it pinned Luke, a bitter smile curling his lips. "I should have known Layla's Bind wouldn't attract weakness. Or humans."

"What's that supposed to mean?" Luke's gaze locked to Adrian's, intensity spiking from him in a crackle of energy once more. At its rise, a whirl of scalding wind rushed out from Adrian. Magic crashed between the two men for the second time tonight and people pulled back as a painful sensation blistered the air. But as Luke and Adrian's gazes locked, Layla had a feeling their battle wasn't exactly about her. Putting a gentle but restraining hand to Luke's shoulder, Rikyava's lavender gaze went to Adrian and Layla saw something pass between them. Setting his jaw, Adrian took a deep breath, then calmed his fierce winds – allowing Luke's energy to settle as Adrian's pulled back.

"Easy, Adrian." Dusk spoke with a warning in his voice, and it was only then that Layla realized he'd subtly built a crystal shield again between both men. "We don't know which way Luke's magic will settle yet. He might be a *nullax* from the Storm Dragon White Chalice, or just a regular Storm Dragon. He might even still become a Blood Dragon."

"Unlikely." Rikyava joined the conversation with a soft snort as she let her hand on Luke drop. Watching him with deep interest now, she swirled her cocktail and sat back in her chair. "We could ask my uncle King Huttr to test him, but Luke's showing Storm capabilities strongly now. We've all felt it."

"Can someone tell me why everyone is so worried about Luke's magic?" Layla asked with a frown, wondering why Adrian was so protective over this.

Adrian's gaze went hard as he set his hands to his chair arms and settled back in a commanding pose. "The problem is Luke's a mutt, Layla."

"Fuck you, asshole." Luke bristled immediately, and Rikyava's hand went to his shoulder again as Dusk's wall firmed between the two men.

"What Adrian means," Dusk spoke solidly, "is that Dragon magic can live latent in humans a long time until it's triggered, especially if that human holds multiple strains of magic. For Luke, that trigger was you, Layla. When your Dragon attacked him in the fall, his own magic opened, trying to protect him. Unfortunately, Luke carries so many strains of magic they went to war inside him, producing the seizures and bleeding you saw in Seattle. Your magic bit him deep… but the rest of what happened in that room was Luke's own power."

"You recognized it when it happened, didn't you?" Layla asked, turning to Dusk and giving him a good stare.

"I did." He spoke quietly, though he held her gaze. "Luke was having trouble remaining stable at the hospital; he kept going into seizures and bleeding from his eyes. I thought it was signs of a Blood Dragon opening to their power and found a talisman, got it to him two days after his surgery. That's why he and I have been speaking on the phone, and Rikyava also. I'm sorry I didn't tell you, but a person's magic opening is a private matter, Layla, it was unethical of me to share that. But now we're feeling Storm Dragon energy from Luke – something his Blood Dragon talisman won't control. And if he truly holds *nullax* like the White Chalice believe they've felt—"

"That scares you. *Nullax.*" Layla spoke, picking up on Dusk's emotions.

"It does," Dusk spoke, eyeballing her with gravitas. "All of us are fearful of a *nullax*'s abilities, Layla. And for good reason."

"Let's put it this way," Quindici DaPonti joined the conversation quietly, though it silenced the table as if a sword had sliced their throats. "Even Master Vampires are afraid of White Chalice Storm Dragons, because they have power like a Vampire Revenant, the evilest of our evil undead. The White Chalice were a nightmare in Europe for thousands of years, not just for Dragons but for every clan, abducting and nullifying the most powerful Royals everywhere until Queen

Justine began to rise to power. Long ago, the Chalice learned to interbreed with Vampire Revenants and create the *nullax*-ability from their founder, the *Sage of the Wilds*. It was a terrifying new magical ability. To have a Storm Dragon who can not only char Vampires with lightning, but also use our own arts against us… even to this day, the White Chalice remain a warning tale among the Vampiric Dark Havens. Our kind owe Queen Justine Toulet much for routing them."

"How was Queen Justine able to beat them?" Layla asked, curious.

"Because of her unique talents reading people, Queen Justine was able to discover their hidden members," Rikyava spoke. "It's the primary reason she's still Storm Queen, because she routed the most frightening cult the Twilight Realm has ever seen. If they're still around, and trying to recruit new people…"

"Then it's bad news." Layla finished.

"Bad news we need to take directly to Queen Justine herself." Dusk's gaze moved to Adrian, intensely sober. "We need to visit the Storm Dragons at Chambord as soon as possible, to find out which power inside Luke is most dominant. Not to mention ask them questions about the White Chalice and see if any really do still exist."

"It's a good place to start," Rikyava chimed in, swirling her beverage as she glanced to Adrian also. "My uncle King Huttr Erdhelm is at Château de Chambord right now with my cousin Rhennic, visiting the Storm Dragons today for Yule. With my uncle and Queen Justine both there, they'd be able to scent out which direction Luke's magic is taking."

"How is everyone so certain my opening magic will be this *nullax* thing?" Luke asked, scowling as he tapped one finger on the rim of his highball glass.

"We're not certain," Dusk spoke, though he kept a watchful eye on Adrian. "*Nullax* is rare, but it's something all White Chalice High Priests have due to their line-breeding. If the Chalice part of your magic steps forward as you mature, you'll be able to nullify any magical ability used against you – draining a person's magical life-force until they're essentially human."

"So why does that have his panties all up in a twist?" Luke snarled, gesturing at Adrian.

"Historically, the White Chalice drank the magic of any Twilight Realm individual they deemed too threatening. Often Royal Dragon Clan Firsts. And Royal Dragon Binds." Adrian's gaze was pinned to Luke, his eyes flinty though he was controlling his power now.

And just as Layla grasped the fullness of the problem arising between Adrian and Luke, Luke did also. Staring Adrian down, he spoke coldly. "I'm not your enemy, Adrian. Or Layla's. If her happiness lies with you, I have no beef. If you fuck up her life, though… I might just learn whatever it is this *nullax* can do."

"Is that a threat?" Adrian snorted, his eyes narrowing as the gold in them brightened, molten.

"Not unless you want it to be." Luke countered, giving Adrian his own hot emerald gaze as he sat back and crossed his arms over his chest, vicious.

"Adrian, Luke – enough!" Layla rose from her chair, staring them both down as she set her fingertips to the table, a rush of spiced wind slapping out from her as her Dragon roared in her veins. Even though Dusk's barrier was still up between both men, they felt it and flinched. But Layla didn't care as they glanced to her – she wasn't about to abide another pissing-match between them.

"Luke is my friend, Adrian." Layla snarled coldly, pinning Adrian's gaze first with her drakaina roaring hot and fierce in her veins. "We will support him through his transition, no matter what his magic turns out to be. And Luke, Adrian is my mate. He's not going anywhere, no matter how much the two of you hate each other. Deal with it."

Adrian's eyes burned as they returned to Luke, and Luke's were no less furious. But Adrian drew a deep breath, and Layla felt him at last pull his magic back. Layla saw Luke shudder, closing his eyes as his magic retreated also, as if putting it away was an immense strain. All around, people watched intently, but as both men finally doused their power, Layla turned a chastising look at Luke. Something in him was stubborn as ever, his hot emerald eyes holding hers without apology, even though Rikyava still restrained him by the shoulder.

As the standoff finally ebbed, Layla's head suddenly lanced with pain. She reeled as exhaustion caught up with her, blinking hard in a swamping fatigue. She hadn't slept last night, she'd been stressed about becoming a Courtesan and having her friends visit, and it was all coming home to roost now. Suddenly, she could see tendrils of energy like colored smoke easing through her vision – the auras of Luke and Adrian's magics still seeking to test each other even though their fight had mostly ceased. It was something Layla had never seen before, and blinking hard, she shook her head as she watched magic move like a tennis match in multi-dimensions – feeling like perhaps she was going crazy in the wake of her friend's abductions.

"Layla? Did you hear me?" Dusk had stood and reached out, pouring a grounding vibration through her.

"What?" Layla blinked, shaking her head again. She hadn't even felt him rise beside her, hadn't even noticed he was touching her until just now.

"I said, you're exhausted." Dusk spoke again, low and kind. "Come, have a seat."

"I'm fine." But as she let Dusk help her back to her seat, Layla felt her body tremble, in the completely spent way marathon runners have after a race. She suddenly didn't feel well at all, and wondered if perhaps something in the food had bothered her. Even as she thought it, she shivered hard, her face and head too hot while her spine between her shoulder-blades felt deeply chill. Layla shivered again and Dusk saw it. Turning his chair, he scooped Layla out of her seat, pulling her into his lap and wrapping his warm arms around her.

Relieved, Layla cuddled back into Dusk's expansive warmth as he shucked his suit jacket and tucked it around her, then reached up, feeling her forehead and cheek. "Jesus, you're burning up! Why didn't you tell anyone you weren't feeling well?"

"I'm fine." Layla repeated, though another deep shudder took her, so hard her teeth rattled.

"Layla? Are you sick?" Luke's wrath had evaporated across the table, as his dark brows knit in concern.

"She's not sick." Adrian spoke softly at the head of the table. "She shifted last night for the first time. It's a shift-stasis fever; she's healing her system after her Dragon's first change."

Silence fell as everyone stared at Layla. But with a hearty laugh, Rikyava was up quickly, rounding the table to wrap her arms around Layla in a tight hug. "Congratulations, girlie! Hope you gave Adrian a little hell as your drakaina."

"I think so." But even though she smiled, Layla's teeth were chattering well and good now despite Dusk's deep warmth, and she couldn't stop shaking. She saw Adrian rise, then Quindici, followed by the Madame and the rest.

"We need to wind this up tonight." Adrian spoke to the group. "Since Imogene is still unconscious, tomorrow if Layla's well enough, we'll take a trip out to Château de Chambord to talk with Queen Justine Toulet and see if she has information on where we can find this White

Chalice group, and the Smoke Faunus working for them, so we can get Layla's friends back as soon as possible. Dusk, Rikyava, Luke – all of you will come with, so we can introduce Luke to King Huttr and Queen Justine and see what direction his magic is taking. Quindici, Etienne, Rake – please hold down the fort here and keep all of this exceedingly quiet, especially from Lulu Duvall. Dusk, make contact with Heathren Merkami in the Intercessoria tonight, to see if we can get backup to go after the White Chalice."

Heads nodded around the table; hands went to hearts as people pledged their allegiance to Adrian. And though Layla shuddered hard as Dusk helped her stand, she found herself pleased watching her Royal Desert Dragon take command.

As Adrian turned her way, giving her a concerned glance, Layla tugged Dusk's sleeve. He came with her as she moved to Adrian, letting Adrian enfold her in his arms as well as Dusk's. Relief breathed through Layla to be held by both her Royal Dragons. Ease washed through her, and somewhere far away, she felt Reginald turn in her mind, regarding her. A wave of dark oceanic power suddenly poured through Layla's muscles, and she let out a sigh. Exhaustion swamped her, and she only had a brief glance at Luke, who watched her with agony in his eyes as her bound men claimed her.

She'd deal with Luke another day – one disaster at a time.

CHAPTER 14 – FEVER

Layla felt terrible, like a chill fever had swept her. A tremor rocked her as they departed the Waterfall Grotto and Dusk swept her up into his arms with his jacket still wrapped around her. She didn't even protest, and neither did Adrian as he flicked his fingers for Guards to follow them back to the Hotel. Shivering all through her core, Layla's teeth chattered as if she was coming down with the flu as Dusk cuddled her close. Moving off through the nighttime winter gardens, Adrian ordered Guards on ahead to prep Layla's room with a hot bath and a fire.

Pushing in the doors of the Hotel, Dusk maneuvered through the halls with Layla in his arms and Adrian at his side, a cadre of Guards still flanking them in a prickling chevron. People stared; guests and staff alike, a number of people bowing their heads to Adrian. Talisman or not, everyone knew he was here now, and Layla was certain the Crimson Circle would hear about it soon. But they were close to Layla's room on the third floor, and shouldering through the doors, Dusk maneuvered into her rooms at last.

At the sight of dragons writhing all over her walls and furniture, Layla was suddenly roaring with fever. As if being reminded of her recent change, she felt herself thinking in her beast mind – in terms of mates, fighting, and fear. Moving quickly to the marble and gold bathroom as if he felt what was happening, everything lit bright and a roaring fire in the hearth, they found the enormous ceramic tub thundering with hot water as two big Red Giant Guards stepped aside.

Layla didn't recall being laid on a velvet resting-chaise in the bathroom as she watched water tumble from the gilded faucet, seeing diamonds fall from the spout with every shimmering wave. His concerned face above her, Dusk laid his hand on her forehead, his blue eyes deeply worried. Breathing had become difficult and Layla suddenly couldn't recall how to do it, her chest struggling to rise. Kneeling swiftly beside her, Adrian set his lips to hers, pouring a reviving breath into her lungs as Dusk's fingers rumbled a bolstering power through her body. It helped, but she still felt cold, Dusk and Adrian's fingers burning upon her skin.

Layla made a pained sound and Adrian ordered the Guards out; they went, closing the bathroom door quickly. She shuddered on the chaise, deep in shift-illness now, her body shutting down. Her head was pounding, her vision strange as she continued to watch magic flow through the air in auras of color and light. Dusk had cast away his jacket, and ripping off his tie, he unbuttoned his shirt fast and stripped it off. His shoes were off, but he didn't care about the rest, for he heaved Layla up from the chaise. Ice seared her as Dusk and Adrian helped her undress, and she shivered hard.

She was only naked a moment as Dusk stepped them into the bath, but it felt like an eternity. Sliding into the hot water, Dusk cradled Layla, humming soothing vibrations through her. Adrian had stripped off his jacket and rolled up his shirtsleeves as he knelt beside the tub, feeling Layla's forehead as he continued breathing his power down her throat. But Layla's heat was gone, no ecstasy surging through her at Dusk or Adrian's touch. She still felt chilly and she blinked, feeling like her entire world had become slow and dark, and strange.

"This isn't good." Lifting an eyebrow at Adrian, Dusk clasped Layla closer to his hot, strong body. "She's not warming up. She should be recovering by now."

"I'm fine…" Layla protested, though her own voice sounded

faraway to her ears.

"You're not. Shift-illness isn't usually this severe when someone is allowed to change fully into their Dragon. Something's wrong." Adrian's gaze was worried as he turned her head to glance in her eyes, one and then the other. "It's almost like what happened a few months ago when Reginald's power was flooding me and it swamped her…"

"But he's all the way up at his clan home in the North Sea, Adrian." Dusk growled.

"Still." Adrian's brows furrowed and then he turned, fetching his cell phone and standing. "I'm calling Deep Harbor, I don't care what Reginald's clan thinks. Hang on."

"Do it." Dusk agreed with a bolstering rumble through Layla's body.

But even in the bath, cradled in Dusk's arms with Adrian's spiced winds breathing into her lungs as he made his phone call, Layla couldn't get warm. She knew the bath was hot, but it was like it couldn't penetrate her flesh. Curling into a ball, Layla pressed to Dusk's firm chest, feeling like her every breath was ice. Inhaling, he rumbled a deep, warming vibration through the bath. But it was as if his vibrations through the water suddenly made Layla's connection to Reginald roar. Like sea-chanties calling through the darkest ocean, she was inundated by the sound of oceanic caverns and the deep tones of whale song.

Layla found herself caught in undersea currents, pulling her like a rip-tide as her eyelids fluttered, sinking like a wrecked ship. She didn't recall fainting until she returned from the deeps, still held in Dusk's arms. She heard someone say something and leave quickly, but couldn't make sense of it. Snuggling close to Dusk with her back pressed to his chest, she turned her cheek to his skin. She felt Dusk's hand settle to her forehead as he spoke by her ear, "Come back, Layla. Talk to me.

What's going on?"

"The sea…" She breathed. The sea rocked her, even as Dusk held her. The sea swirled and breathed with her, making her dive. Layla found her body yoked to the water flowing around the tub and couldn't separate herself from it.

"I've got Caspar Durant on the line, Reginald's cousin," she vaguely heard Adrian's voice say as she dove into dark currents. "He says Reginald is undergoing some kind of trial right now to test him for the position of Clan Second – facing his past. It can't be interrupted. He has to remain in Siren-form until it's finished, and he's currently lodged himself at the bottom of the Norwegian Trench. That's probably what's affecting Layla right now. She's feeling what he's feeling in the deeps – reliving his nightmares as he processes them in the darkness and cold."

"Dammit." Dusk cursed, pressing his hand to Layla's forehead. "She's chill as ice. Layla. Talk to me. What are you feeling?"

"Cold…" Layla smelled nothing but a chill all around her, her teeth chattering as the ocean moved in her veins, deep and dark. "Dark…"

"What else? Keep talking." Dusk urged, something dire in his voice.

"Ice… my blood… ice." She shivered, feeling the cold slide deeper inside her.

"Fuck." Dusk cursed, feeling her forehead again. "Was she like this after you two were together?"

"No." Adrian spoke tersely beside the tub, as he stroked her wet curls. "It's Reginald's energy. He's re-living his worst life-events in these trials, facing them. He's causing Layla hypothermia through the Bind. If we can't get Reginald's Bind with her modified somehow—"

He didn't have to finish the sentence; Layla already knew. She could feel Reginald's rage and ice devouring her. Deep inside, it cored her out, made her feel the Siren's misery and wrath. He was hating himself right now as he relived his nightmarish past in dark solitude at the bottom of the ocean trench in Dragon-form. Layla could feel it going colder inside her, triggering her own dark void and she cried out in pain, shuddering hard. Dusk wrapped her in his arms, shushing her, but he couldn't heat her up – and he couldn't break her Bind to the Royal Siren.

And neither could Adrian.

"Go get Luke." Dusk's voice was tight as he held her.

"You think he can break her Bind to Reginald?"

"He's got power, Adrian. Real power. If it's *nullax*, it might be the only thing that can stop this right now."

A hard silence filled the bathroom. Layla could practically feel Adrian's spiced winds swirl through the air, furious and pained. But through her barely-open eyes, she saw him nod quickly.

He was out the door in a flash. Layla's eyes were clenched tight, her body in rigors by the time Luke arrived. It had only been minutes, but it felt like days. Like Layla's bones were turning to glass, every sinew ground inside her like icebergs cracking in frozen seas. She smelled lemon-balm and clean soap as Luke hurried in through the bathroom door and rushed to Layla's side. Cracking her eyelids, Layla saw him still dressed in his suit from the evening, though his jacket was gone. The rest he quickly ruined as he stepped over the side of the tub, settling into the bath and pulling Layla into his arms as Dusk gave her up.

"You know what you're doing?" Adrian's voice was tense beside the tub.

"I have no fucking clue. Stand back if you don't want to get zapped."

Layla felt Luke rip his shirt open so she'd be pressed to his bare

162

skin; someone must have told him skin contact helped shape-shifters. Luke was in hospital savior mode, holding her tenderly but moving fast as he stripped his bloodstone pendant up over his head and cast it to the floor. As he removed his talisman, his body was suddenly thundering with power. Surges of electricity hammered into Layla and she gave a short scream, but Dusk and Adrian's hands were there, pouring their twinned powers through her body to hold her steady. Both men grunted, hit by Luke's unbound abilities, though they held on. Flashes of lightning ripped through Layla's mind and body as a sound like thunder shuddered her bones, white-capping the water.

"Breathe, Luke!" She heard Dusk admonish urgently. "Slow it down. Panic in your magic will kill her right now. Be the person you are during your rounds in the ER. Slow. Focus."

"I don't know what to focus on!" Luke's voice was tense as he held her. "I don't know how any of this works yet!"

"Love." It was Adrian who spoke urgently, his hand gripping Layla's and draining away some of Luke's furious energy. "Magic is instinct, not mind, Luke. You love Layla. Feel that now. Take all your rage at me and your fury at her situation and transform it. Your rage holds power, but your love holds more."

"I hate you. I hate that she chose you. I hate everything about you." Luke growled, and a vicious spike of his lightning-power made Layla cry out in pain.

"I don't care." Adrian growled equally low, a desperate urgency in his manner now. "You love her, so save her. Save her for all of us. Be the man you were born to be, healer. Because Dusk and I can't help her this time, and you're the one who can."

Layla felt Luke wrap his arms around her, pressing her close in his embrace. She heard him growl, then give a hard sob as he turned her head gently with one hand – pressing his lips to hers. His lips were warm and soft, full and good, and as Layla felt them, they were suddenly her life-line. As their lips touched, as their hearts opened, Luke's lightning blasted the power of Reginald's ocean back in an immense, sundering blitz. Layla felt Luke's furious love jolt through her from his kiss; from his entire body wrapped around her in the bath. She gasped, seeing sky above the ocean now, feeling the rage of a dawn thunderstorm.

Smelling its power.

As that lightning blazed through her, it left a bright white in its wake; a furious clarity that evaporated the crushing blackness of the sea. As it blitzed through her body and mind, Layla felt it blast back Reginald's ice and darkness, even the pit of insanity that was opening deep within Layla's own self. Layla cried out beneath Luke's kiss, the sensation erotic and immense. As he cried out also, pressing harder into their kiss as if he could devour her with his furious love, the blast repeated – devouring Reginald's chill cold with striking hot power.

Layla shivered hard, but as that tremendous blast ran through her core again, it wasn't pain or cold. Her body was ablaze from Luke's power, her chest and heart pumping scalding blood now, her lungs heaving fast. As she cried out again beneath Luke's kiss and he did the same, he gripped her hard, crushing her to his chest. She wound her arms up around his neck, trapping him as their kiss broke, as he bit his power into her neck now and she screamed in a vicious bliss as all that energy went blasting through her.

In a sudden rush, Layla's animal mind took over. In a hot wave of passion, she was turning and Luke was ripping his wet shirt off over his head and Layla was hauling his trousers off in the bath. Need roared through her, hot white and scalding, and as Luke grasped her neck, hauling her hard into his kiss, sundering her with blast after blast of his furious lightning, Layla screamed into his mouth. She didn't know how she'd wound up straddling him. She didn't know whose hands were whose as they tore and raked at each other's skin, kissing hard. But as he crushed her close and positioned himself fast, then thrust into her, the both of them cried out in a furious ecstasy as a blaze of lightning tore Layla to her core.

Fast and hard, furious and deep, Luke's energy devoured her, blazing everything white inside her as they fucked in a scalding, furious lovemaking. Like a leviathan, her Dragon rose, commanding her body, commanding him, pouring through them both in a flooding wave of light and heat. She was wet, so wet despite the bath, and it was like silken coils thrusting through each other as she felt Luke's Dragon respond. Crushing her like some enormous thing made of flashing light and thundering presence, his Dragon was white as staring into the world's worst storm.

As Luke's lightning surged through every part of Layla and her heat went pouring through them both, she suddenly came, roaring. She felt Luke spasm beneath her as he roared also, crushing her close and thrusting up deep into her, coming at the same time. As Layla fell down to his chest in the water, gasping, Luke sobbed like their lovemaking had reached in and ripped out his heart.

It was only then that Layla realized Dusk wasn't in the bath anymore. Layla didn't know when he and Adrian had left, but the bathroom was silent now, the door closed. As Luke's hard, rageful sobs convulsed him beneath Layla's body, her fingertips quietly stroked his chest. She kissed his neck, burying her nose in his good, clean scent, and he clutched her closer, shuddering as if their ecstasy was too painful to bear.

The terrible, contentious desire between them was too much; it had always been too much. And now as they held each other, in the silent bathroom as their heartbeats finally eased, Layla could feel the vast depth of their love, just like it had always been. As she cuddled into Luke's embrace, he heaved a sigh, stroking her hair. She could feel deep surges of his power like a dying thunderstorm in her chest and pelvis, her own energy recovered with a hot roil of scales and fang.

The blackness inside her was banished, along with Reginald's darkwater energy, and a scalding heat spread out to her limbs rather than a black emptiness now. Malaise took Layla in the aftermath. Her head fell against Luke's shoulder, her lips pressed sweetly to his neck as her every muscle went lax in the water. His sculpted arms wound more closely around her, cuddling her to his lean body as he lay quietly now with his head back upon the tub's headrest, still breathing hard from their furious passion. Too much lay unsaid between them with everything that had just happened; too many emotions roiled through Layla. But Luke's incredible power had banished her chill and she could feel the heat of the bath at last.

And the delicious heat of Luke's skin, still smelling of lemonbalm and clean soap even though it held a tinge of ozone to it now.

"I thought I might accidentally kill you there for a moment..." Luke spoke at last.

"I thought I might accidentally kill you." Layla responded, amazed her Dragon hadn't taken a big bite out of him this time. Deep inside her veins, her drakaina coiled over with a lazy movement, opening one big golden eye – and then shutting it again. Apparently, now that his Dragon-magic was open, Luke was a worthy mate. Something about it made Layla sad, as she smoothed her fingers over his strong chest.

"I didn't think we'd ever get to do this again." Luke spoke as she traced his skin, pressing his lips softly to her forehead.

"I didn't know we could." Layla breathed. "Something's changed since your Dragon opened."

166

"Did you want to?" He asked, something in his voice too quiet. "You know, do this again?"

Layla paused, her hand pausing on his skin also. "I don't know if wanting each other is the real issue, Luke."

"I know." He kissed her forehead again, gently, his hands smoothing over her back, mimicking the soothing patterns she was drawing on his chest. Inhaling a deep breath, he heaved a sigh, the same heartbreaking sound as before. "I know we're bad together. Every part of me knows it. It doesn't mean I'm not furious as hell at Adrian – even Dusk, much as I like him."

"You don't have to like Dusk and Adrian, Luke. Just accept that they're a part of my life now." Layla spoke softly. "Just as much as my Dragon is. Just as much as your Dragon is now a part of yours."

"Part of me knows that." Luke spoke with his eyes still closed. "But this world is so confusing, Layla. I don't know what to think or feel. I have all this enormous energy inside me now, my emotions are changing, roiling even though I can feel the talisman working to contain them. I want to do more than fight now, I want to dance and sing and fuck and drink hard, and sometimes I feel like I'm going crazy. I have a hundred times the energy I've ever had, and suddenly I don't even know if I need to exercise or if I want to study, or even if I want to be a doctor anymore. Part of me still loves healing people, saving them. But where do I fit in the human world now?"

Luke's hard sigh held everything he didn't know how to say right now, and Layla understood it to her marrow. As she watched a tear drip slowly from beneath his long, dark eyelashes, she lifted up, kissing him sweetly on the lips. He paused, then pressed into it, touching her gently as they kissed. When they at last pulled away, Luke's eyes were open, and their emerald bleakness cored Layla to her depths.

"Who am I now, Layla?" He rasped as he reached out to touch her face, his dark brows knit.

"Who do you want to be, Luke?" She spoke softly, kissing his fingertips.

Luke inhaled, and Layla watched him think deeply about it. "Dusk thinks I can still be a healer somehow, maybe a doctor in the Twilight Realm. He's helped me a lot, coming to terms with how this is going to change my life – how it already *is* changing my life. His coaching, his information these past months… I don't think I would have been able to help you just now if it hadn't been for him."

"Dusk is good like that." Layla smiled softly, kissing Luke's fingers again.

"He is." Luke sighed, his hands stroking Layla's neck now. They said nothing for a long while, Layla breathing against him in the silence of the bathroom as his hands continued stroking her. The afterglow of their energy was fading and as they gazed at each other in the bathroom's light, Layla saw a deep sadness in Luke's beautiful green eyes. Reaching up, she cupped his face in her hands and he turned his head, kissing her palm. With another deep sigh, he closed his eyes, resting his lips against her hand.

"I love you, you know." He murmured at last, without opening his eyes. "Even through all this fucked-up shit."

"I know." Layla smiled sadly. "I love you, too. Through all *our* fucked-up shit."

It made him laugh. It was a sudden, quiet chuckle, but Layla died inside to see that sweet quirk of his lips, something she had dearly missed. But then he sobered. And then his dark brows drew down in a tight frown.

"What about our friends?" He rasped as another tear slipped from his dark lashes. "If my magic is *nullax*… then their abduction is all my fault. Fucking hells. Fucking, fucking hells…"

168

"We'll find them." Layla shushed, smoothing his tear away with her thumb. "And then we'll make whomever took them pay. I promise."

Luke's eyes snapped open. And in their emerald depths, Layla saw his fury rise in a hot strike of lightning. "They are going to pay – so hard."

CHAPTER 15 – AFTER

As a door opened and closed beyond the bathroom, the sound roused Layla, realizing someone was still in her apartment. With a sigh, she snuggled closer to Luke as he cradled her to his chest in the warm water of the tub. A heavy fatigue held her as she heard more sounds beyond the bathroom, and it was a struggle to come to alertness. Layla couldn't, Luke's body too warm and her own too tired as she languished in vague dreams of white mist.

But as more sounds came from Layla's apartment, Luke shifted beneath her as if he knew their time together had to end. Pushing up from the bath in one smooth motion with Layla cradled in his arms, Luke was stronger than he'd been, with all his furious new Dragon-energy pouring through him. Layla could feel it as he stepped from the bath, helping her out, holding her still curled against his warm chest. He couldn't towel off with her in his arms, but set her feet gently to the marble floor as he pulled on a men's quilted robe, tucking Layla's cobalt silk one around her.

Still curled against him, Layla rested upon Luke as he retrieved his talisman from the wet floor, lowering it back over his head and adjusting the silver pendant on his chest. She felt his energy doused around her, the white mist pulling back. Taking a deep breath, she feared Reginald's darkwater oceans would return to trigger her black void, but they didn't. As if Luke had left some of his *nullax* deep inside her, Layla still felt that swirling white mist move slowly within her, making her want nothing but sleep. She saw nothing when she turned her inner sights to Reginald, except that same blank white field. As Luke set his hand to the gilded door handle of her ornate French Baroque bathroom, he adjusted Layla against him. Taking a deep breath that had a *here the fuck we go* sound to it, Luke pressed the handle of the door and scooped Layla back up into his arms, walking them out.

As Layla cuddled close in Luke's arms, she hoped her apartment would be empty, but knew both Dusk and Adrian were still there. Peeking from beneath her heavy eyelashes as Luke maneuvered her to the bed, she saw Dusk sitting at her breakfast table in a fresh set of grey pinstriped trousers, a white shirt, and pinstriped vest, clothes from his apartment. Reading on a black Hotel-encrypted tablet, a bourbon sat beside him as he held a smartphone to his ear – clearly on hold as an irate energy rumbled from him, his sapphire eyes following Luke sharply.

As Luke laid Layla down on the bed and helped tuck her in, hanging her robe from the bedpost after she shucked it, Layla's exhausted glance found Adrian. Still wearing his shirt and trousers from dinner, Adrian sat in a chair by the fireplace with one ankle crossed over his knee. His high-arched feet were bare, his sleeves rolled up as he cradled a bourbon in his long fingers, staring at Luke with a hard fury to his attention. A tense energy writhed around Adrian, as his Dragon-tattoo seemed to roil in the light of the flames.

No one said anything as Luke finished tucking Layla in and she snuggled down into her duvet, a deep white exhaustion rolling all through her. It was awkward to the max as Luke squeezed Layla's hand then nodded briefly to Dusk, holding Adrian's gaze with a level intensity as tension surged between them.

"Layla will be fine. The cold has pushed back." Luke spoke in a strangely detached way, like a surgeon telling a cancer patient's family that the patient was going to live. Though Dusk nodded, Adrian didn't say anything, still staring Luke down as that churning heat simmered around him. But though she could feel him wanting to, Adrian didn't lash out, and Luke didn't either. With one last squeeze to her hand, Luke released Layla. Some part of her screamed to lose his touch, but she knew he had to go. Crossing the apartment, Luke was at Layla's door with his fingers on the handle when Dusk finally spoke.

"Luke. Be awake early. We're departing for Château de Chambord at eight a.m."

"Sure." Luke gave a nod, and some accord passed between him and Dusk, that he'd managed to save Layla's life. Adrian still made no nod or word of thanks, only watched Luke depart with a tense gaze, still swirling his bourbon by the fireplace. As Luke shut the door behind him, Adrian's gaze met Layla's. But before she could say anything, Dusk suddenly spoke up on the phone.

"Yes. Yes, I have been holding." Dusk growled into the phone, his energy rumbling sharply. Standing and setting his tablet aside, he began to pace by the bank of darkened windows. "No, as I explained to your representative, I need to speak to Insinio Brandfort or Heathren Merkami *in person*. Yes, it's urgent. Yes, they already said both Judiciaries are unavailable. No, I won't hold again! We suspect the White Chalice are involved in this abduction, as I already explained. We *are* talking with the Storm Queen as soon as we can get to her! Inner clan concern!? Three humans were abducted right out from underneath security systems *your people set up here!* No, I won't calm down. I demand—"

But Dusk cut off suddenly. Lowering the phone, heaving hard breaths as the marble floor around him rumbled in a wave, he stared incredulously at his phone. "Fuckers hung up on me—!"

"What did they say?" Rising from his seat at the fireplace, Adrian's brows knit darkly as he took a sip of his bourbon.

"They say it's not an Intercessoria concern!" With a growl, Dusk threw his phone down on Layla's table. "They say any suspicion of the White Chalice resurfacing is an *inner clan concern* to be handled by the Storm Queen. And there seems to be some problem with Heathren and Insinio, because they've not checked in with me, and now neither are answering their direct lines and all the desk people will say is that they're unavailable!"

"We're on our own, then." Adrian swirled his bourbon as he moved to Dusk.

"This is bullshit! Where are those Fallen Ephilohim when you need them?" Dusk was working himself up now, the floor and air shuddering so hard around him that it rattled Layla's windows in a long line. With a furious growl, Dusk ripped a hand through his hair, a wave of iridescence flashing through it. He was starting to vibrate with that un-tuned energy again, and a shiver of alarm passed through Layla as Adrian also perked. She wanted to go to Dusk, but even as she moved to do so, she felt that white wave of mist curl her down again, a deep exhaustion claiming her.

But in a few short strides, Adrian went to Dusk. As Adrian reached out, Dusk tried to wave him off. But Adrian was intent, corralling a hand behind Dusk's head and setting their foreheads together.

"Easy, Dusk. We've got enough leads to go after this thing without the Intercessoria." As Adrian held Dusk, Layla's heart broke, wanting to go join them but strangely unable to.

"I know. I just can't sit idly by while everything falls to shit." Dusk growled, irate.

"Nothing is shit; we don't know anything yet." Adrian spoke quietly. "Imogene said her High Priest wouldn't harm Layla's friends if we go to them promptly, and we have to trust that. We'll set out for

Chambord in the morning. Queen Justine will have information on where we can find the White Chalice."

"I just… I wasn't able to protect them, I can't contact the Intercessoria, and I was useless to help Layla when she needed me tonight. Fucking useless." Dusk spoke again as he flung a hand out, gesturing at the bed.

"You are far from useless, and Luke helped Layla at *your* suggestion. Nothing is shit, just take a deep breath." Adrian admonished again, cradling Dusk's head and massaging Dusk's nape.

Something about Adrian's words eased Dusk, causing the jangled energy to flow out of him. Heaving a sigh, he reached out, gripping Adrian's shoulder. The two men stood together, just breathing, and Layla could suddenly feel their magics flowing through each other in a deeply comforting movement. As if their powers braided together with the strength of their shared emotions and Layla's Bind, she could feel their Dragons sliding through each other's coils in a deep, loving dance.

Layla had never felt anything like it before, and it moved her to quietude as she lay in bed, feeling the emotions of her bound men. She knew they felt it too, because Dusk's breathing had slowed and so had Adrian's, as if listening to each other. Layla wanted to go to them, but couldn't. She wanted to be a part of what they were experiencing, to stand close and feel that energy wrapping into her also, all three of them a part of the Bind and feeling each other's hearts.

But whatever Luke had done to her had left a fatigue so deep in her body that it felt like her passions were swept beneath a dense white fog. Even as she watched her Bound lovers, Layla felt her drakaina stir only vaguely beneath that swirling white blankness, her body still too heavy to rise.

They must have felt it, because both men glanced to her, their moment of sweet intimacy breaking. Layla saw Adrian squeeze Dusk's nape as Dusk gave a sigh, both men sharing deep eye contact before breaking apart and coming to her. Layla didn't know what that sharing had been about; and neither man said anything as they slid onto the bed, Dusk at her front and Adrian moving close to her back. Fully clothed, they eased under the duvet, Adrian corralling her and pulling her naked back to his front, even as Dusk moved in before her, his hips pressed to hers with his strong hand massaging her waist.

But even though it was everything Layla wanted to have them both there, whatever Luke had done with his magics had buried her Dragon well and good. Her passions barely rose as Dusk's sweet lips pressed hers. As Adrian wrapped himself close, spooning her and setting his soft lips to her neck, her body hardly stirred with heat.

"Are you ok, Layla?" Dusk spoke, holding her close to his warm, strong body as his summer-blue eyes searched hers.

"I think so. Crisis averted." Layla murmured sleepily as she gave a smile. Her eyelids were so heavy, and they fluttered closed as Dusk reached up, stroking her cheek with his warm knuckles. "I can't feel Reginald anymore… I'm just tired."

"She feels like she's been drugged," Adrian's murmur was dark at her back as her kissed her shoulder.

"She's alive, Adrian." Dusk spoke calmly as he kissed Layla's lips again. "Be grateful for what Luke did. Don't be a dick. Reginald's self-hate would have taken her down and you know it. And if Layla goes—"

"We all go. I know." Adrian sighed harshly, as if continuing a conversation he and Dusk had had previously that Layla had not been party to. Her eyes fully closed now as she cuddled into them, feeling them so warm and soothing on either side of her that she was almost tipping over that edge of sleep now, she heard Adrian speak again. "I remember the visions Layla had of Hunter's trio. If she falls, or if one of us does—"

175

"It might drive the others insane. Or even kill one of us. Or more." Dusk's words were very quiet now as his sweet river-water breath eased over Layla's lips. "The Bind is giving us insight into each other, letting us feel and borrow each other's magics to some degree, but it truly is a Bind, Adrian. Our life-forces are getting tied together, deep inside."

"I know. I can feel it." Layla felt Adrian reach up, massaging a hand to his chest as if his heart hurt. Sliding that hand around Layla, he pressed his palm to her heart in a deeply soothing gesture. "We're tied to her life-force, too. I can feel Luke's *nullax* inside her, drowning her passion like a vast white mist."

"Like a vast white nothing." Dusk agreed softly.

Layla felt Adrian and Dusk share a look over her shoulder, though she didn't see it. She was already slipping into sleep, tipping over that diaphanous edge with their warmth and safety cuddling her, a vast white emptiness seeping up to claim her. Images of an endless plain rolled through her, emptiness surrounding her like a blank white void. It was serene somehow, and as Layla fell into it, she felt calm rise up to take her. As if her Dragon was the source of her fury, her bright rage, and her darkness also, she felt it all washed away with that smooth white mist.

Empty.

Layla didn't know she'd slept until she woke. Dusk and Adrian were no longer in bed, and she saw through the open canopy-drapes that though a fire still roared in her fireplace, the thin grey light of early morning was rising in the room. Clouds were heavy in the sky outside as she gazed out the vaulted windows, with the dense look of more snow. At the clink of cutlery, Layla glanced over to see Dusk at the table, eating breakfast and studying his tablet. Looking around as if sensing her wake, his summer-blue eyes found her and he paused, then set everything down and rose, coming to her with a gentle smile. Sitting on the bed, Dusk reached out, brushing back a curl of Layla's hair. Layla's inner fire immediately roared, swamping her as a heady citrus scent blossomed from her skin.

"Whoa!" Dusk chuckled, lifting his eyebrows at Layla's reaction to his touch. Her breath heaved and she felt her cheeks flush as her Dragon rolled over deep inside her, fully awake. Luke's mist from the night before was gone, and as Dusk touched her it was as if Layla's passions rose tenfold, the drakaina's heat clenching everything almost like she'd never bound Reginald. It shivered her, but not from cold – from that scalding, delicious sensation sliding all through her body.

"Someone's feeling better this morning." Dusk chuckled, a bit breathless now.

"I feel amazing, actually." Layla blew out a breath, trying to steady her Dragon as the creature roiled. Sitting up in bed and tucking the covers around her nakedness, Layla glanced at Dusk. "My drakaina's back on-line this morning, that's for sure."

"Temperamental little reptile you have in there." Dusk spoke with a grin, though his teasing gaze was also shrewdly assessing. "Any leftover chill? Anything from Reginald?"

"Nothing." Layla shook her head, feeling decidedly hale. Sitting a moment, she eased her way along the golden cord that bound her to Reginald. She could feel him, but when she turned her inner sight in his direction it was still vague, as if swaddled in that dense white mist of Luke's *nullax*, and Layla frowned. "I can feel Reginald's Bind, but... it's like someone's white-washed that entire section of my mind. Luke's magic has mostly washed out of me this morning, or I slept it off, but that area of the Bind still feels vague."

"Nulled," Dusk nodded soberly, his hand touching hers on the covers. "*Nullax* can have either a temporary or a permanent effect, depending on how it's used. Luke stopped by early this morning to see if his power had any… problematic effects on you."

"Diminishing my Bind to Reginald could be a problem if it persists. His magic controls my drakaina from trying to Bind every Royal in sight." Layla frowned, suddenly wondering what Luke might be capable of if he could fully undo one of her Binds. "Do you think it'll persist?"

"I have no idea." Dusk frowned, rocking back and clasping his knee in his hands. "The person who would have that information is Queen Justine Toulet. We need to get ready, Layla. I've already packed a suitcase for you, but you should take a look and make sure everything you need is there. Luke, Rikyava, Adrian, and I are ready to go to Chambord, and Adrian's got his jet warming up at the airfield. But before we go, I have to ask… did you feel anything happen with Luke last night?" Dusk gave her a look, and Layla felt herself blush.

"You mean besides what happened in the tub?" Layla squirmed, suddenly feeling squeamish about her sudden tryst with Luke in the bathroom.

"We heard it." Dusk's smile was wry, and something about it hard-edged, though Layla could tell he was trying to be magnanimous. "And saw the beginning of it. And felt the whole damn thing through our Bind."

"Shit." Covering her face with her hands, Layla massaged her eyebrows then looked back up, knowing she had to face it. "I'm sorry."

"It's ok." Twining his fingers through hers, Dusk's smile was sad but truthful. "Luke saved your life, and a lot of magic is stronger through sex, especially when a person is fully able to use the emotions they carry deep inside. You both still care for each other, and it's obvious."

"Aren't you jealous of what happened with Luke?" Layla hedged, deeply worried.

"I was when it was happening," Dusk reached up, smoothing one of Layla's curls back from her face, "but I can reason through the magical necessity of things. Adrian's stewing, though. He might try to take a chunk out of Luke in the next few days."

"One more problem in a boatload of trouble." Layla sighed, leaning into Dusk's touch.

"But what I was asking before, is if you felt the Bind engage Luke?" Dusk spoke as his touch eased down her neck, stroking her collarbones as he watched her intently.

Stilling, Layla thought about it. Spreading her awareness deep though her body, she could feel her golden Bind-connections to Adrian and Dusk bright this morning, even though the one to Reginald was still dulled. But as she thought about Luke, to feel out and see if she had any magical connection to him, she felt nothing. "No, I don't think we were Bound. I'm not feeling any metaphysical connection when I think about Luke this morning. Just all my regular emotions about him. I wonder if his *nullax* gives him the ability to resist my Bind?"

"Could be." Dusk spoke with a frown. "But I'll thank our stars your magic didn't Bind Luke last night. I think he and Adrian would tear each other to bits. Having Reginald and Adrian trying to get along is hard enough with all their history... but Adrian thinks Luke is a selfish asshole, and I know Luke views Adrian far worse."

"Do you think Luke could break our Bind?" Layla asked, the thought truly scary to her as she felt again the mist still covering her connection to Reginald.

"I don't know, Layla." Dusk frowned as his gaze held hers. "If Luke truly has *nullax*, then he's got more power than any of us. A scary power all Dragons fear. He could take away our magic, our ability to shift into our beast, everything. We would become human, living in a dangerous world that expects us to be a Dragon – weak among the

179

powerful."

"Prey." Layla knew what Dusk was trying to tell her, and couldn't imagine what would happen if Luke ever nullified Adrian's magic. Plenty of bad debts would come home to roost – debts Adrian had been amassing for over a century.

"Prey." Dusk agreed solemnly.

As if that idea broke their sweet reprieve, Dusk gave a hard sigh, kissing Layla on the brow and letting her go. Standing, he took up her silk robe from the bedpost and extended it, gesturing to breakfast. Layla needed no second urging, sliding on her robe and moving to the table. As they sat, Dusk poured coffee and served eggs and bacon and sautéed pears in a brown sugar sauce. Combing through her snarl of hair with her fingers, Layla remembered why she didn't let it dry overnight in bed. As Dusk served her, Layla's hand slid out, stroking one of the gilded china plates. Moving on instinct, she adjusted the silver forks until the setting was perfect.

It wasn't something she normally would have done, and Layla shook her head, lifting a hand to her temple as Dusk sat beside her, watching. But even as she moved, she felt an oceanic presence rise up through her. Reginald's awareness wasn't churning darkwater this morning, but smooth and deep like a calm harbor, and in her mind, Layla saw sunlight sparkle on morning waves. As she turned in his direction, no longer seeing only white but the pale blue-grey of his eyes piercing through that blank fog, something inside Layla breathed deep in relief.

Your friend is a danger. She heard Reginald's smooth voice flow through her suddenly. *Be cautious of what he can do.* And then he was gone, washed away like the morning tides.

"Was that Reginald?" Dusk was watching her intently.

"It was. He's back, and calm finally." Layla blinked, shaking her head to clear it as she took up a forkful of eggs. "I think Luke's effects on our Bind were temporary."

"Small wins, I guess." Taking up his coffee, Dusk sipped it. "I think we need to be very cautious of Luke until we know more about what he can do. Even though he saved your life, it could have come at quite the cost. It was a risk I was willing to take last night, but unless your life is in danger again…"

"Reginald is of the same opinion, that we should be cautious." Layla glanced at Dusk as she took a bite of eggs. "And after what I felt from Luke last night… I believe it."

They ate in silence for the rest of the meal, subtly hurrying as both felt the tension of their oncoming day finally grip them. With breakfast finished, Dusk whisked about Layla's apartment tidying as she checked her suitcase for their time at Château de Chambord. While she dressed in jeans, tall boots, and a grey cable-knit sweater, pulling on her blue peacoat, Dusk and Adrian's luggage arrived with a retinue of Guards. As Layla did a touch of makeup, Adrian entered the apartment, moving to her and giving her a kiss, his aqua eyes sober this morning with deep flecks of gold. Their kiss lingered, but before Layla was able to ask him how he was this morning, a knock came at the apartment door, Dusk opening it to admit Rikyava and Luke.

Dressed in jeans and boots similar to Layla's, though with a rig of modern knives and handguns over her sweater, Rikyava's long Swedish-blonde hair was pulled back in a ponytail as she slung on a beige peacoat and buttoned it halfway, nodding to Adrian. Luke wore his blazer and jeans, and his gaze found Layla's for only an instant before it flicked away. Layla blushed and she saw Luke do the same, his bloodstone pendant whirling. She felt Adrian's energy ratchet up in a hard flash as he stared at Luke, but there was no time for talk. Chambord awaited, and they had to get going if they had any hope of rescuing Layla's friends.

In a moment, everyone was out the door, a cadre of twenty Guards escorting them and carting luggage. Stares followed their party through the morning Hotel, but there were no adverse events as everyone bundled into two of Adrian's black Bentley sedans waiting on the snowy promenade with his personal drivers. Layla took a car with Adrian and Dusk, Rikyava and Luke taking the other. A tense silence filled their car, Adrian not saying anything, though he did slide his hand out at one point, clasping Layla's where she sat next to him in the back seat and twining their fingers together.

But he didn't mention Layla's tryst with Luke, and she didn't know how to bring it up. Before Layla knew it, they were arriving at the Charles de Gaulle Airport, driving to one of Adrian's Learjets waiting on the tarmac, its electronics whining as snow began swirling down from the heavy sky. Rikyava and Luke's car had arrived, everyone up into the jet quickly with luggage stowed. As the Parisian co-pilot secured the doors, she gave Layla a sympathetic smile, feeling the tension in the jet. As Layla took one of the jet's leather chairs across the dining table, Adrian took the seat beside her, while Luke and Dusk settled in the seats opposite. Rikyava buckled in at a writing-desk on the other side of the cabin, though she was close by.

Layla could practically cut the tension in the jet with a knife, it was so thick. No one wanted to engage conversation, Dusk shifting and clearing his throat as Adrian gazed around the group with a simmering hardness. Layla fidgeted while Luke stared determinedly out the window, his fingers tapping on the table. Only Rikyava seemed composed, watching everyone with a Guardswoman's readiness in her lavender eyes, as if she might have to quell a fight soon.

As tension flared to screaming with the roar of the jet's engines, Layla wanted to retreat into the back of the plane and hide – beginning to think this plan with both Adrian and Luke involved was a bad idea. A very bad idea.

CHAPTER 16 – TALK

Adrian's eyes flashed as he settled back in his leather chair on the jet, placing his hands on his chair arms and crossing one ankle over his knee. Layla recognized Adrian's posture as a show of dominance against Luke sitting across from him at the table. As Layla glanced between Adrian and Luke, she saw Adrian simmering with a dark power, though he was trying to contain it. Luke was cool as he gave Adrian hard green eyes back, though his new magic suddenly began to crank up in the relatively small space. Luke's lips quirked, his eyes going two shades more viciously green as the drakes regarded each other. Both Dragons meant business as they stared each other down – Adrian furious that Luke had had sex with Layla, and Luke hating Adrian to his very marrow.

As the jet revved its engines and began to taxi towards the runway, Rikyava spoke up from her seat at the desk. "If you both can't agree to put aside your hatred of each other, our aims in Chambord will go nowhere, and Layla's friends will die."

It was a succinct summary. Layla saw Luke digest Rikyava's statement; she saw it rattle him as Luke closed his eyes and drew a deep breath. "I'm sorry, Layla. I'll try to put aside my grievances against Adrian until we're through all this."

"I won't." Adrian's gaze was pinned to Luke as he spoke quietly, though loud enough so everyone could hear him. "We need to talk through a few things before we get to the Storm Dragons. I think it's high time we had a little chat, Luke." Reaching out, Adrian twined

Layla's fingers in his – another distinctly possessive move that was not lost on Luke.

"What is your fucking problem?" Luke hissed, his gaze fierce upon Adrian.

"You're my fucking problem." Adrian spoke back, simmering with a barely-restrained fury. "You say you support Layla, but all I've seen you do is be a pain in her ass ever since I first met you back in Seattle. Tell me honestly that you support Layla's decision to be a part of this world, or to be with Dusk and I, or to become a Courtesan."

"Hey, I saved her when you could do jack-all about it last night." Luke snarled back, lightning flashing in his hot green eyes now. "You're just pissed that you couldn't help her and I could."

"You *fucked* her." Adrian's gaze was roaring as he spoke coldly back. "Been waiting a while to do that since she left your bed, haven't you? Since when do doctors fuck their dying patients? Oh, I remember – when they have no control over their inner beast."

"You dick—!"

Luke half-rose with a snarl on his face, but Dusk's hand whipped out fast, his formidable Crystal Dragon strength restraining Luke to his seat. As Layla nearly laughed with a bitter gall, that Adrian and Luke had to dig into this now, the plane began to roar along the runway into takeoff. Layla's adrenaline spiked and she gripped the arms of her chair with both hands. It was an animal fear, this panic she always experienced on takeoff. Looking over, Adrian smoothed his hand over hers, soothing her with a curl of spiced wind.

But as she came out of her sudden panic, she noticed everyone around the table was staring at her, affected by it. Across from her, Luke was wound tight, his eyes sparking a fierce emerald as he gripped his pendant in his fist. Dusk was breathing hard, something severe in his eyes as he massaged his chest, as if trying to hold back shattering as his eyes flashed diamond-bright. Beside her, Adrian had set his jaw, gripping her hand too hard now as if he wasn't aware of his tension.

"Look at you four." Over at the desk, Rikyava was watching the entire scene with deep awareness. "None of you can escape Layla's Bind, even though Luke's not even a part of it yet. Best get used to it if you all want to keep it together for this mission."

"My fear. It affected all of you just now." As Layla glanced around the group, she flexed her hand beneath Adrian's. He startled, moving his hand with a surprised look as if he hadn't known how tense he'd been. As Layla watched them, she saw her own primal fear echoed in every face. They were shaking it off, but Layla's sudden rush of animal terror had thrown them.

"Your primal fear brought up our own, I think," Dusk spoke as he let out a long breath through pursed lips, his sapphire eyes finding Layla's. "I was terrified just then that I was going to go full-Dragon right here inside this plane."

Neither Luke nor Adrian volunteered what they'd experienced in their fear, but it was an angle to her magic Layla hadn't considered, that her emotions could affect her Bound men in real time. Luke wasn't even a part of their Bind and he was feeling it, and the thought sobered Layla. An even more dire thought was what might happen if she gave into her blackest fears, the ones that triggered the dark void inside her. She'd never considered it might have more consequences than just her going berserk. That it might cause her Bound Dragons to do so also – and anyone else who could feel her power.

"Do you think we're all being contentious right now because of the Bind?" Layla glanced at Rikyava. "Because I'm upset my friends were abducted, now everyone is feeling it?" If a modest spike in her adrenaline could make them all this tense, they really had no idea how much Layla's black rage at their current situation was pushing them all.

"Maybe." Rikyava spoke with a lift of one blonde eyebrow. "I've never seen Adrian so visibly incensed against someone he knows so little about. And Dusk is famous for his buoyancy in times of trouble, whereas he's cracking now under the strain. And Luke…"

Rikyava's gaze held Luke's a long moment, and Layla felt something pass between them, though she couldn't quite figure out what it was. But at that glance, Luke drew a deep breath, turning back to Layla. "I want to support you, Layla, you know I do. But becoming a Hotel Courtesan? Why?"

"It's a long story, Luke." Layla glanced to him with a heavy sigh. "Let's just say there are reasons for it."

"Layla is now a Courtesan because we're planning a coup against the Crimson Circle," Dusk chimed in quietly. "The Crimson Circle are at the center of the Hotel Board of Owners and want Adrian's head, quite literally, on a platter. We're trying to prevent that, but it means Layla has to go undercover to rout out the specific person or persons who want Adrian dead, and becoming a Courtesan gives her access."

"You're going to become some kind of spy?" Luke's eyebrows climbed his forehead as he gaped at her, horrified. "Were you ever planning on telling me?"

"I wanted to, Luke. I just never found the right moment." Layla held Luke's gaze, suddenly feeling how wide the gap had grown between them since summertime. Despite their tenderness last night, it was as if she and he had both lived numerous lifetimes since they'd last been together. As Layla watched Luke, she realized she didn't know who he was becoming now with his Storm Dragon magic rising inside him – and he didn't know who she was turning into either since August.

"No. No way." Luke spoke at last, a harsh rasp of fury in his voice. "You assholes are so not using Layla as bait to take down a major crime syndicate!"

"I volunteered for this, Luke." Layla weathered his hot rage as his emerald eyes pierced hers. "It's why I was training to become a Courtesan these past months."

"I don't care." Luke growled, fury emanating from him, even though Layla could feel it was backed by his deep protectiveness. But it was like a storm rising inside the plane now, all of Luke's passion for Layla's welfare rekindled in the wake of what they had shared. "I won't be party to putting you in danger like that. And I won't just sit here while everyone else agrees it's an awesome idea. Whoring you out so you can lure supernatural crime bosses into your *bedroom?*"

"I'm not human, Luke. Neither of us is human anymore." Layla spoke back, willing him to understand how invested she was in this, trying to open her heart to make him feel how much Adrian's life meant to her. "I can fight with magic, I can shift into my beast. Everything I've been learning in my life lends itself to this. You've felt your own Dragon-power opening up, how strong it is – mine is no different. I'm not weak, and if I can do something to help get Adrian out of this trouble, I want to."

"I never said you were weak, Layla," Luke countered hotly, gesturing at the group as fury seethed in his emerald eyes. "Only that you sit in company far older than us who have lived in this world their entire lives and *still* not managed to take down this group of crime lords. You've been a Dragon what, six months? And me – fuck, I don't even know why I'm here right now!"

"You're here because Layla's magic called you here." Rikyava's lavender gaze pinned Luke, through there was sympathy in it. "Do you think it's coincidence Layla's Dragon-attack opened up your own latent Dragon bloodlines, Luke? And that you possess magic potentially more powerful than any of us here, including Layla?"

Luke shut his mouth as he stared at Rikyava, and Layla watched the fury drain out of him. Settling back in his chair, he rubbed a hand over his face. Across the narrow aisle, Rikyava reached out, setting a hand to his knee with a gentle camaraderie. Something grateful eased through Luke's gaze though it was still bleak. Looking back to Layla, he shook his head. "How am I supposed to be okay with all this, Layla?"

"You don't have to be okay with it, Luke." She spoke quietly. "Just support me. It's what we have to do to clear Adrian's name, and if we don't strike at the heart of the Crimson Circle, they'll hunt Adrian to the ends of the earth. Me spying among them as a Courtesan gives us the ability to get to them before they get us. Adrian and Dusk and I are not entirely convinced this White Chalice attack on our friends is independent of the Crimson Circle. And if they've come after our human friends to get to us... who knows who might be next on their hit list?"

A heavy silence settled at the table as Luke's gaze swung to Adrian, and Layla felt a heated rivalry spring up again between the two men. "This is all your fault, you bastard. If you'd never come to Layla in the first place, haunting her every move until she joined you in your world, none of this ever would have happened. And now, look where all the dominoes have fallen. Fuck you."

"Curse me all you like," Adrian glared back with a cold quietude, "but what if Layla had opened to her Dragon-powers without the talisman I bought her? What if I had never been there in the art gallery to provide her with the *one thing* that could help control her rages and urges as her magic opened? You've felt your own opening power, Luke. You nearly died in the hospital because of it. Are you saying you would have wanted to stand by and watch devastation like that tear Layla apart? And it's not *my world*, Luke. You're a part of this world now, too, so deal with it. Stop fucking hiding in the human world like a coward, afraid of everything you truly are."

Luke's lips had fallen open, his green eyes tight with fury as he breathed hard in his seat. Layla saw the golden veins in his bloodstone pendant whirl as he fought to contain his power, but even so, a crackle of electricity around him lifted the hairs on Layla's arms. "How can you love this man, Layla?" Luke spoke at last, a devastated fury in his eyes as he glanced to Layla.

"Adrian's my mate, Luke." She countered quietly. "If you've been learning anything about Dragons from Dusk lately, you should know what that means."

Luke shut his mouth. Layla knew it had been the wrong thing to say as he sat back in his chair, staring at her like she'd grown a new, far nastier head. In some ways his silence was worse than when he once might have blown up at her, and Layla felt that devouring blackness open up inside her once more as she felt Luke's heartbreak. She wanted to explain. She wanted to undo that terrible look in his eyes, as if she'd stabbed him right in the heart. But it wasn't a conversation she was willing to have in front of the others, and Layla was left gazing at Luke as some part of her died deep inside.

Staring at her, at last Luke rubbed both hands over his face. "I can't, Layla. I'm sorry. I can't support this; any of it. I'll help go after our friends because it involves me, but after that—"

Luke stopped speaking abruptly. Layla watched him wrestle with the decision they both knew he needed to make – whether he was still in her life, or not. But even more than that, if he was going to join her in this world or not. Layla hadn't considered that Luke had still been trying to live as a human all these months since his power had opened, but it wasn't something Adrian had missed. As a hard shine of angry tears sprung to Luke's eyes, Layla realized Adrian's assessment had been acute – acute like talons shredding into Luke's well-controlled life.

Unbuckling his seatbelt, Luke rose, leaving the table. Layla watched him go, though the only place he could go in the plane was back to Adrian's sleeping area, yanking the partition shut behind him. Rising also, Rikyava glanced at Layla. "I'll go check on him."

"Thanks." Layla sighed, giving her friend a tired half-smile, her heart twisted in knots.

"No prob."

Silence settled around the table as Rikyava left, until Dusk heaved a hard sigh, glancing at Adrian. "Smooth move, Ex-lax."

"He's got to face the truth sometime." Adrian growled, clearly not about to give in on his position. "Luke's in denial about what he is, and what Layla is now."

"Still, you can't just push someone over a cliff and pray they'll fly." Dusk spoke, currying his hands through his hair. "We need him, Adrian. If we're going to face the White Chalice to get Layla's friends back… we could really use someone with *nullax* abilities on our side."

"Luke will come around," Layla spoke softly. "He can't deny his practical side."

But as both her bound lovers turned to gaze at her, a heavy doubt in their eyes, Layla heaved her own sigh. She realized suddenly that she didn't know Luke anymore, and couldn't predict what he'd do in this situation. Once, she could have counted on him even if she knew his rage was going to flare, but now she wasn't so sure.

As she mulled it over, a flare of luminescence suddenly passed through the plane as a wave of vicious disorientation rolled Layla. She inhaled as a high whine hit her ears, thinking the plane had exploded mid-air or something. But then she recognized it for the discomfort of traveling from the human world into the Twilight Realm, and Layla blinked, astounded that they'd made the transition somehow in mid-air.

But as she glanced out the window, she saw sprawling woodlands with fields of impossible colors below. As the jet began to bank down sharply for landing, Layla saw a runway cut through the woods. And there, right next to the woodland was the curved moat of Château de Chambord, with the sprawling grounds of the palace inside it.

The clan-home of the Storm Dragons of Europe.

Layla gripped Adrian's hand for landing, and he gave her a supportive squeeze as her nerves ratcheted up once more. Luke and Rikyava returned to their seats, though Luke studiously avoided all eyes as he sat and buckled in. As they touched down, Layla breathed an audible sigh of relief, feeling everyone else in the jet ease also. Her energy was truly having an effect on them all – even Rikyava more tight-wound than usual as the jet taxied off the runway into an unoccupied space of tarmac near the trees.

Forest surrounded the landing strip, and Layla marveled that the Storm Dragons had their own airstrip at Château de Chambord in the Twilight Realm, something that didn't exist in the human world. A few other private jets waited on the tarmac, with a sizable hangar for more. As the co-pilot opened the doors, everyone fetched belongings, disembarking. Dusk grabbed Layla's bags, leaving only her red purse to claim as they moved down the jet's steps, Layla frowning to see no welcome retinue waiting for them.

But even as she stepped down the last stair, gazing at the snowy woodland, she heard a roar like lions and a lashing sound like whips cut the brisk winter air. Around the edge of the forest suddenly came an enormous carriage pulled by a team of six iron-black manticores. As the lion-bodied creatures whipped their scorpion tails and flared bat-like wings, making the cracking sound Layla had heard through the forest, snarling and pulling in their traces, Layla saw the massive carriage was bigger than a tank, yet crafted in opulent 1700's French Baroque style.

Cobalt blue velvet interiors were augmented by gilded fleur-de-lis carved upon the doors and sides of the carriage, gilded tassels brushing the snow as the carriage arrived. As the driver sawed it to a halt, six footmen in Victorian garb leaped down with deep bows, claiming luggage with flashes in their storm-blue eyes. As the driver hopped down from his high seat, he and Adrian clasped arms with familiar smiles. It was then that Layla saw their driver was the Blood Dragon King Huttr Erdhelm's elegantly sexy younger son, Rhennic Erdhelm. Layla blinked in surprise as Rhennic claimed her hand, bowing over it with a clack of bootheels and a flash of his gorgeously subtle smile – immense pleasure in his vivid lavender eyes.

Rhennic was as immaculately modern as when she'd seen him two nights ago at the Yule Ball, wearing a sleek charcoal suit that looked like Armani with a royal purple tie, gold tie-bar, and gold cufflinks. So tall he towered a full hand even over Adrian, he was fit in an elegant way rather than bulky like his older brother and father. His gladiator-short Scandinavian-blond hair and beard were trim in GQ style, subtle red hi-lights showing in the snowy day. Rhennic smiled, clasping Dusk's hand with a fierce welcome, then embracing his cousin Rikyava with a hearty laugh. The energy of the Erdhelms was infectious; Layla suddenly couldn't be mad with Rhennic's amazing lavender eyes beaming at her, even as he turned back to Adrian.

"Adrian!" Rhennic spoke in a beautiful baritone, smoothly melodious yet fierce. "We heard all about the problems at the Hotel. Layla, my deepest condolences." He turned to Layla with a fierce sobriety in his eyes now. "We will do everything in our power to help find your friends. And to bring them home alive and unharmed."

"Thank you, Rhennic." Layla spoke, her heart suddenly feeling heavy again despite the warm welcome. But she found herself confused it was a Blood Dragon come to greet them at the Storm Dragon's home, even though Rhennic was the son of the Blood Dragon King. Risking committing a faux-pas, Layla asked, "But shouldn't there be a Storm Dragon emissary to welcome us to Chambord?"

"I am your Storm Dragon emissary." Rhennic laughed, flowing and musical, as he smiled at Layla. "Queen Justine is my mother. I'm the Storm Prince, Layla, Justine's only child – my magic has a Storm Dragon affinity rather than Blood. Technically, since King Huttr is my father I'm also a Blood Prince, but my elder brother Halfdir has the honor of being the Blood Throne's Regent should my father fall."

"Oh! Well, I feel like an idiot." Layla flushed.

"You are *not* an idiot." Rhennic spoke kindly, with subtle tones that Layla only now heard held the slightest French accent as he took up her hand, kissing it, even as his lavender eyes flashed with storms like Queen Justine's. "Come. My mother and father await at the Château. Your case takes priority today, and we will devour it to its utmost until we have a valid course of action. The White Chalice will not be tolerated, in Storm Dragon lands or anywhere else. And they will not survive our wrath."

With those bold words, Rhennic gestured towards the waiting carriage. Trying not to glance at Luke, Layla followed the Storm Dragon Prince to his hansom, taking his hand as he offered it to help her up the high iron steps. He was a gentleman as he did so, and Layla felt no mate-taste from him as he helped her up into the massive carriage.

But as their hands released, at the very last touch of their fingertips, a subtle flash of electrifying power gripped Layla. Arrested, she stared at the Storm Prince where he stood beside the carriage, as Rhennic lifted a subtle eyebrow over his arresting lavender eyes, deepened now to a bold royal plum color. A delicious scent of heather and lavender curled from Rhennic as his gaze held hers, as if he couldn't quite contain his magic at the sudden connection of their touch.

And an answering scent of sweet bourbon and bright citrus flowed from Layla, as her drakaina rose high in her veins with eager interest.

CHAPTER 17 – POWER

Château de Chambord was just as incredible as Layla remembered it from the human world. As the carriage drove up over the bridge that spanned Chambord's slow-flowing river of a moat, Layla marveled at the Château beneath the heavy winter sky. A false fortress built in the 1500's with opulent turrets, soaring balustrades, and exquisite French Renaissance facades to mimic Italianate architecture and look like the skyline of Constantinople, the palace was stunning as they approached – just as Layla remembered it as a tourist to France years ago.

Château de Chambord in the human world had been constructed as an ostentatious hunting lodge for King Francis I, and the Twilight Realm version was equally opulent. As they drove around the quadrangle to enter the fortress at the rear, opposite where the false moat surrounded the royal gardens, Layla saw this Chambord was ornate throughout the structure, rather than just in the King's section. That palace had been built of granite, but this one was built of a stone Layla didn't know – shining white in the grey day with veins of an ore that flashed like opal lightning through the walls and turrets.

As if the entire building had been made of pearl then thrust through with storms like fire-opals, Layla found herself gaping at the powerful effect as they stepped from the carriage. The vaulted ebony doors to the palace's rear entrance were thrown wide for their arrival, a welcome-guard of fifty Storm Dragons in charcoal-grey Victorian uniforms waiting at stiff attention in a chevron flanking the ingress.

As Layla took Rhennic's hand, stepping down from the carriage, she saw the rear grounds had extensive stables and out-buildings that didn't exist in the human world. Extensively farmed, corrals of sheep, goats, and livestock were interspersed with sprawling orchards, grape arbors, and berry fields. Most of it was dormant for winter, but Layla saw certain areas still green with production, no snow on the ground as they shimmered beneath some kind of magical barrier that flickered with lightning and sudden rainstorms.

Amazed, Layla realized the Storm Dragons had methods of terraforming their land with magic, and as Rhennic escorted her towards the wide quadrangle of the Château, she saw vast herb gardens flanking the building, blooming in full-summer riot beneath the translucent barriers. As they approached, Layla shivered, feeling like she was about to get lanced with millions of megawatts of electricity, but as she passed through that shifting barrier and into a summer-warm environment fragrant with sun and rain, Rhennic glanced over.

"Don't worry," he spoke encouragingly. "You and your friends are guests. Our storm-barriers don't harm guests."

"Though they're a pretty gnarly surprise for anyone who's not invited." Rikyava snarked with a chuckle behind them as they moved through the chevron of guards and arrived at the palace's rear ingress.

"Indeed." Rhennic grinned at Rikyava as if sharing some private joke.

The magical barriers weren't the fortress' only protection, however. At the ends of the long quadrangle, Layla saw towers that didn't exist in the human-world Château. Atop each tower, an enormous Dragon coiled in beast form, talons bigger than a Buick gouging into the well-scraped walls and turrets. The massive storm-blue and grey Dragon-Guards had an oilslick color to their scales, and as Layla watched one roar, flaring humungous wings and a mantle of brilliant blue spikes like a frilled lizard, she felt a thunderclap hit the air, a flash of lightning blazing in the winter clouds above.

As the Dragon-Guard adjusted its position coiled around the tower, Layla watched the winter storm-clouds far above the Château roil, as if the giant beast was directing them with its power. She suddenly recalled why Storm Dragons were so feared in the Twilight Realm – because they could actually direct thunderstorms, and zap an enemy with billions of volts of lightning.

Beyond the tower, a gargantuan coliseum stood stark against the heavy winter sky. Almost like the one in Rome but styled with French Renaissance details, it was made of the Château's opalescent lightning-stone. Storm Dragons ranging from opal-white to a deep, thundercloud violet-black came and went, perching on the building, preening, and flying in to enormous nests built into the alcoves of the coliseum. Layla blinked, amazed that Queen Justine's people spent so much time in Dragon-form that they needed a place to sleep. But this was the first active Dragon clan-home Layla had visited, and as they entered the double-doors of the fortress' quadrangle, Layla saw a bustling palace of other Storm Dragons coming and going in human form – all of whom glanced with interest and a flash of cunning in their dark blue eyes at their guests.

Passing through the vaulted ingress and into the Château's bailey, Layla saw the area wasn't crushed gravel like in the human world, but an immense courtyard full of herbs and flowers with elegant fountains that rivaled the Palace of Versailles. As she marveled at it, the Château's keep towering over them with flashes of opal lightning flickering through its white turrets, the Storm Dragon Queen herself suddenly flowed out of the keep and down the steps.

Approaching on the arm of the Blood Dragon King Huttr Erdhelm, Queen Justine Toulet was riveting, and Layla was immediately arrested by the Storm Queen's presence. King Huttr wore buckled leathers with a polar bear pelt over his massive shoulders, his beard braided like his mane of fiery red hair, shaven with Dragons on the sides, his strong face beaming to see them. But Queen Justine's iron-hard frame was pure grace as she moved forward. Like Meryl Streep playing the Queen of England, she was a small, fine-boned woman, with long silver hair and midnight-blue eyes. But as she approached in storm-grey breeches, boots, and vest like she'd just been out for a Victorian country ride, her silver hair in a loose braid over one shoulder, her deep midnight eyes flashed with storms so powerful that Layla shivered – a nimbus of energy crackling around Justine as if her body couldn't keep it contained.

Greeting her guests, Queen Justine smiled in a mysterious pleasure, kissing everyone upon both cheeks. As she came to Layla, Layla instinctually balked from the Storm Queen's crackling touch. But as Queen Justine set her thin hands to Layla's shoulders, giving her a peck at each cheek, Layla felt none of the Queen's riotous storms pour through her. Still, Justine pulled back with intense knowledge in her eyes as lightning flashed through them – as if she knew things about Layla that Layla herself didn't even know yet.

The Storm Queen was an enigma, yet as she turned to Luke, she suddenly paused with a frown. Queen Justine's midnight-blue eyes flashed, and she breathed in her heavily-accented alto, "Close your eyes, child of Storms, and come to welcome in your Clan."

Incredibly, Luke did as he was told. As if the Storm Queen had rattled him to his core, he didn't just close his eyes but sank to one knee before her. Layla stood, amazed as the Storm Queen set a hand to the crown of Luke's head, as if he was being knighted.

As Queen Justine lifted her chin, closing her eyes in a sudden ray of sunlight that lanced the clouds, a shudder rippled Luke. Crying out, he fell to his hands and knees upon the gravel, shaking hard. Layla felt a boom of thunder hammer the courtyard, but it hadn't come from the Storm Queen. It had come from Luke, and as he hung his head, shuddering with power and gritting his teeth, his eyes tight as if he was in pain, Queen Justine sank gracefully to her knees before him. Raising his face in her little hands, the Storm Queen smoothed tears from his cheeks with her thumbs. Taking up the bloodstone pendant from his chest, she lifted it off over his head – then cast it to the gravel like so much trash.

Layla hardly heard her words beside Luke's cheek as she cradled his face tenderly. "Do not fear what you are, child. Others will have terror of your power, but to you it will become a blessing. Come. Your Clan welcomes you, and your Queen is glad you are with us."

Helping Luke to standing, the Storm Queen set a hand to his chest, then flooded a smooth energy into him. Luke gasped as he ceased shuddering, blinking in amazement as if relieved. The Storm Queen had somehow soothed the magic that stormed Luke, and as she took his arm with a smile, beckoning for the others, Layla followed in quiet reverence. Even big King Huttr only nodded welcome to them all, though he embraced his niece Rikyava – something about Luke's welcome taking priority to everything else.

As they moved inside, Layla saw massive tapestries flanking the ingress, of Dragons soaring through stormy skies. Leading up the spiraling double-helix staircase at the center of the keep, Queen Justine took them to the second level and into a cozy dining-hall set with heavy ebony furniture carved with dragons. A pleasant breakfast spread awaited them, fountains burbling in the corners of the room, which didn't exist in the human-world Chambord. Inside the palace, every wall curled with greenery blooming behind barriers of flickering energy. Where the human-world Chambord was almost dreary, its gargantuan windows barely enough to let light in to such a heavily-constructed fortress, this palace felt bright and airy – the breeze full of refreshing ozone, the planters giving a warm glow like sunshine.

Layla felt uplifted by the space as everyone took seats around the broad table, servants in Victorian attire moving forward to briskly unveil the waiting spread upon their silver platters. As Rikyava settled to a seat beside her enormous Viking uncle, hugging him again, Layla realized they were being treated more like family than guests. Clapping her hands for servers to start filling plates, Queen Justine began their talks informally, glancing to Adrian where he sat next to Layla – the fiercely elegant Rhennic having claimed the seat on Layla's other side before Dusk could get to it.

"Tell us of your predicament, Adrian," Queen Justine spoke low but with iron-hard intent in her musical French accent. "Let us waste no time in pleasantries while lives are at stake."

"Of course, my Queen." Adrian spoke soberly, even as he took up a gilded china cup of coffee with a nod of thanks to the server. "I believe Dusk briefed Rhennic on the details?"

"And I did also brief our Queen," Rhennic spoke as he began eating a heaping plate of eggs and steak for breakfast with cultured elegance. "But we need to know more about the White Chalice angle of the story, Adrian. What specifics do you have?"

"Few, unfortunately." Adrian spoke as he sipped his coffee. "Only that a sect still lives, that they have a High Priest who somehow noticed Layla is the Royal Dragon Bind, and felt Luke's power come on-line. He wants to meet them, and has abducted Layla's friends as bait. The Intercessoria's recent measures to make our Hotel more secure against Hunter couldn't get a trace on the humans. And our old measures are offline due to Intercessoria involvement."

"And the Intercessoria aren't going to be involved here." Queen Justine purred dangerously as she sat back in her throne-like chair with grace, crossing her knees and sipping her coffee. "I'm sure they've deemed this an *inter-clan matter.*"

"How did you know?" Dusk spoke up, surprised.

"History." Queen Justine smiled over her coffee cup, though it was bitter. "The Intercessoria refused to become involved the first time I sought to rout the White Chalice. Because the Chalice are technically Storm Dragons, the issue falls within the Intercessoria's Articles of Clan Governance. And because Faunus aren't normally aggressive, they deemed the Faunus alliance with the Chalice *unnotable.* Which was why I sought the aid of our clan's ancient enemies at that time for help – the strongest Dragons I knew in my part of the world, besides my own."

Queen Justine gave King Huttr a genial nod, and Layla saw a deep respect pass between the two monarchs as Huttr continued the tale in his booming basso. "Justine and I came to accord in those days, and managed to rout most of the Chalice. But the primary house of worship for their zealotry is guarded by extremely tricky *nullax* magic. Though we had a strong *nullax* in Justine's clan to counter the Chalice's protective barriers, that person died before we could finish. *Nullax* are rare," his astute gaze settled upon Luke, "and we had no others in either my clan or Justine's. If you truly are one, lad, then we have a chance at penetrating the last remaining Chalice stronghold for the first time in three hundred years. But since you're a mix, we'll need to test you first and see which way your magic is leaning."

"But I thought my magic was maturing into a Storm Dragon *nullax*?" Luke frowned as he regarded King Huttr, then Queen Justine.

"You hold numerous Dragon bloodlines, child," Queen Justine spoke softly. "Based on your temperament and any use of magic you may have had recently, your power will shape itself. Though I sense you are currently leaning heavily into Storm Dragon *nullax* magic, to truly determine if you will be Blood or Storm and what focus your magic will have, we need to engage a Trial of Proving. The sooner the better – ideally, this afternoon."

"What does that entail?" Luke frowned, his green eyes sober.

"Facing both Huttr and I in battle," Justine spoke levelly though her dark eyes flashed, "until your magic flares enough to truly scent its direction."

"It's a controlled trial, as much as such things can be," Rikyava supplied as she turned to Luke. "Justine and my uncle know their magics – they won't push you further than you should be pushed. You can trust them."

"What if I hurt someone?" Luke blinked, looking back to Justine.

"That you phrased it that way rather than asking *what if I get hurt*, tells me you know how much power you hold." Queen Justine chuckled, her dark blue eyes knowing. "I sense a tremendous rage in you, Luke Murphy, so enormous it is blinding. And yet, there is also capacity for great compassion. Will your blinding rage win if you are pushed? We shall see."

Justine gave an elegantly French shrug that said little and much, her deep gaze still resting on Luke. Something about Justine's gesture sent shivers rioting up Layla's spine. She saw Luke shiver also, deeply unsettled as the conversation turned.

"In any case," King Huttr continued, "knowing the Chalice still have a foothold in our lands makes my blood boil. Clearly, this was an intentional strike, meant to goad Luke and Layla into making a rash dash to the Chalice's hide-hole. I'm sure it's a trap, engineered by this High Priest. He wants to capture Luke, to turn him to Chalice zealotry, and to eliminate such a strong opposing force as Layla before she's able to be a nuisance."

"Why do you call the Chalice zealots?" Layla asked, frowning.

"Are they deeply religious?"

"In the worst way." King Huttr snorted as his eyes swirled with crimson, disdain in the set of his rock-cracking jaw. "Thousands of years ago, a man came to Europe and Scandinavia, a traveling priest who spoke well and drew many ears. He had no name, but those who eventually became the White Chalice listened to him, calling him the *Sage of the Wilds*. He preached for unity of all magical Lineages, but his words became twisted as the Chalice were born. They believed unity through force was best, and began to line-breed *nullax* against any opposition."

"To quell powerful naysayers." Layla spoke up.

"Indeed." Huttr boomed, his red eyes flashing. "They became a thorn in all the Twilight clans of Europe and Scandinavia. Chalice would surface in an area, nullify any opposition, then rule as if they owned the area, demanding tithes of slaves, wealth, and resources. Which they would receive, though the clans fumed. Essentially, clans were still allowed to govern themselves, but when Chalice traveled into your area, clans had to tread *very* carefully."

"To not lose their most powerful members." Luke chimed in.

"Just so." Queen Justine purred with a sober nod. "The Dragon clans suffered most, since we have the most powerful battle-magics. We lost many to nullification in those days – until my own power proved immune to *nullax*."

"You're immune?" Luke blinked, his eyebrows lifted in astonishment.

"I am, and so is my son." Queen Justine nodded at Rhennic with a small smile. "But I had to wage my fight against the Chalice carefully in those days, to not lose my best fighters. The centuries-long battle I fought against them raised me into Queenship. And now we may have a chance to finish the job."

"Do you know where the last members of the Chalice are hiding?" Adrian asked Queen Justine. "Where they've taken Layla's friends? The Smoke Faunus informant we captured passed out from torture before she could tell us a location."

"I do know where they are." The Storm Queen spoke peaceably. "But getting to that excessively well-protected location requires two things I did not have until now – a *nullax* and a Royal Crystal Dragon." She lifted a cunning eyebrow at Luke, then Dusk. "I was not entirely certain the Chalice were still alive, they have been so quiet these past centuries, but I knew they still had one fortress I had never breached. Now I know they hide there like rats in a sewer – and now we are able to come for them."

"But why now?" Layla frowned, seeing a glaring problem in everything that had taken place. "If they've been so quiet these past centuries, just hiding, why strike now and risk themselves? If they know anything about me, they know I've Bound a Royal Crystal Dragon, and that Luke is my friend. They would know we have the right elements to breach their fortress."

"Which is why it's a trap." King Huttr boomed, scowling. "They want you to come. If they simply wanted to damage you, they would have slaughtered your friends, not captured them and goaded you into coming. They want something else. And it is that unknown something that sets my hackles bristling."

"Just so." Queen Justine continued darkly as she sipped her coffee. "They want Layla and Luke inside their stronghold. Why? We cannot know until we get there."

"But what other option do we have?" Layla asked, her heart twisting as her Dragon roared with a strangled sensation in her veins.

"None." Queen Justine spoke, her gaze formidable but gentle as it settled upon Layla. Suddenly, she flicked her fingers at the servers.

Rushing forward, they filled empty champagne flutes waiting near every plate. As Queen Justine took up her champagne, Layla blinked then followed suit, realizing they were about to have a breakfast toast.

"A toast." The Storm Queen spoke with a subtle smile. "To Layla Price, the reason we are all here today. Who else but a Royal Dragon Bind could bring so many tremendous powers together under one roof?"

Layla paused with her champagne, a horrible roil of energy suddenly passing through her. It wasn't the Storm Queen's, but her own Dragon coiling inside her veins with a roar of pain and heartbreak – knowing the real reason they were all gathered here today. Luke's magic, Adrian on the lam from the Crimson Circle, Dusk cracking with the pressure of too many stresses. And her human friends, abducted like pawns in a terrible chess game they didn't have any answers to, it was all Layla's fault. She felt that pit of blackness open deep inside her, felt it reaching out odious tendrils to try and strangle her Dragon as a tremor passed through her.

"Are you saying I only make friends with people who have power?" Layla spoke as she lowered her champagne.

"Or are powerful friends drawn to you?" The Storm Queen countered, her dark blue eyes flashing with astute awareness. "Beloved of the First of the Moroccan Desert Dragons, a man who rises like a shooting star from an ancient and formidable clan. Cherished by the First of the Egyptian Crystal Dragons, a man so powerful he must keep it a secret so he's not a target to his King. A Royal Siren who would have been King, banished from his clan and become one of the world's most prominent Courtiers. Friend to the Phoenix King before his demise, a battle-lord vanquished by none. Hunted by something dark, called only by the strongest of any century. Friend to a possible *nullax*, even before your powers truly opened. And a Queen of Storms who feels your call, rioting through her aged body from afar. Yes, I feel your magic flooding me like a golden dawn, ever since we met. But I am not the Storm Dragon for you, child – though someone else of great power is."

Queen Justine's eyes filled with dark pleasure as everyone shifted around the table. She knew the avalanche she'd just rolled as everyone thought about the power they had as a group, called together by Layla's Bind-magic. Raising her champagne, the Storm Queen had a demure sip, and everyone followed. As she lowered her flute, her deeply cunning gaze moved around the table with a pressure in Layla's ears like a building thunderstorm.

But as the Storm Queen gave another secretive smile, her dark blue eyes flashing, Layla wondered who the real players were in this game of power – and if she'd just been deeply played.

CHAPTER 18 – PROVING

Standing at the edge of the packed dirt floor inside the enormous Roman coliseum, Layla gazed up at the wide winter sky, seeing storm clouds roil overhead. Waiting with Dusk, Adrian, Rikyava, and Rhennic, Layla fidgeted as she watched Luke move out to the center of the coliseum at Chambord, facing Queen Justine and King Huttr with his breath puffing in the chill air. No one knew how this magical proving was about to go, but as Layla saw the stubborn set of his strong shoulders and the flash of his fierce green eyes, she knew Luke wasn't about to back down.

Whatever the two Dragon monarchs were about to throw at him, he was up for the challenge.

As if responding to the tension building in the coliseum, the winter sky heaved with dense grey clouds. The Storm Dragons at Chambord had been permitted to observe this testing of a potential new member, and in the rows of stone benches that moved up the steep tiers, Storm Dragons in human form settled into a watchful silence. At the higher open-air vaults, Storm Dragons in beast-form perched, flown in at the upper galleries to watch the proceedings. As Layla stood at the sidelines on the main floor, the entire thing suddenly made her think of gladiators facing off with lions and bears in the ring.

Except that for all his fitness, Luke was no gladiator – and Queen Justine and King Huttr were far more dangerous than lions and bears.

As Luke faced the two monarchs with nothing but his bare hands and his magic, Layla's nerves cranked up to an eleven. A scorched bourbon-orange scent barreled off her, and standing beside her, Adrian took her hand with a reassuring presence. Rhennic glanced over at Layla with a thoughtful frown, but Dusk and Rikyava remained riveted, their attention fixed on the scene. Dusk looked pensive as he watched, but Rikyava kept crossing and re-crossing her arms over her chest, moving her fingers restlessly over the knives and guns in her rig as she scowled deeply at the proceedings.

Reaching out, Rhennic griped her shoulder. "Easy, cuz," Layla heard him murmur in his elegant baritone. "Luke's going to be fine."

"I know, I know." Rikyava bit back tersely. "I just wish there was a better way. He's basically never fought with his magic yet, except for a few things I got to show him the other day down in the Guardhall."

Layla's eyebrows raised, having not known Rikyava was training Luke in fight-magic. Yet another secret he'd kept from her, but Layla blinked as she realized Rikyava had been withholding that information also. But Luke was his own person, and this was his magical maturation, Layla reminded herself as her attention returned to the show. Out in the center of the coliseum, Queen Justine was speaking to Luke and he was nodding, as if she were explaining how things would go.

It seemed they hadn't started yet, just preamble, when suddenly Queen Justine set a hand to Luke's shoulder. Luke stood firm one moment, but the next, Layla felt a blast of energy out in the middle of the ring. Luke was suddenly down on his knees with a short scream of pain. Layla felt her heart lurch, but beside her, Rikyava visibly trembled, setting her jaw with a small growl. As Luke twisted beneath the Storm Queen's touch, King Huttr stepped forward. Setting a hand to Luke's shoulder also, Layla saw a quick whirl of blood droplets surge through the air – and then King Huttr's magic hit Luke like a sledgehammer, knocking Luke backwards like a bull, sprawling him onto his back in the dirt.

Beside Layla, Rikyava surged again, and Layla practically felt it when Rhennic clamped his hand down on the Guardswoman's shoulder. Rikyava shrugged her cousin off and he let go, but even Dusk and Adrian had looked over now, Dusk blinking with a sudden awareness on his face as he watched Rikyava. Layla didn't know what Dusk had understood. But as she watched Luke rise from the dirt, fury sparking in his hot green eyes at the treatment he'd just endured, wiping away blood from a cut on his lip, she suddenly felt Luke's power.

It didn't just surge out from him – it roared from him in a maelstrom. Layla's eyes went wide as she felt it hit her, staggering her and Rikyava at the perimeter of the fight-ring, though not Adrian, Dusk, or Rhennic. As Layla watched, something enormous whirled from Luke, rushing through the amphitheater and causing dirt to lift into dust-devils all around him. Rage sparked in his eyes, making them flicker like Queen Justine's as electricity sparked through the cold air. Far above, the clouds roiled into a deep dark thunderhead, where none had been before.

Beside Layla, Rhennic whistled low. "Fucker's a Royal Storm Dragon. Well, I'll be."

"I told you." Rikyava bit tersely, still watching with tension in her every muscle.

"What's happening, exactly?" Layla asked Adrian, still silent beside her.

"Queen Justine and King Huttr both did to Luke what I did to you once – they bit him with their magic. It causes the inner Dragon to rush up, to show itself in a wash of fierce power, chasing the other Dragon out of their body. If we'd seen any blood whirl around Luke, he would have been Blood Dragon dominant, or still undecided. Since we only saw storms, it's clear he's maturing into a Storm Dragon. And from the look of things," Adrian glanced at Layla, "a very powerful Royal Storm Dragon."

"How can you tell?" Layla asked, as she watched King Huttr and Queen Justine face off with Luke again, now that he'd had a breather and his funnels of dirt had subsided. Far above, the dark thundercloud had dissipated, though the clouds still seemed heavier than before.

"Non-Royal Storm Dragons can't call the sky for decades after their power opens, and sometimes never. Royals can do it right away." Dusk glanced at Layla, some deep knowledge in his eyes still. "Royals can also manifest lightning around their bodies, like Luke did just now."

"What are they doing now?" Layla asked tensely as she watched King Huttr and Queen Justine approach Luke again.

"Testing to see what flavor Luke's magic has as a Storm Dragon," Rhennic supplied with a glance at Layla. "It's called the Trial of Resonance. Watch."

As Layla watched, she saw Queen Justine flick her hand, and a fierce rush of wind barreled into Luke in a funnel. It threw him to his ass, but as it did, an answering funnel roared up around him, wild and unrestrained, barreling towards Queen Justine. King Huttr stepped in, throwing up a shield-wall of blood droplets like a surging red rain to block Luke's blast. Before Luke could recover, Queen Justine stepped out from behind Huttr's barrier, gripping her hands into the air and making a ripping motion as her eyes flashed. A deafening concussion of thunder split the air, and even as Layla clapped hands to her ears, she saw Luke's body spasm like a bow, brutalized by Justine's power. He screamed, but even as he screamed, his hands clawed into talons and ripped at the air in a similar motion, throwing a hard wave of thunder back at Justine.

Again, King Huttr threw up his shield-wall of blood to protect the

Storm Queen. But this time, Layla saw Luke's power stagger the big Blood Dragon King as Luke's thunder hit the wall.

"Shit." Rhennic cursed beside Layla, frowning now as if that hadn't been part of the plan.

"I told you Luke was too strong for this kind of thing without a talisman on."

"Justine is old-school, Rikyava," Rhennic spoke tersely, though his gaze didn't leave the show now. "And so is Huttr. Let them do it their way."

"Their funeral." She growled, and suddenly Layla was wondering if Rikyava was right. Alarm filled her as she watched Justine bend her body and then roar at the sky far above, whirling the clouds into a seething black mass above the coliseum. Like a call-and-response game, Luke was somehow compelled to imitate it, though Layla hadn't seen Justine throw any energy his way this time. Throwing her hand up at the sky, Queen Justine raked fingers like talons down from the sky towards the earth. The sky obeyed her command, a bolt of lightning flashing down to blast a patch of sand on the far end of the amphitheater, melting it to glass. Though Layla was nearly deafened, white searing her vision, she heard Luke's answering scream. He'd not been struck by Justine's lightning, but was somehow compelled to imitate her yet again.

Calling lightning down from the roiling black clouds in a furious thunderbolt.

Luke's lightning was not as controlled as the Storm Queen's, blasting the upper ramparts of the coliseum rather than the dirt ring. Stunned Dragons took flight, roaring as they flashed away faster than Layla could blink. On his knees in the dirt, Luke was screaming as if something had gone wrong. Spasming, roaring, Layla thought he was going to shift, when he suddenly staggered up.

Layla inhaled as she heard Rikyava and Rhennic curse beside her, Adrian and Dusk giving stunned growls at what they were seeing. In the center of the amphitheater, Luke's eyes had gone to an emerald fury so wrecked that it shuddered all the way through him, making him look possessed like a demon. All that ferocious rage was trained on the Storm Queen, and as he strode towards her, a white nimbus rose like a mist of flickering opal lightning all around him.

Beside Layla, Rikyava cursed. Queen Justine jolted back, and suddenly a tremendous roar split the air. In a swirling fury of red blood, King Huttr rushed in before the Storm Queen in Dragon-form, snarling as a big snow-white Dragon with geodesic blood-lines racing through his scales. Raising an enormous mantle of blood-red spears, the big King of the Blood Dragons opened a cruel maw and roared at Luke, corralling Justine back behind him.

Huttr was so big he could have eaten Luke in a single bite, yet still Luke came for him. Like a man possessed, Luke's stride towards the Dragon monarchs didn't slow even as Queen Justine crackled with an enormous nimbus of power in human form like an electric sub-station. Layla didn't need anyone to tell her shit was about to go down, as Luke's opal-mist suddenly rushed up around him so hard and fast it looked like a hurricane, his gaze fixed on the tiny Justine as if he could blow her skin right off her bones.

Though Justine stood strong, holding out a pacifying hand to Luke as she stepped back around from behind the snarling Huttr, Luke was gone, Layla saw with a terrible horror. Swallowed by some magic she didn't understand but knew to her bones was absolutely evil, his body was filled with it, his skin bright with a shine like some elder god. As Layla saw his eyes as he regarded his Queen, she saw they weren't green anymore but filled with an awful light, bright white and scalding.

Layla didn't even feel Rhennic change it was that fast. But in a blast of energy like a lightning-bolt, Rhennic was suddenly flashing in before Justine – an enormous white Dragon with a fractal pattern of crimson and midnight blue running through his scales. He made it just as that nimbus of opal-mist lightning around Luke hurtled out. Funneling into Rhennic rather than its intended target of Justine, that massive energy blasted Rhennic's Dragon back against the nearest stone arch – shattering the arch as something deep inside Rhennic broke with a sickening crunch.

Adrian and Dusk ran to Rhennic as Layla stood frozen in horror, watching it all like a bad action film come alive. Rikyava rushed to Luke, who had fallen to his knees, empty of that terrible opal power now and blinking at the carnage as if in shock. As Layla ran to Luke also, knowing she was of no use for the resuscitation efforts happening with Rhennic – human again – she saw Luke's eyes suddenly clear. They were so vibrantly emerald that Layla could have cried, and as she came to him, Rikyava on her knees as she gripped Luke's shoulders, searching his eyes, Layla saw horror devour Luke's face.

"Layla? Rikyava?" He spoke as he tried to catch his breath. "What happened?"

"Your *nullax* rose." It was Queen Justine who answered as she approached, gazing solemnly at Luke, though she did glance at the revival efforts happening with her son. Rhennic was coming to, though he grimaced in pain as Dusk touched his ribs. As Rhennic lifted a hand, summoning a crackle of lightning in his palm and then nodded, relief filled the faces of those around him, and Layla realized what had just happened.

By his last-minute move, Rhennic had taken the *nullax* blow meant for his mother. A blow that might have nullified King Huttr's magics had it funneled into him instead of its intended target, or Justine's *nullax*-immune son. Even so, it had been a vicious blow, enough to end the fight as a number of Rhennic's Storm Dragon comrades helped their Prince limp off the field. Rhennic's lavender gaze caught Layla's for a brief moment before he was escorted beneath the arches of the coliseum back towards the palace. Layla saw the warning in Rhennic's eyes, and the concern for her.

Luke was a terrible power – and in his blind rage, he had no control.

Layla looked back to Luke, still on his knees and breathing hard, his green eyes wide with shock, Rikyava steadying him. Storm Dragons all around the ring were keeping a safe distance, regarding Luke with a dark wariness and whispering. Standing directly before Luke, the Storm Queen knelt, cupping his face in her hands. As Luke gave her a panicked gaze, the elderly Queen smiled, and Layla felt something flow from her body into his. It was like a sleeping-draught, similar to the way she'd calmed him before but far more potent. As Layla watched, Luke slumped, his dark eyelashes flickering with a heavy fatigue. Moving in fast, Rikyava got under Luke's arm, hauling him up by his arm around her strong shoulders.

"Rikyava…?" Luke sighed, barely able to focus as he glanced to her.

"Easy, I got you…" Rikyava spoke low, and the tender way she said it suddenly made everything inside Layla alert. Like a fool, it was then that Layla saw everything she'd been missing, which Dusk had not. The tenderness in Rikyava's gaze as she helped Luke stand. The way his arm curled around her, familiar, bringing their bodies into plenty of contact. Rikyava's no-bullshit demeanor softening as she helped walk him slowly off the field.

The sweet kiss they shared just before they rounded an arch and exited the coliseum.

Layla was left standing alone as a sluice of thoughts raced through her, wondering how long Rikyava and Luke had been speaking since his magic opened, and how many conversations there had been. She wondered if Rikyava had ever gone to visit him in Seattle, or if they'd finally just met in person when he'd arrived at the Hotel. She wondered how long they had been feeling something for each other – and how in blazes had she missed it.

Layla was still staring at the arch they'd departed through when Dusk stepped to her. Lacing his fingers through hers, a deep knowledge filled his eyes as he lifted her hand to his lips and kissed it. Blinking, Layla looked around, meeting his gaze.

"How long did you know? About Rikyava and Luke?"

"I didn't." Dusk gave a sad smile. "But I'm not surprised. They've been talking a lot this fall. I thought it was just about Luke's magic, but… apparently not."

"Was Luke the person Rikyava's been pining for since August?" Layla gazed back to the arch, seeing Storm Dragons departing through it now that the show was over.

"I don't think so." Dusk shook his head, glancing over as Adrian walked up. "That was someone else, but Rikyava's tight-lipped when it comes to people she cares for."

As Adrian arrived, they didn't have time to discuss anything else as he kissed Layla briefly on the lips. "I'm going to go help the Storm Dragon medics heal Rhennic. Dusk? Are you available?"

"In a moment." Dusk gave Layla a glance and Adrian looked to her.

"Layla? Are you ok?" Adrian spoke gently.

"I don't know." Layla blinked, still in deep shock. "It's not every day you find out your ex has power so frightening it nearly made you shit your pants. And is in love with your other friend."

Adrian raised his eyebrows, not comprehending, but as he glanced to Dusk, Dusk said, "Luke and Rikyava are a thing."

Adrian gave a long, slow blink. "Well, I guess that explains a few things."

Layla didn't know how much it explained versus how many questions it created. But as Adrian slung an arm around her and Dusk led her away by their twined fingers, darkness began to core her deep inside as she realized how much of a bad friend she had been to Luke. How self-centered she'd been; how much she had focused only on herself rather than keeping in touch with her friends. As Layla stepped through the stone arch that Luke and Rikyava had departed through, back towards the Château, she felt that cavernous darkness devour her as a vicious self-chastisement rose. Her life had spiraled on in a radical direction since she'd left Seattle – and it was shocking to find out how much the lives of her friends had spiraled on elsewhere.

With a sensation like blackness seized her heart, Layla felt herself being dragged into a dark place. A place that began to fill her like a void as it wrapped around her Dragon's talons and pulled her into the deeps.

CHAPTER 19 – LATER

Layla had been alone all afternoon as Dusk and Adrian helped Rhennic recover. Rikyava was tending Luke, and with the Storm Queen and Blood King marshaling their Dragons for an imminent campaign against the White Chalice, Layla found herself with nothing to do after Luke's testing but fret. Pacing in her tower-suite, she at last slung on her navy peacoat and walked out to the gardens in the bailey, wandering their luscious foliage and burbling fountains. But even that couldn't calm her, and Layla found herself walking out of the quadrangle, nodding to the Storm Dragon guards who came to attention as she exited the Château. Returning to the coliseum where Luke had displayed his terrifying powers, she continued out to the horse barns, but found the barns populated by manticores rather than horses, decidedly not friendly.

Now, Layla was pacing through a winter-dormant pear orchard, gazing up at golden fruits that had somehow been left to crystallize upon the boughs rather than rot beneath the wide winter sky. The sugars within them had preserved into candy, and Layla watched as sugar sparkled on the pear skins in the grey winter light. It was beautiful, haunting and delicate, and for some reason, the sight of the golden pears glimmering in the winter-barren orchards captured her – stilling something deep inside which had been restless all day.

"They're called *aurum*, our winter-preserved pears. They're considered a delicacy throughout the Twilight Realm. We produce only a few hundred each year."

An elegant baritone voice spoke behind Layla, making her turn as her hand came away from touching a crystallized pear on the leafless tree. As she glanced at the intruder, she brushed her fingertips together, sloughing a fine coating of sugar from them. "Aurum, isn't that the Latin word for gold?"

"It is. The pears are named not just for their color, but for the feeling one gets eating it… like a golden dawn opens up inside the body." Standing in the orchard's row with his hands tucked in the pockets of a thick grey peacoat, his collar popped against the cold, the amazingly tall Rhennic smiled at Layla with his lavender eyes bright as violets beneath the grey winter sky.

Twilight was coming, the clouds darkening to a heavy slate color, and a hush had swallowed the fields this far from the Château. Layla turned to Rhennic, her breath puffing in the air as she admired his bright eyes and Scandinavian bone structure. She could see his mother Queen Justine now in his calm posture as he regarded her, silent and subtly amused. Though tall and excellently fit with broad shoulders, he was leaner than his brother and father. Towering over Layla, he was a full hand taller even than Adrian, and would have seemed like a giant had he not been so cut rather than bulky. It was obvious now that Rhennic had Storm Dragon in him, a distinct elegance Blood Dragons didn't have – and a deeper nature as he stood there with his subtly smiling eyes, watching Layla.

"Shouldn't you be convalescing?" Layla asked, somehow not surprised that Rhennic had found her this far out on the property.

"I am." He spoke simply. "Cold helps Storm Dragons recover from injury. I was doing ice baths earlier. You missed it. Made me roar like a manticore, but they work. Though Storm Dragons aren't the most adapted to cold temperatures. Ice Dragons can lounge in a hole cut from a winter-frozen lake for hours, sipping vodka and having pleasant conversation like they're relaxing in a hot tub."

The image made Layla smile, despite her churning. Rhennic was like a combination of Adrian and Dusk – winsomely cheeky and arrestingly sexy all at once. With his own gripping steadiness that reminded Layla of Queen Justine.

"Did Luke hurt you?" She asked, something deep inside her needing to know, as if it was somehow her fault.

"Bad enough." Rhennic's lavender eyes darkened as he sobered. "Six broken ribs, a pierced lung, broke my left tibia and nearly wrenched my shoulder out of its socket from that impact." As if feeling his pain, Rhennic winced, removing his left hand from his pocket and rolling his shoulder. "Luke may not be able to reproduce that kind of power anytime soon without my mother provoking him, but his Royal ability is impressive, Layla. And dangerous."

"So I saw." Layla spoke quietly, still wondering what that meant for Luke. "So Luke doesn't have all those abilities at his beck and call yet?"

"Not yet." But Rhennic's intense gaze didn't ease as he spoke, giving it to Layla straight. "Though now that he knows what he's capable of, he may try to reproduce everything soon. My mother has a unique talent of getting people to show their strongest abilities when her magic bites them, even if they can't consciously use their powers yet. It's helped her sort our Storm Dragons into healthy clan-positions for centuries, and minimizes internal duels, to know how strong someone will be and what their talents are. But Justine almost met her match in that ring today. It's not something that's happened for a long time, Layla. Luke may not be right now, but someday he'll be a monster to be reckoned with. Especially if he can't get that devouring rage of his under control."

"His rage has always been strong; so is mine." Layla spoke

quietly, sliding her hands in her own coat pockets now as she felt that black void reach up, still feeling like Luke's condition was all her fault. "We were a bad pair, way back when."

"You still love him." Rhennic moved forward, something deep in his gaze as he knit his blond brows, watching her. "But your drakaina doesn't want him, even powerful as he is?"

"I don't know. She bit him in the fall, but last night... he was able to help me with his *nullax*." Layla shrugged, feeling hopeless as that cavernous sensation devoured her. She skipped the part about her and Luke having their sudden sex in the bath. That wasn't something she wanted to share with an almost total stranger.

Yet somehow, Rhennic had provoked her with his calm steadiness into digging into places she usually only shared with her most trusted friends. Even though it was uncomfortable, something inside Layla eased, feeling like she could trust him. "Since Luke's Dragon-power opened, my drakaina doesn't consider him an inferior mate, but she still hasn't sought to Bind him."

"His rage would be bad for the group." Rhennic nodded soberly, still watching her.

"I think so." Layla breathed a sigh, her breath puffing in the winter chill. "I've already got one Royal Siren with self-hate issues to deal with in the Bind, and it nearly killed me last night. Perhaps two people in the Bind with that kind of anger would be too many. Plus my own."

The sun had dipped beneath the far edge of the clouds as it reached the horizon, sending long golden rays into the orchard. Layla felt hope for a moment as those rays found her skin, as the light flared in her eyes and the orchard was lit with a radiant glow, making every crystallized pear sparkle on the trees. But the next moment, that hopeful golden glow was doused beneath long blue shadows as the sun dipped

below the horizon. Layla watched those shadows swallow the orchard –
and watched her hope die on the boughs with it.

"Don't lose heart." Moving up behind her, Rhennic eased his arms
around Layla, corralling her into his tall, robust warmth. They stood
together a moment, and for some reason Layla didn't find it strange that
he'd come to her, or that he was holding her now with his calm
steadiness. She found their fingertips stroking each other gently as they
watched the light die beyond the furthest fields, all the lands of the
Château cast in blues and purples now.

"Why did you come out here, Rhennic?" Layla breathed to the
settling evening, feeling like she was lost in some strange winter dream.

"I feel your pull," he spoke simply, heaving a sigh as he wound
her more closely in his arms, cradling her with his enormous warmth.
"I've felt it since the day I first saw you at the Dragon-party. I know it
was bad form to mate-taste you in public like I did when I kissed your
wrist… but I just couldn't help myself. My mother and father and my
elder brother are strong enough to resist your Bind-call, but I'm not,
Layla. I don't know what it means, but there it is. I came out here
tonight because you called me. You needed someone to hold you.
Someone less… complicated than your other partners."

"You're not complicated?" Layla spoke as Rhennic's fingers came
up, stroking her neck.

"I am in my own way," he spoke gently, "but my position in my
clan is determined, and I don't have any undiscovered abilities. After
two hundred years of life, my magic is fully mature with no more
surprises, not like Adrian's or Dusk's. Or Luke's."

"Why tell me this?" Layla breathed, still feeling like she was in a
strange dream.

"In case you Bind me." He breathed back, his lips warm at her
hair.

"Do you want to be Bound?"

"I don't know."

They stood a while in silence, watching the blue darkness deepen over the land. But as glow-lanterns swirled on in the settling dark, lighting the long row of dormant pear trees, Rhennic inhaled a deep breath. Still holding Layla with one arm, he reached up with his other hand, pulling two crystallized fruits down from the leafless tree and tucking them into his coat pocket. Nudging Layla, he nodded to the lit path, swirling with etheric orbs that flickered with liquid lightning, hung from wrought-iron posts.

Setting out back towards the Château, Rhennic walked at Layla's side with his long, calm strides, his hands tucked into his pockets. They didn't say anything as they returned and the guards nodded to their Prince, the Dragon-Guards adjusting their positions atop the towers as they watched their throne's heir return, a flickering intensity in their lightning-blue eyes. The herb garden was quiet in the darkening evening, though Dragons in human form came and went about various tasks amid glow-globes the same as in the orchard. Layla thought Rhennic would escort her back to her rooms, but instead he led them up to the third floor via one of the corkscrewing side-stairwells in the quadrangle, up to the royal suites. Stepping to a massive ebony door carved with Dragons and sporting a snarling gilded crest of arms, he opened it, then turned to Layla. "We have a lot to talk about. Would you indulge me and have a spot of dinner?"

"I suppose so." Nodding, Layla moved into the apartment as Rhennic invited her in.

Layla had toured the royal chambers of the human-world Château de Chambord, but this was something else entirely, she realized as she gazed around. Snarling carvings of Dragons writhed through every arch of white lightning-stone, every tapestry vivid with carnal details embroidered in bright gold thread. The canopy over Rhennic's solid ebony bed was storm-blue velvet embroidered with the fleur-de-lis, with gold tassels cascading from the drapes. Every piece of ebony furniture in his rooms was inset with fire-opal and mother-of-pearl in stunning designs, a low table laden with food sitting before a stone fireplace so tremendous Layla could have walked right into it. Tapers were lit in branched gold floor-candelabra in every corner, low silk ottomans in vivid blues, purples, and gold waiting at the table as seats.

Before the fireplace, roaring with a hearty blaze that warmed the fortress' enormous stone tower-room, sprawled a massive white lambswool rug just waiting for someone to lay down upon its fluffy softness. Layla's lips quirked and her eyebrow raised as she glanced at Rhennic, entirely aware that his private rooms were debonair as shit to impress women. He gave her an eyebrow lift right back – subtle and sexy and unapologetic as he gestured to the low table before the fire.

Layla moved over to it, selecting a seat and settling onto the ottoman's firm softness as Rhennic claimed a stool opposite. The table was already laden with a variety of French traditional foods – from beef bourguignon, to poached pears in white wine, to personal-sized quiches full of bacon and gruyere. As they sat, Rhennic removed the crystallized pears from his pocket and set them on the table, then shucked his coat. Though chilly near the tall stained-glass windows, the tower room was ferociously hot near the fireplace, and as Layla shucked her coat and scarf, she saw how Rhennic gazed at her appreciatively.

As he served her plate, dressed now in a sexy midnight-blue vest and white shirt with his sleeves rolled up, gold pin-striping glimmering in his vest and trousers, Layla admired him back. She knew what was going on here as she took a bite of quiche lorraine, sipping a hearty Côtes du Rhône wine he'd poured. Rhennic was his mother's son, having elegantly maneuvered Layla into having a private dinner with him so he could spend time with her.

But even Layla had to admit it was time well spent, as she admired the way the fire's light caught upon Rhennic's rakishly short blond hair and beard, showing their subtle red Viking hi-lights. Rhennic watched her also, his bone structure strong yet elegant in the way of Scandinavian heritage meets French. His blond brows were level, his cheekbones high, and his lips full, his lavender eyes two shades darker than Rikyava's – a royal purple by the fire's light. As he sipped his wine, Layla saw how massive his fingers were, yet despite his towering structure and fit strength, he had an elegance so cultured it nearly rivaled Reginald's.

Layla suddenly wanted to feel what it might be like to be curled in the arms of such a sexy giant in bed, cradled by a body that could crush her with any too-strong move. It raised her drakaina's heat in her veins and Layla blushed hard as she covered it with a sip of wine – though she couldn't cover the riot of bourbon-orange scent that blossomed from her skin. Nor could she ignore the delicious scent of lavender and heather that blossomed from Rhennic.

"So we're clearly attracted to each other." Layla spoke bluntly, her default as she set down her wine, trying to get control of her faculties.

"Clearly." Rhennic gave her a subtle smile with a lift of one straight blond eyebrow as he sipped his own wine, then set it carefully down.

"Does Adrian know I'm here? Or Dusk?" Layla spoke archly as she took a bite of the delicious beef stew.

"Adrian and Dusk are in conference with my mother, father, and Rikyava." Rhennic spoke succinctly as he ate also. "They're trying to anticipate how Luke might be a blessing or a curse for their upcoming machinations against the White Chalice. I was in conference with them until I excused myself to find you, feeling you out in the orchard. Luke's still sleeping off the antics of this afternoon in his guest rooms."

"Shouldn't you be recovering also?" Layla spoke as she dug into her quiche. "All those broken bones?"

"I did my recovering, and I heal fast." Rhennic spoke back with a subtly flirtatious smile. "Now I want to woo you."

"Careful, buddy," Layla spoke back with an eyebrow lift as she sipped her wine. "I'm spoken for."

"Don't I know it." Rhennic gave her an acknowledging nod as he saluted her with a small lift of his wine glass, then sipped. Setting it down, he sobered as he said, "Your love life is complicated, Layla, and I understand that. But this sensation that compels me told me I had to at least try to approach you, even if it goes nowhere because I am *utterly* see-through with my intentions."

"Utterly." Layla quipped, though she suddenly frowned. "Though your mother isn't."

"My mother is terribly subtle in a way I will never be able to match, being half-Huttr's son." Rhennic spoke levelly now, his sexy flirtatiousness easing as he swirled his wine, regarding Layla with a frank intensity. "Justine has plans within plans and plots within plots, and always has had."

"She's manipulating us to get her aims accomplished against the White Chalice, to wipe them out for good." Layla frowned again as she took another bite of stew. "Me, Adrian, Dusk, and Luke. Even Rikyava. Justine's goading all of us into following through with her plan of attack."

"Manipulation is my mother's favorite pastime." Rhennic chuckled, turning on his stool so he could stretch his long legs out toward the fire. Kicking off his low ankle-boots, he bared lovely strong feet towards the fire, high-arched with long bones. Crossing his ankles, he turned his attention from Layla to the fire, leaning back on one hand upon his ottoman and sipping his wine.

"Manipulation was ever Justine's strongest suit. Take my father, for instance." Rhennic spoke as he gestured at the fire with his wine. "Half the time, Huttr hates Justine, railing against her and roaring. Then she wraps him around her smallest pinky-talon with a flash of her deep blue eyes and he comes to her like a slave, joining the might of his clan to the Storm Dragons. They fight, they fuck, they roar at each other in private or Huttr starts bad-mouthing her in public once again, and yet... he always comes back to Justine's call."

"Sounds complicated." Layla mused, sipping her wine and taking a bite of sautéed pears – which were divine.

"It is." Rhennic glanced back to Layla with a small smile. "But for all that, they respect each other deeply. Justine has had many lovers, most notably your own mother Mimi, but always she comes back to my father, though they never were a mated pair. More like battle-commanders who share a little extra on the side back at camp when they're not campaigning."

"Justine never had any other offspring, besides you?" Layla cocked her head, wondering. She'd had her suspicions about Queen Justine and her mother Mimi, and was interested to know it was true, though she wondered how many other partners Justine had obtained over the years.

"She never did have another child." Something in Rhennic's eyes saddened. "My mother had plenty of stillborns, every time she mated with another Storm Dragon. Finally, she had me when she and Huttr came together, late in life. She's past her estrus days, so my brother Halfdir is all I've got, unless Huttr takes another Queen, which he's not likely to. Halfdir's Blood Dragon mother Losantia died in battle a hundred years back. Huttr has plenty of hot young things to mess around with these days – never when they're in estrus, though."

"And Rikyava?" Layla asked, wondering what the family connection was.

"She's Huttr's sister's daughter. Rikyava's mother died in battle only a few years after Yava was born, so she was raised alongside me and Dir. She's beloved by my father. Maybe even more than his own sons." Rhennic chuckled with a smile, as if he didn't mind. It was clear Rikyava was like a little sister to him. "But yes, you are correct when you feel my mother is manipulating you. Justine's a war-general, Layla, and she's been waging this campaign a long time. She wants to solidify her legacy – to be the Queen who wiped out the White Chalice once and for all. Before she dies."

"Is Justine sick?" Layla blinked.

"Vastly." Rhennic turned quiet eyes to Layla, deeply sober now. "She's riddled with some kind of magical cancer no healer has been able to figure out yet. It's something unprecedented, never before seen in the Dragon world. But Justine's always been an anomaly. It makes a certain kind of sense that her demise would be anomalous, also."

"Hence the stories of rivalry starting in your clan for the top spot." Something clicked into place as Layla regarded Rhennic – that he was already, or would soon be heavily embroiled in dominance-battles for Kingship if his mother died.

"They're not stories." Rhennic drained his wine, then set it upon the table. "There are no fewer than thirty Royal Storm Dragons around the world eyeing my mother's health. So far, she's not infirm, but the fact that Huttr defended her today as she tested Luke, not trusting her to defend herself as her Dragon, tells me much. Her powers are failing. So far, I think she's only entrusted my father with that information, but I have my suspicions."

"What does that mean for us, facing the White Chalice?" A cold sensation devoured Layla's gut as her Dragon turned over inside her veins with a deep, dark fear.

"That Justine's furious storm may have only one blitz left." Rhennic held Layla's gaze with a deep solemnity now, and a ready patience. "I have the feeling my mother has only one blaze of glory remaining in her, Layla, and she wants to use it to take out the White Chalice for good. It's a coincidence that the Chalice have risen again after so many years, goading you and Luke by stealing your friends, but it's a coincidence my mother wants to take full advantage of. Even though this campaign may finally kill her. Afterwards…"

"The Storm Dragons of Europe will be thrown into chaos." Layla understood.

"The Storm Dragons all around the world will be thrown into chaos," Rhennic spoke quietly. "And as Clan Second here and future Regent of the Storm Dragons when my mother dies, I need someone strong by my side to back me up. Or someones."

"You want me to Bind you." Layla blinked, setting her wine carefully aside. Finally, she saw the whole pattern of what Rhennic was about, and why he had come to find her tonight, and invite her to a private dinner. "You want to join our Bind so you'll seem un-challengeable to the other Storm Dragon contenders. So you'll have four notoriously high-powered Royals in league with you against all-comers for the Storm Throne."

"Would it be such a bad thing?" Rhennic continued quietly, watching her with intensity in his dark purple gaze. "I bring steadiness and power to the table, Layla, in a way your other drakes don't have. Dusk is fracturing and Reginald is too far away, and though Adrian is an effective commander, he doesn't have the battle-history I do. I am a tested warrior, calm in my fury, and I would be King of an extremely powerful Lineage if this all settles out right – your Bound ally. Can you say the same for your other mates?"

Layla's mouth closed, considering it as Rhennic watched her. His presence was strong and calm, something she had felt since the very first. He had Justine's subtlety, and Layla saw it in the way he had gently manipulated her into this conversation, into being alone with him to feel the fullness of his ideas tonight. She was compelled by him, she was intrigued by him – and yet.

"I can't Bind you, Rhennic," Layla spoke softly, watching him by the fire's roaring light. "I'm sorry. I don't know you at all. I don't—"

"You don't love me." His smile was wry as he regarded her. "I thought it worked the other way around. That you began to love someone after you bound them, rather than before."

"I can't add you to the Bind right now." Layla spoke again, impressing her point, though gently. "I'm sorry."

Rhennic heaved a sigh. With a wry smile, he gazed at the fire, and Layla smelled his lavender and heather scent whirl. Like a Scandinavian summer mixed with the flooding sunshine of Provence, Rhennic had a good scent, and it almost drew Layla in. She felt herself attuning to it, her drakaina coiling over eagerly in her veins to be inundated by such a powerfully calm presence, and faced with such a strong, handsome man before her. At last, Rhennic glanced around, his smile gentle now rather than wry. His eyes were a dark purple, like plums upon a summer bough, as he gazed at Layla with his sober strength.

"Consider my offer for a year and a day." He spoke at last. "In the meantime, I will be your ally, as I am already Adrian's and Dusk's and Rikyava's. We will find your friends, and bring them home safely. And once it's all over, I would only ask that you come visit me again. So we may speak a while longer… and walk together in the orchards."

"You want to court me." Layla blinked, the thought strangely appealing in an old-world way. "To try and win my hand. To try and win my Bind."

"I do." Rhennic smiled then, and his smile was sexy, strong and deeply radiant. "Give me a chance to be your mate; that's all I'm asking. I won't push you. But I do want a shot."

Layla cocked her head, thinking about it. She had seen how deeply Rhennic was already friends with Adrian and Dusk, and knew how much he and Rikyava cared for one other. He was strong, subtle, attentive, and sexy in that commanding yet debonair way she loved so much. He was asking rather than pushing or fighting for her, or seducing her – asking to be a part of her life in a way no one else had done.

Asking her to be a part of his life also – recognizing the power Layla was becoming.

With a deep breath, Layla rose from the table. As she rounded it, Rhennic's blond brows lifted in surprise, and he pushed gracefully up to standing. Moving to him, Layla stood before him on the sheepskin rug, gazing up at his handsome face. Something tender moved in his eyes as he gazed down at her, not touching or taking advantage, just watching her take him in.

Slowly, Layla rose to her tiptoes, steadying herself with a hand on his broad, well-muscled chest. Something sparked in Rhennic's violet eyes, a deep flash of desire as he realized what was happening. Winding his big hands around her waist, his fingers were so long they met at Layla's spine and navel as she stretched up. With his strength, he steadied her as his chin lowered and his soft lips met hers.

They kissed gently, breathing in each other's scents before Layla at last pulled away. As they watched each other by the fire's light, she felt lightning and passion sear through Rhennic's strong body, but she also felt how well he controlled it. Though his eyes sparked with storms, he merely held her with their intensity rather than rolling her with his power – letting her drown herself in his subtle, strong handsomeness as he held her close.

Layla knew he could take her with his magic; she could feel it. She could feel the Royal power in Rhennic and smell it all over him – the only son of the two strongest Royal Dragons in Europe. Layla's drakaina roiled through her veins in a wave of scintillating heat, so hard that Layla's breath caught. But still, Rhennic held her carefully away – only letting her feel the barest touch of everything he could give her.

In the bedroom and out of it.

Layla was flooded with desire as he massaged her waist with his big hands, then finally let her go. Taking up one crystallized pear from the table, he cupped it in his palms, and she felt a blitz flash through the fruit from Rhennic's big hands. Glancing at her and taking up her hand, he escorted Layla towards the door like he had done this morning for the carriage-ride. Lifting her hand, he pressed the crystallized fruit into her palm.

"For later." He breathed with a knowing look. "When you need some hope in the darkness."

And then Rhennic opened the door and let Layla out of his chamber – though his deep violet eyes followed her all the way.

CHAPTER 20 – CAMPAIGN

Layla slept fitfully that night, one of the tensest, most restless nights she had ever known, even though she was clasped between both Dusk and Adrian in the same bed, sharing their warmth. Over and over she rolled, first facing Adrian, then Dusk, then Adrian again in the ample bed with its thick embroidered drapes drawn against the palace's midnight chill. She turned over so many times that at last Dusk made a low growl in his throat, sleepily turning her and tucking her in against his hard, warm body, wrapping her in his arms and securing her from rolling over again.

Finally Layla drifted, lulled by the smooth rumbles of Dusk's breath as he slept, and the slow flow of Adrian's as it passed from his lips, sweetly kissing hers even in dreams. But when she finally woke to a ferocious winter storm rattling the shutters and swirling a catastrophic white at every vaulted window, her dark restlessness rushed up to claim Layla in force. Snow piled against the window-ledges, the wind howling and whistling through gaps in the fortress' stones. Without saying much, everyone ate a hasty breakfast and dressed quickly in warm winter gear – the first time Layla had ever seen Dusk and Adrian don thick sweaters and parkas against the fierce chill, along with solid winter boots.

Layla did the same for their early meeting with Queen Justine and King Huttr; one last discussion of today's plan to infiltrate the White Chalice's stronghold. As they moved along one narrow corridor from their tower to the central halls on the palace's second floor, Layla gazing out the vaulted windows at the whirling snow, she thought perhaps it was the worst day they could have possibly chosen to invade a Storm Dragon stronghold.

Gaining the vaulted hall where Queen Justine took audience, they were bowed in smartly by guards in blue-grey livery, the massive ebony doors booming inward to admit them. Layla saw as they entered the throne hall that Queen Justine and King Huttr were already there, joined by Rikyava and Luke. Both wore sweaters and parkas and boots like Layla and her men. And though Luke ran an uncomfortable hand through his Irish black hair as Layla entered, his green eyes were clear today as if he'd slept well. Layla wanted to go to him, to say something, when Rhennic whisked into the hall, dressed in his charcoal grey peacoat, a plum cowlneck sweater, and thick winter pants with stout hiking boots.

Rhennic's eyes caught Layla's – a battle-glorious dark plum today – and for a moment she couldn't look away. His smile was subtle as he gave her a nod, then moved up the steps of the throne's dais and pecked his mother on the cheek. Dressed in a long navy dresscoat with 1950's high-waisted wool slacks and a white silk shirt, Queen Justine looked tiny between the two tall Norsemen, King Huttr dressed in his white bear-pelt and rough Viking battle-leathers. But Justine's dark blue eyes were fierce as she beckoned everyone forward, stepping down from her gilded Dragon-throne and sitting casually on the ebony railing that separated the common area from her royalness.

"Good. We are assembled." She spoke in an iron tone like a war-commander as she gazed around the group, her blue eyes flashing lightning to match the whirling storm outside. "If all goes well, today's events will join those of history, my friends, and I intend that they do. I have spoken at length with Adrian, Dusk, and Rikyava last night, and Luke, and together we have formulated a decent plan of attack. Please listen closely, and at the end of my briefing you may ask what questions you need."

Queen Justine launched into the plan without any hesitation. Briskly, she explained that today's storm was the work of herself and her seven top weather-formers – its severe windchill, heavy snow, and occasional lightning a cover to confuse any movement around the Château. Specifically, it was masking the movements of Blood Dragon and Storm Dragon strike teams amassing this morning on the grounds, ready to move at Justine's call.

"As I have already told Adrian, we believe the last of the White Chalice to be holed up at the cathedral of Notre Dame de Chartres," Queen Justine continued, her blue eyes flashing fiercely. "In the Twilight Realm, that cathedral was destroyed centuries ago, along with the entire town. I have felt *nullax* energy surrounding the ruin of Chartres, and believe this is the access-point for our enemies' last stronghold. Though most of that cathedral is gone, the labyrinth upon the floor still holds strangely pristine against time. In addition, the main ruins have oddly disappeared, and I believe that labyrinth is the access-way to our foes, the rest of the cathedral hidden behind a cleverly-wrought magic that keeps it not just hidden but *separate* from both the Twilight Realm and the human world. A phenomenon called a Nexus-space."

Heads nodded around the circle as everyone digested Justine's information. She glanced to all of them, making sure they understood, before continuing. "The plan is as follows. From Chambord, Dusk will use his Royal Crystal Dragon abilities to escort Layla, Adrian, Luke, Rikyava, and Rhennic through the Thin Ways to the ruined Chartres here in the Twilight Realm. You will emerge in an old well that stands inside a warning-barrier that surrounds the ruined town, and proceed to the cathedral. At the labyrinth, Luke will open his *nullax*, feeling for the magical barrier that separates off the Nexus-space. Once his power has opened the Nexus, you should be able to step through into the cathedral, where we suspect the White Chalice are."

But then, Queen Justine's energy sharpened, a pre-lightning sensation shivering along Layla's skin as the Storm Queen glanced to each of them. "This is where our operation becomes difficult. Many elements are unknown, such as whether Luke's ability will be able to open the Nexus into the cathedral, or whether the White Chalice will be laying in wait as a trap. Be prepared for anything. Once you go in the Nexus and are inside the stronghold, the plan is simple. Find Layla's friends; rescue them. Identify the High Priest; kill him. Kill any others who stand in your way. And if you find yourselves outnumbered – Luke will act."

"What do you mean, Luke will act?" Layla blinked, speaking reflexively even though she knew the Storm Queen had asked everyone to hold questions until the end.

"I'll collapse the entire Nexus back into the Twilight Realm with my *nullax* – nullifying the magic that keeps it separate." Luke spoke, holding Layla's gaze with a calm clarity. "Allowing Queen Justine and King Huttr's strike teams access to the cathedral."

"You can do that?" Layla blinked, feeling herself go pale.

"I don't know." He spoke quietly. "But I have to try. I'll do anything to get our friends back, Layla. You know that."

"I have given Luke a talisman imbued with my energy," Queen Justine spoke, looking to Layla, "which when he opens it, will deliver him a very serious bite from my magics. It will draw out his *nullax* just as it did yesterday, and all he will need do is direct his fury towards the Nexus-barrier to bring it crashing down. Though his power is under enough control to tear a hole through the barrier to get you all in, Luke cannot wield enough of his *nullax* yet to cause it to completely wipe out the magics that keep the cathedral separate from the Twilight Realm. Hence, my bite. He and I have spoken, and he has agreed to take this risk upon himself."

"If anything goes wrong, I'll be there to absorb Luke's power," Rhennic glanced to Layla with a sober gaze, "so no one accidentally gets hurt or nullified."

"Bullshit." Layla spoke with a growl, suddenly feeling an intense protectiveness rise for Rhennic's welfare. "You'll be hurt. Badly."

"And you, Adrian, Dusk, and Rikyava will be there to heal me." Rhennic held Layla's gaze with his calm steadiness. "It's a good plan, Layla. And together we have all the right talents to get it done."

"Dusk? Adrian?" She growled, glancing to them. "Rikyava?"

They didn't even need to glance at each other for Layla to know everyone was in accord as Adrian spoke gently, "Like Rhennic said, it's a good plan. As many variables as possible have been accounted-for, Layla."

Layla stood tall, crossing her arms as she fumed. It was a dangerous plan, and gazing around at all the faces of her friends, Layla found she didn't want any of them to do this. She didn't want any of them hurt. She didn't want to place any of them in danger, and if she was the one this High Priest wanted to meet, she would very well march in there by herself and go meet him.

But as if Luke could read her mind, he suddenly spoke. "You can't go by yourself, Layla. Besides, the White Chalice want me, too. The others want to protect you as much as you want to protect them. No one's going in alone. Deal with it."

Drawing a deep breath, Layla felt her Dragon coil through her veins in a wash of protective fear and darkness. She felt a growl rise in her throat, inundated with the overtones of her beast. But reaching out, Dusk set a gentle hand to hers, pouring a soothing wave of power

237

through her sinews. Breathing deeper, Layla was at last able to release her resistance to the plan.

Though not her blackest fears.

"Fine. We'll do what we have to, to get Charlie, Celia, and Arron back safe."

Luke's quiet nod spoke for them all. With a brisker nod from Queen Justine, the plan was set, and as Justine and Huttr stepped aside with Adrian, Dusk, Rikyava, and Rhennic to give them the finer details of the Dragon invasion, Layla was left alone with Luke. As Luke moved to her, she saw agony in his eyes. But he held her gaze without flinching as they faced each other at last.

"So. You and Rikyava are a thing." Layla tried to not make it sound pissed, but she still was.

"You have your love life, Layla, and I have mine." Luke's answer was terse as his emerald gaze went from pained to dark with a reflexive temper. "We don't owe each other any explanations on that account anymore."

Layla felt his words like a dagger in her heart, twisting as she stared at him, at a loss for what to say. "Do you hate me or something? Even after everything we shared the other night?"

Luke drew a deep breath, then let out a hard sigh as he set his hands to his hips. "I don't hate you, Layla. And what we shared the other night… But this isn't about you. You saw my magic yesterday – you saw what it can do. It's dangerous."

"And you don't want me around that." Layla suddenly realized what he was trying to do as she stared at him. "You don't get to push me away, Luke, because you're afraid of hurting me with your Dragon-power. We're friends. That's not something friends do."

"It is when one friend knows they're no good for the other." The edge of his temper flashed in his eyes now, like some massive, simmering beast inside him.

"Do you mean you're no good for me, or I'm no good for you?" Layla countered, feeling her own fury began to simmer in her veins. "Or is it that Rikyava's expendable to your *nullax* so you don't mind being close with her?"

"Don't be mean, Layla." Luke's eyes flashed now for real, sharp as he narrowed his eyes on her. "I'm sorry I didn't tell you about Rikyava and I, but it's not like you were filling me in on your love life with Adrian and Dusk and everyone else this fall. We're just... we're not..."

"We're not friends anymore." What Luke was trying to say suddenly felt like he'd slapped her in the face. "You don't want to be friends with me anymore."

"This isn't about you, Layla!" Luke huffed at last, his temper finally blowing wide open as he raked a hand hard through his black hair. "What is it about my magic opening up that you don't understand?! When was the last time you might have thought, *gee, maybe Luke's dealing with some serious shit right now and needs a good friend for support?* Rikyava was there for me when I needed it. Hell, even Dusk was. But you weren't. And here you are, making everything about you like always, trying to pretend to be all hurt when I can't bend over backwards for you! Don't, Layla. Just – fucking don't. I can't handle it today. Not with everything else going on right now."

Layla blinked, and she couldn't stop the hard wash of scorched orange scent that surged from her as her cheeks flushed from embarrassment – and rage.

"Fine." She snarled at last, feeling her Dragon rise in her veins with a simmering fire that was a furious match to Luke's. "You want to play hard, Luke? Fine. You're right; I'm selfish. I think about myself before I think about others, and always have. Is that what you want to hear? You're right and I'm wrong – your life is way more complex than mine and your magic is harder to bear. If Rikyava's a good thing for you, then I'm happy for you both, but like hell am I going to sit here and let you lambaste me for my choices this past year! I did what I deemed best at the time. Did I forget my friends along the way? A little. A situation I'm hoping to God I can remedy if we ever get them back. You can stand there and be as righteous as you want, you can tell yourself you're right and Layla's fucked up *like always*, but I don't believe it. I have friends in the Twilight Realm who care for me just because of *who I am* – I don't have to prove myself to earn their love. Fuck you. Go take your righteous attitude and blistering hate someplace else, because I'm done. After we get our friends back, I'm done. Fuck you… I am so, so done."

As Luke stared at her like she'd just hit him with a freight train, his green eyes vibrant with a shine of hot tears, Layla turned away. Striding to the end of the throne hall, she gasped as she crossed her arms tight, gazing out the high gabled windows. But all there was to see was swirling snow, and as Layla stared into it, hearing the wind howl outside like tortured animals, she felt only chaos deep inside. As a black pit opened within her, swallowing her heart, swallowing every good feeling in life, she crossed her arms tighter, willing herself to not break. But it just went dark and darker, her Dragon giving a strangled roar as she tried to face it and failed. Layla's Dragon was swallowed into that dark pit – everything was swallowed into it.

As Layla stared at the cruel snow and listened to the vile wind, nothing seemed to matter anymore.

But then warm arms wound around her, and Layla gasped. Adrian and Dusk had come to her, pulling her into their love. As she cuddled into Dusk and Adrian pressed close to her back, kissing her temple sweetly as Dusk kissed her lips, Layla broke. With a hard sob, a tear shed down her cheeks, then another as she buried her face into Dusk's parka, nuzzling in to where she could breathe his clear river-water scent.

But even as they held her, Layla could feel a jangled energy spike inside Dusk. Her black self-hatred had affected him deeply, and as they held each other with Adrian standing strong at Layla's back, she felt how close Dusk was to breaking also. Even with Adrian's warm winds pouring down both their throats, opening their hearts back to a place of love, Dusk's energy still felt like broken shards of crystal spiking all around Layla. As her black pit eased back, her Dragon roaring up in a wave of bourbon-orange scent, Layla felt Dusk shudder and exhale. Corralling her close, he kissed her temple as relief washed through him.

"I'm sorry!" Layla gasped at his chest. "I didn't mean to trigger you!"

"I know." Dusk growled, flooding a soothing vibration through Layla and himself both. "It's not your fault, Layla. I'm just having trouble keeping it together these days myself..."

But even as Dusk spoke, someone stepped to their group. As Layla smelled lavender and heather in the air, she felt Rhennic reach out, gripping Dusk's shoulder. Rhennic didn't touch Layla as she was held by her Bound men, but he poured a deep flow of power through Dusk. It jolted Dusk like the boom of a thunderstorm, but as he shook off the after-effects he was suddenly standing taller, stronger, his magic smoothed and steady deep inside. Looking up, Layla saw Dusk and Rhennic glance at each other, an understanding passing between them. As Dusk let out a slow breath, Rhennic smiled, gripping his shoulder and shaking him before letting him go.

As Rhennic's deep violet gaze found Layla, she saw the incredible steadiness of his character. She felt it, rumbling with a power like rolling thunder over summer fields. She felt her Bind with Adrian and

Dusk become stable again because of Rhennic's magic rippling through them, and on her tongue she could taste lavender and ozone, like a field after a summer rain. It was brisk and uplifting, and as Layla's drakaina raised her head, deeply attentive, Layla shivered. It wasn't from darkness now, or cold, but from feeling this illuminating dark-bright energy calming her like staring at thunderclouds limned by the golden rays of the setting sun.

She stared at Rhennic, feeling the steady power he could give their Bind.

And then he nodded, holding her gaze one last moment before turning to get this show on the road.

CHAPTER 21 – REVENANT

In Queen Justine's royal chambers at Château de Chambord, Layla stood with Dusk, Adrian, Rhennic, Luke, and Rikyava near the massive stone fireplace. Similar to Rhennic's quarters but more feminine, Justine's rooms were the means through which the group would get into the Thin Ways and travel to Chartres. Layla still didn't know what the Thin Ways were – Dusk had only told her they were a method of Crystal Dragon travel through the depths of the earth – but as Queen Justine waited with eager interest, her dark blue eyes alert, Layla realized whatever was going to happen next was a unique event for the Storm Queen.

Stepping into the enormous fireplace, its fires extinguished and the hearth scraped out, Dusk pressed his fingertips to a wrought-iron panel embedded in the stone. The ornate panel depicted a Dragon deep inside the earth, with tunnels moving out from them in a complex Celtic basketweave. Layla had thought it was simply an iron placard to reflect the fire, but as Dusk closed his eyes, he gave a rippling growl. A flood of light passed through his body in a wave, and as the refracting light passed into the panel, the iron shivered – and disappeared.

The entire back wall of the fireplace disappeared with it, revealing a circular stone landing with a corkscrewing stairwell curving down into darkness. Ringed by fifteen dark arrow-slits cut into the wall, the stone room breathed with currents of chill air. Rather than take the stairwell, Dusk circumnavigated the landing and set his hand to one of the far slits, repeating his wave of vibration and light. As Layla watched, the two-inch slit flared, then widened – pushing the others aside in a ripple of light and narrowing them like a fan as the slit Dusk had selected widened into a full hall.

As Layla gaped to see a vaulted stone passage now burrowing into the darkness, Dusk sent a blast of power into the hall from his palm. All along the passage, enormous blue crystals tall as a person flared to life in curved wall-niches, lighting the catacombed hall with a rippling, eerie light. Glancing to Layla and Adrian, then Rhennic, Luke, and Rikyava, Dusk lifted a dark eyebrow. "Everyone ready?"

"Damn, that's insane." Rhennic's soft swear put Dusk's powers in perspective for Layla. Glancing to Rhennic and Justine, Layla saw them both admiring the passage.

The Storm Queen shook her head with a wry smile. Gesturing to the party, she said, "Farewell. You will not see us at Chartres right away, as it will take our cadres longer to fly than it will take you through the Ways. Proceed with the plan when you arrive, as we have no time to waste. Luck be with you all."

"My Queen." Giving her a solemn nod, then glancing around to make sure everyone was ready, Dusk stepped from the stone foyer into the hall he'd lit. Adrian gestured Layla ahead of him behind Dusk, Luke following with Rikyava, and Rhennic bringing up the rear. Gaining the blue hall after Dusk, Layla had a sensation like the entire world had been blotted out as she stepped beneath its vaulted, eerie catacombs. She had a feeling like nothing existed in the world but the endless passage and the deep, seeping cold all around her – even though as she glanced behind, she saw the Storm Queen in her apartment with white snow swirling beyond the windows.

But as Layla watched, the view into Chambord wavered like a mirage, becoming a curved wall of dark stone. As Layla blinked at the sudden magical closing-off of the foyer, Dusk stepped to her, curling her in his arms. She hadn't realized she was deeply chill until his warmth comforted her, as if there existed a cold in this place that only a Crystal Dragon could weather. The silence in the stone hall and foyer was absolute as everyone gazed around, shivering in their parkas as they adjusted to a claustrophobic sensation. Layla had the feeling she was miles beneath the earth, buried in stone and darkness, even though her rational mind told her she was somewhere inside the walls of the Château.

"Where the fuck are we?" Luke's soft breath echoed Layla's thoughts, his voice strangely deadened in the space rather than echoing.

"These are the Thin Ways." Dusk spoke quietly, still holding Layla close. Layla noticed Adrian had moved to her and Dusk also, as if even he wasn't entirely comfortable wherever they were now. "They're ancient passages built by Crystal Dragons, and are only accessible to my kind. Each slit at a node is actually a portal through the earth, taking us to a new node from which we can keep traveling. This one was built hundreds of years ago by Crystal Dragon King Lorenz DuVir, to protect Queen Justine."

"Why did he build her an access to the Thin Ways? Was he in love with Justine?" Layla mused, glancing around at the haunting crystals in their niches, each one reminding her of the deep blue color of Justine's eyes, though they lent a slightly brighter light through the darkness.

"Deeply in love, from all the stories." Dusk gave a smile as he glanced to Rhennic, who confirmed the tale with a nod.

"Lorenz was a Dragon King of voracious appetites," Rhennic took up the tale as he glanced around the vast hall, "and my mother was a strong power in France at the time. Like my father Huttr, King Lorenz loved sleeping with powerful women, but as the story goes, he also fell deeply in love with Justine. Though some passages were already here, King DuVir extended the Thin Ways all over France, even built a few into the Palace of Versailles as escape routes for himself and her, should trouble ever come for them."

"Your apartment at the Hotel is one of those places, Layla," Dusk continued as he corralled her closer in his arms. "It was the main reason I made sure you got that room, so I could have access to you in an emergency. My apartment on the fourth floor has an access, as does Adrian's."

"The Guardhall has an access too, doesn't it?" Rikyava mused as she glanced around, then looked to Dusk. "Down in the Vault?"

"It does, theoretically." Dusk looked at her soberly. "Though that passage is ancient, far older than King DuVir's works, and even I've not been able to locate it. It will take a power far stronger than mine to discover it. It's part of the *Helkafnim Urdo*, the original network of Ways that tunnel through the core of the earth, rather than along its surface. They were made long before my Crystal Clan in Egypt was established, maybe even a hundred thousand years ago. No Crystal Dragon in recent memory has been strong enough to access them."

"Are you sure they're real?" Layla asked curiously. "Not just a legend?"

"They're real. I can feel them." Dusk spoke as he gave a small shiver behind her. "Come on. We should get moving. It'll take us a while to get to Chartres, even through the Ways."

Tucking Layla in beside him, Dusk began to walk down the long passage with Adrian and the others. It was wide enough that they could walk three abreast, and as Layla gazed up, she saw the vaulted stone gables were so high they became lost to darkness far above. Down where the eerie light of the crystals illuminated the hall, she saw each branching blue crystal was inset into a niche in the walls, and sat in a strangely viscous pool of black water. As they passed one, Rhennic wandered over curiously and hunkered as if to touch the pool, but Dusk clamped a hand on his shoulder.

"Not unless you want to get blasted from here to Timbuktu." Dusk spoke with a warning glance.

"You mean it'll teleport me?" Rhennic's eyes widened as he rose.

"No. Just vibrate you apart from your bones out." Dusk spoke with a wry smile.

"Jesus." Rhennic pulled back to a safe distance, with an uncertain glance to Rikyava. She gave her cousin a wry smile as she looked back to Dusk.

"We feel like we're miles beneath the earth." Rikyava spoke with a nod to the seemingly endless hall ahead. "Is that the case?"

"Yes." Dusk spoke, with a deep respect as he glanced around. "The node I opened was actually a mile and a half down, though it seemed like it was embedded in the walls of Chambord. We're deeper now – about two miles. The Thin Ways tunnel all over the earth. Through continents, beneath mountain ranges. Under oceans."

"How do you navigate them?" Luke asked as they began walking again, occasionally passing slits leading off in other directions.

"I find my way by feel and vibration." Dusk spoke as he proceeded, watching the hall ahead. "Crystal Dragons have an impeccable sense of direction underground. We also feel magnetic north like migrating birds. And we can sense stone structures if we focus on them. It's how I can feel the ruins of Chartres where we're headed. Justine needed a Crystal Dragon to get in because the White Chalice alarm-barrier around Chartres goes up in a dome over the ruins. But it doesn't go underground. Hence, using the Thin Ways to get in."

But Dusk went rigidly alert as they reached one narrow slit on the right, holding out a hand and stopping the party. Layla felt him manifest an invisible barrier of crystals in the air, then smooth his hand over that slit from top to bottom, as if sealing it up with his shimmering barrier.

With a tense exhalation and a sharp nod, he hustled them quickly past. Layla felt something swirl far down that black passage as they passed – like a nightmare come to life. Adrian bristled behind them with a desert-wind energy as if he'd felt danger also, Rhennic crackling with a searing alertness and Rikyava tensing as a whirl of blood droplets surged out from her.

"The fuck was that?" Luke asked with a growl as they flanked the passage.

"Something we don't want to tussle with." Dusk spoke softly, as if afraid of disturbing the tunnels as he beckoned them on. "No Crystal Dragon uses the Thin Ways lightly, even if they are strong enough to access them. Mostly because there are far older things that haunt these passages than my kind."

Dusk was still tense as he glanced back. Turning a corner, they took a winding way deeper into the earth. Arriving at another cul-de-sac with numerous slits, Dusk inhaled and closed his eyes, then sent a low rumble of his magics through the node like a subtle earthquake. Facing a direction to Layla's left, he opened his eyes, then moved forward and placed his palm on a slit. Refracting light through it, Dusk widened it, then blasted the passage with a pulse to light the way.

Rather than blue, the crystals in this hall were a solemn, bloody red, the stone vaults of a different shape with less ornamentation. As the hall lit, the passage they'd come from disappeared, blue crystals flashing out to darkness as the hall narrowed – leaving only the circular node with the bloody passage ahead. As if the passage behind had never existed, Layla felt a sudden disorientation, like the tunnel she faced now was the same one they'd come through, despite the color and architectural differences. It gave her a feeling of panic, as if she was utterly lost in the bowels of the earth. Her heartbeat sped, a flush of bourbon-orange scent washing from her as her Dragon bristled.

Curling her close, Dusk poured a soothing rumble through her. "Easy, Layla. Try to stay calm down here. Scents of fear draw the attention of things we don't want to face right now."

"Like what?" Layla cuddled close to Dusk.

"Like you don't want to find out what." Dusk growled. "Come on. We need to move."

But Layla's Dragon was positively bristling with alarm now as the cold scent of something nightmarish like open graves caught her. Adrian had stepped up beside them and set a hand to Layla's back, pouring a soothing desert wind through her as he took a protective stance also, Rikyava snarlingly alert beside him. Even Luke had moved closer to the group with his hands ready, Rhennic extending a palm with a crackle of Storm power rushing through it.

Everyone was feeling whatever lurked in the darkness, and as Layla glanced around, she saw Adrian and Rikyava exchange a glance as if they knew what it was. Leading them at a quick pace through the bloody corridor to another node, Dusk wasted no time, opening a new passage as the one behind them closed, this one lit orange-yellow from crystals like citrine all along its length.

But through it all, Layla could still feel something nasty sliding through the darkness, dogging their steps with a curl of seeping power licking at their heels. It didn't have shape or substance, and as she felt it sliding smoothly through every passage behind them, opened to a full hall or not, she felt her hackles rise to a furiously high alert. Everyone's nerves were ratcheted up hard as they stopped at another node and Dusk set his hands to the wall. Forming a ring facing out, everyone had their hands up, their eyes watchful as Dusk fanned the slits, creating a blank wall of stone before them.

The citrine hall remained, dark beyond the last crystals near the node, and Layla felt that creeping power curl around them from the dark. It was cold as death, a leeching that made Layla feel shaky as a wave of vertigo passed through her. She reeled but Adrian stepped in, catching her by the shoulders. Pouring a blistering wind through her, he steadied her, pushing back that horrible sensation. Flaring a barrier of hot wind around the entire party, Adrian was fierce as he growled in the direction the leeching cold had come from. Layla thought she heard the screech of something dark and angry far away in the darkness as Adrian's scorching power pushed it off.

"They're coming." Rikyava's voice held a growling bite as her eyes went crimson with blood, a fast whirl of blood droplets manifesting around her as she watched the passage.

"What the fuck is coming?" Luke gasped, ashen and visibly shaking as Layla shivered hard in Adrian's grip, alarm racing through her. Dusk was working his vibrations at the stone wall with a hasty feel to his magics, as if pushing himself hard to open it. Clearly, it had not been just Layla the black nightmare had suckled on in its greed.

"A Vampire Revenant. A few of them." Adrian spoke, his gaze fierce as he glared into the darkness of the hall behind them, giving Layla a squeeze and letting her go as he raised his hands in readiness. "Rikyava – blood pool. Spread it wide to distract them. Rhennic, give me the strongest barrier you've got against leeching. Dusk – hurry the fuck up."

"Easier said than done." Dusk was tense as he grit his teeth, continuing to send rumbles of energy into the curved stone wall now at a higher pitch, now lower. His rumbles had cranked up to a fever now as if the passage was proving hard to open, and Adrian's power scalded as he widened his blistering winds around the party. Rhennic had similarly raised his magic into a flowing plasma around the group now, bursts of lightning careening through it. Rikyava had manifested a pool of blood out along the floor, grisly in the light as it moved in rivulets back the way they'd come. Moving her fingers in a flowing dance, she pushed it out further, her crimson gaze focused back along the passage as Dusk continued his attention on the wall.

"Tell me, what's a Vampire Revenant?" Layla spoke softly, fear devouring her as she watched the black passage.

"Vampire Revenants are ancient Vampires who have lost all connection to their humanity, Layla." Rikyava spoke, her attention riveted to the darkness. "There's a reason the Thin Ways are seldom used. Because if a person doesn't have enough power to navigate the Ways—"

"You're dead in them." Rhennic completed Rikyava's sentence soberly. "Regular Vampires drain a person's blood or life-force, but Vampire Revenants don't just leech the body, they leech the mind. Fear is their currency. The more they can make you terrified, the more they own you. If they swallow you inside your fear, there's no coming out of it."

"Once you're paralyzed in your fear, the Revenant has ultimate access to you." Rikyava continued, with a dark shiver as if even she was deeply disturbed. "They drain you – everything you are, everything you were, and everything you could ever hope to be, sometimes stringing that process along for years. It's a very, very bad way to die."

Layla shivered as Rikyava and Adrian shared a long look, and it suddenly hit Layla that when Adrian had been held captive by the Intercessoria, he'd endured interrogation with over a dozen Vampires. Horror flooded her as she turned to him. "Adrian, did you survive Vampire Revenants while the Intercessoria held you?"

"Three of them." Adrian shivered, his gaze fixed on the dark hall. "It's not something I'd like to talk about right now. We've got at least six on our tail, and—"

Adrian was about to say more when Dusk finally opened the wall, causing it to shiver away in a dark mirage. A gloomy stairwell lay beyond with a sheet of ice and half-melted snow at the bottom, mossy stairs curving up to a pale light above. But the scent of winter air outside the Ways was fresh, and with a relieved exhalation, their group moved towards it quickly.

But as they did, Layla felt a surge of powerful intent rush up behind them, as if the coldness of the grave had come to devour their very souls. From all sides it came, as if thousands of hands had been waiting in the dark just outside their barrier for the opportune moment. Intelligence was in that sudden strike, and Layla felt the weight of at least five minds behind it, or more.

Blasting through Rhennic and Adrian's barriers, those dark minds ignored Rikyava's blood-temptation, hammering straight to Layla and Luke. With a roar, Adrian seized Luke's parka and clasped Layla in his arm, running them fast out into the icy stairwell. Stepping in front of the black nightmare, Rhennic and Rikyava hammered up twin barriers of power in a searing flash of blood and lightning-plasma, so thick Layla felt the darkness suddenly caught in that dense force. Struggling as it screeched, it shoved thousands of black tendrils through the layers to try and get to Luke and Layla.

To try and get to everyone.

Rikyava screamed and Rhennic roared, and Layla felt what the blackness was doing to them as they held their barrier – devouring their life-force away as it used its tentacles to suck at their magic, to thin it so it could punch through. But with twin growls, the cousins fought back, blasting the darkness with more and more energy, trying to make their wall hold.

In the icy stairwell, Adrian turned, flaring a scalding wind up at the rear of the party with a blistering gout of flame to sear back the darkness. Rhennic gave a roar of relief, casting a furious lance of lightning from his hand. The lightning flashed deep into the swirling blackness, followed by another and another as Rhennic blasted the Revenants back hard now. They shrieked, and at last Layla felt their group-mind retreat in pain, coiling in on themselves like a writhing mass of eels as if Rhennic's blasts had damaged them.

As they suddenly sucked back into the dark hall beyond the node, Dusk cast his palm up in a warding gesture. Layla saw a barrier of actual crystals fractal out into the air – coating the opening of the citrine hall in a solid, thick layer. Something roared, trapped behind that barrier. Breathing hard, Layla watched a black mass like eels made of smoke writhing behind Dusk's solid, shimmering layer. They had no form, but they had malice as they tried to find a way through with creeping black fingertips. As Layla stared, she felt the Revenants trying to claw their way through Dusk's barrier – six pairs of nasty red eyes rising in her mind.

A hand covered Layla's eyes, quickly – Rhennic's big hand, blocking out those red eyes in her mind. Gasping, a cold sweat had broken out all over her body, and she shivered with terror as Adrian crushed her in his arms, pouring a blistering wind through her – stopping those *things*. As she breathed hard, sightless from Rhennic's hand over her eyes, Layla felt Dusk perform his vibrations, closing the stone wall of the well permanently. The dark creatures were finally secured behind it, and Layla's ears popped as the Thin Ways closed.

She could hear the rustle of trees far above now, and could smell the cool cleanness of snow. As Rhennic's hand came down, Layla saw he'd covered Luke's eyes also. Though Adrian had gripped Layla close, he'd clamped a hand on Luke's wrist, and Layla watched Luke shudder as he blinked at Adrian in astonishment. Dusk leaned back against his stone barrier as if deeply fatigued, wiping sweat from his brow as he opened his eyes in the gloom. Rikyava hunkered on the icy steps at

Dusk's feet, shuddering and breathing hard with her eyes closed, her blonde brows knit as if she was in pain.

"You ok?" Adrian stepped from Layla, kneeling beside Rikyava and touching her gently on her back. Layla felt him pour a bolstering wind through her and Rikyava shuddered hard, finally breathing easier.

"I can't even count all the times my bones have been sucked by those things." She spoke wryly as she stood with Adrian's help. "You'd be surprised how many of those fuckers there are up in my homeland. They just love sucking on Blood Dragons. Like a tic the size of an elephant."

Luke stepped to Rikyava now, supporting her as she gave him a grateful smile, and Adrian pulled away. Glancing to Adrian, Luke frowned. "You saved my life. I could feel those things in my mind, digging… and your winds pushed them back."

"Not the first time I've saved your ass," Adrian spoke tersely, piercing Luke with his blistering aqua-gold stare. "Someday you should try thanking all the people you owe your life to, rather than just pissing them off. Come on. Let's move."

It was a scathing condemnation, and as Layla watched Luke's rage spark all over again that Adrian had been an asshole, Adrian ignored it, moving up the stone stairs that corkscrewed up the old well. With a glance at Layla, Dusk pushed from the wall. Layla followed Adrian with Dusk behind her, choosing her way carefully as they ascended the moss-slick steps.

Ice and snow coated the old stone beneath the dying winter light, and as they arrived above-ground in a thick copse of barren alder trees, they stepped out from a crumbling well carved with dragons and arcane runes. All around lay the ruins of a town, mounds of broken stone walls and foundations spectral in the wan afternoon. Storm clouds were heavy above, beginning to shed a thick fall of snow. Layla realized they were on the hilltop of Chartres, much further north than Chambord and an impossible distance to travel by foot so quickly.

But the Thin Ways had gotten them here in haste, and as Layla glanced to the brooding sky, she estimated it was barely noon. Glancing left, she saw an open space surrounded by trees and dead grass. In a cruciform, the space was exactly where the cathedral of Notre Dame de Chartres lay in the human world, and as Dusk led them along a snowy path towards the ruined cathedral's footprint, Layla breathed deep to be out of the Thin Ways. She couldn't quite shake the terror of it, though, and as she thought about the danger they'd just come out of, she suddenly saw six pairs of red eyes rise in her mind.

But though they were terrifying, they held little power now that they were trapped beneath the earth. All the same, Layla knew what they could have done to her, and glancing at Adrian, she saw the seriousness of his face as they moved into the second phase of their plans. They'd come through one danger, only to be thrust deeply into another.

Another which was entirely unknown, as they moved in to face the White Chalice.

CHAPTER 22 – CHARTRES

Standing inside the footprint of Notre Dame de Chartres in the Twilight Realm, Layla watched snow swirl down as the storm thickened. All around, the cruciform area of dead grasses and winter-barren trees was becoming lost to humped mounds of white, though the infamous Chartres labyrinth they stood upon was strangely untouched by snow. The ancient emblem was pitted and worn beneath their feet, its white stone set in the classic rose design just like in the human world. But as Layla looked out over the ruined town, she saw nothing of foundations that should have been the cathedral itself.

As if the cathedral of Notre Dame de Chartres had simply vanished.

It had been twenty minutes that Luke had been walking the labyrinth, trying to feel for the barrier that kept the cathedral hidden in the Nexus-realm. Twenty minutes that he'd tried to open his *nullax*, and still nothing was happening. But as Luke turned another bend, Adrian suddenly gave a growl where he waited with Layla and the rest, throwing up a hand in exasperation.

"Luke, are you even trying to open your magic?" Adrian called out, as Layla hugged herself to keep warm in the settling snow.

"Show me how it's done, Adrian, and I'll fucking do it!" Luke snarled back as his green eyes pinned Adrian, vibrant and pissed. They stared at each other for a moment, and Layla felt a surge of energy rush between them – though it was only Luke's regular Storm Dragon energy, rather than his *nullax* which responded to Adrian's irate whirl of hot winds.

"This is useless." Adrian growled, turning away from Luke and lacing his hands over his head, staring off at the trees. Luke was similarly disheartened and furious about it as he left the labyrinth, walking over to where everyone waited at the edge.

"Luke," Dusk spoke calmly as he blew on his hands, the cold dropping quickly as a wind picked up. "What triggered your *nullax* in the tub when you helped Layla? Can you recall?"

"I don't know," Luke spoke as he curried a hand through his hair to flick off snow, then drew his parka's hood up and thrust his hands in his pockets. Everyone was huddling in their coats as the temperature dropped fast, even Rhennic and Rikyava. The storm-front Queen Justine and her people had manifested all the way from Chambord was a furious one, and as the wind whipped snow hard through the dead town, Luke's gaze settled to Layla's. In his devastated green eyes, she saw all the pain he wouldn't show the others – that he was failing to rescue their friends.

"You do know," Dusk spoke gently as he watched Luke. "Tell me what happened when you saw Layla in the bath, what you felt."

"Magic is mostly intuition, Luke," Rikyava spoke as she moved closer to Luke, watching him with her strong lavender gaze. "Somewhere inside below your conscious mind, you know why your Dragon rose the way it did to help Layla. Take a breath. Don't think, just relive it. Feel your way back into the moment, and the answer will come."

"I just…" Luke took a deep breath, closing his eyes as he seemed to go quiet deep inside. "When Adrian told me what was going on, I had this rush of alarm. And when I got to the bathroom and saw her – blue in the tub, like the kind of hypothermia you don't survive – I panicked that I was going to lose her. I felt this enormous white electricity surge up inside me. Dusk helped me breathe so it wouldn't swamp me, but the start of it was when I took one look at Layla's face and saw she was drowning… in something that I couldn't heal any other way."

"Healing. Of course." Layla blinked, suddenly understanding the problem. "Luke, the first time your magic rose was when mine bit you – it was trying to heal your body. The second time, you used it to try to heal me. The third time, when Queen Justine bit you, it was trying to heal you also, though it was backed by extreme rage that time. Don't you see? You're a healer. It's not just that medicine is important to you – it's that your magic tries to heal people."

"My god." Dusk spoke, and Layla saw a plan spark suddenly in his eyes. "Luke. Go stand at the center of the labyrinth. Forget walking it, just stand in the middle."

"Ok." Luke gave him a confused glance, but walked back over the worn stone to the center. With a beckon from Dusk, Layla and the others followed, standing inside the labyrinth's boundary, though not in the very center like Luke. "Now what?"

"Close your eyes. Picture your friends in your mind." Dusk intoned in the low, soothing voice people used for hypnotism. As he spoke, Layla felt a slow, strange harmonic moving out from Dusk through the stone of the labyrinth, straight to Luke. Luke closed his eyes, taking a deep breath though his hands were still tucked deep in his pockets. Layla saw his entire body shiver from Dusk's rumbles, then relax as he stood taller.

"Picture Charlie, Celia, and Arron," Dusk continued in that low singsong, "all their smiling faces so happy on a summer day in Seattle. Now see them here in a cold cathedral in the Twilight Realm, scared, taken by predators and not knowing what their fate will be."

Layla saw Luke's body tense. She saw him take a swift breath, his dark eyebrows knitting as if he was suddenly in pain, or furious.

Dusk saw it too, continuing. "See your friends, far down in a black dungeon. Feel them in the deeps, shivering with fear, not knowing if anyone is coming to rescue them. Feel them afraid, cowering against the iron bars of a cold, cruel cell. And then a creature comes for them. A Vampire Revenant with tendrils of black ice and eyes of red flame."

Luke hissed at the center of the labyrinth. Layla's adrenaline spiked as she felt a crackle of electricity spring to life all around Luke. With an outstretched hand, Rhennic eased Layla and the rest back as he watched Luke warily. At the center of the labyrinth, Luke was breathing hard, a seething fury on his face as his hands came out of his pockets – ready.

"Feel the creature come for them." Dusk continued, watching Luke knowingly. "Feel it like ice in your soul as it touches them, as it starts to drain and feed. Feel their fear as its magic touches them; their terror that nothing will ever be right in the world again."

Luke was trembling now, but not from cold – from power. Shivering with a hard magic surging through him in crackling waves, his *nullax* nimbus began to take shape around his body. Forming a ring of white mist, it flowed like ghastly water around him despite the rushing wind. As Layla watched, that deadly mist thickened in currents and eddies like a river of death, blistering with bursts of electricity.

"Feel the Revenant," Dusk continued, his gaze sharpening hard on Luke as his hypnotizing rumbles surged through the stone. "Taste its magic as it takes your friends. Taste that pure cold from which nothing escapes; only dies. They are dying, Luke. Your friends are dying and only you can save them. Their bodies are cast through with the darkest power, eating them like a cancer and making them feel nothing but terror and death. But you can save them. You can heal them. Take your fist now. Take your fist and ready your power. Take your fist – and slam it into the barrier that keeps them from you!!"

As Dusk roared out his final command in a wave of earthshaking magic, Luke gave a horrible roar of his own. Strangled, it was the sound of a thousand beasts in torment as Luke suddenly balled both hands into fists and slammed them down – straight into the stone at the center of the labyrinth. With a deafening retort, the labyrinth cracked in a spiderweb from his impact, shattering to a thirty-foot radius as Luke's white *nullax* thrust into the stone and flooded like a rageful sea beneath their feet. But it did not touch Layla or the others, only flowed out fast all around them – slamming into a shimmering boundary at the edge of the clearing's cruciform in a burst of color and light.

And sending them into the cathedral of Notre Dame de Chartres.

Amazement flooded Layla as the cathedral towered up all around them suddenly. As they burst through into the Nexus-realm, Layla wasn't just amazed by Luke's feat, but also because the cathedral wasn't made of stone and glass. This structure had been built of nature, and as the cathedral was revealed around them and high overhead, Layla was sundered by its grandeur.

All around, the cathedral's stout columns were created from the trunks of enormous trees like redwoods but white. High above, their spreading branches formed the ribs and vaults of gables and domes, walls formed of blossoming vines that had been basket-woven as they climbed the towering trees. Far before them at the chancel where the flowering vines and trees came together, a river rushed down many tiers, sparkling white in its floes. All around, the floor of the sacred space was not stone, but spreading tree roots overlaid by a carpet of moss in so many vivid colors it would have made Japanese gardeners weep.

Beyond the high vaulted windows, it was spring in the Nexus-space rather than winter. But the cathedral's windows weren't made of stained glass, rather formed of the same shimmering barriers Layla had seen keeping the fields at Chambord hale. These barriers flowed with colorful patterns that shifted and danced as Layla watched, forming scenes of Storm Dragons in battle and Storm Dragons in worship. There were scenes of adulation and trial, as a Dragon with a golden halo above his head led the White Chalice through love and fury, battle and revival – and peace.

That peace filled Layla now, along with a deep solemnity in the grand space. As she had felt once walking into the powerfully opulent cathedral of Notre Dame de Chartres in the human world, she felt triply so here, see it all done by nature and magic. As she listened to air flow gently through the ancient vaults of eternal springtime, she saw birds with bright red tails wing through the air, calling out a sweet song. As her heart gripped, she heard the most musical voice she had ever known call out through that vast holiness.

"The Royal Dragon Bind, at last."

Layla blinked as she glanced to the chancel far ahead, seeing a man approach. Walking upon the swirling waters of the river, stepped down through them as if they flowed over unseen stairs. Wearing a robe of diaphanous weave like shimmering light, he smiled at their group with benevolence as he neared. Tall and slender, he was of early-middle years, his hair dark with thick waves, his deep blue eyes sparkling with Storm Dragon energy. As he approached, other White Chalice emerged, wearing similar robes though none as bright as the High Priest's. As he gazed upon her, Layla felt a deep call in her mind – to come be one with the Chalice in peace and plenty.

Layla blinked, realizing something was mesmerizing her, and as she shook her head, she noticed a curling incense wafting through the air. Glancing aside, Layla expected to see a censer, but instead saw

Smoke Faunus dressed in the same robes as the Storm Dragons. They didn't feel threatening, and stopped fifteen paces from Layla's group as they breathed a musky smoke though the air like sandalwood. Waiting patiently as Layla and the others took in their strangely gentle welcome, the tall Storm Dragon man was still beaming at her as Layla glanced back to him.

"How do you know me?" Layla asked bluntly, prickling with a ready energy.

"We have heard tales of the Royal Dragon Bind and her consorts," the man nodded in welcome to Adrian and Dusk, "and of the powerful company she keeps." Here, he nodded to Luke, Rikyava, and Rhennic in a similarly peaceful manner. "We simply wished to make your acquaintance, and that of our newest *nullax* awakening among your comrades."

Layla smelled a rat. Despite the High Priest's pleasant manner, despite the fact that all his host were keeping a respectful distance and not bristling with battle, something still felt way off.

Apparently, Luke felt it, too, because he growled. "If you just wanted to meet us, why not simply invite us here? Why abduct our friends and hurt Layla's co-workers? I want to see Charlie, Celia, and Arron. Now. And they'd better be unharmed."

"Of course. And I assure you, your friends are most hale." The High Priest gave a quiet nod to two Storm Dragons at his right, who retreated towards an alcove. Turning to face Luke and Layla again, the High Priest continued. "As for their arrival here, it was most unfortunately done. It was our intention that your friends would come to our invitation joyfully, yet when we asked them, a few of your Hotel comrades were resistant to the idea. Violently."

Layla felt her blood curdle as her drakaina gave a nasty snarl inside her veins. Of course, the High Priest would try to pin blame on

Rikyava's Guards and the others at the Hotel who had protected Layla's human friends. She was about to say something uncouth when her Seattle friends were suddenly produced by the Storm Dragons.

Layla didn't know how much tension she'd been under until she saw their faces – and saw they'd not been harmed. Clad in the same diaphanous material as the White Chalice, a clinging dress for Celia and loose pants for Arron and Charlie, none had been brutalized, and all looked warm, fed, and in surprisingly excellent spirits. As they arrived, all three beamed to see Layla and Luke, and as they rushed forward, Layla was quite suddenly enveloped in a group hug as she and Luke shuddered in relief.

"Layloo! Lucas!"

Layla choked a sob as she was corralled in their arms, and she felt Luke do the same beside her. All her tension evaporated to feel her friends again, so warm and safe and strangely happy. As tears of relief shed down Layla's cheeks, she hugged petite Celia hard, then Charlie, then kissed Arron full on the lips and hugged him even harder. Charlie's big, buff arms curled around them all as even Luke held the group fiercely.

As everyone finally pulled back from the reunion, Luke spoke incredulously. "How are you all so ok? I thought you were going to be locked in dungeons!"

"Dungeons? No way! This place is rad!" Charlie spoke first, his baby-blue eyes beaming and Adonis blond curls glowing beneath the cathedral's vaults. "They have this whole tree-house setup in the canopy, you guys have to see it. Goes all the way up through the highest vaults of the dome with swings and boardwalks and everything!"

"Did you know you can *paint with air* here?" Celia laughed as she pushed her glasses up her button nose, the only part of her original attire she still wore. "It's amazing! They even let me use it to create a tableau like their stained-glass windows! I mean, they're not stained glass, they're magic, but you get the idea."

"Hey chica, great that you finally made it." Arron pulled Layla into a side hug, grinning as he gazed down at her. "You look stressed, are you ok?"

"Arron, you guys were *abducted!*" Layla blinked up at him in shock. "How could I possibly be ok?"

"We're ok!" He laughed brightly, then kissed the tip of her nose. "No one was hurt. Things were a bit squirrelly when we left the Hotel, but—"

"People were gravely injured, Arron." Dusk stepped forward now, frowning deeply as his astute gaze perused the group. "Don't you remember?"

For the first time, Arron blinked, showing a trace of confusion before he smiled again. "I'm sure it can be sorted out, now that you all have arrived. Layla, come here, I want you to meet someone."

As Arron abruptly changed the subject, he began tugging Layla over to a group of Smoke Faunus, three women and two men quietly watching as they breathed a musky incense up to the vaults above. As Arron dragged Layla over, one Smoke Faunus woman lowered her diaphanous cowl, baring flowing silver hair behind her corkscrewing horns, her big dark eyes smiling at Layla. Like the rest of her kind, her limbs were long and willowy and strangely patterned like silver tree-branches. Her fingers were slender and long like twigs as she welcomed Arron, gathering him close.

Pulled from Layla, he went straight into the woman's arms, embracing her willowy frame. *Really* embracing her. As Layla gaped, Arron and the woman kissed deeply, in a way so completely smitten that Layla felt her world reel. When Arron finally pulled away, both he and the woman were beaming as they gazed into each other's eyes. Turning to Layla, he cuddled the Smoke Faunus close with one arm around her waist, his fingers caressing her hip through her almost not-there garment.

"Layla. May I introduce Giselle. Giselle, this is my best friend Layla."

"It is ecstasy to meet you, Layla." The woman spoke, her voice melodious as a curl of white-blue smoke wafted from her full red lips. "It is such an honor to meet the Royal Dragon Bind."

Layla's mouth fell open as something dark and awful twisted through her gut. Deep inside, her Dragon roared and she felt it bristle with furious heat – fangs bared with talons ready to kill. "Arron. You are *gay*. What the fuck?"

"I know, Layla." He spoke calmly, not smiling now but concerned as if he was hurt she didn't like his new beau. "But Giselle… she just strikes my heart. In a way I haven't felt in a long while. Please, try to accept this."

"No." Layla shook her head in a fast, shocky movement as Luke came to her side, scowling at Arron also.

"Arron, this isn't you," Luke argued low. "She's fucking with your head. We are leaving. Now. And your new *girlfriend* isn't coming with you."

"I don't want to leave." Arron blinked at them, pulling back with a frown as if offended they would even suggest it. Interlacing his fingers through Giselle's, he glanced to her. "This is where I belong now, here with my family. And my wife."

"Your *wife?*" Layla hissed.

"These people are not your family." Luke growled, and Layla felt a crisp wave of power flow from him like a building thunderstorm. "We are. And you are not fucking marrying a woman, Arron, you didn't

265

even like girls when you were twelve. Don't you remember any of that?"

"But we like it here, Luke." Celia had stepped over to them now, trailed by Charlie, and the recognition of what Layla saw in their eyes made her blood run cold – the sweet shine of brainwashing. "High Priest Lodrian even gave us White Chalice membership so we can feel more at home here. We had a ceremony and everything."

"A ceremony." Layla's Dragon snarled hard in her veins, bristling all through her in a furious wave. Turning to the High Priest, she focused her wrath upon him, even as she felt Luke do the same.

"What the fuck did you do to them?!" Luke snarled, a crackle of lightning blistering from his skin with a low roll of thunder.

"Nothing that can't be easily undone." The High Priest's dark blue gaze flickered with lightning now as he gave the tiniest smile. "If you both are strong enough."

And there it was. Layla saw the cold darkness inside the High Priest as he stared her and Luke down. This was a test, to see if they had the ability to break the Chalice's hold over their friends. Suddenly, Layla realized what a dangerous game they were playing. The Storm Queen had said the Chalice used their *nullax* to break anyone they deemed too powerful, and now Layla knew how they dragged a person into a battle of wits with them. They stole someone who was innocent and weaker than the person they wished to break – and used them as bait.

As Luke and Layla both surged with magic, furious, she felt Luke reach out and clasp her hand. Twining his fingers through hers, Layla felt Luke's power roar like a mad thing, bolstered by their touch. She felt his magic leap to her, wanting to be Bound yet hating it at the same time – a surging conflict deep inside Luke that only pushed his magic higher. As a hard wave of thunder boomed from him, echoing high into the vaults and startling birds far above, Layla saw Luke's eyes flash with a horrible power.

"You're on, fucko." Luke snarled in the coldest voice Layla had ever heard from him. "I am going to wipe this hall with your blood. May the best Dragon win."

CHAPTER 23 – BONFIRE

As Luke and Layla gripped hands, facing down the High Priest, Layla felt people's positions change throughout the hall. She thought the Chalice were only the handful who had initially shown themselves, but as Luke and Layla bristled with power and Adrian, Dusk, Rhennic, and Rikyava stepped up quickly to defend their backs, Layla felt a mass of people suddenly move in the hall. As if they'd been disguised by the mind-befuddling powers of the Smoke Faunus, over two hundred White Chalice members now stepped from the vine-woven walls and tree-trunk columns – even soared down from the upper vaults like they danced upon air.

Smoke Faunus were suddenly pouring their poisonous charms into the air from every direction, and Layla reeled, feeling that smoke hit her system like a massive dose of Rohypnol. A blaze of storm-lightning suddenly seared to life all around them, hemming them in from escape. Flashing in every vault, flickering in every window, Layla realized the vast magic that had grown the cathedral into such beauty was also a terrible protection for the White Chalice's last stronghold.

Their only stronghold that had survived Queen Justine's purges – for thousands of years.

Layla heard Adrian's snarl behind her as a searing ring of protective fire flared to life around their group, and she felt Dusk's low, ground-shaking tremors spike hard as he thrust white crystals up through the floor in a barrier that twined into Adrian's fire. Rhennic's vicious storms flashed into Adrian's and Dusk's to form a boundary of plasma-lighting around their group, even though Rhennic wasn't part of their Bind. Rikyava was similarly intent, whirling a tempest of blood through it all, flooding it out over the mossy floor and making Smoke Faunus step back warily.

But Luke's rage was focused on the High Priest, and Layla saw a deadly white mist of flowing lightning manifest from Luke now, easing beyond their group's protection. Seeping like a nightmare, Luke's *nullax* licked out far further than Rikyava's blood-pool. It reached Charlie and Celia, and as it touched them, Layla saw them startle as if they'd been zapped, clearing whatever magical taint had held them. Glancing around, shock was in their eyes as they suddenly realized they were standing in the middle of a war-zone.

"Whoa, shit!" Charlie moved fast with his buff brawn, whisking tiny Celia up in his big arms as he sprinted through the ring of protection, which parted quickly to allow them in. Moving back from Luke's seeping mist, the Smoke Faunus Giselle gave a nasty snarl, twining Arron into her branch-like arms as she poured smoke into him from her lips. But Luke was faster, roaring as he shoved a wave of *nullax* at Arron, who cried out as Luke's power found him. Layla saw Arron's grey eyes clear; she saw him panic that he was being held captive. Arron's lean height was scrappy and he struggled, heaving an elbow into the woman's middle and sending her sprawling to her hands and knees as he sprinted for the group's protection.

Layla saw Luke's *nullax* flow over the Faunus woman. With a shriek, it was suddenly diving in her nose, her eyes – everywhere. As she shuddered, screaming like something was being ripped from her very soul, Luke staggered, faltering. Layla gripped his hand with hers, pouring the wrathful heat of her Dragon deep inside him. Pouring her passion into him, and her anger at everything that had been done to their friends.

Pouring into him all the rage they shared – and their mutual fury.

Layla felt Luke's Dragon rise within him to the call of her Bind, white like a demon of emptiness and mist with flickering lightning-void eyes. It was the most terrifying thing she had ever seen in her mind-sight and as she cried out in horror, Luke cried out also from the devouring presence of his *nullax*. Bolstered by Layla's passion, it took him, and as it did, it took the Faunus woman on the floor. Though their connection, Layla felt the Faunus' magic devoured. She felt the woman's life-force being not just ripped away, but consumed by the *nullax* that lived inside Luke. It didn't feed like a Vampire, only dissolved the woman's magical essence until there was nothing left to devour. Like mist blowing away on a vast storm-wind, Layla felt that essence flow back to the universe from whence it came.

As the Faunus woman passed out cold – smoke no longer issuing from her nose and mouth.

"Impressive, *nullax*." The High Priest's voice was suddenly pummeling all around them like thunder through the cathedral. "But you know nothing of wielding your power, child of my bloodline. It is a wild thing, untamed and raw."

"Fuck you." Luke snarled as he looked up, pinning the High Priest with his furious gaze, emerald lightning flickering as his irises swirled with white mists. His hand was still clamped to Layla's, even though she felt a tremor of fatigue rush through Luke now. He wasn't Bound to her yet, even though her passion had been able to give him strength. Something inside him was still resisting, and with a sudden intuition, she knew the High Priest was right.

Without the Bind, Luke didn't know how to push his power to its true heights.

"Is this what you wanted?" Layla called out to the High Priest, watching him over the seething protection that curled around her

270

friends. "To just see what we can do?"

"I know what you can do, Layla. I have always known it. But you have yet to believe me." All of a sudden, the timbre of the High Priest's voice changed. From its honey-smooth tones, it had gone darker, deeper, and as Layla watched, she saw the man's posture subtly change. Suddenly, he was less holy yet more elegant, more brutal as he gazed upon her from where he stood within the flow of the river.

As if it was enchanted somehow, the river washed away Luke's mist as it seeped to him, washing away Rikyava's blood-pool also. As the High Priest's piercing gaze held Layla's, she watched a tall, slender woman step to his side in the river. A Faunus, her corkscrewing gazelle antlers were twined with golden torques, the same coiling around her upper arms and wrists. Coming to the High Priest's side, her doe-eyes were haughty as she stared the group down. As her gaze pinned Adrian, her perfect lips lifted in a cold disdain, her graciousness obliterated.

Ms. Lulu Duvall.

"The Hunter sends his regards, Layla," she spoke, her words like poison as they flowed from her lips in her purring French accent. "He is impressed that you have managed to push your aims so deeply into his organization."

"What do you mean? What does Hunter have to do with any of this?" Layla growled, blistering with fury now as Adrian and Dusk stepped up beside her with twin snarls, though she still held Luke's hand.

"I have everything to do with this." The High Priest spoke in his strangely elegant, dark voice as he gestured around the cathedral. "This is my Chalice, Layla. And those who keep it for me are my most dedicated servants."

"Hunter!" Layla snarled, though even as she watched the High Priest, she recognized something was wrong. Whenever Hunter had outed himself to her before, his irises had always swirled to their dark forest green and black. But now, the High Priest merely held her gaze, his eyes their regular storm-blue. This body wasn't Hunter, not like the last times he had come to her. The High Priest was merely possessed by Hunter somehow, talking with his voice and seeing with his eyes.

"Yes, you know I am not here in the flesh," he answered, as if feeling her thoughts. "I merely hold sway over my most trusted from long ago, those who accepted my Bind in their bodies. Lodrian was one of the first to come to me in ages long past. He believes in my aims, and has kept the strength of my Chalice, acting as the backbone of my Crimson Circle all these years."

"*Your* Crimson Circle?" Adrian snarled at Layla's side, bristling with a dire heat. "Are you telling us you sit at the pinnacle of the Red Letter Hotel's leadership, Hunter?"

"I am the Hotel's leadership, for the Hotel is mine." The High Priest's gaze pinned Adrian, and Layla felt Hunter's talons in that steely gaze, though Lodrian's irises still didn't change. "I began the Red Letter Hotel long ago. I started its ancient precepts and laid down its laws. I sequestered its first houses and participants, like Lodrian here, and told them of my designs. I shared with them the future of peace I envisioned, and from that vision, two organizations were born, one secular and one sacred. But to me, both are sacred, the Crimson and the White. For me, passion and holy benevolence are as one. And thus, function as one."

Layla reeled, taking it all in as she felt Adrian and Dusk shake hard at this revelation beside her. She suddenly felt sick that she'd been unknowingly working for Hunter all this time; that he probably had methods of spying and infiltration all through every Hotel that no one knew about. Not only had he started the Crimson Circle, he *was* the Crimson Circle. The Hotel and all its egalitarian principles and the utter corruption at its uppermost levels had been Hunter's from the very first – and Layla felt that knowledge shudder through her bones as she stared at Lodrian.

He watched her back, calm and composed as Lulu Duvall stood at his side. Layla saw suddenly why Lulu was the Hotel Board's mouthpiece. Because Lodrian had long stood at their lead just beneath Hunter, guiding the Crimson Circle and White Chalice both – and using the Chalice to do a large part of Hunter's most vicious dirty-work. Quelling opposition. Breaking strong clans, especially Dragon-clans who opposed Hunter's great vision of *peace*. Breaking Royal Dragons and Royal Dragon Binds who would not join him. And Lulu had been Lodrian's lover for eons, working with him to enact Hunter's precepts.

As Hunter remained quietly in the shadows above it all.

Layla felt a deep horror open inside her, blacker than the night was deep. It was a cold, cold place, and she staggered suddenly as it roared up fast to take her. It was only by Luke and Adrian's quick hands that she didn't sink to the floor, as Dusk stepped fast to her back, curling her in his arms. Pouring a bolstering rumble through her as Adrian and Luke growled murderously at Hunter, Dusk set his smooth lips to her temple. Breathing deep, Dusk poured his grounding energy into Layla, and she felt him holding her back from diving all the way into that dark, empty blackness.

And yet, she still felt it devouring her. Despite Dusk's strong grounding and Adrian's bright fury, Layla felt her Dragon swallowed by that vast black nothing inside her, and suddenly her beast went calm rather than furious. Horribly, terribly calm as her drakaina now turned her head towards Hunter – her scales not fiery gold but utterly black, her eyes empty as the endless night. She had no passion as she stared Hunter down where he stood possessing Lodrian's body.

She had no passion now – and it was a terrible, dead thing.

"You and I will never come to accord, Hunter." Layla spoke in a cold, dead voice. "Not now, not ever. No matter how many trials you send my way to shape me, or break me."

"I do not need to shape you," Hunter spoke softly through Lodrian's lips as his gaze became deep upon her. "You are doing it yourself. Your tremendous passion is burning black, Layla, just like mine did long ago. I can feel it in you, staring at me. Your love is turning dark and there is no stopping it now that it has begun. For as a Royal Dragon Bind can burn oh-so-bright, they can also darken oh-so-deep. You will become like me. And then you will understand my aims, and they will be one with yours. I don't fight alone, Layla. There are more people than you've ever imagined who feel as I do. More people who have loved and lost, who understand that the peace of the universe isn't in the passion, but the quiet. Become quiet with me, Layla. Become quiet and understand how strong you truly are – and how far your power can truly go."

As he spoke, Layla knew he was right. Deep inside her soul, she knew it as she stared into the uncaring void-black eyes of her Dragon now. When Hunter imitated someone, or possessed or Bound them, he felt their loves and losses deep inside his soul. Hunter felt their every hardship, fury, and bright loves gone dark – and Layla was the same. As she stared at him, she felt their inner darknesses resonate like harpstrings, entraining with a vast devouring. Even though they weren't Bound, she could suddenly feel Hunter's black coils sliding through hers, moving with her, feeling her. The sensation caught Layla's breath as a dark eroticism slid slowly through her, a deep quiet which had no presence, only void.

She knew then, why Hunter didn't need to Bind her; because his same darkness already lived in her, the flipside to the hot passion of the Bind. It was why Binds had historically turned dark when exposed to too much hardship in their lives; because this inner darkness was always behind the light of their passions. As Layla felt it now, devouring her, she understood that she and Hunter were already Bound. His magic had never taken her and hers had never taken his, but they were Bound all the same. Bound because of what they were.

And how that darkness always lived just behind the light.

"Layla will never be like you, asshole. Not while I'm around."

Luke's snarl was suddenly in Layla's ears, and something about it pushed her terrible emptiness back. As he gripped her hand, digging his nails into her skin like talons, he flooded his power into her through their touch. Hunter's dark coils were pushed back as Layla gasped, as Luke's caustic bright mist seared into that seductive black quietude. As he flooded her with the intensity of his loving fury, Layla suddenly felt his Dragon rear high inside him. Gazing at her, it paused, seeing what was happening as she was inundated by Hunter's black influence.

Luke's mist-white drake lashed out, biting Layla's drakaina through their touch.

And that bite was gasoline on a bonfire as Layla's Bind suddenly opened – and devoured Luke entirely.

CHAPTER 24 – PASSION

Luke's mist-white drake roared all through Layla as her Bind rushed into him, taking what he offered. She felt her magic smash through Luke's last resistance, shrieking like a harpy of golden light as it swept him up. Like a leviathan, Layla's bright Dragon roared up hard from her inner darkness as Luke's white *nullax* scalded Hunter's influence back. Gold and crimson rather than void-black now, the light of the cosmos flooded her drakaina as Layla screamed in ecstasy – all of that terrible power rushing into her men.

She felt Luke's Dragon roar as he screamed, his hand spasming upon hers in a taloned grip as he half-shifted, his body rippling with light. Shuddering in ecstasy, Layla's hand gripped just as tight to Luke's, her body surging with heat and passion. Bent into a bow, she roared with the overtones of her Dragon's voice as the Bind went wild, flooding into Rhennic behind her; shattering any barrier he might have had as it raced into him with soul-shredding heat and sexual winds. Pouring through her already-Bound Royal Dragons, it staggered Dusk and Adrian with the force of Layla's righteous energy. As Reginald's power joined them like a deep, dark wave from far away, Layla felt the Bind respond. Hauling them all close with massive coils of golden light that actually manifested in the air like liquid fire, it flooded deep into their bodies.

Staggering them all as it Bound them fast together.

As Layla's power pushed her men's magic to catastrophic heights, flooding their protective barrier, she felt Luke snarl like a wraith on the winds as his *nullax* expanded tenfold. Like a massive white wave, Luke's *nullax* flooded the cathedral, devouring Storm Dragons and Smoke Faunus on all sides. But though dozens were taken, hundreds remained, shifting fast into enormous storm-colored Dragons and hurtling into the river near the High Priest, using the river's protection to drive Luke's attack back as they funneled up spouts of water to drive off the *nullax*.

Like a hurricane, the High Priest shifted into the most massive Dragon Layla had ever seen. Black-violet with lines of jet running through his scales, he was serrated with nasty ridges as he roared to the cathedral's vaults, tornadoes of lightning shedding from him. He was like a serrated black mamba as he arched above them, pinning them with eyes black as death. As he roared, Layla felt the White Chalice join their searing lightning-power in a vast ring around their High Priest. The energy of a hundred thunderstorms and the poison of a hundred exhalations went pouring in through Lodrian's serrated scales, channeled from his Chalice. As Layla felt that enormous power flare inside Lodrian's black Dragon, she felt her men shift into their own Dragons to do battle against the darkness.

Adrian shifted into his aqua and crimson Dragon at Layla's side, snarling as he sent gouts of white-hot flame out to char enemies, raking talons of tornado-fast power through the air. Like a demon, Rhennic was unleashed into Dragon-form also, a massive creature of white, red, and storm-blue fractal scales thrice Adrian's size, devastating their foes with rolling waves of plasma-lightning and deafening concussions of thunder. Though not part of the Bind, Rikyava had transformed also, flashing through the air in crimson and black geodesic glory, strangling foes with lassos of pure blood.

With a snapping of bones and rush of pain, Layla transformed into her Dragon also. Snarling with terrible instinct, she whirled a hot golden wind through Adrian's fire as she coiled around her human friends, shielding them as she thought *safe, protect, fragile.* She felt Reginald's wrath flow through her from afar, as Dusk's earth-shattering energy shot through her also, spiking out through the cathedral and skewering Storm Dragons and Smoke Faunus in the river. As Storm Dragons blistered them with gales, Layla and her friends resisted – punishing them for their attempts to bring the Bind down.

But as they fought, Layla felt the High Priest's power come to completion. Flaring a mantle of serrated black spines, his eyes sharpened on their group. Layla saw Hunter's mind behind it as Lodrian's Dragon-gaze connected to hers. Taking all the energy of his White Chalice, Lodrian transformed their power into a single, deadly strike. Aimed to take Layla out at the Bind's heart, she felt all that power focus on her. She felt it aim like a spear upon her as Lodrian turned his enormous black head in her direction.

But as Lodrian opened his jaws, lightning and smoke churning in his great maw, Layla heard someone roar like crystals being blasted together in a 10.0 earthquake. The sound came from Dusk as he gave a tremendous shudder, surging up into a terrifyingly huge Dragon even larger than Lodrian. Armored with sapphire-blue and diamond plating, every scale on him was serrated, screaming with diamond-light. Opening jaws with fangs large as mammoth tusks and raking talons of pure diamond through the earth, he roared to the vaults – a hammer of power uprooting trees and concussing the ground, exploding everything into fault lines and making the entire cathedral shudder.

As spears of serrated diamond shot from Dusk's spine and head, creating an armored mantle of light, Dusk heaved with uncanny control, cracking his crystal-spiked tail and skewering Storm Dragons, sending them careening through the cathedral's walls. Turning his furious sapphire-diamond eyes upon the High Priest, Dusk roared with a shockwave of ground-roiling power, cracking the stout trees of the cathedral. Storm Dragons were suddenly shrieking, pummeled by tree limbs bigger than houses as they came crashing down. Layla, Adrian, and Rhennic's abilities were now used only for shielding in a vast dome around their company as Dusk brought the enormous cathedral down by his power – unleashed in its true glory at last.

But even as Dusk raged, Layla felt the High Priest's attention sharpen. Boiling with white *nullax* inside his maw along with that star-bright annihilation now, Hunter's mind guided Lodrian's as the big black drake curved his neck and blasted all that power from his throat. That lance of *nullax*-storm shot not at Layla as Hunter unleashed it from Lodrian, piercing right through the dome of their protection.

But straight to Dusk.

Layla didn't even see the blast hit her Royal Crystal Dragon, but she felt it. She felt Dusk's scream all through her as his power was stolen – as everything that made him a Crystal Dragon was sucked from his marrow like a Vampire Revenant devouring its prey. She felt Adrian scream; she felt Rhennic's shock. She felt Luke's horror and Rikyava's heartbreak, and Reginald's roar of agony far away. But mostly, she felt her own darkness as all of Dusk's diamond-light brilliance was taken from her. All his joy, all his pleasure. All his righteous energy and indomitable strength. All his cheeky laughter and winsome bravado.

All of it, ripped away and casting her into darkness.

Darkness devoured Layla, and she screamed as she collapsed back down into human. Shuddering naked on the broken ground, she heaved as a terrible nothingness filled her from Dusk's energy killed inside her, as he collapsed back down to human also. Protecting her and Dusk as his Dragon, Adrian blasted a gout of vicious flame, charring enemies even as he roiled in pain. Collapsed to his knees, Luke screamed in agonized fury as his *nullax* shot out in a terrible wave, devouring enemies right and left.

But it was Rhennic who roared in defiance as his Dragon flashed to Dusk, fast. Locking his jaws over Dusk's chest, Rhennic poured his magic into Dusk through the Bind. Layla felt Rhennic pouring his *nullax* immunity into Dusk as the final bit of Dusk's magic was devoured by the High Priest's blast. And as Layla felt Rhennic give his all to try and save Dusk, Layla felt Luke's energy roil through the blasted cathedral like a mist from hell.

Layla felt the barrier of the Nexus-space flash out to Luke's ability, returning the cathedral to the Twilight Realm. Snow and winter winds seethed in through the cathedral's broken vaults as hundreds of Storm and Blood Dragon cavalry blasted through. Falling like a shooting star upon the High Priest, Queen Justine dove as an all-white Dragon with piercing midnight-blue eyes, lightning blazing around her in a ball of white plasma. Hurtling right to Lodrian, she smashed into him, bowling his black Dragon over in the river and pinning her jaws to his. Exhaling all her tremendous power, she blasted it right down the High Priest's throat.

Taking him at last.

Breathing fire down someone else's throat could scorch them from the inside, but breathing star-plasma down someone's throat was obliterating. Lodrian's Dragon exploded like a supernova, serrated scales and spines blasting out in terrible black projectiles as his insides charred into ruin. Shields of power slammed up fast from their allies; Layla and her group were saved by a quick lightning-wall from Rhennic. But with a triumphant roar, Queen Justine fell motionless over Lodrian's grisly remains.

Pierced through the heart by a hundred serrated scales and black spines.

Layla heard King Huttr's strangled roar as he swooped in as his massive snow-white drake with geodesic blood-lines, hurling blood-lances in a furious hurricane through the hearts of their foes. Layla saw her human friends cowering in the carnage as Rikyava coiled around them, keeping them safe as the entire cathedral came tumbling down in thundering waves to the Dragon-battle. She saw Adrian coiled around Dusk's body, roaring jets of fire as Rhennic's lightning-wall coalesced around Layla, protecting her from careening debris.

But she didn't see the rest.

Layla felt herself leave, drifting on empty time as sound faded in her ears. She flowed away, wanting to die from all the pain she felt surrounding her, and within her own heart. But even as she despaired, lingering on the brink of an endless nothing, she felt someone call her back. Heat scorching as desert sands flowed into her and Layla gasped. Fire-coils wrapped around her with the tenderest love, hauling her back from the brink. Layla wanted to leave; the destruction was too much.

But with a sweet breath down her throat, Adrian's winds called her back – waves of jasmine and cinnamon leading her back to the light.

Layla came to. His lips upon hers, Adrian was naked in human form as he poured his reviving winds down her throat. Layla gasped, drinking him in as her eyelashes fluttered. Luke was compressing her chest with CPR, and as she coughed, surfacing, he ceased. Kissing her as tears of relief streamed down his face, Adrian pulled her into his arms.

All around, the cathedral was in ruins, silent now but for the groans of the dying. With a massive retort, a tree-limb cracked, hammering the ground nearby and sending up a sluice of dust. The cathedral was destroyed, their Storm Dragon allies erecting a barrier to keep out snow and winter winds, even as Justine's storm-wielders worked to calm the storm itself. Inside the decimated cathedral, bodies of Smoke Faunus and Storm Dragons were now back in human-form, littering the carnage.

Nearby, Layla saw a sarcophagus of sapphire and diamond glowing in the ruins. She could just make out a man inside, in repose with his arms crossed over his chest like an Egyptian mummy. The crystal sarcophagus was so thick, she couldn't make out Dusk's face. But she felt his indomitable energy as the sarcophagus gave a slow pulse. The last fragment of Dusk's magic shuddered with a vicious stubbornness, deep as the earth and just as immutable as it coalesced into a cocoon around him. Layla could just hear the sub-bass notes of his Dragon as Dusk's magic resisted obliteration like a star in the void.

Humming a sweet vibration into Layla's heart.

"He's alive!" Layla gasped, her hand clutching her chest as tears sprung to her eyes, feeling Dusk's light inside her once more.

Nodding, Adrian kissed her brow as his own tears fell. "I don't know what condition he's in, or if he'll recover. But at least he still has his magic and his life. And his Bind is still with us…"

The way Adrian said it broke Layla's heart. Wrapping her arms around Adrian's neck, she held him fiercely as Luke cradled her, setting his cheek to hers. Layla could feel Luke's tears as they slipped down her cheek. She could feel him resonating with their Bind now, with their emotions as his own woe twisted deep into his heart.

But as Layla and Adrian held each other, Layla saw their allies victorious. She saw the White Chalice killed to the last Dragon and Faunus, the High Priest's Dragon-remains charred upon the moss. She saw the Storm Dragons kneeling around the fallen Queen Justine, returned to human-form but with her slender chest skewered by serrated black spikes. Beside her, King Huttr knelt naked, his eyes closed as he held her hand, murmuring a benediction for the battle-slain. Nearby, Layla's human friends huddled in the wreckage, Charlie embracing

Celia and Arron in his big buff arms as Storm Dragon medics wrapped them in wool blankets. Arron's gaze caught Layla's, and she saw shock in his grey eyes – knowing how deadly Layla's world was now.

But as Layla's gaze roved the carnage, she suddenly felt a pull on her Bind. Rhennic's beautiful royal purple eyes found hers where he knelt next to his mother, gloriously naked and covered in battle-gore. Layla felt an indomitable wind move in her, like the breath of evening over summer fields as they watched each other. The scent of lavender rose in her and she caught her breath, unable to look away. As she clutched Adrian and Luke, she felt Rhennic pour his calm strength into her, into them all – unperturbed by her love for her other men.

As their eyes met, Rhennic gave her the smallest nod, like a knight to his lady. Layla's heart swelled, Adrian and Luke both inhaling as Rhennic's energy fed them. Though wreathed in crystal, she felt a flicker in Dusk, saved by Rhennic's selfless act. Somewhere far away, she felt that calm power flood Reginald, brighting his sea-grey eyes.

Rising, Rhennic moved towards them, walking carefully as if everything hurt from the magics he'd expended. As the Storm Prince came to them, Layla rose with Luke and Adrian, facing him. Flashing with lightning just like his mother's once had, Rhennic's gaze roved them as he gave a sad smile.

"I thank you, friends," he spoke soberly, "for delivering to my mother her final wish. The White Chalice are uprooted at last, and we have dealt your enemy Hunter a severe blow. Though my mother is gone, I am not, and as temporary Regent of the Storm Dragons I declare you all heroes among our clan. A tremendous deed has been done this day, and though sacrifice strikes our hearts," he nodded at Dusk's crystal sarcophagus with a deep sadness, then his mother's fragile body with King Huttr whispering death-prayers over her, "we have prevailed. Additionally, we have secured a gift in the ashes – for you."

"A gift?" It was Adrian who spoke, his voice steady now. "What do you mean?"

With a subtle smile, Rhennic nodded to a group of Storm and Blood Dragon guards. Frowning, Layla saw they held someone in manacles that blitzed with lightning, droplets of blood whirling through the chains. As Rhennic nodded, the Dragon guards shoved the bound woman forward, Rikyava snarling with a furious gaze as she hauled the prisoner up. With wide doe-eyes, it was Lulu Duvall who came forward in chains, her thin body stiff and straight.

Luke gave a horrible snarl as Adrian did also. Striding forward, Luke's grip was iron upon Lulu's slender shoulder as Adrian gripped her thin neck. Shoving her back into the Dragon guards, Adrian's eyes flashed molten fury as he snarled into her face.

"We are going to rip you to pieces unless you tell us *everything* you know about Hunter, the Crimson Circle, and how the hell you were involved in all this." Adrian growled, vicious. "I want names. I want positions. I want locations. I want everything you can think of to give me, and even everything you don't know I want – so I can tear Hunter's support structure limb from limb."

"And if you don't give Adrian everything he asks for," Luke spoke with a terrible wrath flashing in his green eyes, "I will suck your magic from your bones until you are raving with madness. And I *will* make it the most horrible thing you've ever felt. Ever meet a Vampire Revenant? Yeah, I'll be worse than that, I promise."

Lulu Duvall's pretty lips quivered as her big does eyes went wide with fear.

And then she was spilling it all – every last secret she hid for Hunter and the Crimson Circle.

CHAPTER 25 – CALM

Back at Château de Chambord, Layla waited in the throne room alone. At the rear of the hall, refreshment had been set up with small bites and warming winter beverages, but they weren't for celebration. As Layla paced before the enormous fireplace, wearing jeans, boots, and a cobalt v-neck sweater this morning, she couldn't touch a bite of food. Her stomach was clenched as her Dragon roiled inside her – knowing what was happening in the room adjacent.

Magical dampening kept sounds of Lulu Duvall's interrogation quiet from the hall, though Layla turned as a Storm Dragon server came to refresh the urn of coffee. At last, Adrian and Rhennic emerged from the tower room adjacent, and with serious faces, closed the ebony door quietly behind them. Coming to Layla, Adrian set his hands to her shoulders, his aqua gaze level as Rhennic took her hand.

"How's it going?" Layla spoke, her voice echoing in the vaulted space.

"Lulu's talking, a lot." Adrian sighed as he smoothed his hands over Layla's shoulders. "We won't need Luke to use his *nullax* on her. The Intercessoria Judiciaries received permission to use their archangelic powers to open her mind for this interrogation. She's spilled the names of central Crimson Circle members, plus locations, habits, and haunts. Not everyone, but everyone she's been party to. She's been a major player in Hunter's game a long while, and is older than anyone would ever suspect; five thousand years and counting. Hunter never Bound her, but she was lovers with the High Priest, who was Bound by Hunter and received orders directly from him through their mind-link."

"I've rarely met anything of so advanced an age." Rhennic spoke as his calm lavender glance found Adrian's. "My mother wan't even that old."

"Neither have I, except Hunter himself." Adrian held Rhennic's gaze with a deep accord, before looking back to Layla. "In any case, the Intercessoria are wrapping up with her now. They have everything they need to engage a massive, imminent sting on the Crimson Circle. Not all the members, but enough to put a serious crippling lance in their side. And in Hunter's central players."

"Will it secure your freedom?" Layla asked, wondering if Adrian's head would still be on the chopping-block after all they had gone through. But at her query, Adrian and Rhennic exchanged an uncertain look.

"It was Hunter who wanted my head, Layla," Adrian spoke as he held Layla's gaze. "He put all his Crimson Circle finest up to the challenge of catching me, to drive you and Dusk and I all further into darkness. Another of his mind-games. One of the most diabolical yet, in addition to abducting your friends."

Just then, the Fallen Ephilohim Intercessoria duo Heathren Merkami and Insinio Brandfort strode out of the magically-secured interrogation room. Enormous like a boulder and fitter than a strongman, the towering archangel Insinio gave Layla a smile from his vivid silver eyes. Moving his big bulk forward smoothly, he launched into his secret handshake, which Layla knew perfectly. Insinio gave a chuckle, though Layla could tell he was tired, seeing in her mind's eye that his ephemeral seven-layer wings dragged as they flowed from his spine, curling across the floor rather than lifting high into the air.

Heathren Merkami was similarly exhausted, for what reason Layla didn't know. Facing them with his pale silver eyes and his tall, heroin-chic grace, Heathren's etheric wings dragged even more than Insinio's in Layla's mind-sight. Clearly the Intercessoria Judiciary duo had been in a difficult situation when Dusk had called for their help, but they'd gotten the memo when Adrian had called again, detailing the battle against the White Chalice. As the archangelic Heathren nodded to them, he set a long-fingered hand to a silver blade on his black leather harness, as if for strength.

Though his full, perfect lips held a hard smile.

"We have everything we need for a full sting operation," Heathren spoke in a viciously resonant voice, like clarion trumpets. "My thanks to all of you – I know how you've suffered because Insinio and I were unavailable when you called."

In his beautifully arrogant way, Heathren didn't apologize for being unavailable, but Layla felt it was more of an apology than he'd ever given anyone. "In any case," he continued, "we have secured the names, fortress locations, access and infiltration information, bank accounts, and far more for ten central Crimson Circle members, all of whom Ms. Duvall interacted with on a regular basis. She has given us extensive details of highly illegal activities, condemning all ten. We have already called in our people; elite squads are being dispatched to arrest these named Circle members as we speak, and the evidence is enough for immediate death trials."

Layla shivered, hearing Heathren's words. Though they were good news for her and Adrian, it was like listening to a honed blade being drawn across throats as the archangel spoke. "What about the Circle members who wanted Adrian dead?"

"The arrests contain eight of those who demanded Adrian's head on Hunter's behalf." Heathren glanced at Layla coolly. "Ms. Duvall knows there were three more who also voted against Adrian, but she does not have names. Hunter was cagey, and kept separate cells of information among his ranks. High Priest Lodrian was head of two cells, but the others were managed by Hunter directly – most likely through the possession of his Bind. Having never interacted with the other three Circle members, Ms. Duvall could give us nothing on them."

"What about Hunter?" Layla's heart leaped to her throat as she glanced to Adrian. "Could Lulu give any direct information on his whereabouts?"

"No." Heathren Merkami continued with a glance to Insinio. "Ms. Duvall never traveled to meet Hunter, because he always spoke with her through High Priest Lodrian. But she gave us a description of how he walked, how he behaved and spoke in Lodrian's body when he came to give missives, and it's a place to start."

"The White Chalice were doing the bidding of the Crimson Circle – of Hunter – for millennia, and my mother never knew it." Rhennic was sober, though his lavender eyes flashed with lightning. "But in taking down the Chalice, she was actually battling a secret strong-arm for the Circle – and Hunter's slave-depots."

"Slave-depots?" Layla blinked, feeling her stomach churn.

"That's where your friends would have gone had you and Luke not freed them," Adrian spoke quietly, though his aqua eyes surged with a vicious golden fire. "To secret slave-depots all through the Twilight Realm run by central Circle members. It's where broken Twilight people and abducted, mind-washed humans have been taken for thousands of years – to toil as slaves for innermost Circle members in works of atrocity and corruption. A grisly operation I had been tracking for years, having discovered decades ago. And now we know it was all Hunter's doing."

"That's why you once thought Adrian was involved in slave

trading." Layla blinked, understanding as she glanced to Heathren. "That's why you tortured him so badly way back when, because you thought he was a Crimson Circle member."

"Indeed." Heathren's piercing silver-white gaze was unapologetic. "I have been tracking this slave trade for centuries, but we have only ever been able to bust individual locations and rescue the broken and brainwashed, who could never remember what had happened. Now we know ringleaders, and will take them down quickly. And we know who is at the top of it all." Heathren exchanged a glance with Insinio, and again Layla shivered at the intensity they shared – as if both fallen archangels were deeply looking forward to that battle in the darkest, most unpleasant way.

"So where does that leave us?" Layla asked.

"With options." Heathren turned back to her. "Eight Crimson Circle members who opposed Adrian will soon be dispatched. Insinio and I will make an announcement throughout the Hotel as soon as it's done – you will hear it. I imagine the structure of the Owners' Board will shift dramatically, and you and Adrian would be wise to step into that dearth of leadership. Pull any strings you have; make arrangements quickly."

Heathren's piercing stare flicked to Adrian then, pinning him like raptor-talons as he gave a lift of one silver-blond eyebrow. "We will be grilling the captured Circle members for the identity of the last three who oppose you, and any more engaged in illegal activities for Hunter. In the meantime, I urge you both to study everything about the *Sage of the Wilds* from your Storm Dragon allies. Perhaps Hunter left clues in the ancient scriptures of the White Chalice – something that might eventually bring him down."

"My mother has a library of writings she collected on the Chalice," Rhennic frowned, though his dark lavender eyes displayed excitement. "Scriptures, and interrogation records of captured Chalice members. I can get you and Adrian copies."

"Do that." Heathren spoke soberly, his silver-white eyes shining with a dark fervor. "In the meantime, Insinio and I must take our leave. Ms. Duvall has already been removed from your residence, Storm Regent – I have taken her into Intercessoria custody. Regroup with your people; mourn your losses. I will be in touch, and promise that if you find any other lingering White Chalice cells, the Intercessoria will lend our full support."

"Thank you." Extending his arm, Rhennic clasped hands with Heathren and the Fallen Ephilohim shook with level frankness.

Staring at Adrian now, Heathren became quiet. "Adrian Rhakvir. On behalf of the Intercessoria, I offer you a full apology for arrests made in the past which have now been revealed to be Hunter's works. Know that you have been cleared of those suspected crimes. We thank you for your cooperation in this investigation, and wish to retain your future help in this matter. Should we find any more information on Crimson Circle members who voted to have you killed or are connected to Hunter, we will notify you at once."

"Thank you." Adrian was as sober as the archangel, and Layla felt a deep accord pass between them. Again, it wasn't exactly a personal apology the Fallen Ephilohim had given Adrian for numerous arrests and weeks upon weeks of Vampire torture, but it was a start.

Glancing at Insinio, Heathren took a step back to Insinio's side. Insinio gave Layla a smile, his natural jubilance shining from his eyes, though he had nothing to add to the proceedings. As everyone clasped hands, Adrian and Heathren were civil, shaking calmly. Stepping back, the two parties regarded each other.

"Battle is ahead." Heathren spoke, gazing at them all. "Perhaps a more trying one than any of us know. Are you ready?"

"We will be." Adrian spoke softly.

With a nod, Heathren perused them with his intense silver-white gaze again. Then with a gesture to Insinio, the two Fallen Ephilohim departed through the throne room's doors, a sensation of exhausted wings trailing in their wake. Layla shivered after they left, feeling the energy in the room brighten as if the two Ephilohim had been draining light from the day to support their drained energy. As she did, Rhennic shuddered as if he'd felt it also, and even Adrian breathed deep beside them.

"We need to get back to the Hotel," Adrian spoke at last, with a glance to Layla. "I need to call the Owners' Board to session immediately."

"You're still a wanted fugitive before these Intercessoria arrests go down, Adrian," Layla spoke, "are you sure that's the best idea?"

"I want to see their eyes as their syndicate falls, Layla," Adrian spoke with a dire heat in his eyes. "I need to watch Hunter's machinations burn. Please."

Gazing at him, Layla saw the vindication Adrian needed. She saw the tense set of his shoulders, the way he held himself so rigid from breaking, especially now that Dusk was cocooned in crystal. No one knew when Dusk would wake, or if he would; Crystal Dragons were notorious for going into spontaneous cocoons when gravely injured – sometimes dwindling until they died.

Reaching out, Layla clasped Adrian's hand. "We'll go. Let's gather everybody and get Dusk's cocoon loaded up, and we'll go."

"Thank you." Adrian was quiet, but as Layla squeezed his fingers, he squeezed them back, then moved in and gave her a sweet kiss. "I'll go see Rikyava and find out if Luke and your friends are well enough to move. I'll find you in an hour."

"Okay." Layla agreed quietly.

With another kiss, Adrian was out the door. It left Layla alone with Rhennic, and as he turned, watching her with a calm elegance, Layla heaved a deep breath and met his gaze. His eyes were a royal plum in the morning light, the day free of storms with sunshine beaming in from every window. Smiling softly, Rhennic extended his arm in a gentlemanly fashion.

"Walk with me, Royal Dragon Bind."

With a nod, Layla took his arm, feeling a thrill of energy roll through her as they touched. Exiting the hall, they passed down the center stairwell into the bright day. Leaving the Château and wandering the snowy fields, Layla and Rhennic strolled, breathing deep in the glorious winter day. He glanced at her, and she snuck glances at him, but neither said anything. Though something dark still stirred inside Layla with Dusk in a coma and Luke needing deep recovery after the battle, Layla felt more calm than she had in ages. Taking a breath and seeing the sunny day bright all around her as the snow sparkled like diamonds, she felt something lighten in her soul.

Glancing to Rhennic, she found him watching her as they gained the dormant pear orchard. Stopping, he turned Layla gently to face him. Gazing up, she saw how his brush-cut blond hair and beard shone beneath the bright winter sun, his eyes a luminous lavender. Reaching out, he brushed her cheek with his knuckles, an amazed look on his strong, handsome face.

"If every woman looked at me the way you're doing now, I would have found a mate far earlier in life," he spoke in his elegant baritone.

"I bet lots of women have looked at you like this," Layla joked mildly, though she still felt caught in Rhennic's pull.

"Not like this," he spoke, his lips curling into a subtle smile.

"What are you thinking?" Layla spoke, feeling a strange energy pass between them in the bright winter day.

"I'm thinking I don't regret stepping in when your Bind called me yesterday." Rhennic spoke, his lips still holding a hint of a smile. "I know I did what was right, and I'd do it again if faced with the same decision."

"You saved Dusk," Layla spoke, a deep gratefulness welling up inside her as her eyes pricked with tears. "I will never be able to repay you for that."

"You don't have to." Rhennic replied gently, stroking a curl of Layla's sable hair back from her face as a breeze wafted through the snowy orchard. "I did what I did because it was right, not because I seek compensation from you, or Adrian, or even Dusk. There are some things a man must do, when life calls him to be brave."

"It hurt you, didn't it? Pouring your magic into Dusk as his power was stripped away?" Layla knew how weak and in pain Rhennic had been after the battle, his every movement carefully controlled as if everything in his body hurt ferociously. She hadn't seen him at all last night after they had returned to the Château – he'd spent the night being treated by his Storm Dragon healers and fight-medics.

"It hurt like the seven hells of Tirennia," Rhennic spoke soberly, though his lips still smiled. "But I wouldn't have held back, not for anything in the world."

"Because you knew how much I love Dusk?"

"Because I knew I could never face you again if I hadn't given everything to save him."

It was a deep sentiment, and it pulled at Layla's heart. She found her breath quickening, curling out in a steam of sweet bourbon scent as she watched Rhennic inhale, opening his lips as his eyes brightened. His breath quickened also, and Layla could smell a heather-lavender fragrance on the air. It made her body heat, as her Dragon curled over inside her veins with a pleased, eager smile.

"What about courting me?" Layla spoke, feeling this deep intensity between them. "Where do we stand on that whole thing now that you're part of the Bind?"

"I promised you a year and a day to get to know me," Rhennic chuckled, his eyes luminous upon her, "and I hold to that, even though we're Bound now. I won't interrupt your life, Layla, or force myself into your bed. I know my place is here at Chambord right now, acting as Regent while my Lineage undergoes a fractious transition. But I want you to know… I will be dreaming of you. And wishing I could stand at your side. I will be here for you, anytime you need me – all you have to do is call. I can feel you now, deep inside my heart from the Bind. And I will know when you call for me."

Layla swallowed hard, feeling the honesty of Rhennic's words as they curled around her with a subtle passion in the bright winter day. Like a white knight, he seemed to shine in the morning light, and Layla thought back to his Dragon-form – his ferociously bright white scales edged in royal blue and crimson fractal patterns. She could feel the complex simplicity of Rhennic's personality, just like the fractals on his Dragon-scales. He was a steadiness she needed in her life, in the Bind.

Even though there was so much more to discover about him.

She felt the golden cord between them then, and Rhennic felt it also, reaching out to corral her around the waist with his big hands as their bodies pulled closer. He exhaled, and Layla saw him fight an urge to pull her close and kiss her. To break all his gentlemanly composure and throw her down, taking her like a wild thing out in the silence of the Château's orchards. She felt the power in him, the power she had seen and felt in action during the battle yesterday, the force of nature he was, so elegantly contained.

Rhennic was the son of two of Europe's most powerful Royal Dragons. And now he was Regent of his Lineage, holding the throne until someone challenged him. Breathing out, Layla suddenly felt how many dominance battles Rhennic would have to undergo in the coming months. It unsteadied her, and she blinked, feeling tears gather at the corners of her eyes.

"What's that look for?" Rhennic breathed, his big hands pulling her closer to his tall, rock-solid body.

"I don't want you to get hurt." Layla spoke briskly, swallowing her tears back. "You're going to face a lot of challengers soon, and I don't want you to get hurt."

He blinked his long blond eyelashes, a shocked amazement filling his handsome face – followed by a soft wonder. "You wouldn't have said anything like that to me yesterday."

"Yesterday, I didn't feel what I feel now." Layla whispered, feeling their golden cord pull tighter like it pulled directly on her heart.

"Yesterday, you didn't love me." Rhennic spoke with a subtle roguishness lifting the corners of his lips. "But today…"

"Don't push your luck, buddy."

Rhennic laughed, a bright, lovely sound that reminded Layla of Adrian. But in the next moment, his big hands were pulling her in, cradling her close to all that amazingly tall, strong physique. Layla tasted heather and lavender on his lips and he kissed her deep and slow. Pulling her into his storm winds, a swirl of air surrounded them as a roll of thunder rippled through the orchard. Layla found herself kissing him back, tasting his lips and body with a slow, deep passion, as if the blessing of him would never cease. Curling her closer in his muscled arms, Rhennic crushed her to his amazingly powerful yet elegant body. Layla melted, moulding to him as she drank his kiss like lavender honey on her tongue.

It was a long while before Rhennic pulled back. With a deep sigh, he kissed her lips one last time. "Where have you been all my life,

Royal Dragon Bind?"

"I've been here," Layla spoke with a strange mystery, "waiting for you."

"Waiting for me." With an equally mysterious smile, Rhennic cradled her closer to his body as he reached up, caressing a curl of Layla's hair back from her face. "I have duties here at Chambord. But will you wait for me? A year and a day... that's all I ask."

"Yes." Layla was surprised at how quickly it tumbled from her mouth, yet also not surprised. Something deep inside her wanted Rhennic, in a calm, amazing way none of her other Royal Dragons had. "Yes."

"Yes." With that same incredible smile, he nuzzled her nose. And then kissed her again, deep and thorough, before pulling back and escorting her to the Château like a knight with his lady.

CHAPTER 26 – RISORGIMENTO

Back at the Paris Hotel, Layla faced the gilded mirror in her apartment, finishing affixing her mother Mimi's black diamond earrings on her ears, and clasping the waterfall necklace of black diamonds around her neck. She was dressed all in black tonight, in respect for the dead. Head Clothier Amalia DuFane had created her a stunning garment to show mourning for all that had happened – and all that was about to. Made of exquisitely ornate black lace, the gown was fitted off her shoulders, torso, and hips, with long, draping sleeves and a trumpet shape with a modest train. Layla's curls were up tonight, and with her Dragon's austere bone structure since October, she looked both stunning and terrifying in the ensemble.

This was not a night for romance – this was battle, and Layla had dressed accordingly.

Setting a hand to Mimi's black diamonds and glancing in the mirror, Layla paused, thinking back over the past few days. Queen Justine Toulet's funeral at Château de Chambord had been astonishing, the day after Lulu's interrogation. Even though Adrian had been eager to get back to the Hotel, everyone had stayed for it, and in the coliseum, the European Storm Dragon clan had gathered to pay their respects to their fallen Queen. The amphitheater had been filled with people whose eyes flashed with lightning, as well as hundreds of Blood Dragons come to support King Huttr in his grief for his slain ally. As Layla sat with Adrian, Luke, Rikyava, and her friends, gazing down upon a beautiful bier of woven branches and flowers that Queen Justine's body had been prepared on, Justine had been surrounded by her top lightning-strikers in the middle of the amphitheater as King Huttr and his elder son Halfdir looked on from the sidelines.

Dressed in crisp militaristic uniforms of storm-blue, medals of valor had been clipped to the lightning-strikers' breasts, and Rhennic had been among them. In a similar outfit of pure white, the Storm Dragon color of mourning, a dark storm-blue sash had complemented Rhennic's stunning array of medals. Layla knew now why Rhennic had been so heavily decorated over his past two hundred years, and had been his mother's Clan Second. He was a force of nature in a fight, calm but terrible. As she watched, he had given a crisp command, himself and the lightning-strikers raising their hands as one. Together, they had called down an astounding array of silent lightning from the blue winter sky, and moving as a group, had worked together to weave that lightning into a bright dome around the bier.

Smoothing it, braiding lightning into ornate patterns and flows with their movements, they had formed an enormous yet intricate plasma-sphere around the fallen Queen. As Layla watched, they released it in unison, and it took on a life of its own. Beautiful films of rippling lightning had flushed through the translucent sphere, lancing Queen Justine's body in flowing waves. Eerily silent, it had been haunting, the enormous coliseum filled with people who hardly even breathed. Gradually, the Queen's body had been desiccated by the lightning, then charred into white ash. None of the herbs on the bier had been touched, but as the dome dissipated, a heavenly scent of flowers, ozone, and thunderstorms had filled the space.

Layla had never smelled anything like it, the strongest, most delicate perfume she'd ever scented. She doubted she'd ever smell anything like it again, and as Rhennic had quietly gathered his mother's ashes by moving his hands to summon a cool wind to caress them into a pile with the flowers and herbs, Layla had breathed a deep sigh. Rhennic had swept everything up into an urn made of opal lightning-stone like the Château, and the unworldly fragrance had gradually cleared from the air. With a bow to the lightning-strikers, then a deep bow to the coliseum and to his father Huttr, Rhennic had lifted the urn and carried it from the hall, off to be deposited in the King's catacombs beneath the Château.

Everyone had dispersed after that, and Layla and her friends had taken Adrian's jet back to Paris. Celia and Charlie had opted to fly all the way home to Seattle after everything they had endured. They were on permanent guard now with three of Rikyava's best, hired away from the Hotel by Adrian. But Luke and Arron had decided to remain one more day at the Paris Hotel to watch history go down.

And now, it was time.

A knock came at the door and Layla turned, already feeling Adrian standing on the other side. Moving to the door, she opened it and he stepped inside, kissing her sweetly. Pulling back though leaving one hand at her waist, Adrian stroked her neck, watching her with his incredible aqua eyes. Dressed in a classic black tux with a deliciously slim fit and black satin lapels, plus sapphire and black diamond cufflinks, he looked every inch the renegade billionaire – about to cause a storm.

"Are you ready?" Adrian's energy was quiet tonight, flowing with gentle intensity as his magic curled around her.

"Yes." Layla spoke, ready to face what was coming. As Adrian extended his arm, Layla took it, and he ushered them into the hall. A retinue of twenty Guards stood by her door, Adrian's escort since he was still technically a fugitive. But they had received word from Heathren Merkami that the ten Crimson Circle members Lulu Duvall had named were all in custody, and the announcement of their sentencing would go out tonight.

Layla didn't know how that would happen exactly, but Adrian assured her they wouldn't need to leave the party to receive the message. As she took a deep breath, she watched Rikyava approach from Luke's apartment, dressed in a stunning blood-red silk gown with Luke in a classic black tux on her arm. Arron was with them also, though his tux had a bit of flash in the royal plum lapels. The color reminded Layla of Rhennic's eyes, and she took an inhalation, summoning herself back to the moment.

With a nod from Adrian, everyone continued down, surrounded by Guards. The Hotel was intensely quiet tonight, all activities suspended in the wake of Adrian's summons. Restlessness moved through the Hotel, still packed after Yule, but with everyone simply mingling and drinking tonight at the copper hall-bars. Eyes followed the heavily-guarded group as they moved through the Hotel's main floor. Those who recognized Adrian gave a solemn nod, and with curiosity, began tailing the group. At last, Adrian's retinue gained the Diamond Ballroom where Layla's debut had been at Yule. It felt like a lifetime ago as they gained the ornate entrance – Hotel Owners turning and all talk silencing as the billionaire Royal Desert Dragon renegade and his Bind moved into the hall.

Stepping aside with Luke and Arron, Rikyava went to a niche by the main doors with a good portion of the Guards – protecting Layla's friends, though Luke was entirely capable of protecting himself now. But the Hotel Owners didn't know that, and it was a good ruse to have a locus of power near the doors if Adrian needed it.

Layla could feel her golden Bind to Luke, simmering like a kettle about to boil as he gave her a subtle nod, ready. Leaving their Guards, Layla and Adrian proceeded into the Diamond Ballroom, still sparkling with Yule decorations. No one spoke as they made their way to the stage, some faces scowling as they tracked the renegade duo, others attentively curious. But no one made a blatant move, and as Layla and Adrian arrived at the stage where the Madame and Quindici DaPonti waited, the Master Vampire stepped forward.

Dressed in a stunning dark maroon tux with black satin lapels, Quindici handed Adrian a lapel mic, which Adrian clipped on. The Vampire's eyes were dark, their onyx depths intensely sober as he gave Adrian a nod, then gestured to center stage. With Layla on his arm, Adrian took the middle of the stage as spotlights went up, catching Adrian and Layla in their hot flare though dim enough that they could still see the hall. As Owners moved forward with drinks in hand, scowling or curious, Adrian raised his voice with smooth power.

"Owners of the Red Letter Hotel, thank you for coming to this emergency meeting tonight." He spoke calmly, his baritone voice resonant as it moved through the room. "You have been called here this evening by the Barone Quindici DaPonti, but in reality, it was I who summoned you. You all know my story; you all know I have been declared anathema among you. Yet many of you do not know the entire tale. I will not be the one illuminating it for you. Please, open your ears, and hear of the treachery behind our beloved organization."

As if it had all been planned to the precise moment, Adrian suddenly stepped back, moving Layla back with him. As the spotlights died, an eerie series of piercing chimes sounded all around Layla, and deep inside her mind. She wanted to clutch her ears, she wanted to shudder away from the sound, but there was no escaping it. As if someone had invested the sound through the very air inside her head, it was like Dusk's rumbles but piercing, clarion – a riveting sound like trumpets flaring through the world.

Every person in the hall came to intense attention, many of them shivering like Layla as they jerked, shocked to stillness. In that moment, a voice suddenly flooded the air like the voice of God come alive. It was a voice Layla knew, cutting and clear, and as Heathren Merkami began to speak via whatever magical mechanism had flooded the Paris Hotel, Layla watched the Owners.

"Ladies and gentlemen of the Red Letter Hotel," Heathren spoke in his clear, viciously angelic voice, "this is the Intercessoria. You are being informed as per the Annihilation Code seven-oh-one-point-oh, that eleven members of your pinnacle leadership have been arrested for crimes against the Twilight Realm and the Human world, and have been put to death. The list is as follows: Lulu Duvall of the Faunus of France. Remi Dufresne of the Molennics of Europe. Bintni Rabii of the Kali-Makti. Lawrence Koss of the European Fumaroles. Mikhail Korotnik of the Russian Ice Dragons. Dina Armann of the Crystal Dragons of the Czech Republic. Muni Barba of the Blue Tempests of the Caribbean. Roman Adario of the Sirens of the Mediterranean. Angela Kona of the Royal Tempests of Hawaii. Maya Benny of the Desert Dragons of Nevada. And Letitia Armani of the Dark Haven of Rome."

All around, Layla watched faces of Hotel Owners open in horror and shock, as drinks and plates were set aside. A number of Owners were glancing to the doors now as Heathren's announcement paused, as if wondering if they could make a quick escape before the Intercessoria's message concluded.

"This is only an initial list of the accused," Heathren Merkami's disembodied voice continued, cold with righteous wrath. "We have over fifty additional names of Owners involved in illegal activities and crimes punishable by death according to Intercessoria laws. We have incriminating details and have already raided numerous illegal operations around the world, both in the Twilight and Human realms. Run, and we will find you. Disappear, and we will hunt you. Your days of disrespect for international law are finished. That is all."

As the announcement ended with the same series of ear-piercing chimes, many things happened at once. A number of Owners tried to dash for the doors, and found themselves blocked by a veritable horde of Intercessoria enforcers, snaring them into white cubes moving with gilded sigils that they cast beneath the feet of those running. The Owners that had tried to flee were incarcerated as the cubes expanded fast, trapping them in a magical gel and immobilizing them. Others who had merely spooked were surrounded, Intercessoria spears with white-gold sigils thrust around them to keep them still.

As Layla and Adrian watched from the stage, Heathren and Insinio marched in through the ballroom doors and began making the rounds in their black battle-leathers with their seven-layer wings visible tonight, spread wide with a dark grey-opal hue like angels of death. Flicking their fingers or nodding at incriminated Hotel Owners, their Intercessoria enforcers rushed in, incarcerating Owners right and left.

It was a rout. There were a few magical blowups as certain Owners tried to fight, but the Intercessoria presence was efficient and overwhelming, and those who tried to do battle were quickly subdued. As Intercessoria began magicking the incarcerated from the ballroom via their golden cubes, off to be interrogated or put to death, Layla felt a dark tension inside her begin to ease. As the process finished, Heathren finally mounted the stage with Insinio beside him. Gazing at the less than thirty people left, Heathren flared his wings in a terrible spread, Insinio crossing his arms over his battle leathers and scowling in a dark angelic fury as he did the same.

Lifting his voice in a clarion archangel wrath, Heathren's piercing silver-white gaze swept the nearly empty ballroom. "Choose your next actions carefully. Many of your names came up during interrogations as related to quasi-illegal activities, or illegal actions for which there was no immediate proof." Glancing behind him, Heathren's silver-white eyes fixed on Quindici, though the Master Vampire stared him down with a cool, grave-like ease before Heathren turned back to the hall. "Restructure your organization, and keep its activities clear of the law. Or I will return. That is all."

With one last long look at Quindici, then a nod to Adrian and Layla, Heathren flicked his fingers at Insinio and they departed with the rest of the Intercessoria – sweeping from the hall as if they'd never been.

Layla felt a shudder pass through the ballroom as the Intercessoria departed. As enormous eyes stared back to Adrian, shocked at what had just happened, he stepped forward once more. "Friends, we have a responsibility to the Red Letter Hotel. From ancient times, this organization had been one of amnesty in its day-to-day principles, each Hotel a place where enemies could come and relax, and find solace in times of strife. At its core, our beloved organization concerns itself with peace and plenty, with re-shaping the way a person sees the world in a way that fosters community, goodwill, and an uplift of heart. The crimes many of our Owners were involved in were anathema to our Hotel's heart, and it was for this reason that I aided in exposing their corruption. Though that corruption goes all the way to the pinnacle, to the very creature who founded our Hotel, it is not what our organization is on the day-to-day. I have a sincere wish for the Red Letter Hotel to survive this, and thrive in a way it never truly has before. For how can we tolerate corruption at our heart when our mission is so beautiful? I hope you agree, and that you will join me. I do not intend to give up on our beloved Hotel, and I hope you will not allow me to."

It was well spoken. Layla saw a number of eyes shining at Adrian's speech, heads nodding in accord. There were still a few angry faces but they were the minority, and as Layla gazed around, she realized Adrian had far more allies among this crowd than enemies now. Stepping quietly to Adrian's side, Quindici surveyed the room, then raised his voice.

"Fellow Owners and members of the Hotel Board," he spoke in a pleasant way, smooth and cool. "A motion has been put forward to absolve Adrian Rhakvir of his *Punizione Completa*, and to re-instate him into both full Hotel Ownership and as Head of the Red Letter Hotel Paris. Please think for a moment on your decision, and we will put it to immediate vote."

As Quindici stepped back, Layla saw movement in the hall. People frowned, they glanced at Adrian, they sipped drinks or spoke low words with a neighbor. As talk finally silenced, Quindici engaged the vote. The vote in favor of re-instating Adrian was nearly unanimous, with only four dissenters. In a quick moment, it was done. As Quindici stepped back, his onyx eyes glittering with pleasure, he turned to Adrian with a slow smile that showed his fangs.

Reaching out, he clasped Adrian's hand. "Hotel Head. Welcome back."

"Thank you, Quinn." Adrian spoke quietly, and Layla felt his deep breath, as if a great weight had fallen from Adrian's shoulders as a warm desert wind full of jasmine suddenly flowed all around him.

Turning back to the assembly, Adrian stepped forward and spoke one last time.

"Friends. I thank you for the opportunity to be a part of this Hotel once more. In the coming days and weeks, I intend to call a series of meetings to create a firm, egalitarian, and equal structure of leadership among us. Too long has our Hotel been ruled by a shadowy elite, most of which are now removed. This is the true meaning of *Risorgimento*, my friends, the re-structuring of everything we are as we remove that which corrupted our heart. Which leaves the rest of us, to take the Hotel forward into the future. Come together with me; help me create this new chapter of our existence. And we shall have true peace and plenty, as was intended at the very beginning of the Red Letter Hotel's formation. Thank you."

With one last solemn survey of the crowd, Adrian let the power of his presence sweep the room. And then extended his arm to Layla, escorting her from the hall.

CHAPTER 27 – PARTINGS

After the Owner's meeting, Adrian escorted Layla back up to her rooms, where they stood a long while, kissing. As his sweet lips finally parted from hers, Adrian drew Layla close, and she laid her head on his shoulder. Nuzzling his nose into her hair, he breathed deep, then let it out in a long sigh. Layla heaved a sigh of relief also as she felt the tension gradually draining out of them both. Slow and calm, she could feel her Dragon and Adrian's sliding through each other's coils – not a dance of hot passion tonight, but of deep solace. Layla closed her eyes, drinking in Adrian's warmth as she felt him close his eyes and surrender to her also, pressing his lips to her temple.

"Are we out of hot water?" She asked, still cuddled close, not wanting to let him go.

"I don't know for sure." He murmured, his resonant baritone beautiful in the quiet of her rooms. Reaching up, Adrian stroked her neck, and Layla shivered in bliss at his touch. "It's a good sign that the remaining Owners accepted me back into their ranks. Whether they'll let me re-organize them remains to be seen. But many of those left have been friendly to me in the past, and it's encouraging. With Quindici's help, I think we can get it done."

"Do you think you still have enemies among those left?" Layla asked, soothed by Adrian's caresses.

"Maybe." Adrian frowned slightly at her cheek. "Heathren said there are three more Crimson Circle members out there, as yet unidentified, who worked directly for Hunter. We still need to find them, and rout out any supporters they have on the Board. But all this is uncharted territory for me. Plus, we've dealt Hunter a severe blow that I'm not entirely certain he saw coming, and I can't predict what he'll do next."

Layla knew what Adrian meant. With the White Chalice fallen, the Storm Queen dead, Layla bound to both Luke and Rhennic now, and with Dusk in a coma, his crystal sarcophagus under heavy guard in his rooms on the fourth floor, everything seemed upside-down. But all the same, a deep quietude had taken Layla to know Adrian was no longer being hunted. At last, he could stand at her side out in the open.

At last, they could hold each other and be together – just like this.

As Adrian set another kiss to her temple, Layla sighed again. Lifting up, she kissed his lips, then pulled back to see his eyes. "What now?"

"I believe Arron and Luke are eager to return home to Seattle," he spoke quietly, his fingers still stroking her neck as he watched her. "And I need to meet briefly with Quindici and the Madame. You should go say goodbye."

Layla nodded, heaviness in her heart. She wasn't looking forward to either conversation. She'd barely said three words to Arron and Luke after the battle at Chartres, and neither had really wanted to approach her. Giving her a kiss on the forehead, Adrian led her towards the doors. They exited, and after kissing him goodbye and watching him depart down the stairs with a retinue of Guards, Layla moved across the hall to knock on Arron's heavily-guarded apartment doors.

Arron opened his doors, still dressed in his tux from the evening. With a lack of surprise in his grey eyes, he ushered Layla in, then moved to the bed and sat down, clasping his hands over his knees as Layla sat beside him.

"Hey." Layla spoke softly, glancing at Arron.

"Hey." Arron smiled wryly as his grey eyes glanced to her then back to his clasped hands, tension stretching between them. But the only thing that had ever solved tension between her and Arron was touch, and as Layla reached out, clasping her hand upon Arron's, he gave a deep sigh. Layla felt something tight in him begin to unwind as he chuckled wryly. At last, he looked up, meeting her gaze in a way Layla knew meant they were going to have a no-bullshit heart-to-heart.

"So you probably think I'm a fool. Marrying a woman." Arron spoke quietly, watching her with a deep vulnerability in his grey eyes.

It was the last thing Layla had been thinking, and she blinked in astonishment. She had thought Arron was going to chastise her for getting involved in all this. She had thought he was going to be furious that her new life had put him and Celia and Charlie so deeply in danger and cast them into a war-zone. But it struck Layla suddenly that Arron had been avoiding her because he was deeply embarrassed about things that had happened with the Smoke Faunus woman Giselle. As Layla's heart opened wide for her best friend, she inhaled a choking breath, turning and gathering him into her arms as they sat upon the bed.

"You're not a fool, Arron. Gods, you're not!" Layla breathed as she stroked his soft ash-blond hair. "You were taken advantage of, drugged and under magical coercion. It's not your fault. None of anything that happened is your fault."

"I had *sex* with that woman, Layla!" Arron rasped, even as she felt him wrap his long arms around her, clinging to her suddenly as he released his emotions at last. "Sex. I haven't had sex with a woman... ever! And now I did it with a... a *thing*. A tree-thing. God, I don't even know quite what she was."

"It's not your fault," Layla repeated, stroking his hair as he gave a hard sigh. Tears pricked her eyes, but she didn't let them shed, staying strong for her friend. "You were under magical sway, you couldn't have helped it."

"Is this how it feels?" He rasped with a sad, dire chuckle. "Is this how being in a world of magic goes? This horrible feeling like you can't control anything?"

"Sometimes." Layla admitted, knowing that sensation of helplessness like there was nothing she could do against certain sways. In so many ways, the human world felt predictable to her now, the rules defined, the laws set. But the Twilight Realm was a wild place, and it felt wilder, more dangerous to her now than ever before, since her human friends had gotten so disastrously hurt. As she held Arron, stroking his hair, she felt that knowledge seared deep into them both.

Layla's new life was dangerous – and humans didn't belong anywhere in it.

"Well, I don't want it, honey." Arron was resolute as he pulled away, briskly wiping tears from his cheeks as he regarded her with red-rimmed gray eyes. "This is shit. I wish you could just come home to Seattle… come be with us again."

"Some part of me wishes I could, too." Layla spoke, as she and Arron twined their fingers together. But she knew she never could. Layla was in too deep – and too deep in love to leave. Adrian's beloved face rose in her mind, then Dusk's. On its heels from somewhere far away came Reginald, turning to look at her through their Bind, then Rhennic, lifting his head with a sharp vibrance in his lavender eyes as he felt her presence.

And then Luke's green eyes, piercing her with a vivid intensity.

Quietly, Layla banished them all, sitting with Arron once more. They were both gazing at their twined fingers when he spoke again. "I want to stay friends, chica."

"I know. I do, too." Layla spoke earnestly.

"No matter all that's happened. No matter how dangerous your world is, or your magic. When you come visit the human world, please come see me. I just… I don't think I can come here again." Arron looked up, and the look in his grey eyes was so haunted, it broke Layla's heart. She felt her love for her friend expand as she reached up, cradling his cheek with her hand.

"I will come visit you," she spoke. "I promise."

Nodding, Arron brushed away more tears. Rising, he drew her into a deep hug, holding her close. Layla felt the finality in it; he was never coming back to the Twilight Realm. Once he left, that was it. But Layla could visit the human world, and she promised herself she would, firming her intention to not leave Arron behind as a friend – not like she had done with Luke.

"Be good, chica. Don't do anything I wouldn't do." Arron spoke softly as he kissed her hair.

"I promise."

Layla hugged him harder, but as a knock came at Arron's doors, they parted. It was Rikyava, still in her gown from the night coming to summon Arron and bundle him into a car that would take him to Adrian's jet waiting at the airport. Rikyava's lavender eyes met Layla's as Arron welcomed the Guards in to fetch his suitcases and his new Amalia suits in their crystal bee-venom cases. As everyone exited the apartment, Arron drew Layla into one last hug, kissing her cheek.

And then he was gone, moving down the stairs with Rikyava's Guards.

Layla heaved a sigh, then felt Rikyava looking at her and glanced over. Her heart surged, not feeling animosity towards her friend that she had found something good with Luke. Her emotions wide open tonight, Layla moved over, drawing Rikyava into a deep hug. As they held each other, Layla felt Rikyava relax her strong Swedish frame as Layla petted her long blonde hair.

"I thought you were pissed at me, girlfriend." Rikyava spoke at last with her chin on Layla's shoulder, as all the Guardsmen looked away, pretending to be interested in frescoes in the hall.

"I could never be pissed at you." Layla laughed sadly, gripping her friend's shoulders and shaking her a little as Layla pulled back. "I love you, Rikyava. I love Luke also. You two should be together, you might actually drive a little sense into him."

"Fat chance." Rikyava chuckled, her lavender eyes bright now as she set her hands to Layla's shoulders also. Squeezing Layla, Rikyava gave her a little shake back. "You're a hell of a woman, Layla Price. You're a hard act to follow. I watched you in the battle at Chartres – you've come a long way from where you were, and your Dragon with it."

"I'm not what Luke needs." Layla spoke soberly, holding Rikyava's gaze as she impressed her point. "You are. I saw how tender you were with him after he was hit with the Storm Queen's energy in her test. I saw how you protected our friends as everything came crashing down inside the cathedral during the battle. Luke needs that in his life – protection and tenderness. Lord knows he and I were never able to be tender with each other. Things are better this way. You're good for him; good for his life in a way I never was."

"And your Bind?" Rikyava held Layla's gaze intently, and Layla knew what she was asking.

"I don't know." Layla sighed. "Maybe Luke's magic will help the Bind, but... he and I won't be lovers. You can count on it."

"Thanks." Rikyava smiled softly. "Normally, I'm not against Dragon men having a few lovers, but in this case... I think it's just weird. You Binding my boyfriend and all."

"Yeah, weird is one way to put it." Layla laughed sadly. "I need to go say goodbye to Luke. Do you mind giving us a moment before you fetch him down to the car?"

"Sure. Have at it, girl." Rikyava gripped Layla's shoulders with a smile, then let her go. Layla nodded, knowing she had Rikyava's permission to see Luke alone, but still dreading it.

Drawing a deep breath, Layla faced Luke's apartment as Rikyava moved a distance away with her Guards. Knocking on Luke's door, Layla felt him move close, then throw the door wide. His green eyes were bright as he beckoned her in, and she saw he'd already changed back to jeans and a blazer for travel rather than wear his tux. As Luke shut the doors, Layla moved into his apartment, but didn't sit. Turning to face him, they regarded each other as Layla felt the Bind move like a golden cord between their hearts.

"So what now?" Layla asked as she gazed into Luke's vibrant green eyes and saw them shift with a flicker of lightning.

"I'm going back to Seattle." He spoke quietly, as he curried a hand through his Irish-dark hair, mussing it. "Since I never used it in the battle, I asked Rhennic to modify his mother's talisman for me, so her power could disguise my magic in the Human world. He did, and it works." Extending his left hand, Luke showed Layla a cuff on his wrist made from the same opal lightning-stone as Château de Chambord. "It'll look like plain ivory to anyone who doesn't know, but it contains my magic so at least humans don't feel anything, and can't see my eyes flash."

"What's your plan?" Layla asked.

"Finish my grad studies, get my medical license." Luke spoke, heaving a sigh with a slight frown. "Complete my initial ideas for my life and then we'll see."

"Sure." Layla couldn't fault him for his desires; Luke had always been a methodical creature to help control his blazing emotions, and routine helped. He was facing his Dragon now, but big change came

313

slowly with Luke, and always had. He would hold to his routine until he figured out a better plan for his life – one that could account for the creature he was becoming.

"What about Rikyava?" Layla asked.

"She's got a good talisman," Luke spoke, holding Layla's gaze. "She's already come to visit me twice in Seattle. We'll keep dating, but keep it on the DL."

"Cool." Layla nodded, her hunch confirmed that Luke and Rikyava's relationship had been kindled prior to him visiting the Hotel. Rikyava's welcome at the Hotel's gates for Yule had been an act – neither of them wanting to spill their relationship in public yet. But as Layla stood with Luke now, awkwardness stretching at their imminent leave-taking, Layla knew there was something else she needed to atone for.

"Luke I... I want to apologize for Binding you."

"Don't, Layla." He spoke quietly, holding her gaze with his intense green eyes. "I did what I wanted to do at the time. What I needed to. What we all needed me to do."

"Still. I would release you, if I could. If I knew how."

"Thanks. I appreciate that." Luke nodded, taking in her words as a sweet tension stretched between them. But as Layla watched him, seeing how well he was trying to take it that he was Bound to her now, she knew he didn't want to be. She could feel it rioting all through him that he was trapped, that part of him would never be free of her, that he could never live his own life. Luke's emotions were open to her now through their Bind, and she could feel his heart. He had done what he'd done in the moment because he loved her and always would love her, and the part of him that saved lives couldn't have engaged the battle any other way.

But he didn't want to be hers anymore – despite how much his

Dragon felt like it should be.

"Luke…" Layla spoke suddenly with a slight frown. "Do you remember when you helped me overcome Reginald's cold, in the tub?"

"Yeah?" He spoke, cocking his head and setting his hands to his hips. "What about it?"

"I… for a while afterwards, it was hard for me to feel Reginald's presence through the Bind." Layla continued, not quite knowing where she was going with this but needing to hear her thoughts out anyway. "Our Bind felt thinned, obscured by this white void in my mind and in my body… faraway. After your *nullax* touched it."

Luke blinked, and Layla saw it dawn on him what she was trying to say. "Are you saying you think I could break our Bind? Or… thin it with my *nullax?*"

"I think so." Layla continued, moving closer. "Would you like to try?"

Luke blinked again, and Layla saw him draw a deep breath as his emerald gaze pierced her, flickering with lightning. "That could kill you, Layla. When the High Priest's *nullax*-lance hit Dusk during the battle, you collapsed. Your heart stopped. I had to do CPR while Adrian revived you with his magic. It didn't take long, but still…"

"I know. But would you like to try?" Layla spoke, coming close enough that she could reach out and take Luke's hand. The Bind thrummed as they touched and she saw Luke sway, his lips falling open as a deep passion surged between them. His emerald eyes lit, and then darkened, as Layla watched him try to resist her call.

"I would like to try." He spoke softly, closing his eyes to steady himself. "I can't—"

"Can't live like this. I know." She spoke gently. "I feel your heart Luke, though the Bind. I can feel how much you want to be free. I can feel what you truly desire, despite all the passion between us. And it's ok. I understand."

His eyes opened. They were the most impossibly vibrant color as he gazed at her, his dark brows knitting as he tried to form some kind of placating statement and failed. Staring at her, Luke's gaze became furious, then bleak – then finally soft. Reaching up, he pulled a few pins from Layla's hair. Her sable curls fell down around her shoulders and over her back, and Luke combed his fingers through them, watching the passage of his hands as he drew a deep breath. Layla felt his heart open as something beautiful and sad moved between them.

"God, I love you." Luke murmured at last. "So regal. So beautiful. So terrible."

"I know. I love you, too." Layla spoke quietly as she reached up, taking his hand.

"Are you sure you want to try this?" Luke regarded her, caressing her fingers with his thumb. "What if you need me in the future? What if not having my power in the Bind makes you vulnerable against Hunter or other foes we know nothing about yet?"

"I'll take that risk." Layla spoke again, gripping his fingers tenderly. "If you love someone, you let them go, Luke. We need to let each other go. It's long past time."

He nodded, and Layla saw him process. Glancing down at their hands, he heaved a sigh. When he looked back up, his eyes were clear. "Maybe we should sit."

Layla agreed, and together they moved to two high-backed chairs by the fireplace. Pulling them close, they faced each other, reaching out to hold each other's hands as they took seats.

"Open the Bind." Luke spoke, watching Layla with an intense emotion.

She nodded. Closing her eyes, she felt for the golden cord that bound them together now, that bound their hearts and bodies, their souls and magic. Layla felt Luke's enormous white Dragon of lightning-mist rise in her mind; she felt it coil all around her as she summoned it. She felt that sensation hit Luke and rock him as he felt her Dragon coil around him also, fire-bright in its crimson and gold glory. She felt how their beasts twined together, writhing through each other's scales as they bound close through Layla's magic. She felt their energies sliding hot and smooth through each other, in an intricate dance of passion and need.

Though their true desires lay elsewhere.

"I'm ready." Layla spoke, though it was with effort. A part of her had already dropped so deeply into her Dragon-mind that she couldn't think like a human anymore.

"Open to me." Luke breathed, and Layla felt his breath like a curling white mist as his *nullax* eased out around her.

A part of her tensed, resisting that dire sensation, but Layla forced her Dragon to be calm as she felt Luke's diabolical power slide out, coiling all around her. In her mind's eye, she saw Luke's mist-white Dragon surround her crimson and gold one, growing enormous as it reared its head and flared a white-spiked mantle. In its eyes, she saw death and the void, an endless diamond night of cold and loneliness as the lightning of creation and eternal destruction flashed in its gaze.

Towering above her, the white Dragon lowered its head as Luke's fingers gripped Layla's before the fireplace. As the enormous white drake of endless nullification bent Layla's drakaina backwards, making her surrender as they locked jaws in a kiss, Layla suddenly understood. Her power was not the master here, not anymore. As Luke breathed his drake's magic deep into her drakaina's body, Layla surrendered, not fighting that energy but allowing it to flow through her – and to go where the mist-white drake wanted it to go.

Layla felt Luke's *nullax* pour through her like a cold mist beneath an endless swath of midnight stars. It had no time and it had no boundary as it moved, seeking magic to unmake. Layla felt it touch upon her heart, her own Dragon's life-force, and move on with a shake of its mist-swirling mantle. It didn't want her life, or her magic. She felt it slip into Dusk through their Bind, deep in his coma in his crystal cocoon yet still alive, and felt it pass him by. It didn't want to hurt a friend. She felt it pass into Rhennic and make him shudder with alarm far away, but again left him behind as an ally. She felt it ease into Reginald, facing off with the Siren's blackwater tides, and decide that this was no foe to tussle with, not at the moment.

And then she felt it pass into Adrian.

She felt Luke's power hesitate. As that white, creeping mist paused inside Adrian's body, Layla felt it think thoughts like *enemy, arrogant, demolish.* But something fierce rose inside Layla, her drakaina breathing back against the dire mist as she struggled beneath the drake's massive white jaws. Layla fought Luke's power with everything she had then, instinct filling her as she struggled for Adrian's life, thinking *mate, honor, love.*

Beloved.

Beloved? She felt Luke's magic pause, terribly still.

Beloved. She confirmed, exhaling a burning golden light deep into the drake's mist-white body. She felt him shudder. She felt him lose all hope for their reunion, him and her.

And then, she felt him let her go.

With a sweet exhalation down her throat, Luke's power eased deep into Layla's body, finding the Bind between them. Part of Layla felt Luke draw near in the real world, standing as he pulled her to her feet. Pulling her close to his body by their twined hands, he wrapped an arm around her as he drew his lips to hers. She felt him kiss her, one last soft kiss as he exhaled deep down her throat in both the physical world and the metaphysical. And then his white *nullax*-mist found their Bind, curled into it.

And devoured it from the inside out.

Something inside Layla screamed as she felt it go. And something inside Luke breathed deep as he was released – as his lips lingered upon hers, pressing her one last time before letting her go. Setting their foreheads together, Luke released his magic. Layla choked, rubbing her chest, feeling something beautiful stolen from her, far deeper than any death. Sweetly, Luke kissed her forehead, his lips lingering.

And then he pulled back.

"Goodbye, Layla." He breathed.

"Goodbye, Luke." She choked, still clutching her heart.

Luke's gaze went long, watching her suffer, his green eyes intense as a flicker of lightning moved through them. But Layla couldn't feel him anymore, and his thoughts and heart were closed to her, as he at last turned and walked away.

She didn't see him leave, as she heard the door open and Luke stepped out into the hall.

She didn't want to, as her friend and first-bound Royal Storm Dragon was taken from her – forever.

CHAPTER 28 – CRYSTAL

Moonlight flooded down through the crystal atrium at Riad Rhakvir, a night-whisper of palm fronds easing to Layla's ears as a cool desert wind flowed through the space. Jasmine and honeysuckle were fragrant in the air as Layla stood by a column in a flowing Moroccan silk caftan gown in a deep royal purple, feeling the night. Sipping an after-dinner Prosecco, she lingered in the airy hall with its burbling fountains and sculpted gardens, staring at its central fixture. All around the broad atrium, crystals thrust up through the alabaster floor, some massive, some spreading and branched, as soothing water-sounds eased through the columns. Fireflies moved in lazy patterns, swirling slowly around the crystals as they reflected an unearthly light from the high desert moon.

Swirling her Prosecco, Layla stared at the crystal sarcophagus glowing softly beneath the atrium's high dome. As if Dusk felt her watching, the beautiful cocoon gave a slow pulse, shimmering through its depths with a deep sapphire light. All around the vaulted room, crystals reflected that light; towers of ruby and emerald, massive fans of sapphire and citrine, swirling columns of onyx and amazonite. It was haunting and beautiful, and as Layla watched the light move like a living thing through Dusk's room in Adrian's palace, her Dragon curled up inside her with a keening sound.

As she watched the night, warm hands found her shoulders, and a tall, strong presence stepped to her back, curling her in his arms. His cinnamon and jasmine musk stole in her nose as she breathed, his soft desert winds moving all around her with a deep comfort and scintillating passion. Wearing a vest and trousers in a dark navy with gold pinstripes to match her gown's beadwork, his white sleeves were rolled up at the elbows as his strong arms curled around her, baring a snarling crimson, gold, and black Dragon-tattoo winding up his left forearm. A slow smile curled Layla's lips as she turned slightly in Adrian's arms, lifting her chin. Setting soft lips to her neck, he kissed her gently.

"I thought I would find you here." Adrian murmured, cradling her as they watched the crystal sarcophagus glow beneath the moon. "Will you come back to the party? Rachida is asking for you, and Emir wants you to regale him with the tale of our victory at Chartres again. He's furious I didn't call the clan in to help for the battle – Rachida, too."

"I'll go back to the party in a moment." Layla spoke low, something about this room and her mood demanding quietude beneath the moon tonight.

"Dusk's not going anywhere, Layla." Adrian spoke, kissing her neck again with his sweet, smooth lips. "His condition hasn't changed for three weeks, and the Arizona Crystal Dragon healers we had come take a look at him couldn't make any definitive diagnosis on his condition. He's stable, and for now that's good enough. Come back to the party. Your clan is asking for you."

"I just wish there was more we could do." Layla sighed, staring at the sarcophagus. "It feels like he's a coma patient… and we're just waiting for him to wake up."

"We are." Adrian spoke simply. "But Dusk would want us to live our lives in the meantime. Rachida and Emir and the clan are guarding him now, day in and day out. They'll tell us the moment anything changes."

"I'm glad you invited the clan to come stay at Riad Rhakvir these past weeks. It's been nice having them around, getting to know them." Her gaze breaking from the sarcophagus at last, Layla turned in Adrian's arms, setting her wine aside on a teakwood table by the column and lifting her arms up around his neck. They kissed, gently and decadently, before she pulled away. "When do they go home?"

"They don't, not unless they want to." Adrian spoke with a smile as he brushed one of Layla's curls back from her face. "Rachida and a number of others want to take up residence again in the palace, and I said yes. Like you said – it's been nice having them around."

"Adrian Rhakvir!" Layla spoke with a growing smile as something lightened inside her at his words. "Solitary bachelor billionaire no more, I guess."

"Not since I found a good mate."

With a tender grin, Adrian nuzzled her nose, and Layla felt her mood lighten despite the somber beauty of Dusk's atrium, and everything that had happened recently. Layla and Adrian had been together these past weeks, day after day, standing at each other's sides and sleeping together at night. After her friends had left the Paris Hotel, Layla had gone to the Madame and put herself on indefinite sabbatical. Without Dusk, she hadn't wanted to return to Concierge Services, and with everything that had happened, she didn't feel ready to launch into her new role as a Courtesan. With the Desert Dragon clan now back in residence at Riad Rhakvir and Dusk's sarcophagus being protected there, Layla and Adrian had done most of his Hotel re-org work from Morocco – all while perusing documents late at night from Rhennic about the *Sage of the Wilds* to figure out more about Hunter. But as everything had shuffled out, it had given Layla and Adrian a new life together.

For the first time, Layla felt like Adrian actually was her mate and she his.

And despite their sacrifices, it was a cherished thing.

She felt Adrian share her emotions through their Bind as he wrapped her in his arms, kissing her deeply now as his hands netted her close at the waist, his warm desert winds easing all around them. It was heady and decadent, and Layla felt herself melting into it as she breathed him in, as she touched his infinitely soft lips and enjoyed his incredible scents breathing into her mouth and all around her body. She felt his strong coils of heat and power slide against her as they kissed, trapping her close to his body, stroking her with deep pleasure.

Kissing Adrian was always a pleasure – especially now that she got to indulge in it daily.

"Besides, I'm still a billionaire, you know." Adrian spoke at length, as he grinned deviously between kisses. "Even despite what I spent on you for Yule, Courtesan-in-Absentia."

"And I didn't even get a Rolex or a Ferrari for sleeping with you." Layla grumped teasingly, winding her arms more solidly around his neck as she grinned back.

"You're still sleeping with me." Adrian growled with an even wider grin. "And you can have fifty Ferraris if you want. Though Rolexes are completely passé."

His mood was lighthearted, and even as Layla laughed, she realized it was something Dusk might have said. Winding her arms tighter around Adrian's neck, she sobered. "You sound like him sometimes."

"I find myself almost thinking like him sometimes," Adrian agreed as he nuzzled her nose. "Which tells me more than anything that he's still in there, Layla, still fighting – still him. Dusk is a stubborn bastard, and more of a fighter than anyone I know, possibly excepting you and Rachida. He'll wake. I know he will."

"But when?" Layla asked, turning in Adrian's arms so she could see the crystal sarcophagus once more, glowing softly beneath the high desert moon. Reaching one hand up behind Adrian's neck, her fingers stroked his nape, feeling his soft hair. Turning his lips into her, he kissed her neck as his hands kneaded her waist, making her body tighten deliciously even though her mood was still strange.

"Can you feel him, Adrian?" She asked suddenly. "Out in the dunes, at night?"

"Dusk?" He paused, and Layla felt him frown.

"Hunter."

Layla felt Adrian draw a deep breath by her neck. "You've been reading through all those documents Rhennic sent us too late past bedtime, Layla."

"But is Hunter the benevolent saint he preached back then, creating the White Chalice to unite the clans?" Layla mused, moved by too much wine and partying with their Desert Dragon clan, and the lateness of the night. "Or is he the mad thing I witnessed in the Phoenix King's bower? Or is he this shadowy puppet-master who has been orchestrating the Hotel for thousands of years?"

"I think Hunter is all those things," Adrian continued, as he cradled Layla in his arms and watched Dusk's resting place. "I think he is so many personalities, and has been over the years, that he's lost. Hunter tried to start a religion to fill some empty place deep inside him when he lost his original Bind-mates, but it never worked because he was too far gone when he started it. Thus, a beautiful idea was enacted in a terrible way, producing a result that had to be torn down."

"The Red Letter Hotel was similar," Layla mused. "Except Hunter kept his hands out of the Hotel itself, only used it to further his shadowy aims in other ways. So the Hotel began to flourish without him, to create its own culture and momentum. A culture that stands to this day for actual peace and prosperity."

"I'm glad it does." Adrian murmured by her neck. "There are many good people who work for the Hotel, Layla, at all its branches. They believe in peace and love, in joy and redemption. It's a beautiful place for those who have day-to-day stock in it. The Paris Hotel is not the only site that houses refugees from feuding clans, or people finding redemption from some ancient tragedy. The Hotel protects them. And that's my job as an Owner, and as a Hotel Head."

"I'm glad." Layla smiled, stroking Adrian's neck. "You're a good Owner, Adrian, and a good Hotel Head – now that you have Quindici to keep a weather eye on the daily management."

"Quinn is astute at business, I'll give him that." Adrian chuckled as he kissed Layla's neck. "He's an excellent Associate Hotel Head, even with his responsibilities to his Dark Haven in Florence occasionally occupying him. I know Dusk doesn't care for him, and Quinn has a dark side, but he's never given me a reason to mistrust him."

"Heathren Merkami has his suspicions about your ally." Layla frowned, thinking back on the way the Fallen Ephilohim had stared at Quindici during the purge. And the darkness Layla had seen in the Vampire when he had interrogated Imogene Cereste in the Guardhall. Though Quindici was Adrian's staunch supporter, Layla still felt a chill in her gut when she thought about him. As if summoned, she suddenly felt the Vampire's kiss he'd given her in his office before her debut. Smooth and supple, a sensation of warm breath eased in her lips and Layla shivered – seeing Quindici's onyx eyes in her mind as if he were watching her from afar.

"Heathren Merkami has suspicions about everyone." Adrian kissed her neck, winding her more solidly in his arms, and the sensation of Quindici's dark magics was banished from Layla's skin. "If Heathren had anything concrete on Quinn, he would have been arrested, Layla."

"Too bad the Intercessoria were trigger-happy with their executions before we could get more detailed information." Layla frowned, still wondering what it was she had just felt.

"But because they were trigger-happy," Adrian admonished, "we are free. And have more support on the Hotel Owners' Board than ever before. Which reminds me." Behind her, Layla felt Adrian slide a hand into a pocket of his trousers and take something out. Sliding his arm around her once more, he pressed something into her palm, warm from his body heat.

"Congratulations." He breathed by her ear, with a renegade smile.

"Congratulations?" Layla blinked, frowning as she lifted the object up to the yellow lamplight streaming out from the hall behind her, to see it better. As she gazed at it, she saw it was an 'R' pin from the Hotel done in platinum, made from rubies edged in diamonds. It looked similar to the employee pin Layla had seen the Madame wear, but this one had a central line of black diamonds running through the letter.

"What's this? A Madame's pin?" Turning in his arms, Layla glanced up at Adrian, confused.

"It's an *Owner's* pin," he chuckled softly, a devious humor flashing in his aqua-gold eyes. "Congratulations, Layla Price, newest Owner in the Red Letter Hotel. You don't have to wear the pin to Board meetings; everyone knows who you are. It's more ceremonial than anything. But still, you should keep it safe."

Layla gaped at the object in her hand, then stared up at Adrian. "But… I don't have enough money to buy my way into Hotel Ownership, Adrian!"

"I know." Adrian grinned slyly with a devious chuckle. "Quindici heads up the New Owner's Committee, and I may have gotten him to put your petition forward. Quinn did a little accounting and found the Paris Hotel didn't really need your Courtesan's Debut money with all Quinn's new changes, so he simply didn't report your Debut to the Board, or its earnings. Between me and Dusk putting in that hundred million Euros, a generous contribution from Reginald's ample savings, and a sizable donation from Rhennic – we bought you in to the Hotel. Together."

"But…" Layla blinked incredulously, feeling her world spin, though not in an unpleasant way as she thought about joining Adrian in the fight against Hunter on the Hotel Board. Not to mention the significant generosity of her Bound lovers to pony up what she knew was multiple billions to get her a seat. "Aren't I supposed to be a Courtesan now, to help you infiltrate the last three members of the Crimson Circle?"

Adrian chuckled, his aqua-gold eyes flashing with a dark knowing as he wrapped Layla closer in his arms. "Do you *want* to be a Courtesan, Layla?"

Layla paused, frowning, feeling all the tumult that decision had led her into since the fall – a tumult she still had yet to reconcile. Deep inside, she churned thinking about it. And even though her Dragon coiled eagerly in her veins, there was a darker sensation beneath it, as if that pit of black self-hate and emotionless nothing could rise more quickly, should she actually step into becoming a Courtesan.

"No." Layla spoke at last, knowing it was true. "I never wanted to become one. I was doing it for you, and because my Dragon is intrigued by sleeping with new people. But the saner side of me that's not my beast feels like it's just way too much. I can barely handle being Bound to a number of men. I mean, there are four of you now, and would have been five if Luke and I hadn't parted ways. Juggling that much Dragon-testosterone in my life is already insane. I can't imagine what would happen if I really moved forward with being a Courtesan. I think my life would explode or something."

"I thought as much," Adrian smiled at her gently, though his eyes were beautifully bright now, as if her words were everything he'd wanted to hear. "Because Quinn had an impressive idea in that calculating mind of his. He thought perhaps now that your Bind-magic is under control and already Bound to four powerful Royal Dragons, that being a Courtesan is not your best avenue in this battle we're waging against Hunter and the last three members of the Crimson Circle. You're not a *femme fatale* of the bedroom, Layla – you never were. You're a cojones-busting drakaina who comes in like a wrecking ball, clearing a room and making all heads turn. You're a woman of battle and direct power, not a seductress. And you belong in an arena where battle happens directly. In the Boardroom. And nowhere else."

Layla blinked at him, then at the crimson and diamond pin in her palm.

And then threw her arms up around Adrian's neck, kissing him deep and taking no prisoners.

Adrian kissed her back, renegade and wild, before sweeping her up into his arms as she gave an *eep* of surprise, her drakaina roaring like golden fire in her veins.

"I love you, Layla Price." Adrian growled sexily at her lips. "And I am taking to you to bed, right now."

"What about the party?" She laughed, breathless as her heart pounded like fire for the man she loved.

"Fuck the party." Adrian growled with a deadly, panty-dropping smile. "I'm ready to make our own rules about how to party down and get what we want."

"You've always made your own rules, Adrian Rhakvir."

"And now you're going to be beside me, helping me set those

rules all the way." Adrian spoke, holding her gaze by the glow of the high desert moon. "You in?"

"All the way." Layla breathed, joy spilling from her in a wave of golden glory.

With a vast fire in his beautiful aqua eyes, Adrian kissed her, hard and deep.

And then turned, taking them back to his new bedroom in the palace to fuck her rotten.

The story continues in *Crystal Dragon King: Royal Dragon Shifters of Morocco #5*
A Red Letter Hotel Paranormal Romance
Find out more at www.avawardromance.com

Love this series? Help Ava write more by leaving a review for this book on Amazon and Goodreads!

COMING SOON!

Crystal Dragon King: Royal Dragon Shifters of Morocco #5, the next book in the Red Letter Hotel Paranormal Romance series is coming soon.

Find out more at www.avawardromance.com

GET NOTIFIED OF NEW BOOKS

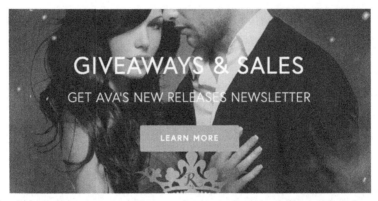

Get the latest giveaways, sales, and new releases delivered right to you!
Sign up at —> www.avawardromance.com

Follow Ava on Amazon to be notified of the latest releases in Kindle
Unlimited —> www.amazon.com/Ava-Ward/e/B07KX8NB3M

Follow Ava on BookBub to get notified of all new releases —>
www.bookbub.com/authors/ava-ward

Join Ava's reader group on Facebook for the latest sneak peeks and first
looks —> www.facebook.com/avawardromance

ABOUT AVA WARD

AVA WARD writes hot & sexy paranormal, fantasy, and sci-fi romance, and is the pen name for Amazon bestselling and award-winning fantasy author Jean Lowe Carlson. From dragon-shifters to otherworldly hotties, there's no limit to the heat! Discover the Red Letter Hotel romances, the decadent world of four bad-boy dragon shifter billionaires and the one woman who keeps them in line! **Discover more at www.avawardromance.com**